Hate Crush talks about topics some readers may find difficult, including suicide and miscarriage.

HATE CRUSH

———

ANGELINA M. LOPEZ

carina
press

Recycling programs
for this product may
not exist in your area.

ISBN-13: 978-1-335-45950-3

Hate Crush

Copyright © 2020 by Angelina M. Lopez

Carina Press
22 Adelaide St. West, 40th Floor
Toronto, Ontario M5H 4E3, Canada
www.CarinaPress.com

Printed in U.S.A.

To Mom and Clay, these books wouldn't exist without your "crazy" idea to plant a vineyard. Thank you for including me in your dreams.

The Monte del Vino Real is my make-believe kingdom in the mountains of northern Spain, but I leaned on the real and gorgeous wine-growing region of Rioja for inspiration. Go visit. Send pictures.

HATE CRUSH

Prologue

The second bottle of fermented celery root gin went down much easier than the first.

His stylist was going to kill him for trading his Cartier sunglasses for the bottles. But as he slumped on a vegan leather couch in the VIP tent with his arm slung around his new best friend—a hemp-wearing gin maker wearing thousand-dollar shades—Aish Salinger thought the trade was totally worth it. After a year of sobriety, the foul-tasting liquor blurred the edges of his vision so the open flaps of the tent, the gyrating dancers in the distance, the burning fires, and the endless expanse of hot, white, flat Nevada desert looked like it used to. Exciting. Welcoming. Like a place he wanted to be.

The liquor pillowed him in the memories of the other times he'd attended this art and music festival with John Hamilton, his bass player and lifelong best friend, at his side, groupies and hangers-on answering every beck and call. The liquor convinced him that he wanted to be here, dressed like a Mad Max tool in graffitied leather jeans and no shirt, flashing his famous tattoos, instead of being home. Alone.

The liquor gave him his new best friend.

"Got a question," his new best friend said above the

distant beats of techno coming from the main stage. Propped against Aish, the man reeked of pot and patchouli and unwashed days in the desert. But that's what you did for your best friend. You accepted them, stink and all. You never pushed them away.

The man's name was Buck. Or Steve. Aish called him *dude*. "What's that, dude?"

"Who'd you guys write that song about? You know the one, 'In You.' Song's good for rubbing one out."

Aish tugged his head off the couch and looked blearily around the tent. The festival headliner was playing so the velvet couches and satin play pits were empty in the glow of the chandeliers. And Aish's once-packed entourage had disappeared with the stink of scandal and a failing career.

Still, he couldn't be too careful with a secret he'd kept close for ten years, a secret that journalists and groupies and spies had been trying to squeeze out of him since 'In You' exploded on the charts and unleashed their band, Young Son, on the world.

But as Aish smacked the taste of spoiled celery root in his mouth, he thought he'd never met a trustworthier guy than Buck. Or Steve.

"Dude, not naming names, but she was amazing," he said, closing his eyes as he settled his head back on the couch, feeling soothed and tied in knots like he always did whenever he thought of 'In You.' The song was pure sex, summoned the sensations of the purest sex with her.

He never should have let the label release it. "I fucked up so bad."

"What'd you do?"

"Broke her heart." He used to think it was the worst

thing he'd ever done. "I was a douche. Young, so stupid." Memories of her lit like a constellation in his brain. "She was one in a million."

"You sound like you loved her. I thought she just rocked your cock."

Rocked your cock. Could Aish turn *that* into a song? It was better than what he'd been coming up with on his own.

"Yeah, she did," he said, dragging his fingers through his hair the way she used to, slow and tugging. "I miss her."

"I'd miss her too if she was as hot as you say in that song. Miss her on my junk, you know what I'm sayin'?" He laughed and elbowed Aish.

His new best friend was kind of an asshole. But his old best friend had been kind of an asshole, too.

At the disloyal thought, Aish tried to straighten. "Don't talk about her like that," he grumbled. When had his neck turned to jelly? His best friend had turned into quadruplets.

"Sorry, man, no offense," Buck or Steve said, raising his eight palms into the air. "What's she doing now?"

Buck or Steve was a good guy. And there were so many of him. It'd been a long time since Aish had talked to anyone but his manager. It'd been a long time since he'd talked about her. "She's opening a winery."

"For real? Classy for such a dirty girl."

"Yeah. Yeah, she's real classy. Royally classy." He huffed at his own joke. Could that be a song?

Buck or Steve laughed dirty. "I bet you'd help her open her winery real good."

"That'd be nice," Aish said dreamily. "Soaking in the Spanish air, getting my head on straight…"

"Wait a fucking second." His new best friend's sharp voice forced Aish to focus, forced him to see that he was just one man, one man with eyes that weren't as blurry and red rimmed as they'd seemed when they'd first started drinking. "A rich slut into wine? In Spain? You're not talking about that princess, are you? What's her name?" He snapped his fingers and the sound was percussive over the thump of the headliner's beats. Then he pointed a dirty fingernail at Aish.

"Princess Sofia! That's who 'In You' is about."

"Shhhhhhh," Aish said, trying to concentrate as he looked around the tent again. But when he steadied his head, the tent kept swirling. He closed his eyes. "Dude, keep your voice down."

"Princess Sofia. She's starting a winery? I thought she was in rehab." Aish tried to open his eyes. But the gorge was rising in his throat. And the man's words were crowding his ears. "Motherfucking Princess Sofia. Wasn't she caught fucking an entire boy band? Her winery's gonna be a 24-7 orgy. You think you can get me in there, too? Damn, I'd like a go at her."

Aish was going to kill his new best friend. He was going to shove his hand down Buck or Steve's throat, rip out his tonsils, and dangle them in front of his eyes as the first body part he'd lose if he ever touched her or thought about her or told another living soul.

But a familiar sensation welled up in Aish.

And instead of violence, the video from the camera hidden in a fern would show rock star Aish Salinger lurching out of view. The mic hidden in Buck or Steve's poncho would pick up—over the thump of techno-surf—Aish Salinger heaving in a corner.

* * *

The viral video might have actually carried a virus. Because when the woman they were discussing saw the video the next day, a woman with a kingdom on the line and nothing going her way, a woman who'd blocked that catastrophic first love from her thoughts, she had to run for the bathroom, too.

Mid-August

Princesa Sofia Maria Isabel de Esperanza y Santos stood in the arctic cool and ancient dark of her wine cellar, a hub for the endless tunnels that ran beneath her repurposed monastery, and tugged out the thick bung from a barrel. She purposefully placed the bung next to the hole—she'd lost them to pockets and distraction in years past—and stuck the wine thief into the barrel. The Tempranillo that slowly filled the glass tube sparkled like a ruby in the dim light of the LED lantern. She pulled the thief out when it had been filled to a precise amount, immediately plugged the barrel, and emptied the wine into her glass.

She gave the wine four hard swirls, the exact number she'd given wine from the other barrels she'd sampled, and studied it in the lantern light for imperfections. No off coloring. No unexpected lees or residue. The wine slid silkily down the inside of the bowl, just as she wanted it to.

She leaned her nose and upper lip into the bowl and inhaled, mouth open. Dark plum, cherry, tobacco, the rich, decadent aromas had been subdued by the year in American oak barrels. Screw the Consejo Regulador del Monte, the regulatory board that demanded the wines age in French oak to get their stamp of approval. These grapes from a sunny northern corner of the Monte del Vino Real cried for a different technique to display their best flavors.

Sofia was princess of the Monte del Vino Real, the small winegrowing principality nestled high among the Picos de Europa in Northern Spain, and legend had it that the juice from the grapes flowed through her family's veins. Since it was her lifeblood, no one knew better than her what the grapes of the Monte del Vino Real needed to become great wines. No one cared more. No one had trained harder or convinced more people or had more at stake. It was up to her, the first winemaker in a five-hundred-year legacy of royal winegrowers, to convince the world that the Monte del Vino Real was capable of creating some of the most sophisticated, palate-tempting, tourism-building, and revenue-generating wines on the planet.

With a careful and restrained breath, Princesa Sofia put the glass to her lips and upended it, chugging the wine down like *una cerveza light*. She drank until the glass was dry. Just as she had from the other wine barrels she'd sampled.

She rubbed her sleeve across her lips and burped.

Overhead lights flared on as the cellar door at the top of the stairs crashed open. *"¿Dónde demonios estás? ¡Sal ahora mismo!"* yelled her winery manager.

Only the constant state of horror, shock, and fury she'd been living in for the last forty-eight hours kept Sofia from reacting to the crash, the blinding lights, and her employee telling her to "Get your ass up here."

And the wine. The wine helped, too.

"It's fine," said an all-business voice, also from the top of the stairs. "I'll meet her down there."

Sofia slumped on the closest barrel and kept her focus on her empty wineglass instead of on the improvements she'd made to this chamber beneath the medieval monastery. The spectacular cathedral space now boasted a two-stories-high wood-beam ceiling and black, Corinthian marble floors. Barrels branded with *Bodega Sofia* were stacked two deep on the sides. At the room's edges, cut-stone archways led to tunnels that ran beneath the Monte, providing an underworld of primeval pathways that Sofia knew like the back of her hand.

This was the heart of Bodega Sofia, where the stone and the cold blocked out everything and allowed Sofia's sensitive nose and palate to do the intricate work of creating great wines that proudly displayed the thousand-year history of her land and people.

Sofia shut down the images of this space filled with people relishing their first sip of Bodega Sofia wine. She wished her brain was as empty as her glass.

As they descended, the boots of the PR woman rang louder against the metal and the winery manager's grumble grew more distinct. "… Just been hiding down here and I can't get her to do anything…"

"I'll take care of it," the American promised as they turned the corner of the stairs. Sofia marveled again at how tiny and delicate the woman who was taking on the Herculean task of managing Sofia's PR woes appeared to be. In an emerald-green baby doll dress, her black hair cut into eyebrow-brushing bangs and a bob, Namrita Mirakhur looked like a fragile hipster butterfly. What Sofia had come to realize after months of working with her on a winery launch plan was that the PR exec was about as fragile as a steel-punching drill bit.

Sofia propped her back against the cold rock walls

of her cellar and tipped her empty glass at the women as they noticed her.

Carmen Louisa, her winery manager, stopped in her muck boot tracks. "*¿Estás borracha?*"

"No, I'm not drunk," Sofia replied in English, for the sake of the PR rep. "Not yet."

Sofia had known and looked up to Carmen Louisa for the entirety of her twenty-nine years; it was immensely soothing to play the teenager around her. With her caramel and curly shoulder-length hair and a body used daily as a tool, the forty-eight-year-old woman looked like a model hired to play the role of a winegrower, rather than the accomplished grower she'd been all of her life.

Right now, she looked like she was going to seriously blow her top.

Namrita put up a calming hand. "How's it going?" she asked, tucking her arms around herself.

It was chilly down here, just like Sofia needed it. "*Bien*," she replied through a fake smile.

Carmen Louisa scoffed. "No, she is not *bien*. She's ignoring the phone and her emails, thank God you sent that press release or people would think she was dead, *no sé cuando* she ate last *y* she says she's topping off the barrels, does she look like she's topping off the barrels to you *y no sé qué hacer y ella no me habla…*"

Carmen Louisa's university-learned English went to hell when she got wrought up.

Both of her brothers and her best friend Henry had given up texting or calling. They didn't try to visit. Sofia knew the tunnel system that ran into the mountains better than anyone. When she'd played *escondidas* with her brother Mateo in it, she'd always won. Not even the power of being the next king gave Mateo the confidence that he could find Sofia if she wanted to hide.

Namrita put up a slender hand again.

"I know this is rough," she said, in her trademark not-going-to-sugar-coat-it voice. "You've been working your ass off and then this video comes out two weeks before launch. Things might seem hopeless but they're not going to get any better with you hiding down here."

The majority of the wine world had already treated Bodega Sofia as a joke, calling it the worthless vanity project of a party-girl princess. Wine industry influencers had essentially ignored her invitation to take part in an all-expenses-paid launch of the winery and its adjacent luxury hotel. And here at home, many in the village were concerned and suspicious about Sofia's efforts to innovate Monte winemaking.

"I'm sorry to ask, but I have to," Namrita said. "Is it true? Were you in a relationship with Aish Salinger?"

His name. A name she'd successfully blocked out for ten years. Sofia slipped her hand into her front pocket, palming her hip, and pressed back against the cold rock wall. She nodded once.

"Okay," Namrita said, gentle for once. "And have you seen him since the relationship ended?"

Gracias a Dios, no. She'd thought the universe had been kind.

After that disastrous autumn, Sofia put her energies into getting her dual degrees in enology and wine chemistry from the University of Bordeaux, learning all she could apprenticing to top winemakers, and filling in for her absent brother and careless parents as a leader for the Monte. Once her brother, Príncipe Mateo, found his brilliant billionaire bride and took his rightful place at the helm of the kingdom five years ago, Sofia had left the Monte and filled her days developing a chemical to correct a wine fault that had long harassed the industry. Her nights…well, she'd learned in her wild-child teen years that pretty boys and parties were an effective distraction from whatever she didn't want to think about.

When she perfected her chemical compound that revolutionized the wine industry and became instantly and magnificently wealthy, she turbocharged that wild child with an Amex Black. She worked with top winemakers, went clubbing with the worst of people, advised in creating exciting wines, and let the paparazzi catch her in compromising positions. For three years, she enjoyed the work-hard-play-hard behavior that would have been celebrated in a man. When Sofia did it, they called it antics.

She'd put all that aside two years ago when her brother had shown up at her Tuscany villa and asked her to come home. He'd asked for her help to secure a better future for the Monte.

Two years of quiet living and unrelenting effort to build the winery weren't enough to erase Sofia's wild child from the wine world's collective consciousness or cool the rumors that her invention relied more on her billionaire sister-in-law's money than Sofia's wine expertise.

The wine world was making her pay now for her behavior then.

But at all those parties with all of those boy toys, she'd never heard Aish's name. She'd never been haunted by his voice in a dance club. She'd remained blissfully unaware that Young Son was a worldwide sensation.

The universe hadn't been kind; it had been cruel, hiding a secret until its reveal was the most disastrous.

Sofia shook her head no. She'd had no contact with him.

"Okay," Namrita said. She paused for a beat and then said, "I think I figured a way out."

"We delay the launch," Sofia said. "We wait a month for some other stupidity to attract people's attention."

"It's not that simple," Namrita said. "You don't understand how big the mystery of that song is. 'In You' was Young Son's breakout hit; a really hot guy sang about a very hot relationship in a lot of detail. He wouldn't deny that she was real but he also wouldn't name her, which only made it more catnip-y for everyone. There are websites and YouTube documentaries dedicated to discovering her."

Sofia scrubbed at her thick hair, cut into a bob that ended at the top of her neck, and wished she could brush it forward and hide her eyes with it.

"Now to discover that the woman is you, a *princess*, who had a romance with a *rock star* when you were teenagers, well…people are losing their shit. The hashtag #Aishia is trending worldwide. The *Daily Telegram* paid someone from that fall $500,000 for a fuzzy Polaroid of you two. His video has been viewed millions of times."

Sofia had only deigned to watch the video once, caught a glimpse of him—drunken and half naked and covered in ink—before she'd turned away, nauseated. She wanted to run into the darkness of her tunnels with the hope that when she emerged, blind and grey, years from now, the world will have forgotten that her name was ever linked to Aish Salinger.

"We've struggled to get attention for the launch. Now we have more attention than we know what to do with. Even people who turned down your internship invitation are calling."

That snapped Sofia's head up. They'd invited a pool of fifty people to take twenty spots as superstar interns who would enjoy a luxurious, all-expense-paid, month-long trip to assist Bodega Sofia with its inaugural harvest season. The last time she'd checked, only two had RSVP'd. These wined and dined interns—wine writers, hospitality up-and-comers, travel bloggers, and young winemakers—would be the first guests at Bodega Sofia's luxury hotel, would take part in the entire winemaking process, and would be the most powerful bullhorns declaring the potential of Monte wines and tourism.

Namrita continued, "So how do we take advantage of the attention, transform it into something positive, and work the public's sudden empathy for Aish?"

Sofia's combat boot slipped off the barrel. "What?" she asked. "Empathy for Aish?"

"That's right," Namrita said, shaking her head. "Don't ask me how, but he made vomiting on camera a positive. His vulnerability hit a chord and reminded fans how much they used to love him. People are so giddy about you two that it's drowning out the rumors that he stole songs and was involved in his bass player's death."

"What?" Sofia asked again, thoroughly confused.

Carmen Louisa waved an irritated hand at her. "She doesn't listen to any music made after 1965. Or that doesn't have something weird in it, like a rain stick or a *gaita, un como se dice* bagpipe." She sighed at Sofia. "The guy he started the band with, John Hamilton. He killed himself last year."

Sofia dug her blunt nails into her jeans. "John?" His name echoed in her ancient chamber. "He's dead?"

Namrita nodded. "Did you know him?"

Aish's blond and blue-eyed best friend went everywhere with Aish. So of course John joined him as one of the student-laborers Aish's winemaking uncle recruited every year to help with harvest at his California vineyard. That fall of her nineteenth birthday, Sofia had also joined the group. And Aish found her in a wine tank.

John had been friendly, funny, accommodating. And he'd disliked her. Probably even hated her.

She nodded. She'd known John Hamilton. But she didn't elaborate.

"Production on Young Son's fourth album has stalled," Namrita said. "There were nasty rumors that Aish couldn't write a song without stealing it, that he was jealous and convinced his friend to kill himself, but now..."

When she paused, Sofia felt the hairs stand up on the back of her neck.

"There's a growing romanticism that only the princess who inspired his most famous song can save him."

Sofia slid to the front of the barrel and put her feet on the floor, shock biting at her numb fingers and toes. "What are you saying?"

Namrita didn't blink. "I'm saying we should invite him to be a part of our internship program."

"No," Sofia said, standing slowly.

"We can use the public's fascination with you two. If we suggest that there are still feelings between you then we can..."

"No!" she shouted, a flare of heat burning through her cool as she flung her wineglass down, shattering it against the marble, flinging crystal like shrapnel.

Namrita gasped. The PR rep looked down at her smooth, dark shin.

Blood was welling in the cut across the middle of it.

Sofia stared, horrified.

"*¡Dios mio!*" Carmen Louisa said, the first to react as she led Namrita to sit on a barrel then slapped the woman's hand on top of the cut. "I'll get the first-aid kit."

"I… I'm sorry," Sofia stuttered.

Namrita blew out a breath. "Believe it or not," she huffed, planting her boot on the barrel then tucking her dress around her thigh, "I've had clients react worse."

It was almost a challenge to that wild child in Sofia, that little monster that bit back, to break more, to kick her combat boots into the barrels, to stomp and scream and shout until wine ran like blood over the marble. And this, at the end of the day, was why her winery—and her hopes for her people—were doomed.

Because millions of new dollars and a lifetime in the role hadn't magically transformed Sofia into the princess her kingdom could depend on. There was a reason they no longer leaned on her after her brother returned. And yet, she'd shackled their future to her ankle. When she went down, the kingdom would go down with her.

She wrapped her hand around her forearm's blazing red tattoo to hide it from sight.

As if hearing her fear, Namrita said, "You've got to look at the big picture. You have options if the winery fails. But your growers who've invested their life savings don't."

Sofia narrowed her eyes, but grabbed her cargo coat off a barrel and stooped to wrap it around Namrita's chilly legs.

"I know it seems extreme," the PR rep continued, her eyes dark and serious as Sofia pressed the cloth against the wound. "But fake romances are used all the time to create diversions in high-profile situations. A pro-mance with Aish Salinger for a month could mean the difference between Bodega Sofia's success or failure."

She nodded toward Carmen Louisa clanging down the stairs. "Do you hate him more than you love her?" she whispered.

Namrita had been recommended by Sofia's sister-in-law because she pulled no punches. Right now, Sofia didn't need the low blow. "I know what's at stake," she hissed.

Her reputation. The future of her people. A legacy that stretched back a millennium.

For centuries, the Monte del Vino Real had grown the most admired Tempranillo grapes in the world. Winemakers from Madrid to Bordeaux, Napa Valley to South Africa, transformed their grapes into incredible wines. But here in the Monte, owners of generations-old wineries—or *bodegas* as they were known in Spain—stayed fat and rich producing low-quality wines sold in jugs. They've loved proclaiming in the village square that the Monte was known for its wine*growing* not wine*making*. As the leaders of the Consejo Regulador del Monte, the regulatory board that in centuries past had ensured that only the best wines were sent to Spain's royal family, these winemakers turned laziness into law and used their power to trap the Monte in old-fashioned ways.

The instant Bodega Sofia was announced, they'd harassed Sofia's efforts every way they could. They'd denied her their stamp, making access to materials and shipping difficult. Their leader, Juan Carlos Pascual, appeared repeatedly in the press harping on her party-girl past and casting doubt on her winemaking abilities. And they bold-faced lied to her people, claiming she would insist on prohibitively expensive vineyard changes that would beggar them.

The Consejo sowed fear in the Monte, when Sofia wanted to add strength. She and her brothers feared that their sleepy little kingdom would become comatose without the money and tourism of a reinvigorated wine industry. While the finances of the Monte had stabilized, the kingdom was still losing its young people to the greater world. A local wine industry focused on Monte winemakers could bring in money, tourists, and jobs.

Without it, the Monte del Vino Real would become a ghost kingdom in a matter of years.

Namrita slipped the coat off her legs so Carmen Louisa could clean the wound. Confident the cut was clear of glass and didn't need stitches, Carmen Louisa began to apply butterfly tabs and a larger bandage. She shoved alcohol swabs into Sofia's hands to clean Namrita's hand.

"You're going to clean this mess down here, too," Carmen Louisa said angrily. "*Actúas como si fueras la única que tuvo un mal día. También estoy teniendo un mal día y...*"

Sofia ignored her as she swiped at Namrita's palm. "Aish Salinger knows only how to take; he believes everything is his due." How dare she make her say these things. How dare she make her remember this. "He's never had a contrite day in his life. How do we know he'll agree to any of this?"

"Because he's already said he would." Namrita fingered the large white bandage on her leg. "His manager said he'll be here for the launch."

Sofia stood up, hooking her thumbs into her jeans and gripping her hips. "You...you had no right!"

"I know," Namrita nodded, lowering her legs and pulling down her dress. "But I couldn't present such an outrageous solution unless I knew he was on board."

She effortlessly pushed Sofia into a corner.

"But...but..." *Jesucristo*, she might actually be sick again. "But how do you know this will work? What if you manufacture this spectacle and the wine world doesn't care?"

"I sent an email to the intern candidates and asked if they'd join if Aish was here." She crossed her wrists in her lap. "They all replied yes."

Carmen Louisa gasped.

Sofia felt shock like lightning bursts in her chest. "All fifty candidates?"

Namrita nodded.

"But we...we only have twenty spots," Carmen Louisa sputtered.

For the first time since her descent downstairs, Namrita smiled. It caused her cheeks to bloom roses, a sweet look inappropriate for this wrecking ball. "Then we'll be able to pick and choose the best people, won't we?"

Repeating that she hadn't the right to contact the candidates was worthless at this point. Staggered, stunned, and feeling like her life was unraveling, Sofia looked openmouthed at Carmen Louisa for...for what? For the straight-talking rationalization she always provided as her mentor? The morale-boosting confidence she gave as her dear friend? The motherly guidance that her own mother was never there to provide?

But right now Carmen Louisa was neither her mentor, dear friend, or mother. Carmen Louisa was her partner and her employee. And her partner and employee had put her future in Sofia's hands.

So had her brother and his wife, who believed Sofia's efforts were the best course to bring industry and revenue to the kingdom. Her people looked to her, their *princesa*, with eyes filled with equal parts distrust and hope.

She'd wanted to be needed. And now she was.

Her kingdom needed her to spend thirty days faking a romance with a man who ripped out her heart.

She mentally embraced the cold and the dark of her cellar, the heart of her dreams and her kingdom's hopes, and let it suffocate her panic. Let it make her numb.

She lifted her chin. "*Vale*," she said. "Tell him to be here the first of September." She gathered herself and focused the power of her royal gaze on Namrita. "But he is going to sign off on some rules before he steps a foot into my kingdom."

Knowing when to cede ground, Namrita nodded.

When Sofia went back upstairs to the sunlit winery, to the clatter and dust of the workmen wrapping up construction before the launch in two weeks, she would throw herself into unraveling this mess. In an hour, she promised Carmen Louisa. Just one more hour, and then she'd be up.

She wanted to be alone in the dark and the cool. She wanted to surround herself with her wines, the only children she'd ever have.

Protected by her mountain's rock walls and surrounded by the only thing that would ever truly need her, she would shore up her defenses and renew her most important vow: to never fall in love again.

September 1

Aish Salinger sat in the back seat of a black Mercedes sedan that crawled down a narrow cobblestone street in the Monte del Vino Real. The cheering villagers and fans packing the lane made it impossible to go any faster. He couldn't even see the famous mountains Sofia had talked about because of the bodies pressed against the car.

He squeezed his forearm and gripped his jaw against telling the driver to move his ass. It wasn't the driver's fault Aish was late.

"She's gonna be so pissed," he muttered to the darkly tinted window. All he could see through his Ray-Bans were a press of bellies, bodies, and smooshed faces.

"She's not going to fall to her knees and ask you to marry her," his manager said in his Brooklyn-tinged accent.

Aish turned on him and glowered. Devonte Mason, their manager since Young Son's first album, was built like a linebacker and Aish, at six-foot-four, found few back seats comfortable. With his elbows up in Aish's space as he worked his phone, Devonte was too close, too calm, while Aish was a nervous fucking wreck.

He went to run his fingers through his hair when he

remembered, at the tacky feel of gel and product, how long the stylist had worked on it. Fuck. He was a year out of practice with this shit.

"Really wish you hadn't brought so many people, man," he grumbled, wiping his hand on his jeans and thinking about the entourage of stylists, makeup people, and wardrobe crew they'd left in the village.

"And I wish you'd gone outside in the last six months," Devonte said, his thumbs still flying over the screen. "You look like shit; you need that many people to clean you up."

Would Sofia think he looked like shit?

It was the entourage Aish had been trying to escape yesterday when he rented a car after landing in Madrid instead of piling into the private plane with everyone. Google Maps had insisted it was only going to be "4 h 46 min" from Madrid to the Monte, giving him a chance to get his bearings and clear his head before arriving in Sofia's kingdom.

But after making a pit stop and grabbing a coffee in a village, he'd felt awful, like he had food poisoning although he'd barely eaten, like he was still suffering from the aftereffects of that evil vegetable gin. He'd had to pull over on the winding mountain roads—and over, and over—until he'd startled awake this morning with goats bleating at the rented Porsche. So instead of arriving yesterday, attempting a night of sleep, and then meeting with Sofia and her people this morning, he'd screeched into the Monte an hour ago, unwashed, nauseous and bleary eyed.

Now Aish was late and apparently looked like shit for Sofia's big day.

He aimed his frustration at the one person who didn't

deserve it. "I don't need your crap right now," he muttered. "Lie to me and tell me I'm pretty."

Devonte snorted and finally put his phone down. He narrowed his eyes at Aish. "You're a perfect meat of a man," he said, his voice going Barry White deep.

Aish rolled his eyes and looked out the widow again. "Fuck you."

Devonte tsked through his teeth. "You don't pay me to blow hot air up your ass. You pay me to tell you the truth."

In the last year, Devonte had been the grim reaper of truth telling. He'd been the one who'd banged on Aish's hotel suite door in Memphis and peeled him out from under a pile of naked bodies to show him John's suicide note. It was Devonte who'd driven them down to the park by the Mississippi River in a panic, who'd first seen the pile of clothes. Over the next months, it was Devonte who told him, in the closed-curtain dimness of Aish's living room, about the growing plagiarism allegations and the rumors that Aish was responsible for John's death and that John—six months after he left a note—was legally declared dead although a body had never been found.

That shitshow in the desert was the first time Aish had left his house since John's casketless funeral. Devonte had ordered him to the festival as a last-ditch effort to drum up some positive publicity before the label, worried about a threatening rain of lawsuits, terminated his contract. Aish had promised for months to deliver Young Son's fourth album, an album that he hoped would wipe away the rumors and allegations, renew Aish's career and John's reputation, and firmly plant Young Son among the rock 'n' roll stars.

Problem was, down in his basement studio, Aish had barely been able to strum two notes.

"Truth is man, you gotta get yourself together," Devonte said. "You got an opportunity here to clear some of the stink off you." The public's seismic excitement over #Aishia had bought him a few more months with his label. "But no one's gonna buy it if you keep pissing her off. Her ground rules make it seem like you're starting with negative yardage."

At the thought of her ground rules, Aish rested his knuckles against his teeth.

The first time he'd ever seen Sofia, she'd been like a sparkler that he had to touch, all glowing skin and long gleaming hair. He'd wrapped her in his arms within minutes and she'd stretched his T-shirt tugging him closer. That's how it had been with them—instant obsession, unrestrained need.

Aish had ruined that when he'd broken her heart three months later. And any hope that she might have softened over the last ten years was demolished when Devonte slapped down the packet of her ground rules.

Rule 1: Aish Salinger will only speak to Princesa Sofia de Esperanza y Santos when it will benefit the arrangement. Therefore, there will be no personal interaction unless the media, the intern corps, tourists, or other public influencers are present. There will be no private, one-on-one conversation.

The rules forbade Aish to touch Sofia, required him to cover his tattoos, and demanded that he learn the scripts for five-minute daily interactions that were supposed to look like romance to the press and interns. The rules wrapped layer after layer of barbed wire around a woman he'd been desperate to be near for ten years.

Sometimes, when memories of her popped into his brain when he was on stage in front of a sold-out crowd, when he was accepting another platinum album, or when the paparazzi bulbs blinded him, his unending yearning for her felt like the worst thing that ever happened to him.

"*La bodega está allá*," said the driver. "There is the winery, señores."

Aish and Devonte scrambled lower into their seats to look out the windshield.

Beyond a rock wall and a gate scrolled with a large S was an ancient monastery of pale stone with windows of stained glass. A modern building made of the same pale stone stood beside it, with people leaning from the balconies and waving. A vineyard-covered hill rose up behind the winery, and a mountain with harsh peaks dominated the sky.

She'd whispered about this, about the winery she wanted to open and the wines she hoped to create, when he'd held her delicate body in his arms. She'd inked her stories into his brain—about her mountains, her people, the thousand-year history she was buoyed and weighted down by—as she'd licked and bit his ear.

Aish felt the anticipation of ten hungry years, and the nerves of one isolated one, in the back of his teeth. The gate opened and they drove into a sprawling courtyard.

The press was cordoned off on one side. A large group of people with wineglasses in their hands stood to the other. A line of people facing him stood in the center.

As the car slowed, Aish closed his eyes behind his

Ray-Bans and took a couple of deep, jittery breaths. The moment he'd craved every day since the second he'd left her was finally here.

The door opened and Aish stepped out into the Spanish sun.

He was blinded by it. But he hid behind his sunglasses as he lifted a casual hand to the cheers of the guests and flicked his trademark side grin.

He hid behind his sunglasses as he hunted.

A dude—a huge blond dude who'd opened the door—was leaning close to say something when Aish saw her.

She stood in a ray of sunshine.

He felt her eyes on him like a shot to his heart. Gone was his erotic woodland fairy girl with her butt-length hair and miles of exposed golden skin, replaced by a badass woman who looked firmly sick of his shit. She'd cut her gold-brown hair short and right now it was slicked back from her perfect face. She wore a snow-white button-down shirt that covered her to her wrists, wide-legged pants that hugged the curves of her waist, and a heavy silver necklace in the open collar of her shirt. Her kohl-lined eyes, the firmness of her wide mouth, and the jut of her sharp chin told him what she thought of his late arrival.

Deaf to whatever the dude was saying, he turned and moved over the cobblestones to get to her with all the speed and compulsion she'd inspired in him when they were kids.

Her wide eyes flared as he came toward her. He put his hands on her warm, strong biceps and took in her gorgeous face. Thick-lashed cat eyes, pert nose, wide mouth that could stretch into the most peace-giving smile. She wasn't going to smile for him now, and that was okay as he looked down to rememorize her. It was shocking to realize how small she was when she was so huge in his mind's eye. He leaned down to brush his lips against the velvety softness of her ear, to say "I'm sorry" before he kissed the fine edge of her jaw.

I'm sorry I'm late, he wanted to say as he inhaled the treasured memory of her cinnamon-sugar skin. *I'm sorry I released that song,* he wanted to plead against her neck. *I'm sorry I hurt you. I'm sorry I broke your heart.* He wanted to paint her in sorry's and drown in her wide wise eyes and discover forgiveness and redemption in her.

He wanted to stop feeling so fucking shitty.

He moved to pull her into a much-needed hug when Sofia's hands come up to rest on his chest—God, *yes*—then she wiggled out of his hands as she stepped back. She did give him a smile, then.

Oh no.

"Welcome to Bodega Sofía, Aish," she said softly, nodding to encourage his grin. He gave it but dreaded what was coming next.

"We're going to smile for the cameras," she said in the same soft voice, her Spanish accent purring over his skin. "But next time you touch me, I'll knee your *polla* so hard you'll taste it. *¿Comprendes cabrón?*"

September 1
Part Two

Only a lifetime's worth of practice keeping it together while her parents humiliated her in front of the cameras kept Sofia from vibrating apart as she stepped away from Aish Salinger. Kept her from shaking into tiny pieces as the entire world watched with bated breath.

#Aishia was a fever and it seemed like every living soul was sick with it. According to Namrita, the past and speculative future of the wounded rock star and party-girl princess had infected the nightly news and entertainment tabloids and social media. Both camps had remained silent, so it made minor celebrities of every vineyard worker or coffee shop barista who'd known them that long-ago autumn. A part-time pot salesman was getting a spot on a reality dance show.

Her winery launch that couldn't get the attention of a Reddit board a month ago now had coverage from every major news outlet in the world and the enthusiastic presence of nineteen superstar "interns," movers and shakers from the wine and hospitality industries, who watched from the VIP section.

Sofia felt the weight of the world's gaze as they recorded her first interaction with a man she hated. She did the one thing she never wanted to do again. She touched Aish Salinger.

For the benefit of her people, she hooked her hand into the crook of his elbow, fought back the sensation of heat and muscle, breathed through her mouth to avoid the scent of him, and moved to his side.

Henry, who was supposed to have escorted Aish through the receiving line before presenting him to Sofia, stepped to her opposite side.

"That slippery fucker got away from me. You okay?" her best friend whispered in her ear. He was head of her sister-in-law's security, but Sofia had borrowed him for the launch. She'd wanted Henry's intimidating bulk and bullet-chewing smile to be the first thing Aish saw when he stepped out of the car, wanted Henry to relay warnings and orders as he walked the rock star through the line of Sofia's family before Aish got anywhere close to her.

Now she had to improvise. She couldn't lean on Henry's hulking protectiveness. She had to stand alone just as she had when Aish had abandoned her.

Sofia kept the placid smile on her face as she nodded then tugged Aish toward the other end of the receiving line. Henry walked just behind her.

Low, Aish said, "I'm sorry I—"

"Shut up. Smile." She kept her eyes forward as she smiled warmly and tipped her head toward him. "Don't talk to me unless it's for an audience. We have nothing to say to each other."

She could do this for a month, project a royal demeanor and blur her vision when she had to interact with him. She'd made a mistake when she'd watched him get out of the car, hoping to see the depressed, disregarded rocker Namrita described. Yes, he'd changed, stuffed his distinct beauty—a combination of a Japanese-American mom and a Jewish-American dad, all soaked in the California sun—into the costume of any overindulged rock star. Mirrored sunglasses hid his eyes and the ebony hair that once brushed his jaw-line was now short and pompadoured. His once-tanned skin looked pale in his black V-neck T-shirt and tight black jeans, looked pulled too thin over biceps and vein-throbbing forearms, now covered in indigo ink.

But still, he was beautiful.

When her eyes had helplessly trailed over his long, leonine nose and slashing cheekbones and plump bottom lip and wide shoulders and endlessly arousing height, she realized she would be attracted to him if he painted himself polka-dotted and wore a clown's wig. When he pressed against her—too rangy, too hard, too rough ridden—she realized her body's reaction to the smell and feel of him was programmed into her DNA.

She relied on her hatred to cool and calm her as they walked in her kingdom's sunlight.

At the opposite end of the receiving line, she let go of his arm and wiped her hand against her hip, steadying herself to begin the introductions. This was fine. This was good. The cameras were going to love it and Sofia could talk around him while almost ignoring him. She'd positioned them so the lenses would catch the winery and her luxury hotel, the Hospedería de Bodega Sofia, the red-tile rooftops of her village, and the limestone outcrops of the Pico Viajadora, that mountain that had defended them for centuries.

In a manner uglier than the Moors' cannons that

tried to blast out her ancestors, Sofia would punch a hole through it and expose them to the world.

The first person in line looked at her with worry crinkling the lines that winged out from his handsome green eyes.

"This is my brother, Roman Sheppard," she said, her tone different than her camera-friendly smile as Aish shook his hand. "He and his security team will keep an eye on you while you're here. If you touch me again without my permission, I'll ask him to break something."

Aish stiffened beside her, but her half brother gave a begrudging huff. "We're also here to keep you and your people safe," Roman said, his gravel voice tinged with Texas.

Strong, dark haired, and dressed in black, the brother they discovered five years ago was head of a security firm that protected magnates and sheikhs. When #Aishia began to scream across the internet, Roman pulled his best people off other assignments and brought them to the Monte. Neck deep in winery preparations, Sofia hadn't even conceived the need for security until one of her growers' teen daughters was offered twelve hundred euros for her invitation.

Now, Roman was ensuring that the descent of a rock star, frenzied tourists, and roaming press on their village occurred without incident.

"But I am ex-army ranger," he said. "So if she asks me to hurt you, I can make it real creative." A taciturn man who seldom smiled, it was hard to know when he was joking.

Wisely, Aish stayed quiet.

Sofia motioned Aish to the next people in line while Henry stayed just behind her.

The crowd noise rose inside the courtyard walls, and outside, where a live stream of the event was being shown on screens throughout the village as rock star Aish Salinger stepped in front of her brother, Príncipe Mateo Ferdinand Juan Carlos de Esperanza y Santos, the next king of the Monte del Vino Real, and his billionaire bride, Roxanne Medina. The couple who had taken the world by storm five years ago with their fake then very real marriage looked so blindingly beautiful—him in a cream-colored suit with his gold-tipped hair held back by his sunglasses, her in a white, body-hugging dress with an artful blue flower painted over the side—that Sofia and Aish were the only ones close enough to see the annihilation in their eyes.

"Príncipe," Aish said, clipped. His welcome here—or the lack of it—seemed to be finally sinking in.

"Aish," Mateo said, clasping Aish's long hand in both of his work-hardened ones. Mateo had stepped away from his role heading one of the world's top winegrowing labs to focus on the Monte, but he still liked to work in the fields. While he pumped his hand, he said, "I should kick your ass for writing a song like that about my sister."

"Look, Mateo, I was young and—"

"*No te preocupes*," Sofia soothed her brother, telling him not to worry while preempting Aish's excuses. He'd always had so many excuses. "I've never heard it and won't. I haven't heard any of their albums. I didn't even know Aish was alive." Out of her peripheral vision, she saw him jerk to look at her. She hoped the consummate performer remembered to keep smiling. "Let's just get through this month and then we'll go back to ignoring Aish Salinger and Young Son."

Roxanne gently extracted Aish's hand from her husband's death grip and took it into her own. "Aish, you might feel that she owes you because of the attention you've brought to the Monte," her sister-in-law purred in her throaty voice. Sofia had seen the billionaire cry during movie trailers and drop into the snow to teach her twin toddlers how to make snow angels. But right now she was every bit the world-dominating mogul.

"We want to correct that assumption," Roxanne continued. Her thick brown hair was twisted into a sleek bun on top of her head, which she bobbed at Sofia. "She's precious. Her goal, to improve the future of our kingdom, is precious. Behave and you can win here, too." She gave him a lush grin and a wink. "Misbehave and there's no limit to the ways we'll destroy you."

Sofia kept her smile while she blinked back tears.

No one—not Henry or her family or Carmen Louisa—had asked what had happened with Aish. Only Roxanne knew a hint of it, had seen Sofia fall apart when she'd asked her, years ago, if she'd ever been in love. Her family and dearest friends had no details, and yet they stood resolutely by her. Loyally at her side.

As if Sofia, her mistakes and her missteps, wasn't the reason their kingdom's future was partially in the hands of an out-of-control rock star.

Her mistakes and missteps were about to be showcased as Aish moved stiffly to the last grouping of people. They'd stationed themselves a few feet away from the others. Sofia took a steadying breath before she followed.

King Felipe and Queen Valentina did their best to

look down their noses at a guy who towered over them. Aish gave them each a quick bow; he'd apparently done enough homework to know not to try to shake their hands. After getting caught blackmailing her brother and almost bankrupting the Monte five years ago, her parents had been stripped of their power and put on a strict allowance. The king and queen now had to satisfy themselves with petty displays of dominance. Like demanding bows and curtsies on introduction.

But the silver-mustached man who stood next to the queen, a person who should have never been standing with the royal family, stepped forward to grab Aish's hand.

Her mother had always liked attractive men whispering in her ear.

"Aish Salinger, this is Juan Carlos Pascual, owner of the Familia Pascual Bodega and head of the Consejo Regulador del Monte," Sofia said. She was okay with everyone seeing her smile dim.

"Mr. Salinger, *bienvenidos*," Juan Carlos intoned as if *he* was the king. As the leader of the Monte's most prominent winemakers, he was almost as powerful and twice as wealthy. In a double-breasted suit and royal red tie, his full mane of silver hair swept back from his face, the sixty-something-year-old winemaker looked magisterial. It was a look he used to great effect slandering Sofia. "Welcome to our beautiful village. Hopefully, you will pull our *princesa's* attentions away from changing generations of tradition and focus it on something else."

She wanted to slap him. He had a chokehold on Monte winemaking. And yet, by invitation of the queen, he stood on the cobblestones of Sofia's winery, among Sofia's people, preening amid everything he was using innuendoes and rumors and lies to stop.

"I'm just here to help Sofia," Aish said in his low, slightly scratchy voice.

"Indeed, Mr. Salinger," the queen said. "My daughter loves the help of rock stars. You might have seen the help she got from that Irish boy band."

Her mother's white sparkly dress, brightened teeth, and sheet-straight platinum hair shone against her bronze skin. If Aish Salinger hadn't gotten involved, she would have never had to invite her mother either.

Sofia had only slept with two members of Starting Five—at separate times—but the photo in the Jacuzzi overlooking the Dubai skyline suggested she might have been sleeping with all five of them. She'd been wearing a bathing suit, but the bubbles and the hands and everyone's expression made her look very, very naked. The photo had sent the queen into apoplexy, probably because she hadn't been the one in the Jacuzzi. But in recent weeks, it was the main image the press had been trotting out to remind everyone of Sofia's party-girl reputation.

The Consejo and the queen were only hanging Sofia with the rope she'd given them.

"I admire the intentions that brought you to our little, insignificant corner of Spain," Juan Carlos said, a derisive smile on his face. "But take my advice, señor. Cut your losses while you can. She knows little about quality winemaking. About love, even less. While she might have once called you her *fuego,* I assure you she's allowed herself to be heated up by many others since."

Sofia stiffened. *Fuego,* the Spanish word for fire that she'd called Aish, how did Juan Carlos—

The song.

Aish had used her love name for him in his song.

She made herself as impenetrable as the limestone walls that protected her wines.

"What the fuck?" Aish muttered. "Look…"

Henry moved his bulk so it blocked Aish from the view of the cameras, nodding sternly when it was safe to go on.

"How Sofia spends her free time is not your fucking business. No one's going after me, and my stories are ten times wilder than hers. And about her winemaking? Sofia's ideas about aging wine in something other than French oak are great. Tempranillo is better in American oak. And you guys won't even try stainless steel barrels? At Laguna Ridge vineyards, we've been aging in stainless with oak staves for years. It gives us a lot more control…"

"Aish…" Sofia hissed, her eyes on the cobblestones.

"What?"

"*Cállate.* Shut. Up."

She didn't want him defending her. She didn't want to know that he'd read about her winemaking techniques. She didn't want to know why he'd said "we" when he talked about his uncle's winery, the winery where they'd met. The Aish she knew had always viewed working at Laguna Ridge Winery as a good time with lots of pretty girls, clueless to how much his childless uncle enjoyed having him there.

"Sofia, how can you let him…"

"Stop," she demanded.

"I want to help you."

"Then be quiet."

"But…"

She turned, ready to march into her winery and barricade the doors, when she saw them. The interns and her grower-partners. They stood near the winery entrance, far enough away to have missed the growing tension. Carmen Louisa, who could track Sofia's emotions with one glance, gave a worried frown. But the rest of them, they grinned. Cheered. Waved. The superstar interns smiled with excitement, finding themselves in the middle of a media circus and eager to see Aish and Sofia jump through hoops for the next thirty days.

The growers smiled with hope.

It had been an act of bravado and stupidity when— instead of going to lenders—she'd convinced fifteen of the Monte's top growers, including Carmen Louisa, to form a cooperative with her to create the winery and luxury hotel. Ready to enjoy the spoils after years of watching their best fruit go into foreign bottles they couldn't afford, the growers committed money, their grapes, and their hopes for their children's future to Sofia. She'd resisted when they'd nominated the name Bodega Sofia for the winery, and had swallowed her tears when the vote had been unanimous except for one.

Now, their winery was ground zero for the biggest pop culture spectacle in years. And every available room in the Monte was full.

This was what the world wanted. Aish, the disgraced rock star, standing next to Sofia, the party-girl princess. This was what Namrita and Aish's manager, that muscular man who'd snuck out of the black car before it rolled away, had agreed to. Sofia and Aish would play out some farce of a romance for the next month—a pro-mance, Namrita called it—and maintain the public spotlight long enough to repair his crumbling reputation and gain positive exposure for the winery. Right now, Sofia had too much on the line to order Henry to toss Aish out of her kingdom.

And Aish was just playing his role to the max. He'd researched her parents' peccadilloes and Sofia's wine-making efforts, then playacted her defender when the situation called for it. She'd seen him perform, knew how good he was at working a crowd.

Sofia could pretend, too. This is how she became the princess her kingdom needed her to be. This is how to show them that their faith in her hadn't been misplaced.

Chin high and shoulders relaxed, Sofia took Aish's arm once again and walked toward a winery side door, Henry on her heels. Namrita and a cadre of security guards herded the press toward another door, where they would wait in a conference room for Sofia and Aish to join them and say a few words. A few well-scripted words. Then Sofia would ignore Aish for the rest of the night at the private launch party for interns, growers and friends.

The instant Sofia was inside the winery's processing facility—a high-ceilinged, concrete-floored room full of large tanks and equipment and the home of Sofia's glassed-in office—she dropped Aish's arm. She embraced the dim and the cool as she moved away from him and into the protective shelter of Henry's hulking shadow.

"How you holdin' up?" he asked. Henry was way more Texan than her brother. Blond and burly, he looked like the kind of American she might have mistrusted before he opened his mouth. Within minutes of their first conversation, she discovered that below his thick neck was a big squishy heart. He protected Roxanne, and now Roxanne's family, with his life. He was one of the dearest friends Sofia had ever had.

"*Estoy bien*," she said, rubbing her forehead. "I'm fine."

"Sofia?" Aish's voice echoed through the empty warehouse.

She ignored him.

"No you're not," Henry said, squeezing her shoulder, forcing her to look up into his quarterback-pretty face. "But you did good out there. You pulled it off."

Sofia let out a breath she didn't know she was holding. She covered Henry's big hand with her own. "Gracias," she murmured. "I…"

"Sofia," Aish called again, louder this time. A spark of anger tried to catch in her chest. She breathed in the cool.

Henry's slate blue eyes looked into hers. "You know," he whispered, "at some point you're gonna have to for real talk to him."

"Talk to who?" she said without smiling. "Now, has all the security been set up for the—"

"Sofia!" Aish's voice rang off the steel fermenting tanks and the concrete floors, shot off the rafters and the stained windows. That demand vibrated through her winery. Polluted it. "Would you, just…would you look at me?" he said.

She turned and looked, refusing to let him make her a coward in her own castle. He stepped out of the shadows, tall and lean in his dark clothes. His manager had snuck in and muttered urgently behind him. She raised her chin and didn't say a word.

He took off his sunglasses. His manager went silent.

For the first time in ten years, she met those black eyes.

"I'm sorry." Those dark, sparkling eyes, moving over her face, still had power.

"You should be."

Too sharp, too drawn, his face was still painfully beautiful. He revealed his dimple in a sad side smile. "You don't even know what I'm apologizing for."

She was stone. She gave him nothing.

His sleek black eyebrows quirked. "Why'd you let the guy talk to you like that?"

"That's not your concern."

He huffed a frustrated breath. "Well… I'm sorry about the song. I'm sorry about this whole—"

"We're not discussing that."

"Goddammit, Sofia!" Aish burst out.

Henry came to her side. "Watch yourself."

"How the fuck is this supposed to work?" Aish asked, throwing up his big hands, his irritating tattoos flashing like contrails. "You won't look at me, you won't talk to me, I can't ask a single fucking question."

"You can ask questions," she said coolly. "They will be in your daily scripts."

"Scripts? Sofia! Between you and me?"

Her stomach dropped as he looked at her with everything they once were. They once had. Ten years ago, she'd been overwhelmed and honored by the naked way he'd looked at her, soul-deep stares, unashamed and obvious. His open adoration had worked powerfully on a young girl desperate to be loved.

"I know I've fucked up, over and over again," he said, and his voice, *Dios mio*, she'd forgotten how his low voice with just a touch of roughness had lured her. "Just give me five minutes to apologize without…" He motioned to Henry.

Five minutes? After what he'd done to her, he thought he only needed five minutes and an empty room to bring her to heel?

How could she have ever loved this selfish, conceited, narcissistic man-child? How could she have let him back into her life?

Sofia, I fucked up, he would moan from his bed when he was too hungover to cover his interning shift and needed her to cover it for him.

I fucked up, he'd begged when he'd forgotten about their one-month anniversary date at Fisherman's Wharf and played a gig in Santa Cruz. She'd wandered the piers for hours, certain she'd gotten the meeting spot wrong, holding twenty-four glittering "I Love You" balloons.

I fucked up, he'd pleaded when he'd wandered off with a female lead singer at a music festival. He'd cried against Sofia as he reeked of patchouli and swore they only talked managers.

For ten years, despite how she'd deny it, she'd been haunted by the ghost of Aish Salinger. Now he was here, in the flesh, and she could effortlessly become spellbound once again by him. It was almost relieving to verify, once again, how craven and untrustworthy her needs were.

"*Verdad*, you fucked up," she said. "*Pobrecito.*" She used to make this "poor thing" come with her voice. She walked toward him, her heels echoing off her concrete floor.

"You fucked up thinking your help was needed here."

She moved through pools of soft warehouse lighting. "You fucked up believing your apologies were wanted."

She inhaled the toasty char of barrels stamped with her name. "You fucked up imagining *my* kingdom was a place that would give you welcome or rest or redemption."

She stood directly in front of him. It had been a while since she'd worn four-inch heels, but never had she been gladder for her ease in them. "You won't talk to me or touch me or ask me a single question unless it's written in the script. Those are my rules and you will follow them." She let her eyes stroke over his arrested face, his tempting lips and nose, and that black hair she used to grip in her fingers and pull. "Right now everyone feels pity for you, the broken rock star who's come to find his spark in the arms of a party-girl princess."

She fisted his black T-shirt and pulled him down to her. Underneath the pomade and the aftershave and the artifice, she could still smell him, skin smelling of sun and salt. She pressed against his heat, foreign yet so familiar, so she could whisper in his ear. "They've stopped wondering if you're a thief. I can remind them. I have proof that Young Son stole songs." He jerked but she held him close in a tight grip. "You'll stick to my rules or I'll ruin your life. Just like you're trying to ruin mine."

She bit his jaw, a mockery of the kiss he'd given her outside, before she pushed him away and turned on a heel.

"Aish will need a minute," she said as she returned to Henry and wound her arm through his. "Let's join our guests."

For a decade she'd hated her memories of Aish Salinger. Today she discovered that the essence of him still called to her as strongly as it did that fateful night ten years ago.

But for the first time, she was grateful for the brokenhearted reminisces of a spurned little girl. And she was exultant about the box full of treasures she could never bring herself to throw away.

Ten Years Earlier

Nineteen-year-old Sofia stood in the humid semidarkness inside a stainless-steel tank, reaching overhead with a long-handled brush to scrub off the shiny glasslike crystals of wine tartrates. The crystals glistened in the evening sunlight coming through the hatch at the top of the tank. She'd rinsed the tank down with warm water before she started, and the residual heat made her oversized sleeveless T-shirt and ragged jean shorts stick to her skin. Her arms ached—she'd arrived at Justin Masamune's Laguna Ridge Winery a week ago and had been plunged into body- pummeling, twelve-hour days. The other student-workers, most of them in college or older with a few harvests under their belts, told her she'd be numb by mid-September. She focused on the Galician music blaring through her headphones and made long sweeps to the rhythm of acoustic guitar, hand drums, and bagpipes. As she moved, her long, heavy braid beat at her back.

The snapshot image of how Queen Valentina would react if she could see her now added a feral grin to the happiness she was already feeling.

When she'd finally deigned to answer her mother's call several days ago, the woman had screamed that

Sofia would rather be a "grubby laborer" working at a winery in America than taking the tour of the continent that she had arranged for her. As if the grubby labor of winegrowing wasn't the source of the woman's wealth. As if touring the continent still was a cherry-popping experience for a girl born in the era of the Internet and transatlantic flight.

Sofia had actually considered forgoing the job to go on a rare trip with her mother. She'd thought—for a brief, foolish second—that perhaps her mother was interested in getting to know her now that she was an adult. Then she discovered that her mother had also invited a Portuguese infanta and her wealthy and powerful uncle.

Queen Valentina just wanted to use Sofia for convenient cover as she lured another man between her legs.

When Sofia realized the whole trip had been a ruse, that the woman had never wanted to spend time with her, she'd grabbed the first train to Madrid, gotten her first tattoo, showed it off to the first paparazzo, and then taken the first plane she could to the United States.

The only thing she regretted, she thought as the urgent beat of a hand drum filled her ears and the last of the tartrates fell to her brush, was that she hadn't been there to see her mother's reaction when the blood-red "The Queen is Dead" inscription on her forearm appeared all over European tabloids.

A finger tapped Sofia's shoulder.

She whirled around, holding the long-handled brush like weapon, and would have clobbered the tall boy if he hadn't blocked it with a thick forearm. He grabbed the broom handle, pulled it down, then immediately let go, mouthing urgent words as he raised his hands—big, big hands—palm up in front of him. His thick, dark hair fell into his face and framed his cheekbones, hard jaw, intense eyes, and full bottom lip. He was tall, really tall, with broad, muscular shoulders in a black T-shirt.

The frenetic, Celtic-like rhythm of her favorite Galician band rose to a crescendo.

She yanked her headphones out of her ears and pulled the broom handle closer to her.

"Whoa, whoa, sorry," he said, shoving his hair out of his face while he kept the other palm up to her. "I'm not going to hurt you."

Her heart pounded. But after a lifetime of being on the defense, she knew it wasn't because of fear.

"Who are you?" she scowled. "What are you doing in here?"

The 3,500-gallon tank was only six feet across; he backed up, but could only move a couple feet away. She still had to look up at him, still felt covered in his shadow.

"My uncle, Justin, he wanted me to check on you," he said, voice low and a little scratchy.

Ah, so this was the owner's nephew. *Aish.* The student-workers who came back harvest after harvest had repeated his name breathlessly over the last week while they waited for his arrival. He apparently sprinkled excitement, hijinks, and orgasms wherever he went.

"Justin said you'd volunteered to clean some tanks, but when you didn't show up for dinner he got worried." His eyes narrowed at her, eyelashes black and thick. "You know you shouldn't be inside here too long."

Carbon dioxide gases could build up inside tanks and asphyxiate the people cleaning them. Sofia had been a sidekick to winegrowers and winemakers her whole life and knew the hazards. At his assessment that she was some amateur, she relaxed the handle and settled it against the bottom of the tank.

"I might not be the great Aish Salinger, but I know how to stay safe in the tanks." She cocked a hip as Aish lowered his hands. "I tested the atmosphere levels before I got in, I've got airflow——" She jerked her head up to the open top hatch. "And I'm keeping track of the time I've stayed in here." She watched him bite into his plump bottom lip, watched a dimple try to appear in his firm cheek. "Why didn't you just knock on the tank and stick your head in? You didn't have to frighten the *mierda* out of me."

"I tried," he said, finally letting that dimple dig in. He pushed a hank of hair behind his ear. His smile was wide and easy as he looked down at her. "You couldn't hear me. What're you listening to?"

Tinny sound still came out of the headphones looped around her neck. "Milladoiro," she said. He was so tall. There was something about looking up at him, about being the recipient of that smile and the focus of those dark eyes that made her a little breathless. Maybe the oxygen was getting thinner than she realized. "They're a Galician folk band."

"Oh." His eyes watched her mouth. Had he moved closer? "Can I listen?"

She nodded, and he did move closer as she leaned the broom handle against the side of the tank and handed him her earbud. She felt a flare as their fingertips brushed. He stooped down to put it in his ear. With a lack of self-consciousness she'd never known in boys her age, his eyes stayed on hers as the headphone cord leashed them together. His skin, deeply tanned, glowed with the moist heat inside the tank. She wanted to dig her hands into that thick, black hair and anchor him there. She wanted to lick the long, straight line of his nose.

His eyes—black but light reflecting—traveled over her face like he had the right to stare.

"Never heard this before," he said softly, puffs of his breath hitting her skin. "It's good."

"*Es mi favorito.*"

"Yeah," he said, his eyes watching her mouth again. "Can you make a mix for me?"

"*Sí,*" she said. "Yes." She felt six years old, like they'd just met playing *la rayuela* on the sidewalk and then declared themselves best friends.

He pulled the bud out of his ear and straightened, never taking his eyes off her as he held it out. When she took the bud from him, she let her fingers linger. His fingertips were warm and that tiny touch sent a frisson down her arm.

She unwrapped the headphones from around her neck and stuffed them into her back pocket. But she didn't move back.

"I'm a musician," he said, voice low.

"I know."

A corner of his mouth went up. "What else do you know?"

That he made every millimeter of her skin buzz. That he smelled like boy and sweat and ocean salt. She hated the nose-clogging scent of cologne. There was nothing fake about the way this boy smelled.

She pulled her long braid over her shoulder and tugged on it. "You're from LA, your father designs clothes, your mother is a famous fitness instructor. *Y...* you're very good at surfing, singing, partying, working harder on less sleep than everyone else and...oh, *sí*, ménage à trois."

Shock, mortification, and humor created a palette across his expressive face. "Who said I'm good at three-somes?"

Sofia ran a hand down her braid and shrugged, all Spanish cool. "*No sé.* I keep my nose to myself. It's everyone else who talks."

When he grinned this time, he looked like he might lean down and taste her. "And what does everyone say about *you*?"

Sofia worked to maintain her smile. She wanted to be no one to nobody. She wanted to have nothing said about her. But even if she'd lived a cloistered life in a high tower, her story would be marred with her parents' dramas and affairs and fights, ugly public episodes that stripped Sofia of dignity without her involvement. And Princesa Sofia hadn't lived a cloistered life. Maintaining her dignity hadn't been high on her list when she'd mooned the crowd from atop a Semana Santa float in Cádiz or when she'd waved drunkenly to the paparazzi from a movie star's hotel balcony when she was supposed to be presented to the Queen of England. She'd been neither drunk nor sleeping with the star. But her humiliated mother had abandoned the duke's bedroom she'd been occupying to drag Sofia back to the Monte.

She didn't want to think about her scandalous past. She didn't want to think about the demands of her future. All Sofia wanted right now was to be a dirty, half-naked girl wrapped around a beautiful boy in a wine tank.

"I know some stuff about you," Aish said quietly.

Sofia focused on the air in front of his face and ran her hand down her braid.

"Your name's Sofia. That's…really fucking pretty." He hadn't said Princess Sofia. He hadn't said Sofia de

Esperanza y Santos. Just Sofia. And he thought it was pretty. She focused again on his eyes.

"You've got a great accent." The air between them felt like it was warming up. "You like grunt work, which is so hot it kinda hurts."

Nothing about her royal status. Nothing about her reputation. He'd just arrived; perhaps none of the interns had told him about the princess in their midst. Perhaps his uncle had just said, "Make sure the new intern hasn't passed out. Her name is Sofia."

"You're not wearing a bra." Her mouth opened at that, surprised, as his eyed gripped shut. "I noticed and if you noticed I noticed, I'm sorry 'cause I don't want you to think I'm a total fucking creeper and scare you away…"

"I don't think you're a creeper," she said, reaching to brush her fingers over his clenched fist. Her breasts were so small she seldom wore a bra. But this boy acted like they were an irresistible temptation.

Aish opened his eyes. "Are you for real?"

Sofia smiled up at him, feeling helpless and foolish and floating.

"I mean, am I having some weird acid flashback?" His urgency seemed to express that it was a real possibility.

"Wouldn't I be having one, too?" she asked. "And I've never done acid."

"No, no." He was a lit fuse aimed in her direction. "This could be my own personal hallucination. Because, what the fuck. My uncle tells me to go check on the new intern and inside a tank is a kick-ass, bareskinned fairy girl listening to elf music. I feel like I'm tripping. Am I?"

With amazement beaming from her, Sofia shook her head.

He reacted like she'd punched him. "Fuck. Your smile. Can I kiss you?"

Before he completed the question, she stepped into him and pulled him down by his black T-shirt. Hard body and hot hands and soft, soft lips engulfed her in sensation.

His lips were buttery-leather smooth and she licked at the plush bottom one, sucked at it before he licked in return, making her lips tingle like he'd touched raw nerve. She went up on her toes and burrowed her fingers in his hair, got two handfuls and tugged him closer, wanting him deeper, and he gave a thrilling gut-deep grunt before his tongue pushed into her mouth, before his big hand gathered her shirt at the small of her back and arched her against him.

She was instantly addicted to his taste of wine and salt and smoke.

He crushed her close, his touch hard and necessary as his free hand claimed her thigh. She threw her arms around his neck to eliminate any space between them.

He pulled off her mouth with a suck that bounced off the inside of the tank. "Can I see if you're wet?" he panted, searching her eyes. "Can we make you wet?"

She nodded frantically before he got it all out. She craved anything he wanted to give her.

He pushed her back against the wall of the tank, knocking the brush handle over with a clatter, before swooping down to his knees, pulling her cutoffs and panties down, not even bothering to tug them over her muck boots before he was separating her pussy lips and licking in. She'd been so self-conscious when other boys tried to do this and never understood what the fuss was about but there, down there with his gorgeous face between her legs and his soft lips mouthing at her and his calloused thumbs holding the seam of her body apart...

"Tell me," he whispered against the softest part of her. She scratched her fingers against his scalp, used him to keep her upright when he nuzzled his lips into her. The steel at her back alone couldn't keep her stable. "I don't know what I'm doing unless you tell me. Do you like it like this?"

Normally, she didn't know what she liked, although she definitely liked that as he flicked at her fast but she was too stunned to say it as she looked down and found him watching her, his eyes black and hungry with his pink tongue on this pink part of her.

"Or do you like this?"

And her whole body went to water as his tongue did this rolling, stroking thing, poking in deeper, melting her against his hands as she gripped his hair. "Yes, yes," she moaned. "*Ese. Así.*"

"Yeah," he said, trying to push her legs wider and then growling, thrillingly, at the clothes that still held her knees closed. He ripped her shorts and panties off one boot, pushed to standing as he raised her knee and pulled her against him.

"This is insane, right?" he asked, searching her face as the heart of her throbbed against his cock, hot and hard through his jeans.

"Definitely," she gasped, hips rolling against so much lean, muscular boy.

"Is it too fast?"

She groaned and felt him clench her ass in his big hand. "Not fast enough."

"I have a condom."

She felt him kiss the top of her head; she was sweating at her roots.

"Can I be inside you?"

She slid her hand down his torso and tugged at his jeans' button.

Hands wild, they got his jeans and boxers down around his thighs, they got the condom from his wallet covering his long, thick dick, they got his black T-shirt halfway up the abs she was trying to lick and suck before he stopped her, groaning, claiming she'd have him coming his brains out before they got started. He picked her up rather than fighting her, got her thighs around his waist, his hands squeezing her ass, his tongue deep and rich in her mouth. She shuddered against him, instantly compliant as the hot tip of his dick brushed her pussy. She folded her elbows around his wide shoulders as he pushed inside.

She felt incandescent.

"Tell me if—" He stopped. Panted. Leaned her against the tank wall and licked her nipple through her T-shirt. He pushed in again and stretched her a little further. "Tell me what—" He moaned, stopped again, and moved his mouth until he found skin in the sleeveless arm of her T-shirt, sucking his mark on her.

Arms raised to engulf his head, shuddering between him and the warm tank wall, Sofia felt light-headed with pleasure. She gripped him with her knees and circled her hips once to work him deeper.

He clenched her ass and buried his face against her neck. "I'm sorry," he whispered into her skin. "I'm going to come."

His helplessness made the muscles inside her surge, muscles she'd never known she had, and she squeezed them again, gripped and stroked him inside of her, wanted him more helpless, wanted him at her command, and he cried out, sound bursting in the tank, and then he pushed hard and fast, hard and deep into her, pounding into her body as she used all of her strength to hold him against her, and that wetness he promised made the way sleek and fire-cracking and then he was grunting through his teeth as his penis swelled then jerked inside her body, the thick, long, hardness like an arrow of pleasure.

She circled her hips frantically as he cursed and came.

He sagged against her swearing promises into her skin. "...fuck...fuck...sorry...so good...you felt... Gimme a minute, just a minute, and... I promise...fuck, you feel so good..."

Sofia hooked her ankles around his back and bathed in his worship. As she held him close, her body trembled with the promise of more. It was a journey she'd never completed, but she'd been further down the road with him than with anyone.

As he regained his breath, he turned his head and nuzzled into her neck. "Your tattoo...it's so fucking cool," he murmured. "The Smiths?"

She nodded, torn. That he'd recognized the red script from The Smiths' *The Queen is Dead* album cover was one more sign that her instant lust for this foreign boy was right and good and true. But she didn't want the outside world to start creeping into their warm and musky tank.

She seldom got what she wanted.

"Aish!" a male voice called out in the winery.

They both startled. When Aish jerked up his head to look at her, she was doused in cold reality. They were strangers. Fucking. In a wine tank. Among a gossipy group of twenty-somethings. He eased out of her gently, but she grimaced at the wet, uncomfortable pull.

He set her down on her feet. "Are you good?" he whispered, his shaggy, surfer hair falling into his eyes. She nodded, although her legs quivered beneath her. He took his warm hands away.

"Aish!" the guy called again.

"He's not going to leave until he finds me," Aish whispered, and Sofia wondered if the low voice was to protect her reputation or his. Maybe he didn't want to be discovered with the girl in the tank.

She reached down to pull up her shorts and panties, struggling to get them over her boots, as he took off the condom. He tied it off, but then looked around, nonplussed about where to put it. Realizing she was going to have to redo the cleaning and sanitizing of the tank anyway, she nodded at her bucket. "*Allá.* Put it in there."

"Sorry," Aish muttered, dropping it in.

"Where the fuck are you, man?" the guy yelled. "The girls are waiting…"

Sofia turned her back on him, picked up the brush, while he buttoned his jeans. "Just…one second…" he murmured before he crossed the tank. He grabbed the handle above the open porthole and swung his legs then his torso through.

"John," she heard him call from outside the tank. "What do you need?"

"Dude. What're you doing?" She'd heard of John, Aish's best friend and constant companion. They'd obviously spent a lot of time together; from outside the tank their voices were eerily similar. "Jackie and Betty already have the sleeping bags—"

She heard Aish cut John off with a "Shh."

"What? Wait—" John's volume went down. But the

open hatch of the tank magnified his voice. "Is she in there?"

Goose bumps erupted over Sofia's skin.

"No way," John said, an awed smirk in his voice. "You're all sweaty. Did you already…"

"Shut the fuck up."

Then there was a tussle outside of the tank before she heard a clang and a grunt and then another boy—an all-American boy about Aish's age, good looking in that blond and bland way—stuck his head into the tank.

"Hey, Princesa," he called, looking her over and grinning from ear to ear. "How's it goin'?"

Cold encased her. Aish had known who she was the whole time.

The legendary Aish Salinger had stepped into this tank to add a little Spanish princess to his conquests.

With a lifetime of experience, she reacted to defend herself from the pain. "It's going *fabulous*," she drew out, smiling, making the word drip with pornographic pleasure. No one could accuse you of what you'd already admitted yourself.

"These tanks are a bitch to clean," John drawled in a bastardization of Aish's voice. She imagined his act got him lots of his best friend's leftovers. "You need any help?"

With a yelp, his head and torso were tugged out of the hole.

"Don't be a dick," she heard Aish curse him. "I'll meet you in the bunkhouse." There were some angry murmurs, this time too quiet for her to hear, before there was silence. Numb, Sofia began to gather the cleaning equipment.

"Sorry 'bout him." When Sofia didn't respond, Aish said, "Here, let me help."

She turned to see Aish with his hand on the handle, about to pull himself back inside.

"Why?" she asked.

He stilled. "You have to start over because we—"

"I was bored." She cut him off. "I'm not bored anymore. So you can go."

She knew from gossip that he was twenty-one, that he was almost done with his music degree at UCLA. But his perfect little life hadn't exposed him to what Sofia had been exposed to, and his surprised naiveté showed in his face. "But, baby, I thought…"

She burst out a laugh. "Baby!" He must have been accustomed to so much more devotion from his hookups. She made a face. "Ah, *cariño*, you thought you'd get your dick wet again. Not tonight, *mi amor*. I'll find you the next time I get bored."

Her smile, the ease of her body, the surety in the knives she was throwing almost had *her* convinced that she was this steely woman.

When she said, "*Buenas noches*," and added a meant-to-be-irritating wave, his face hardened and he jerked his head out of the tank. The concrete pad of the winery hid his steps as he walked away.

She refused to let herself think as she picked up the equipment and shoved it outside the hole. She'd have to wash down the tank again. She refused to let herself think when she picked up the empty condom wrapper and stuck it in her pocket. And she made herself numb when, late that night, the bunkhouse already murmuring with rumors about her and Aish, she opened a carved, two-hundred-year-old box hidden in the footlocker at the end of her bed and slipped the stupid, pathetic wrapper inside.

September 2

Aish had the multiple espressos the wardrobe assistant poured down his throat and the B6 shot from the dietician to thank for being upright and heading to a vineyard in an open-air Jeep the next morning. The last year's insomnia had him out of practice with mornings.

And the we-will-cut-you hatred from Sofia's brothers, bodyguard, billionaire sister-in-law and—oh yeah—Sofia had made him want to suffocate himself in the bed's pillows.

People used to like him. His parents were successful business owners in LA and he was the only apple of their eye and he'd grown up anticipating smiling faces whenever he walked into a room. People liked his looks, his dumb jokes, his dependable hook shot, and the way he stayed in the curl on his board. They liked it when he opened his mouth and sang a pretty tune. It had all been so easy.

That was before John had looked into the fast-moving current of the Mississippi River and decided it offered a solution.

"She has proof Young Son stole songs?" Devonte asked, sitting in the seat next to him. His manager kept his voice low so that the wind swept his words away from the driver in the front seat. "What proof?"

Aish kept his eyes on the deep green vineyard rows that raced by and shrugged. Now, he could see those snow-tipped mountains Sofia talked about.

"I mean, you didn't copy any songs, did you?"

Aish turned and glared through his sunglasses. "Fuck you."

Devonte raised his dinner-plate hands in surrender. "No judgment. Whatever you say stays with me. But I can't keep this ship from sinking unless I know where the holes are." He was wearing a shiny suit and dark sunglasses; he looked like he hadn't gotten much sleep either.

"I never copied a fucking thing."

Aish wished he could unspool from his chest the years practicing his guitar and days perfecting a song and the endless hours spent in the studio. Shove them into the face of anyone who doubted him.

"And John?"

Aish turned to look at the vines again. "John's dead," he said, shutting down the conversation. Devonte had been the one person who'd been cleaning up his mess all year, the one person beside his parents he'd let into his house. He didn't want to punch him. "John didn't do anything wrong."

Aish had wanted to prove it by recording a fourth album that cleaned the muck off Young Son and made John's legacy gleam. Young Son was a duo, with studio musicians filling in for the other instruments, and all songs were credited as Hamilton/Salinger, with no preference given to who actually wrote them. Aish didn't plan on changing that for the fourth album, fuck everyone who demanded to know who wrote what when.

Rumors of plagiarism had always circled them like flies. He'd ignored them, drowned them out with the songs in his head and the roars of the fans in his ear. He had relied on Devonte and the label to manage the rumors while he and John made them millions, focused on writing and recording and performing the perfect harmonies that helped define their sound, their voices so similar because of the years spent at each other's sides.

But when John's death caused Young Son to go quiet after a decade of ceaseless chart topping, the plagiarism rumors gained volume. Now, several performers—bar bands and street musicians and the kinds of people who'd fling CDs at them as they raced on to their tour bus—were claiming that chunks of their original songs had appeared on Young Son's albums. The media was pointing at Aish as the person to blame. And the fourth album, the best way to resurrect his career and John's reputation, was an empty file on his studio computer.

"You know her," Devonte said. "You think the Princess really has something she can use against you?"

Aish closed his eye to block out this place that was drenched with her. "I thought I knew her. But I don't. Not now."

What had he thought when he'd arrived yesterday? He thought she'd heard his songs. He thought she'd seen his tattoos. He thought she knew. She'd made it clear that she didn't know, hadn't seen or heard, that although Young Son had hit the number one spot in thirty-eight countries, she'd kept herself in the dark and hadn't cared whether Aish was alive or dead.

He'd hoped that because everyone else had effort-lessly loved him that Sofia had held on to a little love, too. That with the distance of a decade and the understanding that he'd been young and stupid—because who isn't at twenty-one—she'd forgiven him although he'd never picked up the phone to beg her for it.

He'd believed that after a good talk and a better grovel she would set aside her rules and open her arms and let him rest. Let him get a decent night's sleep for the first time in a year.

Instead, shame had him tossing and turning in his high-thread-count sheets. For a decade, he realized, he'd clung to the childish idea that Sofia wanted him back.

In reality, she hated him. She hated him and hated that he'd intruded on her life. And if he didn't stick to the rules keeping her away from him—away from a woman he had an addict's need to touch—she would use whatever proof she had to destroy him.

His depression over the last year had nothing on the oppressive weight holding him down now.

"Let's go back," he said to Devonte.

"What?"

He reached out to tap the driver's shoulder. "I wanna go back to the—"

Devonte grabbed his hand and shoved it back at him. "No. You gotta show up."

"I can't," Aish said, shaking his head, his shoulders bending. "She fucking hates me and I can't—"

Devonte pushed him back against the seat, jolting the breath out of Aish. "Yeah, she fucking hates you. And you're gonna take it because she fucking needs you. If you abandon her, you'll ruin her. The cameras will leave, the interns will go home, and everyone's gonna laugh at her for being rejected by a rock star who sleeps with anything with a pulse.

"And you. This'll be it. The label's not giving you another chance."

His last chance to resurrect Young Son. His last chance to rescue his best friend's reputation. But Sofia...

"I don't know if I can stand it, man. She looks at me like I'm shit she stepped in. I shouldn't be here. And I don't know how're we supposed to look romantic with her scripts and her rules and..."

Devonte took off his sunglasses. "You let me handle that. You just keep putting one foot in front of the other."

He'd been good at putting one foot in front of the other—writing his music, singing his songs, smiling his trademark dimpled smile—while he let his parents or Devonte or John clear his way.

Would Devonte still be as loyal to Aish if he knew the truth about John's death?

Aish shied away from that hammering thought as the Jeep crested a rise and he saw a Mercedes bus parked on the side of the road. Beyond it, the interns were gathered at the edge of a vineyard. The cameras in the press area swung on Aish as the Jeep parked.

Devonte had arranged for their own transportation so Aish could have time to read over the scripts. When they got this morning's packet, however, they realized an extra ten minutes was not going to be enough time to memorize the choreography Sofia demanded.

Glad he was still wearing his sunglasses, Aish followed Devonte up the gravel road.

Calling the nineteen adults gathered near the vine row "interns" was ridiculous—Aish had been surprised last night when he recognized some of the heavy hitters Sofia had convinced to come to her "internship." His uncle didn't have any kids, so it had been Aish that Justin Masamune had explained winemaking to at a young age and Aish who'd gone along to the occasional wine conference between tours and Aish who helped out at Laguna Ridge Winery when he had the time or wasn't barricaded in his house.

As he joined the group, he nodded at a former-actor-turned-winemaker he'd partied with and an elegant French woman who was the wine director for an international hotel chain. The large, black eyes of the cameras tracked his every move. Sofia's eyes barely touched him.

She motioned at her mountains and continued to talk. "So it's these mountains that allowed those ninth-century peasants to believe they could grow grapes here in the Monte del Vino Real. We're thirty kilometers from the ocean, but the Picos de Europa create a barrier and a bowl of warmth that give the grapes enough sun to ripen."

Aish caught the winemaker stifling a yawn behind his hand. He glanced around. It had been a late night for some of them—Aish had made a limp appearance at the launch party then escaped to his room—but they all looked a little sleepy.

He returned to watch Sofia and nodded like he'd caught every word.

"Now, as an Esperanza, with the vino that runs through my veins, I believe the quality of the wine begins and ends here. In the vineyard."

She looked chic as hell in overalls and a long-sleeve T-shirt, her neck wrapped in a turquoise scarf and sunglasses holding back her short hair. She stood in front of a waist-high vine, its thick, gnarled arms hanging with almost-black clusters. For the first time in his life, Aish was seeing the Tempranillo fruit that Sofia used to talk about with the excitement usually saved for a lover.

Right now, though, she sounded as exciting as someone reading a textbook.

"As a winemaker, my duty is to ensure that the *calidad* of the water, the soil, the sun—the *terroir*—shines in the glass. So if I must get out of the way, ferment the juice in stainless steel and barely age it, I will. If it needs a year of American oak and a year in the bottle, that's what I will give it. But I let the grape tell me; I don't try to boss it around."

What she said was interesting and smart, the same philosophy of minimal winemaker intervention that he'd learned from his uncle. But she was so…muted. She wasn't smiling, those river-ripple eyes of hers didn't flash the way he knew they could. She was working so hard to bury the good-time girl that she was mimicking everyone's most boring aunt.

Devonte nudged him.

"What?" Aish whispered.

Devonte leaned toward him. "She said, 'Boss it around.'"

Boss it? Oh yeah. "Boss it around" was the cue from his script.

Devonte had promised to talk to Namrita about how stupid—he was going to use *unconvincing*—these scripts were. Sofia was trying to plan to the second how she and Aish delivered five minutes of #Aishia time for the press and public. Today, Aish was supposed to praise the fruit, laugh at Sofia's lame joke, then allow her to punch his bicep. His *right* bicep, as was highlighted in the script.

Everything in Aish shrank away from faking it with her.

Feeling like his balls were in ice water, he called out, "So these are Tempranillo grapes?"

Her wide eyes blinked at him like she hadn't known he was there. "Yes, the world-famous Monte del Vino Real Tempranillo grapes." He moved toward her as the script dictated, trying to judge the three feet of space it demanded. "*Temprano* means early, and these ripen earlier than other grapes, therefore, Tempranillo."

Impossibly, her voice grew more robotic the closer he got.

He stood with the bush between them, facing their audience. "These vines look really old."

"Yes, they are." They sounded like pro athletes in an insurance commercial. "They are the oldest in the Monte. They were planted by Carmen Louisa's great-great-great-great..."

She looked to the side where Carmen Louisa stood in the rows with other locals. The woman who'd glared daggers at him yesterday shouted out, "*¡Dos 'greats' más!*"

The interns gave an actual real laugh.

"As you can see, the yield on these vines are incredibly low," Sofia continued. "But the quality is high. These are the grapes I choose when I need to add a bit more *sabor* to a blend. When I need it to pack a Monte punch."

A memory had Aish rubbing his bicep. "You don't need any help with your Monte punch," he said, winging it. "I still have ten-year-old bruises."

It was supposed to be Sofia who joked and Aish who responded, but the opportunity was there and she seemed to recognize it, so she laughed at the bad joke along with their audience and then leaned over to lightly tap his right bicep, her fist touching his skin in his short-sleeve T-shirt.

"As long as you behave, I won't have to remind you," she said with a swagger. It was convincing, drawing a laugh from a cameraman, and reminded him of the girl he knew. But she was looking over his shoulder, not directly at him.

She couldn't even stand to look at him.

"One question, though," he said.

The script hadn't called for another question from him. The joke and touch was to be their #Aishia time for the day.

"The Monte's regulatory board has got pretty strict rules about how you're supposed to make wine," he said. "You're supposed to use a certain blend of grapes, age them only in French oak, and age them in barrel and bottle for a specific length of time."

He took off his sunglasses and used the opportunity to really look at her. He let his eyes soak in her strong chin, those wide soft lips, that perky nose, and her big dark eyes aimed over his shoulder. He let himself stare, even if she wouldn't. "Why are you so intent on breaking them?"

"The old rules no longer allow for wines that meet modern needs." She seethed behind her set smile. "We have better-developed palates, world competition, and climate change affecting the grapes. Let's just say that the Consejo Regulador del Monte and I have agreed to disagree."

"But it's more than that," Manon Boucher, the French hotel executive, spoke up. Others murmured behind her. "They won't give you their stamp. Without that stamp, you can't export your wine. If you can't export it, I can't buy it."

The round eye of the camera recorded it all.

"Currently, the Consejo has expressed some reservations about my intention to forge a new way." He wondered if anyone else could tell she was barely clinging to her smile. "I believe that in time, they will see the wisdom of my plan."

She said so many words while saying nothing. These were nineteen knowledgeable wine folk with valid concerns. Sofia couldn't gloss over their skepticism with idyllic storytelling.

Aish pushed her. "So you think you know better than people older than you, who've been making wine longer than you, who are drawing on generations of wine-making experience?"

"Yes," she flared. Now he had her full attention. "Tradition has bred complacency and laziness. The entire world has changed but the Monte is stuck in amber. By letting the grapes lead, not the rules, I will create wines that people crave to drink." Her eyes promised him fire and brimstone. "The Consejo can keep their stamps when my wines are streaming out of here in the suitcases of people desperate to get their hands on it." She snapped her fingers in the air.

"*¡Eso!*" yelled one of the locals as her people hooted and clapped, breaking the tension and causing the group to laugh. The journalists got every word. Sofia dropped her glare from Aish, and he felt like a cloud had moved over the sun.

In her natural state, Sofia was Spanish to her core, full of bravado and hyperbole. Playing the restrained instructor wasn't her gig. And as an expert in reading a crowd, Aish knew the act wasn't going to change her interns from skeptics to believers. Only her passion would do that.

But if he kept pissing her off to prompt it out of her, no one was going to buy #Aishia. So he stepped close to her, fuck the three feet of space, and reached for her arm. It was warm through her sleeve, strong although he could wrap his entire hand around it, and he stroked down until he lightly gripped her hand. Folded his big fingers through her delicate ones.

"Sofia. Of course, you know better than a bunch of old guys," he murmured to her bent head, intimate but loud enough that the others could hear. "But I had to give you crap about it." The sun had warmed her hair and he wanted to bury his nose in its cinnamon-sweet scent.

When she punched him in the right arm this time, there was nothing light about it. "Just you wait, Mr. Salinger," she said, her grin manic as she looked up at him. "Revenge will be sweet."

She dropped his hand and moved away from him, looking again to the interns. "Today, we're going to perform a green harvest. We will clip some of the underperforming clusters so the remaining clusters receive more of the vines' energy and nutrients. Each of you will be working with one of our vineyard crew…"

Her people paired with an intern and she handed them gloves and hand clippers. Carmen Louisa appeared at Aish's side. "You're with me, señor." She didn't look happy about it.

Aish wasn't happy about the Timberlands, tight jeans, and skintight white T-shirt he wore, clothes he'd let the stylist put on him without thinking about spending hours bending over in a vineyard.

Devonte joined him as they followed her to a row.

"All you had to do was stick to the script, man," he whispered.

"I know but...they're not buying what she's selling. You see that, right?"

Devonte pointed a finger at Aish. "Whatever steam's building in your head, stop. We've got a plan; we're gonna stick with it."

He flipped around and walked toward the Jeep, where he was going to sit in the shade and work his phone. Aish adjusted his balls in his ridiculous jeans and wished he could join him.

As he slipped on the gloves, a frisson went up his spine. He looked up and saw Sofia watching him from another row. Even from here, he could see that little troubled line she used to get between her eyebrows. Her quick brain was working on a problem she hadn't figured out.

That she was cogitating him gave him his first spark of hope since he'd stepped into Spain.

Aish began clipping off the grape clusters with too much shatter—fruit that didn't fertilize—or that had a predominance of unripe fruit. Carmen Louisa watched him for a minute, gave a huff, and then left him alone.

Aish distracted himself from the growing burn on his pale arms and the discomfort in his too tight jeans with the spark growing in his chest.

He could help her. He'd come here to help her. Yeah, he'd ignored a couple of her rules and, yeah, she might make him pay. But he knew how to make a crowd love you—he'd been practicing it all his life—and he could put that knowledge to use helping her, even if she was too goddamn stubborn to realize she needed the help.

September 7

Sitting at her desk in the winery's glassed-in office, Sofia watched the popular entertainment news channel on mute, her stomach in knots since Namrita had run in twenty minutes ago with a reporter on the phone. The reporter had waited until the last second to call; Sofia had given the *hijo de puta* a firm "No comment."

Namrita and Carmen Louisa watched from behind her. The grower squeezed Sofia's shoulder when *Disgruntled Interns Threaten to Abandon Party-Princess's Winery* appeared at the bottom of the screen.

Sofia turned up the volume.

"...felt like they'd received a golden ticket when they were invited to front-row seats with free wine to watch this generation's hottest love story unfold," said the smarmy American reporter in his overtight suit. "But after five days of backbreaking labor, average wine, and the relationship between the down-on-his-luck rock star and the petulant princess showing as much passion as roadkill, some interns are complaining that this party in the mountains feels more like purgatory. There's talk privately among the group about going home."

Namrita hadn't heard any such talk until the reporter called. She'd been monitoring the interns' social media accounts and most had seemed okay with the work and complimentary of the wine.

The reporter zeroed in on the one thing the interns had complained about as images of Sofia and Aish appeared on the screen. "A lust affair had seemed inevitable between the reunited duo; individually they're known for having a hard time keeping their pants on. But the intern we spoke to said the interactions between Aish Salinger and Princess Sofia are as awkward and uncomfortable behind the scenes as they are on camera."

Image after image showed Sofia smiling grimly at Aish, shrinking back from his unexpected touches, and glaring at him when he went off script, as he did day after day. Aish was refusing to keep the bargain he made. But the cameras were catching Sofia failing at it.

"Many blame the princess. Although Aish has thrown himself into the difficult vineyard labor—as well as the hard work of wooing the princess—he's been getting nothing in return but a cold shoulder."

Aish was being portrayed as the innocent. After what he'd done. After he'd left her alone and afraid when she'd needed him most.

Sofia hid her hands in her lap so her friend couldn't see them shake.

"Some interns are concerned about their ability to leave. After an inn in the backwater kingdom closed for unexpected repairs, the inn's guests found themselves struggling to find flights out of the rural airport. Some say the Monte del Vino Real is not ready for the tourism the princess wants to force on it."

The reporter failed to mention that Sofia fixed the inn's unexpected problem within two hours of it happening, reopening the inn and placating the guests with free cases of wine and tours of El Castillo del Monte, their six-hundred-year-old castle. Her repair involved bribing the inn owner, who was suspicious of Sofia's efforts, with more money than the Consejo had bribed him with to close.

They'd modernized the airport before the winery was complete. There'd never been a problem with flights. Whoever was speaking to the media was doing it with a bile that Sofia hadn't noticed among the interns.

"None of the interns were willing to go on record about putting an end to their month at the winery. For perspective, we spoke to the top winemaker in the Monte del Vino Real, Juan Carlos Pascual."

Carmen Louisa's colorful cursing filled Sofia's office.

"I'm not surprised the interns are unhappy." Juan Pascual appeared on the screen in all of his Spanish hacienda owner glory, silver haired, handsome, unquestionable in his misogyny. "Even if Aish and Sofia had hopped into bed in the middle of the village, it wouldn't have covered up the fact that Princesa Sofia is unqualified and ill prepared. She harangues our winemakers to change techniques passed down from their grandfathers because, why, she invented the chemical to eradicate cork taint? What proof do we have it's even her invention?"

Cork taint, a naturally occurring fault that made wine smell like moldy basements, used to plague the wine industry until the chemical Sofia developed eliminated it. She leased the chemical's license to a manufacturer and received a percentage of every vial sold. Since a drop was now injected into almost every bottle of wine produced, that percentage added up to a pretty penny. The rumor that her billionaire sister-in-law's company had developed the chemical and given credit to the spoiled princess was an old and tired one. Men in the wine industry loved to trot it out to discredit Sofia's hard work, training, and years of experience.

"The larger concern is how Sofia's delusions have affected her brother Mateo, the future ruler of our kingdom," Juan Carlos said, his brow furrowed in a mockery of worry.

Sofia shot Namrita a glance. This was new.

"He's ripped out many of our vineyards and installed his own clone. Has our fruit quality improved? Many think no. I worry that these children's effort to modernize centuries of tradition will ultimately damage the Monte del Vino Real's reputation for excellence in the eyes of our fruit buyers."

"*Joder*," Sofia breathed through her teeth. Juan Carlos had taken off the gloves.

The Monte had one thing going for it: a successful winegrowing industry. Her brother had replaced tired and underperforming vines with his Tempranillo Vino Real, a clone bred to grow higher quality grapes and withstand climate change. His new clone and careful financial management had brought the kingdom back from bankruptcy.

But Juan Carlos and the Consejo winemakers, all intimate friends with her parents, wanted to undermine any change and maintain a status quo that allowed them to keep wealth among a powerful few.

"Unfortunately, the Monte is being torn apart by a woman with too much time on her hands. We'd hoped Mr. Salinger would help her fill it, *pero no*." Juan Carlos chuckled. "Without proper distraction—a man, a family—our *princesa* makes up fantasies about a kingdom on the brink of ruin with her as its only savior. Our future king would be best served distancing himself from the delusions of his sister."

Juan Carlos was drawing a line in the sand and telling Mateo to choose a side.

Sofia hit the off button, wishing she could erase Juan Carlos's words just as easily. He'd publicly voiced the worry that sometimes smacked Sofia awake at night.

Had she insisted on a winery and a new way of winemaking as the only way forward for her kingdom because it forced her people to need her? Had she handcuffed them to her success or failure—even knowing her reputation would make success harder—so they couldn't get away?

When she'd been the only one caring for the kingdom in her early twenties, she felt like she was flapping a fan at a forest fire: listening to her people's woes that she couldn't fix, trying to keep her brother's head out of the sand, and attempting to circumvent her parents' worst abuses of power.

But when her brother returned and took his place with his billionaire bride at his side, Sofia had felt unnecessary. Unneeded. So she'd left.

She spun around in her chair to seek reassurance that this all wasn't just her "delusion," but the worry on Carmen Louisa's face had her shutting her mouth. Her winery manager and lifelong mentor had entrusted Sofia with her life's savings, several harvests of top-quality Tempranillo fruit, and her family's reputation as legendary winegrowers. For so long, Sofia had been in the woman's care. Now the woman was in hers.

Sofia straightened in her desk chair and set her chin. "Okay," she said, looking at Namrita. "What do we do?"

"Well…" Namrita said. Her long pause and the way she stroked her bob told Sofia more than anything else how desperate things were. "Maybe this pro-mance wasn't the way to go."

Sofia's eyes widened. "What do you mean?" He was here. His feet had walked her winery. His hand had pruned her vines. She'd had to endure his voice and his touch and glimpses of him out of the corner of her eyes for the last week. Now Namrita was saying it was a mistake?

"Maybe we ask Aish and the interns to leave and we launch again in six months on a quieter—"

"No," Sofia shot out angrily. She'd spent the last week running from one task to the next: checking the grapes then holding workshops for the interns then prepping the winery then writing scripts then faking two hours of sleep in her *hospedería* bed. She'd done everything Namrita had asked of her. "How can you suggest giving up?"

Namrita looked surprisingly vulnerable for a woman in a Chanel blazer, a stack of pearl bracelets, and over-sized ripped jeans. "I've let you down. I didn't take seriously how hard this was going to be for you, and I asked you to do the one thing that was intolerable. If this fails, it's my fault. You've worked too hard to fail."

Sofia was surprised by Namrita's concern. The PR rep was an unrelenting whip cracker and Sofia resented every second she was forced away from harvest preparations to impress the unimpressionable and fake an attraction to a man she hated.

Now she had to accept the responsibility that, no, she hadn't done *everything* Namrita had asked of her.

She'd actually lulled herself into believing that #Aishia was going okay. Those images proved it wasn't. And the world's gaze was going to wander off her winery—her "purgatory" winery in her "backwater" kingdom—if she didn't improve the view soon.

"*Mira,* look," Sofia said, raising her hands to clasp the women's in her own. "I can fix this. I just need to give the interns a reason to stay. So what do we do?"

Namrita gave her a grimace. "I need to find out which intern the press is talking to. I had no idea they were that unhappy."

Carmen Louisa nodded in agreement. "Manon has said nothing." They'd all been encouraged by the way the French hotel executive had sought a friendship with Carmen Louisa. Having a second luxury hotel in the Monte besides Hospedería de Bodega Sofia would be a coup.

The grower grimaced before she said, "I hate to suggest it, but maybe we allow Aish to lead some demonstrations in the field. I've been surprised by his wine knowledge."

Sofia fought her sneer. She was saved from answering when a door leading into the winery crashed open.

"Sofia!" Aish yelled.

She could hear Roman trying to stall him.

"Dude." Aish's voice echoed through the winery. The processing facility was empty; employees and interns were taking a well-earned siesta after spending the morning prepping equipment for harvest. "The only way you're keeping me from her is if you hog-tie me and lock me in my room."

Henry's thick drawl was coming closer. "We can stuff him in a closet until everyone's gone to bed."

She spun around in her chair as Aish came into view through the glass. When he saw Sofia, he charged forward, his manager, Roman, and Henry on his heels.

The glass walls shook as he threw open the door. "Can you call off your fucking…"

Abruptly, he stopped. Blinked. And stared at her from the doorway.

In a black oxford shirt buttoned to his neck and rolled-up sleeves exposing his forearms, artfully faded jeans, and manicured black scruff he hadn't been able to grow when he was twenty-one, he looked like he'd just walked off a *Rolling Stone* cover shoot.

Feeling pinned by his gaze, she asked, "*¿Qué?*"

"You're wearing glasses."

She raised her hand to the round tortoiseshell frames on her face. "And?"

"You didn't used to need glasses," he said. His stare was unapologetic. "You look hot as fuck."

"Man…" she heard Devonte groan as Roman and Henry each grabbed a shoulder.

"Wait, fuck, I'm sorry…" They got him turned around as he struggled, a giant man between two titans.

He should be sorry. But his base compliment had unwanted heat flaring through her. Aish always had a filthy mouth, no filter between his wants and his lips, and it had driven her crazy. She'd craved anything he commanded when he talked dirty.

"Sofia, please, I'm sorry," he called over his shoulder, almost at the door. "I saw that news story. We've got to figure out a way to make this work."

Namrita put a hand on her shoulder. Carmen Louisa

leaned toward her ear. "*El tiene razón. Escucha lo que tiene que decir.*"

He's right. You should hear him out. Aish didn't speak Spanish, so it was their go-to when he was nearby.

The PR exec on Sofia's right had put together a plan that successfully drew the world's attention. The grower on her left depended on Sofia to steer that attention correctly. Sofia could prove to herself now that she was the princess her kingdom needed.

"I know exactly how to make this work," she said. Roman looked at her and she nodded. He let Aish go and the man shrugged out of Henry's hold then turned around. For an instant, she met his sparkling gaze. "Follow my rules. Stick to the script."

She caught Aish's struggle with patience before she unfocused her eyes. She looked-not-looked at him in a move she'd perfected.

"The script's not working, Sofia," he said. She hated the way he kept repeating her name. "We can't convince people of anything when we're reciting lines and judging feet of distance and trying to remember which fucking elbow I can touch."

How dare he be frustrated with her. "You haven't once tried."

"Yes I have."

"No you haven't." Her voice wanted to rise, but she forced it cool, shoved it like a hot iron into ice water. "You won't even follow the simplest of my rules."

She pointed at his rolled-up sleeves.

Rule 8: Aish Salinger will wear full sleeves and keep his tattoos covered in all spaces outside of his private quarters. He will resist unveiling himself to 'explain' his tattoos. For the purposes of hygiene, he will maintain a long-sleeve shirt at all times.

When she'd seen the glimpse of him in the video, she hadn't seen the details of his tattoos. But the ink running all over his torso and down his rangy arms had been instantly provocative, even when he'd looked too skinny and too pale. She didn't want to be intrigued by what the ink drew across his velvety skin.

And she shouldn't be confronted by it in her own fucking kingdom, she wanted to shriek and pound against her desk.

"It's hot," he said between his teeth. "Outside."

Sofia breathed through her nose. "You show up late for my workshops dressed for a music video. Are you taking this seriously at all?"

"I show up late because I'm trying to memorize your script," he said, voice rising. "And I'm working just as hard as everyone else even when I'm wearing leather. I'm doing my part, Sofia, and you're still trying to punish me with your rules. They're all stupid."

She made herself ice against the surge of anger.

"I have been patient. I've asked politely. There were terms, and you agreed to them. So stop behaving like a child and do as I asked. Or we end this charade and I share my information with the press."

"You can threaten me." His large hands gripped his hips. "You can refuse to look at me and ignore me and sic your brother and your bulldog on me full time—"

"I'm more of a golden retriever," Henry interjected.

"Whatever you do," Aish growled, "it doesn't change the fact that this *isn't working*. That news story is my problem, too. And it just announced that we're not convincing anyone of anything. If everyone goes home, I'm also fucked."

His problem? How could he in any way compare his responsibilities to hers?

She raised her chin regally. "It's working just fine."

"Can everyone wait outside the office?" he asked.

Jolted, she met his gaze. His eyes were dark, bearing down on her, his hands still gripping those swaggery hips.

"Just gimme a few minutes," he said. "Just stand outside the door."

When she looked at her brother, already shaking her head, she was shocked to see that Roman was considering it.

"But the ground rules…" she said, heart racing. The most important rule.

Aish Salinger will only speak to Princesa Sofia de Esperanza y Santos when it will benefit the arrangement. Therefore, there will be no personal interaction unless the media, the intern corps, tourists, or other public influencers are present. There will be no private, one-on-one conversation.

Namrita, who Sofia had just begun thinking of as an ally, betrayed her. "Maybe it will be good for you to clear the air."

In Spanish, Carmen Louisa said, *"We'll be right outside the door; we can see everything going on."*

She turned back to Henry, her only remaining support.

He studied her, rubbed a hand across his mouth, then turned on a heel.

Roman said, "You got five minutes."

Looking more than a little guilty, both Namrita, Carmen Louisa and Devonte followed him. They walked out and closed the door behind them.

And then, for all intents and purposes, Sofia was alone with Aish Salinger for the first time in ten years.

She felt herself pressing back into her leather seat as he fell into the chair in front of her desk. He spread his knees, rested his elbows on them, entwined those long, tactile fingers. His hair glistened blue-black in her fluorescents as he stared at the floor. His scent reached her sensitive nose across the desk—seawater and sunlit air.

"My uncle says hi," he said to the floor.

It was like he reached across the desk and took away her gun.

Aish's uncle, Justin Masamune, was one of the top winemakers in California and a champion of wine innovation at his Laguna Ridge Winery. As a Japanese-American in an industry with few minorities in the United States, he enjoyed bucking the system. He'd written Sofia's recommendation letter for the University of Bordeaux and had provided her some info as she was planning the winery, which was how Aish had probably learned about it.

Carmen Louisa was right; Aish did seem to know an uncomfortable amount about the wine industry. When they'd been together, he'd taken his uncle's devotion and his easy access to a fascinating winery for granted.

"Um…" Sofia stuttered, staring at Aish's black hair. "Tell him hi."

"He'd love to come and support you but he won't be able to get away. He's doubled the number of vineyards he farms since you were there. He's doubled the harvest

crew, too. Asshole put bunk beds in the bunkhouse instead of enlarging the space."

When Aish raised his head, his grin and his dimple
were like a sword through the middle of her.

"He still makes me sleep out there when I piss him
off. You can guess I sleep out there a lot."

Sofia's heart jackhammered in her chest. She felt actual pain behind the bone. She didn't want to share this
memory lane with him. She didn't want to know that he
was involved with his uncle's winery. She didn't want to
think about the bunkhouse and all the memories under
its roof. She didn't want…she didn't want him here.

She lurched to standing, her chair rolling back and
smacking against the file cabinet. "What is this?" she
spat. "What are you doing?"

"I just want to… I'm trying to…" He ran his hand
over his forearm, a move she remembered when he was
stressed. He stilled and gripped it hard. "I'm trying to
reach you, Sofia. I'm trying to get you to hate me a
little less."

Hijo de puta. Anger roared through her. After what
he'd done to her.

She put her hands on her desk and leaned toward
him. "That will never happen. You can fool the interns
and the public and the press, but I know the truth about
you. When push comes to shove, you don't care about
anyone but yourself. The rest of the world can call you a
down-on-his-luck rock star, but I know you are the most
selfish, self-involved man-child I have ever met." *Aish
has thrown himself into the vineyard labor,* they said.
He's been getting nothing in return but a cold shoulder.
"You have turned me, my winery, and my efforts into a

farce for your own benefit. You'll destroy a kingdom so you can record another album of pop ditties."

His stood and dropped his hands on her desk, too. "You won't listen to Young Son so you don't know what I'm recording," he said, his powerful jaw flexing. "And you've got me all wrong, I am trying to help. If you would just start working with me instead of against me..."

Let him playact caring for the cameras. Let him touch and stroke her when it felt like being raked over coals.

"Follow my rules and—"

"They're not working."

"If you would stop going off script then we could—"

He laughed, harsh and cynical. "The script? Sofia!" He shook his head and she wanted to launch herself across the desk and claw his face. "You already hate me, so I can say what no one else will. You're boring. You're stiff and wooden. The interns are falling asleep out there. You look even less interested in entertaining them than fucking me. It's not fair what people were saying about you before the launch, but trading in the party girl for the automaton isn't working either. It's like you unscrewed the real Sofia's light and stuffed it in a drawer."

Sofia slammed her palms against the desk. "The 'real Sofia?'" Fury tinged her vision red. "You think the real Sofia is that girl who scraped and begged for your attention. That girl hasn't existed in ten years and good riddance. Especially when the real Aish is this man-child who cowers behind his manager and hides in his house for a year."

"Stop calling me a man-child," he said, his black eyes flashing.

The rage washing over her was cleansing and glorious. "You're not one? Only a man-child needs a crew of people to dress him every morning. Or needs special arrangements so he doesn't catch *piojillos* from the interns. Or needs a constant companion. With John gone, you're turning your manager into your new lap dog?"

"Fuck you, Sofia."

"*You're* the princess here. The pretty California boy faces one storm in his entire sunny life and dissolves into a puddle."

He shoved his face, harsh and gorgeous, toward her. "Better a puddle than a fucking ice queen. You think this act is going to make people forget that you made out with that married soccer player or danced naked in that fountain or…how many people were at your orgy in St. Moritz?"

His checklist paused her anger. Yes, an orgy had broken out at her ski chateau. But Sofia hadn't been there; she'd been in Madrid, consulting for her chemical's manufacturer, who'd been opening their third processing plant.

The words escaped her mouth without her permission. "You said it wasn't anyone's business what I did."

"It's not!" He stopped and swallowed. "That doesn't mean I don't care."

"Why?"

"Because I never stopped caring."

All the anger whooshed out of Sofia's system. "What?"

The muscles in Aish's jaw did a jig. "I should have picked up the phone ten years ago." Then his black-eyed stare became resolute. "I should have said I was sorry for—"

"No," she said. Pain sluiced through her.

"Sofia—"

"No! Roman!" Her brother immediately put his hand on the door handle.

Moving quick with his surfer's grace, Aish came around her desk toward her, his hand reaching out. "Sofia, please, there's things I need to—"

She scrambled to the other side and grabbed an empty wine bottle by the neck. She lifted and waved it at him. "I swear if you say another word I'll—"

Instead of coming in to thrash him, Roman spoke to someone outside the glass. Sofia froze. And saw intern Amelia Hill staring in at them with huge eyes.

Amelia was a wine blogger and a voice Sofia desperately wanted on her side. As one of the few black female master sommeliers, she was a writer who championed innovation over tired traditions. But she'd been skeptical of Sofia's efforts so far. This morning, Amelia had sharply questioned the wisdom of putting a state-of-the-art winemaking facility in the bones of a medieval monastery. And she always looked embarrassed when Sofia tried to banter with Aish.

Was she the one talking to the press? She'd certainly have a story to share now. It looked like Sofia was about to brain Aish Salinger with a wine bottle.

This was why Sofia wanted rules and scripts. Yes, to manage their interactions. Yes, to control him.

But mostly to control herself.

Because left to her own devices, abandoned to her needy impulses and unruly emotions, Sofia destroyed her world better than Aish Salinger ever could. Proof was here, right now, as she gaped impotently at the wine blogger, quivering in anger and terror, so overcome with emotion, she could do nothing to save her kingdom's imploding future.

Long arms surrounded her, pulled her arms down and against her body, dragged her close against taut, warm muscles, and tugged her head down so she could hide her face against his chest. "I'm sorry, I'm sorry," he said against her temple as he held her close, surrounded her in darkness and heat as the bottle dropped from her nerveless fingers. Her glasses pressed into his chest. "I'm sorry, shit, I didn't want to…" He muttered against her hair, words meant only for her as he rocked her. "Things keep getting fucked up with you and I'm sorry." It was dark here, overwhelming with the smell of him, shocking with the lean hot familiarity of his body wrapped all around her. "No, no, don't pull away," he said, rubbing her back. His hands always felt Atlas-size against her body. "She's…okay, she's looking away."

The rocking, *Jesucristo*, she'd forgotten about that, the soothing dance to the constant rhythm in his head. He tucked his head close to her ear. "Let me help you." His breath tickled her pulse. "I can help you. I'm an entertainer, Sofia, I know how to entertain. You gotta let me loose from some of these rules. You gotta…" She was shaking her head no, rolling her glasses against his hard pecs as she resisted that voice formed to compel her. "Yes, just show them more of who you are. Who you really are. Show me." She shook her head harder, inhaling the sun-soaked scent of him, and he captured her neck, calluses against her skin. "Okay, okay," he soothed. "Then…" That scratchy voice licked directly into her ear. "I'll do what I can and if you've got to punish me, you punish me. But I'm not trying to hurt you, Sofia. I never want to hurt you again."

Light doused her like ice water as Roman ripped Aish off her and shoved him back against her desk.

Roman turned her to face him. "You okay?" he asked, glancing at Aish like he was waiting for an excuse to tear him apart.

Devonte pulled Aish upright and behind him.

"I'm fine," Sofia said. Strengthened her voice. "It's fine. It was only for show." A show. A play. Aish's unbelievable one act. "What did Amelia say?"

Namrita sounded shaken. "She was flustered. She apologized for intruding."

Sofia breathed an exaggerated sigh of relief. "Well, that's good. Another crisis narrowly avoided." She glared at Aish over her brother's shoulder. "*This* is why we're going to avoid any impromptu conversations." Then she caught everyone's eyes. "And this is why I don't want to be left alone with him."

She grabbed Henry's arm and forced him to walk with her, her head held high.

She'd almost escaped when Aish called to her. "I mean it, Sofia. I'm going to help any way I can. You do what you have to do."

She plastered on a smile for employees and interns and shooed Henry away at her suite door. She slumped back against it once it was closed.

When Aish Salinger had wrapped around her, surrounded her in the smell and strength and heat of him, it felt like being able to breathe after slowly suffocating for ten years. At that moment, she realized that it wasn't Aish she despised.

Ten Years Earlier

Sofia combed out her long, wet hair in the silence of the girls' bathroom in the bunkhouse, dripping faucets and her exhausted thoughts her only companions. It had been a rough week. An unusual August cold snap had hit the Russian River Valley, with daytime temperatures only getting up to the high sixties. So on top of all of the regular duties the Laguna Ridge Winery student-workers performed to get ready for the September harvest, they also had to assist the vineyard crew with leaf thinning twenty-five acres so that the pinot noir clusters could get enough sun to fully ripen. The group prayed for more sun so they could get more than a couple hours' sleep a night.

Sofia liked the hard work, liked the uncomplicated this-equals-that result of her efforts during her waking hours. The vines had needs; she could provide them. She also liked the fact that the workers were spread so thin she never ran into Aish Salinger.

His uncle had taken pity on them tonight and given them a few hours so they could drive into Sebastopol and dance off some steam at a local bar. She'd take advantage of having a bunkhouse free of twenty-nine other people's smells. And she'd never position herself

alone, drinks in her system, with Aish Salinger somewhere in the dark and smoky.

Rumors had run rampant the first couple of days
after the incident: "Did they really do it in a...tank?"
But Sofia had managed rumors since she was old
enough to walk, so her careless shrugs and dismissive
looks had quieted much of the noise. The fact that she
hadn't tried to lay claim to Aish also quelled the more
malicious rumors. Aish Salinger was free to sleep with
whomever he liked. She honestly seemed not to care.

People believed she didn't care.

It was a tactic she'd learned from her mother. Or
rather, learned behaving as the polar opposite of her
mother. Queen Valentina would scream at reporters
who asked about her latest lover, would organize a
photo shoot dressed in virginal white, and then would
be caught clawing at a woman in the lap of the lover
she originally denied.

At nineteen, Sofia was beginning to understand that
life was a series of choices. She could live the bored
life of a royal representative of a kingdom. Or she could
squash grapes and study why their spoiled juices tasted
delicious. She could cry and wail over a man who
fucked her under false pretenses. Or she could throw
him away as effortlessly as he tossed her.

Did her mother see these options? And if so, why did
she always pick the one that was the most destructive?

You like grunt work, which is so hot it kinda hurts.

Cross-legged on the bench in the bathroom, Sofia
pulled her brush out of her hair and hit herself in the
forehead with it. *Stop thinking about it. Stop thinking
about him.*

She stashed her brush in her shower kit, drank out

of the faucet to wash down her birth control pill, and walked out of the bathroom in her oversized black top and wide-legged black pajama pants, vowing to turn off her brain until dawn.

"Hey," a deep voice called, startling Sofia. There, standing barefoot on the old boards of the bunkhouse, was Aish Salinger in jeans and a black hoodie, his thumbs in his pockets.

Warm honey moved treacherously through her veins.

"I heard you were staying in," he said.

Her brain did an instant calculation: she was easy tail in a convenient location.

She smirked. "Oh, *pobrecito*. I'm tired and you're predictable. I'd rather lie on my mattress than bounce on you. Keep begging and perhaps—"

"No, that's not—" He took a couple steps forward then stopped, ran his hand through his thick black hair to get it out of his face. The overhead lights bounced off his fascinating combination of strong bones and velvety tanned skin. "That's not why I'm here. I…"

He jabbed his thumb back over his shoulder and, unable to help herself, Sofia looked. There, on his bed on the boys' side, was a giant pizza box, a bottle of wine, and a bunch of white daisies in a mason jar.

She'd known exactly where his bed was in the long bunkhouse.

"I heard you weren't going out, and you need to eat, so I figured…" He crossed his arms over himself and squeezed his left forearm with his right hand. It was a surprisingly boyish gesture on a man so big. "I figured I'd feed you. We're too tired to go on a real date."

Mentiras, a voice whispered. *Lies. He lied to you.*

He doesn't want you. He just wants another go at a princess.

Sofia looked down at the ground, shaking her long, wet hair. "No, I…"

"I'm sorry," he said urgently. "John can be a prick and he totally was last time and, if it'll help, I'll get him to apologize because I've been on his ass about it and he feels really bad and…"

She scowled at him. "This isn't about John."

He let out a gust of air. "No, I didn't think it was." He took a couple of cautious steps toward her. "But to be honest, I'm not sure why you're so pissed at *me*." He put those big hands up when her eyes flared. "I want to know. I want to apologize and make it right. Can you tell me how I fucked up?"

A male had never talked to her like this before. Open, vulnerable. Her father barely acknowledged her, too caught up in his ego and his women and his efforts at whipping her brother into perfect princely compliance. Her brother Mateo was an incredible man and scientist, but he was so distant. He was halfway through his PhD work in America and seldom came home anymore. And she had more honest conversations with the men who made her *café con leche* in the *cafeterías* than the boys she slept with.

Out of her element, Sofia shook her head at Aish. "It doesn't matter," she said, turning toward her bed.

"It does," he said, moving closer to her before stopping, leaving a good two meters between them. Sofia realized he was trying not to get to close. This big boy was resisting making her feel forced or pressured. "Sofia, it really does matter. If it's the sex that's pissed you off, then I wish we hadn't done it. I don't want to do it tonight."

When Sofia peered at him, Aish stumbled. "I mean, I do want to. I want to every time I think of you, but not if... I mean not every time, but...most times. But..."

Sofia found it harder and harder to resist her smile.

Aish trailed off. "Tell me what I did wrong." He took another step closer and his black hair stroked his sharp cheekbones.

Sofia looked down to the shower kit in her fists. "I thought you didn't know who I was."

"I didn't. I don't," he said, sounding confused. "I mean, I knew you were that princess from Spain, but that's it."

"Then you knew about my parents' affairs and my tattoo and that stuff I did in Prague and..."

"Oh, that." She was surprised when he scoffed. "Look, in LA, everyone's got a story. My parents are public figures—they've got a story. It's got nothing to do with who they really are. All my friends whose parents are in the industry—they're either *waaaaay* crazier or way more boring than the public knows. I never thought twice about what the media says about you."

Sofia stared as he effortlessly lifted the weight of her history off her shoulders. "So you weren't looking to screw a princess?"

He showed a dimple as he shook his head, his big shoulders shrugging in his worn sweatshirt. "Justin was worried about you. I never thought I was going to run into a fairy I couldn't keep my hands off of." Those shoulders slumped. "But if not having sex with you means we could have been hanging out for the last week, then I wish we hadn't done it. As good as it was, I'd trade it in a second for time with you."

She could feel her heart growing with the sincerity of his words, like a vine unfurling toward the warmth of the sun. If she was honest, her heart reached for him the instant she saw him standing alone in the middle of the bunkhouse.

"Well," she said, catching her smile with her teeth. "You could bribe me with pizza now."

Delight burrowed in his dimple. "Yeah?"

"*Sí*." She motioned with her shower kit toward the girls' side of the bunkhouse. "Let me just..."

He followed her to her bed, and Sofia couldn't believe he was right behind her, smelling like a boy washed clean with seawater. Sofia was conscious of the warmth of his big body. She was conscious of his eyes on her as her wide-neck lounge shirt exposed her upper back and collarbones and one shoulder.

When she opened her footlocker to stash her shower kit inside, Aish walked around her unmade bed to pick up a book half hidden among the covers.

"Is this in Spanish?" he asked, pointing at "Munduaren euskal historia." His hands made the hardcover book look small.

"It's Euskera," she said, closing her footlocker. She walked toward him and pulled her long, damp hair over her shoulder. "It's the language of the Basque people in Spain."

"Is that that area above Portugal? Like..." He screwed up his face. "Like west of where you live?"

"No." She smiled, looking up at him. He really was very tall. "The Basque Country is below France. Above

Portugal is Galicia. They speak Gallego. I speak that, too."

He looked at her sharply. "How many languages do you speak?"

"Enough to know that *Aish* means fire in Hebrew."

As his grin grew devastating, she helplessly asked, "Why? How many do you speak?"

The bunkhouse was huge and cavernous. But their voices grew quieter and quieter. His eyes were warmer than a campfire.

"Let's just say Aish is one of the few words I know in Hebrew."

"*Como un Americano*," she chided gently.

He stepped closer to her and there was hardly room in her chest for breath. "And you're a gorgeous nerd," he said.

She wondered if she was glowing in the reflection of his dark, sparkling gaze.

They settled on his bed at the foot and the head, facing each other and separated by the pizza box. Sofia and Aish used the torn lid as plates and his bath towel as a napkin and they passed the wine bottle back and forth, the glass growing slippery with the grease from their fingers. The rich smells of tangy sauce and spicy sausage helped to block out the cloying odor of John's cologne. He was always heavy-handed with it, and his bed was next to Aish's. Aish, an only child, loved John like a brother, he said unabashedly.

Sofia had to cover her mouth to prevent a piece of meat from flying out when he got her laughing. He drew a picture of what it was like growing up wealthy, handsome, the only child of adoring parents in the California sun. He painted it with family dinners and surfing before school and two people telling him he was capable of whatever, whenever.

Sofia planned to stay quiet about her own family. But then she found herself telling a story about her next-door neighbor, Carmen Louisa, who'd found Sofia when she was hiding in the grower's vineyard. Carmen Louisa had lain down with her in the dirt, taken apart an ugly grape flower that looked nothing like a flower, and explained why it was the most beautiful sight in the Monte del Vino Real.

"Why were you hiding in her vineyard?" Aish asked her.

Again, despite herself, Sofia described how the queen had been roaring through the vineyard in a golf cart, screaming Sofia's name because the ten-year-old had hacked into the queen's computer and broken up with all of her lovers over email.

Aish laughed so hard she had to grab his knee to keep him from tumbling to the floor.

She told him, shyly, about her plans to be a winemaker and he told her, reaching for his guitar, about his dreams to be a rock star.

She watched him test the strings. "You could be a winemaking rock star."

"Why would I do that?" he asked as he adjusted a knob.

"Your uncle admires you very much," she said. While she'd been able to avoid Aish this week, it had been impossible to avoid her boss and his constant references to his talented nephew. "He's built something he loves; he probably would like to know that, once he's gone, it's going to continue to thrive in the hands of someone he loves."

Aish strummed his fingers over the strings while he looked at her. Finally, he said, "I never thought about it that way. About…legacy." His mother, father and uncle had started their own businesses in California, the land of fresh starts. How freeing it would be to grab for the opportunity in front of you without the pressure of history guiding your hand.

How directionless.

Aish pressed his fingers to the fret and strummed a beautiful note. "I wrote a song for you."

Surprise sparkled through her. "You did?"

"Actually, I wrote three." He bit into his full lower lip. "This is the best. I hope."

Once, thirty male *coros* sang to Sofia from the top of a *Semana Santa* float. It had been embarrassing. Now, with Aish's inescapable gaze, this had the potential to be excruciating.

But when he began to play, he wasn't looking at her. He looked down at his strings, his dark hair trailing over his cheek and jaw, and picked out an evocative melody that floated through the bunkhouse. Still focused on his guitar, he began singing.

Make a map and show me
Where you want to be
Make a map and I'll show you
Where you can find me

I'll always be there
Hanging around
You won't need a compass
Not lost, just found

Sofia loved music, loved the fast percussion of Galician music and the scratchy moan of old American blues albums, loved David Bowie in his Ziggy Stardust days and the folklore tunes that girls still sang in her village as they walked arm in arm to school. She had strong opinions about music, knew what she liked, and had decided at twelve that the last great year in music was 1988, when Jane's Addiction released *Nothing's Shocking*. After that, music died.

So while she was predisposed to hate all modern music, she knew her massive pounding crush on Aish worked in his favor. Still, she was overwhelmed by how delicious his voice was. It was like flan, warm and smooth and soft. She wanted to bathe in it. She wanted to smooth his voice over her skin. His voice surrounded and overwhelmed her like his ghostly twin, and now she had two gorgeous and tempting Aish Salingers to contend with.

Make a map and show me
Where X marks the spot
Make a map and I'll be there
I can be caught

Watching his beautiful mouth sing as his nimble fingers played, she couldn't believe he had this voice, this ability to play a guitar and write an evocative song, on top of everything else he had: beauty, strength, ease, charm, sweetness. Uncommon good fortune.

Beyond a meaningless crown and a bad attitude, what did she have? How could this song be for her, a girl he fucked inside a wine tank?

His eyes lifted to hers.

I found you in the day
Without a star in sight
I need my North Star
Lead me with your light

Please make a map and show me
The way to your heart
Cause you've got my map and already
You've got a head start
You've got a head start
You've got a head start
You've got my map and already
You've got a head start

The bones of his face, she realized staring at him, were actually quite brutal—long nose, high cheekbones, a carved jawline that could cut concrete. It was the tanned, velvety skin, the plush lips and the devoted eyes that made him look…safe. That made him look loving.

"It's beautiful," she sighed as the song strummed away, not caring that she sounded like every groupie who would come after her.

"I've never written a song that fast before." His voice rumbled out of him. "I think you're my muse."

"Am I?"

"Yeah." He rested his long arms over his guitar. "My North Star."

She could feel her heartbeat in her fingers and toes as he stared at her. She wanted him to touch her. Instead, he gripped his left forearm with his right hand, and looked down into the shadows between his arms and the guitar.

"I'm not trying to get in your pants again," he murmured toward his lap. His knuckles turned white as he clenched his arm. "I'll wait as long as you want to show you—"

She launched off her knees and tackled him, grabbing him by his hair to bring his mouth up to her as the guitar thunked between them.

He grunted in surprise. And then opened for her.

She'd been starving for his mouth, and now it was there, open and talented beneath hers, twisting to give her pleasure. He tasted like pizza and wine and spice, some secret ocean spice she couldn't get enough of, and she ripped her mouth away to bury her nose in his neck, to greedily inhale what she'd been missing for a week.

"Fuck," Aish groaned. "Wait…" He had to push her away, his hot hand against her naked shoulder, as he pulled the guitar from between them and propped it against the bed. The instant it was steady, he grabbed as Sofia leapt, falling back among his covers. He caught her head in his big hands and brought her lips back to him, tasting them and then licking inside them, holding her mouth captive for what he wanted to do to it. Sofia had never felt anything better than Aish Salinger's tongue stroking against hers. But she wanted to feel his fiery heat against her skin. She pushed against his chest, ripped out of his hands until she was upright and straddling him, and whipped her pajama top over her head.

"Jesus," Aish breathed as he looked up at her. "Jesus." In her frenzy, Sofia had forgotten that she was self-conscious about the size of her breasts, the small scoop of an A-cup with dark, tight nipples. Now she was in bright, fluorescent barn light, but when she tried to lurch down to him, he pushed her back, a hot hand against her sternum. It felt like he could span her torso if he spread his hand. He stared at her, and she knew she was panting and that her nipples were hard and she made her eyesight go blurry in case there was something awful on his face.

"You're gonna make me blind," he said. When she focused on him, he was staring into her eyes. He raised his other hand and lightly stroked his thumb over her nipple. "How do you say star in Spanish?"

"*Estrella*," she said, trembling as he continued to stroke her nipple, her body growing wet with the thick feel of him between her thighs.

"Right. *Estrella. Mi estrella.* You're so bright I can barely stand to look at you." He let go and lifted up on his hands so he could tongue at her nipple, sweetly, delicately, making her shiver, before he wrapped his arms around her and pulled closer, brought the heat of him closer to the heart of her. He sucked on her and she buried her fingers in that soft, thick hair, rolled her hips to make him ease the ache.

"Your cock is so hot through your jeans," she purred into her ear. "Like fire. *Mi fuego. Que calor.* You'll burn me up from the inside."

She bit his ear and he crashed her back on the bed, his weight holding her to the Earth. "Stop it," he moaned, licking the words out of her mouth. "I've listened to Spanish my whole life, but when you speak it, my dick feels like it's gonna explode."

She'd never laughed before as she got naked.

He was velvet end-to-end, endlessly long and strong as he stretched over her. But any impulse to laugh ended when he kissed her belly button then determinedly slung her thighs over his shoulders.

She actually squeaked when she looked down, caught the resolute gleam in his eyes as his mouth hovered over her. He was separating her with those long fingers.

"You don't have to... I don't..." she murmured. "I've never..."

When he smiled and licked his bottom lip, she thought, *Maybe I could...*

"Tell me what..."

"I don't know what I like..."

"Wet and tasty, cinnamon-sweet, do you like it like... *ungh...*"

"It's never felt like this, I don't..."

"God yeah, pull my hair, show me..."

"Oooh, there, your tongue, yes, yes, *unh...que fuego, demasiado calor..."*

"Deep, gonna tongue fuck you so deep...*umm, estrella,* baby. Fuck..."

"Me gusta eso, eso. Mi fuego, más, más. Te necesito."

And as pleasure ripped away her words, she screamed into the bunkhouse, filled it with the glory of what he did to her, the first to care enough to seek it from her, and he scrambled up her body, slipped on a condom and was inside her, hot, hot heat and fire for only a moment before he also was coming, his shout helpless and a little defeated.

His body trembled as he pulled off the condom and then pulled her into his arms. He muttered against her temple, "Stay with me. Be with me." He squeezed her tight. "Need you."

Unable to speak, Sofia just nodded against his naked shoulder.

It was simple. It was inevitable. She was his. And he was hers.

September 8

After a sleepless night thinking about Sofia's accusations, her anger, and the haunting feel of her in his arms, Aish dragged himself out of bed at 5 a.m. and called Devonte. He'd been making notes on the morning's script and mainlining espresso when Devonte stumbled in with a still-yawing makeup girl twenty minutes before the bus was supposed to leave. She'd barely had time to cover the yellow bruises under his eyes and flat iron his hair. The sprint to the bus had made Aish feel like hurling.

Maybe it was time to start working out again.

Now, Aish had to nudge a snoring Devonte awake as the luxurious passenger bus came to a stop beside a vineyard.

Canceling their private transportation was probably cruel to his overworked manager. But as much as that news story wanted to put the blame on Sofia for the interns threatening to go home, Aish knew it was his fault, too. He was so good at wooing a crowd that he'd been offered acting gigs, and yet, here, with his music career on the line, he was forgetting to entertain. He was only around the interns when they worked; he'd skipped the "fun" activities and took most of his meals in his room. Solitude was a hard habit to break.

But he needed the interns to stay so he could keep the cameras on. He needed those cameras sending sparkly vibes to the public. He needed the public to keep him in their good graces long enough so the label would accept a reputation-cleansing fourth album.

He needed Sofia to give him a chance to apologize.

And none of that was going to happen if Sofia kept thinking of him as a "selfish, self-involved man-child."

So he'd canceled their car and torn up his room looking for the intern schedule and buttoned his long-sleeve cuffs at his wrist.

He walked off the bus and stood outside with the group in the morning sunlight, getting a few "good mornings," which was progress over the shocked stares when he got on. A low, hazy fog lingered among the rows. Like California's Russian River Valley where his uncle grew grapes, the Monte had cool nights and warm days, which made for great grape growing. But the day was warming up fast and Aish could tell it was going to be another scorcher.

In a vineyard was one of the few places he didn't miss his best friend like a missing limb. John hated the work, and once Young Son had made it, never returned to Laguna Ridge Winery with Aish to lend a hand whenever their recording and tour schedule allowed it.

Aish sometimes thought the repetitive, exhausting, exhilarating work was what allowed him to withstand a decade of nonstop rock 'n' rolling. John never needed a break from the booze or the drugs or the sex or the limelight. Especially not the limelight, which, as the years went along, started casting John in an uglier glow.

Aish felt a stab of guilt at the uncharitable thought toward his best friend. His brother. He needed to clear up any public doubts about John and he wasn't going to do that focusing on what his best friend had done wrong.

Instead, Aish would focus on helping Sofia. He could help the interns see her talent, help the world see how interesting and compelling she was. Squash the rumor that they were going to pull the plug early on the internship, forcing him to lose his one best chance with her.

This morning, she looked unbearably sexy in oversized canvas work pants, a long-sleeve white T-shirt, and swept-aside bangs as she began to motion to vines trained on wire trellises. But his heart sank when he realized she was doubling down on the stilted-somber performance. *Nothing* of what he'd said yesterday had sunk in.

A few gnats buzzed above her soft, sun-streaked hair.

Aish began to sidle around the group to get closer to her. Devonte caught his arm. "What're you doing?"

"My cue's coming up."

"No, it's not. What're you up to?"

Aish tugged his arm away and kept moving. Devonte muttered behind him.

From the other side of the group, he could see Namrita trying to head him off. But he was closer to Sofia.

Within handholding distance from her, he stopped and adopted the look of a captivated audience member. Sofia side-eyed him but ignored him.

He raised his hand and gave a swipe at the gnats above her head.

Sofia startled back, brown eyes wide. "Aish!" she said, under her breath.

"Sorry," he said quietly. "Just…" He pointed at the gnats that had regathered above her.

She huffed and kept talking.

He let his eyes wander over her face. With her hair short, her delicate cheekbones were more prominent. Her eyes bigger. Her skin was as fine as porcelain with a healthy olive tan.

Holding her close yesterday, stroking his nose into her soft hair, filling his lungs with the spicy-sweet scent of her, had overwhelmed him. Memories had carpet-bombed him, tried to convince him of the insane: that she still wanted him, that he was essential to her. He lost all sense when he touched her. Always had.

Sleepless in his bed last night, that senselessness tried to convince him that he could make the insane true.

But here and now, Sofia was academically and long-windedly taking the group through the history of vine-yard trellising.

Aish waved away the gnats again.

"Aish!" she said with more irritation. A few of the interns chuckled. They probably thought the down-on-his-luck rock star was as high as a kite.

"Sorry," he said. "I thought they were annoying you."

"Something is annoying me," she shot back.

This time, she got a genuine laugh from the group.

"Forgive us. He's regressing." And she said it just right, pointing her thumb at him, good-natured exasperation on her face. Aish couldn't have scripted it any better. Amelia, the wine blogger, was scowling, but the French hotel exec gave them a warm smile.

Sofia launched into the warming global climate and how it had changed Monte winegrowing. He could hear the pride, history, and resolve bubbling behind her words. Could the others?

When he looked around, most of the interns were eyeing him. Waiting to see what stunt he pulled next. And the cameras in the cordoned-off media area…shit. They were stuck on him. They probably missed her whole fucking speech.

Might as well get it over with.

He stepped closer and waved his hand above her head one last time before he planned to retreat to the back.

She grabbed his hand like it was a gnat she was going to crush. "Stop it!" she snarled, pushing his hand against his chest. She shoved, forcing him to stumble back.

He heard a chorus of sharp inhales.

Her eyes were meteorites. "Stop playing the idiot," she said. "You can do better than this. I deserve better than this!"

A sharp, feminine sound of affirmation shot from the group.

She stepped away and his hand fell, burning, to his side.

No one around them breathed. The gnats were gone.

Thank God for the roar of a vehicle coming down the gravel road. It gave people something to focus on as a white truck came over the rise.

Shit.

Shit, shit, shit… He stared at the back of her head, at her slight body in grower's clothes. He kept his face impassive, aware of the cameras.

Shit fuck.

Stop playing the idiot. Was that what he'd been

doing? For the last ten years, he'd done whatever he wanted—wrote songs, fucked, partied, performed, dicked around at his uncle's winery—and received nothing but praise and money. Then John's death had pulled back the curtain of how much he'd been ignoring.

You can do better than this. When they were young, Sofia had always made him feel adored and admired. But she'd also pushed him. She expected more of him than others did.

She'd been the one person who thought he was capable of being more than just perfect.

I deserve better than this, she'd insisted.

Aish needed to take a good, hard look at how he was fucking this up—his one, best, *last* chance.

Devonte nudged him out of his existential crisis as the truck, its windows heavily tinted, parked. People craned their necks and the media—thank Christ—turned their cameras.

The truck doors cracked open and a man's heavy work boot appeared on one side, a woman's high-heeled boot on the other. There were murmurs and high little voices.

Then the world's most admired couple—Príncipe Mateo and his wife, billionaire Roxanne Medina—emerged around the truck doors holding their never-seen toddler twins. The birth of Liliana and Gabriel Esperanza y Medina three years ago had involved a breathless, worldwide countdown that ended with a gasping whimper because of the lack of photos the royal couple shared with the public. The two munchkins now wore sunglasses and ball caps—their dad was famous for his unprincely ball caps—but they were still painfully cute with their round cheeks and matching overalls. They waved excitedly at their aunt as they wriggled in their parents' arms.

"*Buenos dias,*" Mateo called to the slack-jawed crowd, sunlight shining in his blond-streaked hair. Aish now got the whole "Golden Prince" nickname. "I'm getting the impression Sofia forgot to tell you we were coming?"

All eyes turned to Sofia.

She gave a cool Spanish shrug. "I thought they could use a surprise," she said. And then she hurried over and embraced them all.

The interns murmured with excitement as the cameras focused on the beautiful bunch.

In the interview yesterday, that Consejo dickhead had threatened Mateo right along with Sofia. The fact that the royal couple were here, revealing their kids to the interns at the same time as the world, proclaimed exactly what the Consejo could do with their threats. If this was Sofia's idea, it was a brilliant one.

The beefy bodyguard—Sofia called him Henry— also stepped out of the truck. Aish didn't like how he popped up at random moments, keeping an eye on him like Aish was going to go claw at Sofia's door. Aish didn't like how blond and milk-fed he looked, like he could chew through linebackers with his strong white teeth while lobbing touchdowns. And Aish *really* didn't like the way he touched Sofia, like he did now, walking up to her and squeezing her against him and running his hand over her waist while Sofia leaned effortlessly against him and chatted with her family.

"Who's this Henry guy?" he whispered to Devonte.

"I don't know."

"Find out."

"Excuse me?"

"I mean…shit. Sorry." He took a breath and shook out his fists. "Could you find out what his story is?"

"Yeah. If she's sleeping with him, do you want me to tell you?"

No. Yes. Then he could kill him. Although a body that size would be hard to hide…

"Just…just let me know if it's serious." The hulk swept Sofia's bangs out of her eyes just like Aish wanted to. If it turned out Sofia was in love with the giant… well, it wouldn't be great for #Aishia. And personally, it would send Aish fetal.

Sofia laughed, head thrown back and beautiful. Happy. It was the first time he'd seen her genuinely smile in the week that he'd been here. Then, thank God for small favors, she stepped away from the behemoth and claimed Liliana from her mother. The little girl wrapped chubby arms around her aunt's neck and squeezed.

When Sofia began walking toward the group, her family and the beefcake following her, the excitement from the interns became palpable. Namrita told them, quickly and quietly, that they would be introduced to the little prince and princess one by one then escorted into the field for that day's duty.

Aish was thrown when he realized that Sofia and her troop were headed straight toward him.

Sofia looked over his shoulder and Mateo shot him death-ray glares. But they were still coming. Aish almost took a step back in surprise before Devonte stopped him with a hand at his back.

With the bland grin of a dinner hostess, Sofia said, "Aish, you remember my brother and sister-in-law?"

"Yeah," Aish said, stupidly. Roxanne, in a floral red dress and leather boots, was woman incarnate as she leaned against her golden husband. He held her possessively close with one arm and carried his son in the other.

Aish was suddenly, blindingly jealous.

"I would also like to introduce you to my niece and nephew," Sofia said, her smile growing real as she looked at her niece in her arms. Aish couldn't believe this was happening. "This is Liliana and Gabriel Esperanza y Medina."

She said their names solemnly.

The little girl held out her hand. Multicolored wisps peeked out from her ball cap. She had the same hair color as her aunt.

"Should I bow?" he asked Sofia. He really had no idea how to greet the three-year-old princess of a kingdom.

But the girl giggled. "No, you just shake my hand," she said, her words high and lispy. "Like this…" She took one baby-chunky hand in the other and then shook them up and down.

Aish was mesmerized. "Like this?" he asked, holding both of his hands together and pumping them.

And everything wrong with the last week evaporated with the kids' squeals of laughter.

"You gotta hold hands with me," Liliana cried, her aunt wincing at the volume.

Aish took her hot and tiny hand in his and allowed her to shake it. "Thank you," he said solemnly, looking into her black sunglasses, their lenses the size of quarters. "You have a very good handshake."

"*¡Prueba el mío. El mío también es bueno!*" shouted the boy from his dad's arms, waving his hand around.

Aish remembered to look questioningly at Mateo. "He wants you to try his handshake," Mateo said gruffly. He looked uncomfortable having to move closer to Aish. "He's decided he doesn't like English. Won't speak it no matter how much we bribe him."

Aish shook the little boy's hand. He had brown curls, dark as his mom's, erupting from his cap. "English is for the birds," he told the boy. "You stick to your guns, buddy. Your aunt used to tease me for not speaking more languages."

As the boy tried to choke the life out of his hand, Aish remembered. "Oh yeah, you've got a good handshake, too."

The boy beamed. "*Me gusta tu canción.*"

"We like your map song," Liliana said, excited from her aunt's arms. "Can you sing it?"

Sofia's eyes went saucer wide, and she whipped to glare at her brother. He promptly nudged his head and threw his wife under the bus.

Roxanne looked gorgeous even when she was caught out. "I have a couple of their albums. I didn't know! A few of the songs are okay for the kids to listen to."

Most of Young Son's songs, about sex and love and loss, weren't okay for three-year-old ears, but he'd recorded "Make a Map," the last song on their first album, like a lullaby, sweet and sad over his simple piano playing.

It was the second song he'd written for her. The first one he'd played for her. And the lip-gripped set of her mouth told him she remembered.

"Maybe I can sing it for you later," he said to the kids. "You've got a lot of people excited to meet you and—"

Their twin groans were in as much harmony as his and John's ever were; they had matching pushed-out lips.

"It's fine," Sofia said, her eyes on his chest and her niece on her hip. "You can sing it."

She'd asked him to *do better*. He couldn't have scripted this better to benefit him. But he was trying to peer through a decade's worth of desires to see what this was doing to her.

With the cameras and the interns and the two baby faces all focused on him, all he could do was open his mouth.

"Make a map and show me, where you want to be..."

He was singing in her kingdom, in front of her, in front of her family and the world. He kept his eyes on her niece and nephew, on their rapt faces, who watched him like there was magic coming out of his mouth.

For the first time in a week, he focused on *not* looking at Sofia.

He drew it to a close after the first chorus, wrapping up as quick as he could. For a moment, there was no other sound than the quiet clucking of the chickens the workers let loose in the vine rows every morning.

Then the kids and the interns and even the media began clapping. The toddlers whooped and bounced.

This time, he did bow when the prince and princess thanked him for their song, which set them to laughing and squealing even more. He didn't know how the adults' arms were going to survive meeting nineteen more people.

He caught Sofia's eye as her group began to move

away and a grower stood beside Aish to lead him into the field. Carmen Louisa had shed Aish as her intern, now working regularly with Manon.

For once, Sofia looked back. Without a word, he tried to say sorry. He tried to say, "Not like this. Not in front of so many people."

And, for once, Sofia gave him honest sadness from her dark honey eyes. With a nod, she gave him forgiveness.

As the group moved on to the next intern, Aish pushed past the grower and Devonte to head into the vineyard rows, wanting to get out of the camera's sights before he knuckled at his eyes.

September 10

Two nights later, Sofia stood alone at the balcony railing of Restaurant Martín, a bistro built on a stone bridge, and watched the small river that flowed beneath it. The Río Cristo was the lifeblood of the Monte del Vino Real and mountain runoff from the winter's heavy snowfall had the river running high and fast, providing plenty of water for her growers' irrigation. It was a blessed thing. It was getting hotter every day, which was worrying this close to harvest.

Sofia took a deep drink of the Cerveza Estrella in her hand. Now was not the time for worry. She—along with her interns and employees—were here to celebrate.

Her ploy had worked. While she'd been loath to drag her niece and nephew into her media circus, when she mentioned it to her brother and sister-in-law, they reminded her that they'd been looking for a controlled environment to introduce the twins to the public and press. And Mateo had agreed that it was time to bring out the big guns.

The big guns had squeezable bodies and smelled like almond cakes and powdered sugar.

Namrita reported that the next day's news cycle was dominated by images of the adorable prince and princess meeting the interns, stories about their delightfulness, and—thanks to the uncontrollable spontaneity of children—the video of Aish singing to them while Sofia looked on.

Namrita said the video's numbers were surpassing the video that had gotten them into this mess. There'd not been another peep from the interns about going home.

Sofia turned around and leaned back between the railing's flower boxes dripping red bougainvillea down the balcony. Through the crush of people laughing and talking and drinking, she met Namrita's eyes and raised her beer in salute. This impromptu tapas crawl through the Monte's taverns was keeping the good vibes flowing.

All she had to do was copy the behavior of the man she hated.

Aish liked to go off script. She could go off script, too, rip the interns' attention away from him and his antics and focus it back on the real reason they were here—to help a royal family create a better future for their kingdom. She could pretend some affection for him just like he was pretending a yearning for her, give him the honor of meeting her *muñecas* first, and wipe away the discourse about her being petulant and cold.

She could hide her trembling as the degenerate rock star spoke to her precious ones, as he sang to them, soft and sweet, a song that he once sang soft and sweetly to her.

For a masochistic second, her masochistic mind wondered if they'd had a daughter, would he have sung to her, too?

But Sofia would never, could never have a daughter. And Aish was not a man who hung around to sing lullabies. Aish was the man who'd turned his back on her when she'd needed him most.

As the fairy lights strung around the balcony twinkled and a busy waiter slung garlic-soaked *gambas* on her high-top table and the conversation on the packed balcony swelled, Sofia put one hand over the other on her bottle to cover their shaking. She could do this. She could control her emotions and playact with him and be the princess her kingdom needed.

As if daring her to prove it, she looked up to find Aish Salinger staring at her as he lounged in the shadows of Restaurant Martín's awning. Leaning against the stone wall, he was black clothes and black hair and intensely focused eyes, watching her through the vibrancy of the crowd.

She refused to be intimidated by his stillness when she'd only known him as kinetically energetic. She let him stare, raised her chin so he could see fully the deep V of her plum velvet dress, the heavy silver hoops that brushed her neck, the magenta lipstick at her mouth.

His side grin appeared as his eyes grew dark and devilish. He pushed off the wall and started toward her.

She grabbed the first people in reach. "Manon, Amelia." She directed the hotel executive and wine blogger to the dish of sizzling shrimp on her table. "*Por favor*, don't make me eat all of this by myself."

Startled, the carefully coiffed French woman looked at Carmen Louisa, who they'd been talking to. They all gathered around.

Searching for a topic, Sofia nodded at the rustic glass tumblers they held. "How do you like the wine?" The Monte's taverns served wine made locally as well as imported Tempranillo. Sofia hoped to shorten the distance their grapes had to travel to become great wines.

Amelia swirled the wine in her glass, took a sniff, tasted it along with a sip of air. "It's jammy," she said. "Lots of American oak."

Sofia pointed at her glass. "May I?"

Aish joined them as Sofia took a sip. She noticed he carried a water bottle, then ignored him.

"That's from the Villalobos vineyard on the sunny side of the Monte. They do high quad trellising to get even sun disbursement without having to drop leaves or fruit and they never…" As she spoke, Manon looked away and then down at the terra-cotta dish of shrimp, picking at it with a spare fork. Amelia narrowed her eyes behind her big glasses.

Aish drummed his long fingers on the table.

Show them who you really are. Show me.

"If you don't like it, you can always offer it to the holy men who live in our mountains."

She turned, held the glass over the balcony, and waited for the group to join her at the railing. Aish gave her the courtesy of not standing directly next to her. She closed her eyes and spoke:

"A los de las montañas
Quien nos abrigó y nos alimentó
Acepta nuestra ofrenda
Pero quédate ahí, entiende."

Then she tipped the glass and poured a small measure of it into the river below.

"What does it mean?" Manon asked as Sofia returned Amelia's glass.

"We believe our mountains are haunted by the hermetic monks who used to live in them," Sofia said as she watched the water froth. "They were the first to teach us how to survive in this valley. So we empty the last of the vino from our glasses and bottles into the Río Cristo with the belief that it will flow to them. We say:

> To those in the mountains
> Who sheltered and fed us
> Accept our offering
> But stay there, understand."

As the group laughed and others joined them, Sofia settled back against the railing and began to entertain them with legends about the monks who haunted the mountain caves. These monks taught early settlers how to make sacramental wine; the early settlers taught them how to enjoy it. The caves were the entrances and exits of the many natural tunnels that ran through the limestone foundation of the valley. The ghostly legends kept most from exploring, but Sofia knew the pathways better than anyone.

As more people joined their group, Sofia stayed relaxed and smiling, shared the myths and fables, and held her breath as she waited for Aish to interject himself.

But he didn't. He stayed quiet as he drank from his water bottle and watched her.

Del amor al odio hay un paso, a few Spanish tabloids had declared under two images of Sofia and Aish: one where she glared toe to toe at him, the next where she wistfully looked up at him as he sang, her hands twined around her niece's back.

There's a fine line between love and hate.

#Aishia, they reported, was showing signs of life.

She could do this.

He took a step closer toward her.

"*¿Estamos listos?*" she called, straightening. "Are we ready for the next stop?"

For the first time, these people gave an enthusiastic reply.

She gathered a group of interns around her and turned, her velvet dress whirling around her shins. Feeling like *el flautista de Hamelín*, she headed for the back stairs, knowing that *ratón* was going to follow.

Goddamn, it was something to chase a woman like her, Aish thought as the laughing, chatting group walked through the village plaza. He had no practice with chasing; from that first moment in grade school when he became aware of dazzled grins aimed his way, people treated him like he was their gold-medal prize.

But here he was, a guy with a Grammy, an Emmy, and the panties and private phone number of a Hollywood A-lister, crossing centuries-old granite in his steel-toed boots to literally chase after her skirts.

It was more exhilarating than those podium walks and that limo blow job.

He didn't care that she all but ignored him when she told her stories, stories from the heart of her, stories that made her shine. She'd be so pissed if she knew he was proud of her, but he hoped that some of her irritation with him had channeled into proving him wrong.

She ignored him, was annoyed by him. And yet, when she'd caught him staring at the bar, when she leaned back and taunted him with the unending sweep of skin from her breasts to her sharp chin, she beckoned him. Saliva had filled his mouth, and he had a drunk's thirst to grab a handful of that cropped hair, arch her head back, and taste every inch of skin the velvet exposed. Fuck the crowd and the employees and the suspiciously absent security and media that had to be lurking somewhere. Fuck that big blond bodyguard that kept touching her.

You can do better than this. I deserve better than this.

And that was why Aish let her have her distance. Because he was trying to haul himself out of a year's worth of thinking about nothing but his miserable self to spend a little more time thinking about her. About what she was asking for and why.

At this point, all he could realistically fantasize about was one decent conversation.

Sofia stopped outside a stone-fronted shop that looked centuries old. A few young guys came out of Bocadillos de Hernandez with trays of paper-wrapped baguette sandwiches and alcohol. Aish moved toward her as he watched Sofia greet a tiny, elderly lady with helmet-black hair. In a huddle of locals, it was a pleasure to watch Sofia speak a happy and knee-weakening Spanish.

He was such a fucking kid that her voice still did that to him.

As a waiter teased a young *hospedería* employee about moving to the big city, Aish saw Sofia's happiness fall away. "Lourdes?" she asked the girl. "What's he talking about?"

The girl—in her early twenties, round and cute—gave a retributionpromising glare to the waiter before she put her hand on Sofia's sleeve. "You know my last semester is this spring. I have to start applying now if I want a teacher training position in the fall."

Sofia smiled weakly. "The Monte needs teachers."

"*Si*, señora," the girl said. She could have been talking to the elderly lady, the way she was gently letting her princess down. "I might move back one day."

What had Sofia thought, that a few smiles from the

interns and couple of good news cycles had changed the tide working against her? He knew one of her hopes was stopping the flow of young people out of the Monte by providing them the jobs, opportunities, and fun that could come with increased tourism.

But everything was still on shaky ground. He and Sofia still needed each other.

He hated watching the little bit of joy he'd seen in her fade away.

He sidled in, brushing his leather-jacketed arm against her velvet sleeve, and said, "What's a *boca-dillo*?" He made sure to give the double *L*s a flat *L* sound.

Sofia's spine straightened. When she was annoyed at him, she was too puffed up to be sad.

"It's *bo-ca-diyyyyyyyyo*, señor," the older woman said in a heavy Spanish accent, stressing the *y* sound in the double *L*s. She barely came up to his chest but her dark-eyed glare was formidable. "It's a sandwich. This is my shop. Try one."

She took a sandwich from a tray and handed it to him. Aish loved a late-night *bocadillo* when they were touring Spain, but this one—with crunchy-crust bread pillowing a perfectly seasoned *tortilla española* fixed up with paper-thin tomatoes and red onions—was truly superior.

He said as much through a full mouth. "Damn, that's good!" he exclaimed before opening his water bottle to wash it down. "You can make a sandwich!"

The woman smiled at him patiently. Aish took another gigantic bite and forced Sofia to fill in the silence.

"She's the finest *bocadillo* maker in Spain," she said finally. Begrudgingly. "Aish Salinger, this is Loretta Hernandez."

"Titi?" Truly surprised, a crumb flew out of his mouth. "You're Titi?"

The smile of Sofia's former nanny became real and glorious. "*Sí*, señor."

This was the third most influential person in Sofia's life—next to Carmen Louisa and her brother—a person who'd calmed the chaos created by Sofia's dickhead parents. Without the nanny's warm heart and firm demands, Sofia might have lost herself to her worst intentions.

Aish might have lost her before he'd gotten to love her.

He swallowed, gathered his sandwich and bottle into his arms, and then held out a hand. "It's really nice to meet you," he said, kissing both of her violet-scented cheeks and gripping her small powdery hand in his. He hoped she could forget the fool she'd met.

When she smiled, it made him miss his mom. "*Y tú tambien.* What do you think of our little village?"

"It's fu—really beautiful," he said, coughing away his curse. "You better watch it; you let people get a taste of your *bocadillos* and you'll be overrun." He said the word the right way this time, and he saw her dark eyes narrow on him.

It really was cool, being in this old plaza with its arches and stairways leading off to ancient streets, surrounded by these beautiful Spaniards under the stars, eating an everyman's meal with Sofia's people. Even with the big glaring thing that was missing—Sofia's affection—it was kind of perfect.

Titi tugged him close. "I have one question for you, señor."

"What?" he asked, leaning down. Had Sofia told

her about him? He thought he was Sofia's dirty secret. "And please call me Aish."

"Señor Aish," she whispered conspiratorially. "Do your tattoos go all the way down?"

"Titi!" Sofia gasped.

She shrugged as everyone but Sofia laughed. "*¿Qué?*" With the tattoo coverage over his top half, it was a question he got a lot, though never from an octogenarian.

She winked at him. "I am single."

"Titi, I would show you," he murmured. "But I'm not sure my heart could take it."

She patted his cheek with a chiding "*Sinvergüenza.*"

"*Vale*, that's enough, *vieja*," Sofia said, the color high in her face as she kissed her goodbye. As she turned and walked away, Aish discarded his half-finished sandwich and hustled to catch up.

He matched her stride as her high-heeled boots— black leather that caressed her up to mid calf—cracked against the stones.

"You can ignore me," he said, under his breath. "We can clock some #Aishia time for the interns and paps without saying a word."

He assumed she was going to ignore him. But, as they went under an archway and out of the plaza, the group laughing and chatting behind them, she said, "We don't have to worry about the paparazzi tonight. I paid to have the bars open just for us and Roman and his team are keeping a perimeter around us clear of tourists and the media. Everyone deserved a night off from the scrutiny."

He said nothing as they continued walking down the winding street, aged copper street lamps glowing against the ancient granite buildings. He couldn't say anything.

For the first time in ten years, Princesa Sofia Maria Isabel de Esperanza y Santos talked to him like he was a normal human being. For the first time on this odyssey, she spoke to him without a script or a plan, and without her words stinging with hatred. Energy filled him to his eyeballs. He wanted to ask about a storefront they were passing. He wanted to tell her about his boots. He wanted to find out if she'd rather be walking alongside that Texas He-Man. He wanted to wind his fingers through hers and pull her to him and whisper against her neck.

He wanted to apologize.

But thinking quickly on what *doing better* involved, he did nothing and absorbed the marvel of walking quietly beside her through her hometown streets.

Sofia kept her mouth shut for the rest of the short walk to Vino Secreto and was thrilled when she walked down the steps into the subterranean bar to see that its candlelit crannies and nooks were already stuffed with growers and winery staff who'd forgone the tapas crawl. The interns exclaimed at the winding brick and stone bar with its wine barrel tables and cracked leather chairs and iron-gated arches that were entrances into the tunnels. Early villagers had recognized that the subterranean space directly under the village made for excellent wine aging and storage.

Among the heat and the noise and the crush, a favorite three-piece band—*gaita*, hand drum and guitar—played in a little room that dead-ended at one of the gates, creating a gothic echo, and Sofia snuck through until she could squeeze in behind a high-back armchair, hoping she'd lost Aish in the crowd. The miasma of sour beer, candle smoke, and good-time sweat drowned out the scent of him, the wildly thrumming music the sound.

Aish, however, had stayed on her heels and the crowd squirmed and squished to make room for him next to her. Suddenly, she was trapped between old leather and Aish's long body. He wasn't pressed against her, but she could feel the open edges of his leather coat when he moved. And the smell of him, salt and sea, settled over her like a personal fog.

A strolling waitress handed her a glass of Manzanilla Pasada and Sofia grabbed on to the glass like a lifeline, downed the rich, nutty alcohol in big gulps. Aish, she noticed, didn't take one until Sofia shot a desperate glance at the departing waitress. With a grin she caught over her shoulder, he grabbed two more glasses off the tray.

Staring resolutely at the band, she took the full glass that appeared over her shoulder and handed her empty glass back. There. That was plenty of #Aishia action for the night.

What was that in the plaza with her Titi?

There was nothing online about Loretta Hernandez, no refresher course Aish could have taken about the woman both Mateo and Sofia had relied on to be their soft landing when their parents dropped them from perilous heights. Titi had been paid to be their *niñera* but she'd loved and disciplined them like her own.

Aish remembered that. Confusion and his nearness created an unsettling buzz in Sofia.

The room was already warm, but he was the sun behind her. She knew without looking that his head was rocking and his shoulders were moving to the rhythm of her kingdom's music. His hand—big, with long, elegant fingers and veins that popped out because of his guitar playing—probably tapped against his thigh. Inches from her body.

She remembered the way two of those fingers could exploit a crazy-making spot inside her.

I should have picked up the phone ten years ago, he'd said in her office. *I should have said I was sorry for...*

The band's song crescendoed and ended with hoots and applause as the singer announced, "We're going to take a short break and we'll be right back."

Gracias a Dios.

But as the band left the tiny room to go to the bar and the sweaty audience followed them out for drinks, air, and cigarettes, Sofia found herself staring at her empty glass. Aish settled on the arm of the armchair, stretching his long legs out in front of him. Sofia leaned back against the wall.

He plucked her empty glass out of her hands and replaced it with a full one.

"You're not having any?" she asked and caught the shake of his head as he put her empty glass on the ground.

"I stopped drinking a year ago."

Quick and angry incredulity made her meet his eyes. His presence in her kingdom proved that to be a lie.

His lip tilted self-mockingly. "Besides a slip a few weeks ago, the only thing I've had to drink since John died is half glasses of your wine."

Sofia didn't have many memories of him at meals from the last ten days; he either wasn't present or she was ignoring him. But he'd never seemed drunk. Or hungover. And tonight, she'd only seen a water bottle in his hands.

"Why?" she asked, despite herself.

"Because I wanted a drink so bad," he said simply. "Because I was tired of the way drinking sometimes made me an asshole."

A decade ago, he'd never behaved like an asshole in the typical way drunk men throw around their bravado and fists. He'd been helpless. Embarrassingly slurring and boneless and careless with his words and behavior. Worse, there'd been no way to monitor when it was going to happen. She'd seen him walk a straight line after she'd shared two bottles with him and mumbling on her shoulder after two glasses.

"Should you be drinking my wine?" she asked.

The glint in his eye showed he'd read her unwanted concern.

"I'm not an alcoholic, Sofia. But I don't want to become one. I wouldn't be any good to my uncle. With John gone—" He cut himself off like he was surprised at his words; his broad shoulders tightened. He dropped his eyes to his hands. "It'll be easier to tone down the partying on the road."

She didn't care about that. She had no interest in his future. But there was something she needed to say about his past. She should have said it ten days ago, blurted it out on the first day rather than letting it guiltily fester.

"I'm sorry. About John. I'm sorry he's gone."

When he raised his eyes to hers, the look in them had her pressing her shoulder blades back into the stones.

All he said was "Thank you," soft and deep. But she had to look away. She looked through the gate, down into the tunnel. It was long and instantly dark, eating up the light. Half-full glasses and bottles congregated on one side of the arch, placating the ghosts who wandered this far.

"You know I borrowed from this style of music for our sound?"

That caught her by surprise. "How?"

His eyes took on…a look. Just for a beat. Then he gave a quick smile—dimple—and said, "Do you know about microtones?"

She shook her head.

He smiled wider and she'd forgotten how much joy he could pack into his cockeyed grin.

"Actually, you do," he said. "You introduced me to them."

She took a deep drink as he sat up to curve his fingers over an imaginary keyboard. "Think of microtones as the red keys between the black and white keys. Microtonal music is prominent in the Arab world. They have an ear for it; the western world doesn't. But you hear it in Irish music and in flamenco and definitely in Celtic-style folkloric music popular in Northern Spain."

He used his hands when he spoke—it had always been imperative for him to speak with his body—and nudged his hair off his forehead. He'd left it loose, with less product, and the blue-black thickness looked as soft as her dress.

"The music you introduced me to that fall, the world music I hadn't heard before, a lot of it had microtones. So after we…after that fall…"

Queen-like reserve stomped out her flare of anger, allowed her to stutter-skip over the wound.

"I reworked our songs to put microtonality in them. It was one way to stand out among the millions of talented bands. And it worked."

She shrunk back as he seemed to reach for her. But he just tapped the silver ring he wore against her glass, making it chime.

"That music helped me create something unique that still appealed to the masses. I have you to thank for that. I've always wanted to thank you."

Sofia remembered one of Aish's favorite quotes from that fall. "Music's just sound if no one is paying attention," she said.

His eyes went wide and bright. "Right." His dimple dug deep.

She looked down in the amber depths of her glass. "You certainly have my niece and nephew's attention."

"About that… I'm sorry—"

She shook her head. "You're good with them. I was surprised." She was floored. She was agonized.

"You know me, Sofia," he chuckled. "I know how to kiss babies and press the flesh. I should run for president."

She was surprised by the mockery in his voice. "Those kids can smell *mierda;* they're not sweet to frauds."

She felt a miniscule tug on her skirt. He'd reached over and taken an inch of the plum velvet near her thigh between two long fingers.

Heat like a summer breeze blew through her.

"Then maybe you could listen to my music with them sometime." His voice was dropping low, dipping into the depths of her.

"Why is that so important to you?"

He slowly moved those tactile fingers until he'd pleated her skirt around his knuckle and held it between three fingers. "You have good taste in music." She watched as his thumb stroked an inch over the fabric. "I'm hoping you'll be a fan."

"A million adoring fans aren't enough for you?"

She made the mistake of raising her eyes. She made the mistake of feeling want when he—lightly, letting her deny the pull—tugged her toward him.

"You were the first fan that mattered."

Self-destruction was a practiced art. She put her talents to work as she allowed him to reel her in between his thighs, as her mouth fell open at the feel of him running his big hot hands, never-forgotten hands, up her hips and sides.

She slid her hands into his thick, finger-encasing hair and tugged his head back.

He groaned a guttural sound of shock and pleasure against her lips. The warm burst of his breath felt like relief. The grip of his hands around her waist felt like law. All of her rules, all of her scripts and machinations, had been useless. They'd been careening toward this since the second he'd stepped out of the car.

A cloying tang of cologne made her wrinkle her nose, made her jolt back with its odd familiarity. Laughter burst into the room and then choked off as a group of people rounded the corner.

Sofia leapt out of Aish's hold. She squeezed her eyes shut and froze, wishing those ghosts would carry her away.

She heard the group murmur and leave.

"Sofia," Aish said.

She turned and fled. She tried to appear calm as she escaped the bar, but once she was outside in the deserted streets, she slipped out of her boots and ran. She ran over cobblestones and vineyard roads until she reached a secret side entrance into El Castillo, ran until she could shut herself in her childhood bedroom.

It was a room she hated. No matter how many times she'd ripped the silk and lace canopy down, her mother had always forced the staff to put it back up. But it was here, staring at its detested flounce, that she could remind herself of all the things she never wanted to need.

September 11

Aish was sitting barefoot on his balcony, plinking at his guitar and watching sunrise turn the mist and mountain gold, when the balcony door opened.

"Hey, man, you need to—"

Aish turned and nodded at his manager. "Morning. I ordered us coffee."

Devonte's eyes stuttered as he took in the two cups and coffee service, the fruit and the sliced meat and cheese set up on a table; he'd been the one making room service orders.

"I, uh..." Devonte slipped his phone back into his inside suit pocket. "How ya doin'?" His question was tinged with concern.

"Great. Awful." Aish smirked at his own stupidity and ran his hands over the strings. "Who the fuck knows."

He'd been using the view since dawn to even him out after a night of roller-coastering from peaks of hopefulness to pits of dread. The morning sun made the delineated green vineyard rows, lush hillsides, and the craggy mountain yellow and hopeful, birds twittered, and he'd heard snatches of workers giving each other shit as they headed to a field. The air was warm and soft against his T-shirt-exposed arms. The day was going to end up hot, but he'd dress proper before he saw Sofia.

Devonte made himself a coffee then unbuttoned his suit jacket to sit next to Aish. He nodded at Aish's guitar.

"Haven't seen that in your hands in a while."

Aish nodded. He'd watched phenomenal Arabian musicians play in tiny *teterías* in Granada, and jaw-dropping *taiko* drummers play with the New York Philharmonic, and the Rolling Stones from the front row. But it was the band last night that had rocked him. To hear her music from her people in her village, to be at the source of what had made it click for him musically, had lit an urge that he hadn't felt in a long time.

"I stayed up most of the night working on a couple of things."

"That's good," Devonte said, surprised and gruff. "Real good." He paused before he said, "Make sure you write it down."

As kids, John used to record them practicing and performing all the time, already prepping for documentaries about the band. Once they were signed, the chronicling stopped, and, when the actual documentary makers came knocking, John told them he'd lost all the audio and video several laptops back. Aish had always worked out lyrics, chords, progressions, in his head, and the first lyrics-and-music-sheet draft he put into his computer was the final version. He'd never questioned when John presented songs to him the same way.

It meant that Young Son had no proof of drafts or revisions, and no time stamps of their early stuff, to battle the plagiarism claims against them. Aish had no proof of songs that were solely his, that carried his heart and soul, beautiful babies that now looked like someone's second-class clone.

He inhaled the spicy evergreen scent of growing things and said, "I tried to kiss her last night."

"I know."

Aish blinked. "You know?" He'd told Devonte to mingle and his manager had hung out with Namrita most of the night.

Devonte pulled his phone out of his jacket pocket and handed it to Aish. *Princess Pr!!! Tease: #Aishia Almost Hooks Up in Crowded Bar* was the headline that yelled from the screen.

There were two blurry pics, one of their almost kiss, her hands in his hair, and the other of Sofia fleeing. The story was about how the "pornographic" princess had forced the "teetering-on-alcoholism" rock star to get drunk, teased him throughout the night, and then pushed him away just as they were about to mount each other in public.

"We all know about the revolving door on Princesa Sofia's bedroom—maybe it's time for our poor boy to get off that ride."

"What the fuck?" The tapas crawl had been a closed-door event. Only someone on the inside, someone supposedly loyal to Sofia, if only for a month, could have taken those pictures.

Devonte pointed at his phone. "Don't break that. Give it back."

Aish released his white-knuckle grip. "Why do they keep going at her?" Whoever was talking and lying to the media consistently made Sofia looked bad and Aish looked pitiable.

He cursed under his breath, focused on the sunrise, and fought off the self-pity that had become as comfortable over the last year as an old cardigan.

Last night, his newborn effort at restraint had been overwhelmed by…everything: her earthy eyes looking into his and her wide, soft mouth talking to him and her cinnamon-sweet smell and her questions—fuck, she'd been curious about him—and her skin and the velvet purple dress that begged for his touch.

He wanted to blame her for the inch. But he was the asshole who took a mile. They'd come together instantly and intensely as kids, but he had to be better than that twenty-one-year-old walking hard-on.

She was going to be so pissed today.

"It's time to send the stylists home," Aish said. His dependence on others to see to his basic hygiene and maintenance collided with her *do better* directive.

"You sure that's a good idea?" Devonte protested. "Probably want to look your best this morning."

"I gotta stop playing the movie version of me," Aish said. "The stylists are doing their jobs, but why would they think leather pants are a good idea when I'm going to be in a field for four hours? I had to cut those motherfuckers off."

Devonte snorted into his coffee.

"I'll have them pick up some stuff for me before they go," Aish said. "But I look better, don't I?"

He put his chin up, mugging for Devonte, but it was a serious question. He was doing better, wasn't he? He wasn't that ghost who'd haunted his own house for the last year. He wasn't that man Devonte had barged in on a few times when Aish hadn't opened his door, when Devonte's face had showed what he was terrified of finding.

His manager huffed and smiled at him now. "Yeah, man, a little sun and work, you're getting those *GQ* looks back." He rose as a ringtone on his phone let him know the stylists were outside the door. "You sure?"

Aish nodded. "Sofia's been putting in the work, every day, to show them how much this means to her." He clenched the neck of his guitar. "I gotta show them how much it means to me, too."

Today's work, Aish realized exhaustedly as he watched Sofia in the winery courtyard, was going to involve lobbing fireballs at Sofia's icy wall. Again.

She'd mortared up the light and charm she'd begun showing the group, showing him, and she was monotone and academic as she explained the purpose of the mammoth crusher-destemmer set up in the open bay of the processing facility.

When he thought of her last night—velvet-dressed, grinning, softly content in the arms of her people and village and music and legends—Aish wanted to sit on the cobblestones and cry.

The interns had been surprisingly welcoming when he and Devonte had appeared on time for that morning's workshop, showing none of the snickering from that fucked-up article. He got handshakes and good mornings, maybe a smile or two that was a bit more teasing, and even a nod of approval from the wine blogger.

"I like you better without eyeliner," Amelia Hill said. Her no-nonsense manner was ruined by a mild grin. "I think she'll like you better without it, too."

In ungelled hair, a worn long-sleeve Cowboy Surf Shop T-shirt, jeans, and old Blundstones, clothes he'd thrown into an overnight bag when he left LA, Aish had felt like the goth dude who'd shown up in an oxford to ask out the prom queen. The whole senior class was rooting for him.

All of his fantasy about the situation faded, however, the moment Sofia opened her mouth. As she robotically recited the manual about the huge machine that was so much cooler to see in action, Aish raised his hand.

She aimed scorching hate in his direction. She flicked her head away, showing him a sliver of tender, sensitive neck. She'd once been sensitive all over to his touch, like a bare nerve.

He kept his hand up. Devonte nudged him. "Dumbass. Put your hand down."

But it was an easy hop for him to touch a basketball rim. He was a hard man to ignore.

"What?" Sofia shot out, startling them all. "What do you want, Aish?"

"Are you worried about the heat?" His question sounded like a demand. He needed to pull back. But dammit… "It's hot so close to harvest."

A hair's breadth from harvest was an anxious time for growers and winemakers, when the fruit was days away from full ripeness and vulnerable on the vine. Wind gusts, rainstorms, unexpected cold, or heat spikes could ruin a crop. Laguna Ridge Winery once lost 75 percent of a year's fruit thanks to a thunderstorm and the subsequent mildew.

The increasing heat in the Monte could burn Sofia's not-quite-ripe fruit before it was picked.

When Sofia glanced at Carmen Louisa, he knew the answer was yes. She was worried.

Aish had spent night after night in his uncle's truck, nodding off as they drove from vineyard to vineyard, his uncle nudging him awake as they obsessively checked the grapes. Here, he'd spent sleepless nights in bed while Sofia, who had yellow smudges under her furious eyes, had spent those same nights running from field to field. How many vineyards was she taking harvest from? Fifteen?

She spoke through gritted teeth. "We're keeping an eye on the temperature and putting together a contingency plan. Now, back to our crusher-destemmer…"

"What contingency plan?"

Goddammit, Sofia. He felt the urgency, the frustration, in his spine, his clenched fists, his molars. *Goddammit, Sofia, let these people help you. They want to help.*

Let me help you.

He could see her anger, equal to his, as she glared back.

But Namrita, who'd been on the phone, moved quickly to Sofia's side and murmured close to her ear. Sofia's mouth dropped open with dismay. Then her narrow shoulders slumped and she nodded.

Namrita spoke into her phone.

The black-iron gate that barred the entrance to the winery slowly opened. A gleaming red Mercedes-Maybach rolled in and purred up to where the interns were gathered. When the car stopped, Juan Carlos Pascual, that slime bag who was head of the Consejo, slid out. He strolled around the back of the car—the picture of power in a morning-grey double-breasted suit with a fuchsia tie and pocket square—and opened the door.

A feminine leg that ended in a white-glitter heel stepped out onto the cobblestones.

Juan Carlos helped Queen Valentina out of the car. Aish looked at Sofia.

She was still as a statue.

Queen Valentina and her husband had once regularly made the list of the world's worst royals for their gross extravagance, showy extramarital affairs, ugly fights, and snobby lack of interest in their own people. They'd gone quiet after their son took control of the kingdom several years ago.

Privately, Aish knew that Queen Valentina had made her affection something impossible for Sofia to gain. In the spaces between Sofia's stories about the fights, parties, and ever-changing hair colors of her teen wild-child days, Aish had heard a girl who'd decided that if she couldn't get her mother's attention through pleasing her, she'd get it through pissing her off.

As she'd told him her stories, whispered them to him, he'd run his nails up and down her tattoo and squeezed her tight.

Now her mother had brought Sofia's enemy into her camp.

Juan Carlos and the queen stopped just short of Sofia, forcing her to move to them. They exchanged stiff air kisses. The queen looked into the air as if she were tolerating her daughter's affections.

Her smile for the interns, however, was full and slick lipped.

Sofia introduced them tonelessly while Juan Carlos and the queen nodded with matching smirks. Aish could imagine what temper tantrums they'd threatened if Sofia hadn't let them in. Without any warning, already exhausted, and on the day that the world's tabloids called her a drunk cock tease, Sofia had to deal with the head of the regulatory board that had been doing all it could to badmouth her.

This was no fucking coincidence.

But Aish saw none of his building head of steam in Sofia. She was good at aiming anger at him. But toward her mother and this asshole actively trying to make her winery fail—nothing. She was the star that had winked out.

The queen pressed a manicured hand against her diamond necklace. That was a lot of carats before noon. "Forgive me for not returning sooner. The king and I have been waiting for an invitation." Her accent was affected, semi-British. She sounded like American celebrities when they'd spent too much time in the Hamptons. "But a princess who shirks her duties as hostess does not mean I can shirk mine. Please, at long last—" she swept her hand away from herself "—let me welcome you to our kingdom, the Monte del Vino Real."

Her hand waved over the winery built by her daughter.

"We have a rich tradition of working together as a village, a community, and a kingdom, despite what you may have heard from my daughter. When a person puts her own selfish glory in front of the kingdom's needs, she breaks us into pieces." Sofia slid her hands into her front pockets and looked down at her boots. "I would like you to hear from a winemaker whose family has been setting the standard for Monte del Vino Real wines for centuries. Juan Carlos?"

The winemaker stepped forward. "*Mil* gracias, *mi reina*," he oozed. He swept a hand toward Queen Valentina. "Isn't she gorgeous?"

As she was put on display to bring credit to this slea-zeball, Aish felt a surprising tug of pity for her. Smiling widely, she looked like the unhappiest person he'd ever met.

"I'm disappointed the press is not here," Juan Carlos said as he looked around. The press portion was scheduled for the post-hangover second half of the day. "*Pero vale*. Perhaps one of you will share my words with them."

That motherfucker.

"Our kingdom has been growing grapes and making wine for a thousand years," Juan Carlos said, the rings on his fingers catching the sunlight. "The Consejo Regulador del Monte was given the noble duty of ensuring only the highest quality wines went to Reina Isabel. We chose the barrels that the conquistadores carried to the New World to bargain with the *indios*."

Bargain. Aish felt the group twitch. Dude. Read a textbook.

"Now, every century or so, we have a prince who thinks he can reinvent the wheel, that he knows better than hundreds of years of communal experience. Call it youth. Call it naivete. Some call it…delusion." He spoke behind his hand. "Those are the Esperanza strains we don't talk about. But each time, the people relied on the Consejo to bring him back to sanity. Why waste our fruit, the sweat from our growers' brows, on an experiment? That is why, *por ejemplo*, my family's *bodega* is called Familia Pascual. *Porque la familia es lo más importante.* The family, the community, the kingdom is what we value. There is only one *bodega* in all the Monte that is named after only one person."

That one person was still looking at her boots.

Enough.

"*El Gato con El Queso?*" Aish called in an American accent. He'd noticed the Cat with the Cheese *bodega* on the way to the square yesterday.

The interns laughed, breaking up the tension. But Sofia shot him a dark look. Like *he* was the one being a dick.

Juan Carlos gave him a patronizing smile. "Señor Salinger, you have the leisure time to make jokes, but these good people do not." He looked around. "You've been lured from your lives to prop up a charade. I encourage you to end it and go home. If not for your sake, then for the sake of our villagers. Let's end this media circus and allow them to get back to work. Then they can focus on their real futures and not the fantasies of a princess who imagines herself the hero."

This fucking guy. "You can't come in here and say shit like that."

"Aish," Sofia reprimanded quietly.

Her mother's eyes narrowed at him. "I am the queen and it is my duty to defend our home and our people. I brought Juan Carlos to make you and the others see the truth."

Aish scoffed. "The truth? You're only in *your home* and with *your people* because your son cut the purse strings. You and the king *defended* the Monte so well you almost bankrupted it."

"Aish!" Sofia spat his name, loud and clear.

"What?" he said, arms out.

She was trembling, twin spots of color high on her cheekbones.

It was with rage. At him. "Stop. Talking."

He shook his head at her. "Why aren't you saying anything? Why are they even here?"

"It's none of your business." She could barely choke out the words. "Why are *you* even here?"

Speechless, Aish slapped his hands against his jeans. The sound cracked off the stone surrounding them.

"*Que vergüenza*," Juan Carlos purred. "Is this the end to #Aishia?"

Sofia turned on her heel and walked through the open bay door, into the dimness of the winery.

No.

How could he do better when she wouldn't give him a chance?

Aish went after her, blind to everything but the darkness that she'd disappeared into.

September 11
Part Two

Fury shook Sofia as she sped through her winery, desperate to reach the cellar door, desperate to disappear down into the dark. As her fingers grabbed on to the cool metal of the handle, she heard Aish's urgent "Sofia!" burst through the empty warehouse.

With a barely repressed snarl, she wrenched open the cellar door.

She grabbed a LED lantern hanging on a hook and flicked it on so she wouldn't kill herself running down the steps to the cellar floor. Once there, she could turn it off and disappear into a dark so complete that Aish would never find her. Would never come near her. Would never come close enough to warm her again.

As she tried to tug the heavy door closed, a hand caught it on the other side.

Abandoning it, she began to race down the metal steps as fast as she could.

"Fuck! Sofia!" Aish cursed. "I can see you." He pulled the door closed and then she heard the steps clang above her. They were in absolute darkness except for the hovering glow coming from her lantern.

He was taking the steps two and three at a time.

Gasping, her heart pounding in her ears, her feet flying down the steps, she felt like she was shooting off sparks.

No. No, no, no, no... She'd made herself cold. During the humiliations handed out by her mother and Juan Carlos, degradations she'd become accustomed to and been anticipating and just wanted to get over with, she'd made herself ice. Ice hurt. But fire.

Fire burned.

And Aish was setting tinder and kindling and match to her when he thanked her for his music or pretended to care about her vines. When he played the rocker-in-shining-armor in front of the interns. When he demanded more of her, demanded *she* do better—*"Why aren't you saying anything? Why are they even here?"*—without giving her a way to see it as self-serving.

He blew life into the flame when he'd made her believe, just for the tiniest second when he'd defended her from her mother, that he really did care.

She heard a clatter directly above her and her heart lurched at the thought that he'd fallen. But no, he kept coming, and that, that impulsive concern, made her consider for a moment simply pulling herself over the railing.

But then her feet hit the black marble floor she'd paid for, an extravagance she'd financed from her own account, and her suicidal self-pity disappeared in a flood of righteous fury. Fuck him, she thought as she turned and strode backwards into the center of her cathedral-size marvel. Fuck him for being here, for challenging her, for making a difficult job impossible. Fuck him for using his joy and his beauty and his American goddamn good fortune to destroy her ten years ago, and fuck him for trying to do it again now.

She dropped the lantern to the floor and stood in the circle of its light. Let him come.

His steps were cautious, so different from the heavy weight of him as he chased her down the metal stairs. As he walked into the light, he looked like the boy she'd known, with the tan of her valley's sun on his skin, his soft black hair, worn surf shirt, and work boots. His long-fingered hands were palm up, and she hated him for it, hated that he surrendered his big body when it would have been so much easier if he used it against her.

Anger stoked the flames higher.

"You've broken every rule you agreed to," she said, clenching fists that dug her short nails into her palm. "Leave now or I'll give my evidence to the press."

"If that's what you have to do," he said, his deep voice echoing in the massive chamber. His breath moved deeply in his lean chest; he still held his hands up. "But I'm not leaving."

Leaving had been one of a million crazy thoughts she'd had last night in her canopied princess bed. She'd considered chartering a plane and disappearing into the world. Abandoning years of effort and the best hopes for her kingdom's survival because they'd almost kissed.

His inescapable relentlessness, the injustice of it after what he'd done, made her want to howl. "I hate you," she spat. "I wish you were the one who'd died."

Pain like she'd punched him creased his beautiful face before he smoothed it out. "I wished that some-times, too, baby," he said, coming closer, putting him-self in range of her fists. "But I wouldn't have done it. Not when I still needed to tell you how sorry I am."

The sound she let out was animal. "Don't." It was the plea of the thing that couldn't claw itself free.

"What I did to you was the worst mistake of my life."

She took a step toward him and raised her fists.

"Sofia," he groaned, the animal too. His eyes were bright in the darkness as they searched hers. "Why won't you let me apologize? Why won't you let me try to make this better? Talk to me. Tell me how I can make this better."

"Tell me," he'd whisper to her in the dark. *"Tell me what feels good. Tell me what you need."* Their love-making had been crowded with words; Aish's mother had told him that women make love with their minds, and he'd put that advice to good use when he'd talked to her in his thrummingly low voice.

"Your round little clit...tell me if you like...you squeeze me so tight...does it feel good when I push... your cunt is so soft...tell me what you want...lick you for days...tell me if this feels...tell me...tell me..."

That boy melded with this man, bigger, broader, more intent and demanding, and what she wanted to do was tear him apart. She wanted to rip and demolish him into tiny pieces that she could scatter in the dark, sprinkle through the tunnels so that he could never tempt her again. Never make her want, never ever make her need.

She wanted to destroy him with her hands.

She leaned over and flicked off the lantern. Then she dropped to her knees and pressed her palms against the front of his jeans.

He jerked. His grunt of shock echoed through the darkness.

Blind, she cupped him with one hand, at his balls and base, and used the other to stroke up. And up and up. He was hardening beneath her touch. So thick and long. So hot and familiar.

She leaned in and pressed her face against that hardness between her hands, rubbed her lips against the warm denim and inhaled that basic essence of him, salt and sand. All the memories of a decade ago came crashing back.

He gave a sound like she'd stabbed him.

She reached for his button.

"Sofia, I—"

"*Mira, guapo*, if you talk, I will stop." She felt the heat of her breath against his clothes. "*Y no creo que quieras que me detenga.*"

"And I don't think you want me to stop," she said in Spanish to ensure that he wouldn't, regressing to that nineteen-year-old girl who believed in the power that her words, her voice, her mouth, and body had over him. Who'd believed without a flicker of doubt that he needed her.

As she pulled down his zipper, she gloried in the hitch of his breath like he couldn't decide.

She knew exactly what *she* wanted. She stroked her lips over the skin of his abdomen, silky and tight and as familiar as her own skin, as she pulled down the elastic of his briefs in the V of his jeans.

His hot cock reared up against her knuckles, kicked into her fist, an eager old friend. Sightless and fascinated by the memories stored in her touch, she stroked down it, up it, focused her attention there at the rim, wondered if running her thumb over the velvety head still…

Ten years older and a million lovers later, he gave a full-body groan like she knew he would.

"Are you safe?" she asked him, her words haunting in the chamber. He'd always been adamant about this, a kid who'd seen a lot in LA, and she and Aish had been tested before they'd gone without condoms. About protection, he'd taught her a level of self-respect that she carried to this day. She wondered if this rock-and-sex god remembered the same level of self-respect.

Stroking and punishing his gorgeous cock for all of her abiding and unwanted affection for it, making him speechless and gasping above her, she leaned close and gave one tiny, delicate kiss to the steely shaft. "*Hermoso*, are you safe?"

His words were strained babble. "Yeah, I was tested a year ago and that was after the last time I—"

She put her mouth around his cock and swallowed him down.

"Fuck," he yelled, and tunneled his fingers into her hair.

This was what she wanted. She wanted him filling her mouth and hitting the back of her throat. She bobbed over him, rememorizing the feel of him with her lips and tongue, relearning the sounds of his gasped breaths and caught groans. She pulled back when he was wet all over and licked at his tip, tasted the salty precome beading in his slit, worked her flat tongue all over his shaft and head. He was delicious in the dark, like he'd always been, but she could feel the razor-thin restraint in him. He panted her name above her, petting her scalp, combing through her hair.

She didn't want his restraint. She wanted him desperate with need.

She took him deep again, worked him roughly until he was dripping, reduced to grunts, until those big hands clenched in her hair.

The pull on her scalp made her drop a hand between her legs.

She wanted mastery over him. She wanted him and could use him this way, could get herself off getting him off. Down here, in her ancient cellar, the dark behind her closed eyelids was the same dark when her eyes were open and it was like a dream she'd deny she had: Aish Salinger in her mouth with no responsibility or repercussions, only taste and feeling and his ocean smell.

Sofia unbuttoned her pants as she relaxed her throat, breathed through her nose as she slid her hand into her panties and spread her thighs. A wisp of cologne—who'd dared to wear cologne down here?—had her pressing her nose against his skin. Aish's sea-salt smell was the only oxygen she needed.

Tears streamed down her face as she fingered her clit.

With a grunt, Aish yanked on her hair hard enough to hurt and pulled out of her mouth, then fell to his knees in front of her. He surrounded her jaw in his big hand and titled her head to the side.

"I can hear you fucking yourself," he said against her neck, his breath against her windpipe. "You're sloppy wet." He grabbed her hand, pulled it out of her panties, and raised it. Then Sofia felt his hot, wet mouth surrounding her fingers, pulsing over them as he sucked them clean. His dirty words, his rough grip in the dark, were her filthiest fantasy.

She whimpered as her hips gyrated helplessly, her head still caught in his big hand.

"Goddammit, Sofia," Aish groaned against her neck, dropping her hand to grab at her hip. Now it was him who sounded like he hated her. "Goddammit."

Sofia willfully ignored the reminder of what was inked under his grip.

And then he was lifting her to her knees so he could shove down her pants and panties and she was leaning behind to flip off one shoe and they were struggling together to free her leg and then he was pulling her into his lap, thrillingly strong when she'd assumed he was weak, making her straddle him where he kneeled, all of it in the deep cool dark, a secret they could hide, and his lean hips between her thighs felt like the best kind of dream.

The familiar but unbelievable heat when he slipped inside her slapped Sofia with an icy dose of pragmatism. Aish Salinger was the flame she couldn't put out? Then she'd feed it, get it high and hot, and incinerate this want out of her.

But when he tried to tilt her lips to him, she wrenched her face away. "*No me beses*," she hissed. "I don't want you to kiss me."

The sound he made against her neck was awful. But he moved. Lifted slightly to surge that thick, long, hot cock inside her, that cock she measured all others against. And gave the gentlest of kisses to her neck.

When he surged again, she fell forward, pulled his shirt to the side, and sank her teeth into his collarbone.

"Fuck," he groaned. Then he grabbed her by her hips and began to use her like she wanted to be used, like the sex doll mailed to his house for his pleasure. His jeans scraped the inside of her thighs and his fingers gripped bruises into her skin and his cock flashed fast and deep into her pussy. So good and deep. She clung to his biceps and let him fuck her.

She went off like a rocket after ten strokes. He went off after fifteen.

Their orgasms were searing. Earth melting. And silent. Sofia bit her lip bloody to prevent herself from making a sound.

As she pulled off him and stood, the taste of warm iron was in her mouth.

She worked to keep her gasping breaths shallow as she fumbled her pants back on. Fortunately, she bumped the lantern as she moved around. She turned it on, but kept her back to Aish. Found her shoe and headed to the stairs.

At the top of the stairs, she flipped the lights on and forced herself to look down. There, in the middle of her Corinthian black marble, small in her mammoth cathedral space, was Aish Salinger, head bent, still on his knees.

Head held high, Princesa Sofia went through her cellar door then pulled it closed behind her.

Ten Years Earlier

Sofia stared fixedly into the bonfire and tugged on her own braid to prevent herself from looking for the millionth time to see if the only missing worker's truck had pulled into its space. Her crew, unfortunately, had been one of the first back, and over the last couple of hours—while more and more workers had joined the bonfire to drink and get high because no one planned to sleep in the few hours before harvest began—Sofia had gone from chatting with her coworkers between glances at the gravel parking lot to morosely yanking on her hair to stop herself from obsessing.

Que estúpido. Being in love was stupid.

This hole in her stomach and buzz around her heart, this ache she'd pulled her thighs against her chest to soothe while she sat on the cold ground and watched the flames snap, it was like suffering physical withdrawal from the few-hours absence of a boy she'd known for a month.

She'd been surprised when she saw the roster this morning. Then hurt. Then worried. Justin had said he had no problem with Aish and Sofia working together to monitor the grapes as long as they actually completed their monitoring, and Sofia had been diligent about feeling every grape for texture and ease of skin collapse, performing every test that determined sugar and acid and pH levels, and tasting the grapes for that hint of black cherry and spice that was essential to Laguna Ridge Winery wines. Only when their work was done would she attack Aish.

Nights alone in the truck or the fields or whatever dark spot Aish chose had been a gift; privacy was hard to find living in a bunkhouse with thirty kids. They'd done it a couple of times with the covers over their heads, both of them biting back the moans and words essential to their lovemaking. *Tell me if you like...yes, there, faster...mi estrella...mi fuego.*

She wondered, for the millionth time that day, if she'd done something wrong. She was depending on Justin Masamune's recommendation for her University of Bordeaux application; French winemaking academia were unimpressed by her princess credentials. Once harvest began before dawn, it would be a crazy all-hands-on-deck scenario as the interns hauled and processed hundreds of tons of wine grapes, and alone time would be even harder for Aish and Sofia to find. Why hadn't his uncle allowed them to spend this calm before the storm together?

And why was she acting like some moony-eyed Juliet over a few missed hours when they still had two months? She tugged on her hair again.

This, this impossible high when he was looking at her or laughing with her or listening to her—better than anyone ever had—and this bone-deep low when he was away, this was love. She'd never felt it before but had known it, had understood it, the moment she'd met him. She loved him. It filled her until it made her float, it weakened and flattened her, it energized her to her fingertips in the morning, and it made her communicate love songs with her body when she was with him at night. She loved him.

She was certain he loved her back. Although, for all their talking, he hadn't said so.

She gave a little pant she hoped couldn't be heard over the laughter and flickering flames. That click of thought—*maybe he didn't need her the way she needed him*—made anxiety prickle all over her body, and she sucked down half her beer to drown it.

Was this the sensation that had driven her mother to become the vain, adulterous, egomaniacal woman she'd become?

Sofia knew a secret about her, a secret she didn't know if the queen remembered giving up. The queen had been drunk when she revealed it, miserable, crying, her face still beautiful in the year before she began her addiction with plastic surgery. Sofia had been seven. They'd both been so young.

The queen had been so young when she'd married Sofia's father, only three years older than Sofia was now. So young. So stupid. Her mother had married a prince who would be king. Sofia had fallen in love with a boy who wanted to be a rock star.

Staring into the flames, she angrily wiped a tear from her cheek and cursed herself for ever comparing her beautiful boy to that cheating, vainglorious, self-involved man.

Like an autumn leaf thrown into the flames, all her ache and worry disappeared the instant she heard the rise of happy voices around the bonfire. Only one person had the power to elevate the mood of an entire group like that.

Sofia jumped to her feet. Looked through the roaring flames.

And saw Aish, lit by the glow and the moonlight, carrying his guitar toward the fire, fist bumping and hand clapping the people who greeted him, John trailing behind and carrying his little video camera. Aish never took his eyes off her.

She ran to him. And it was like no one else was there.

She jumped and his strong arm grabbed her around the waist and then he was kissing her and she gripped him with her thighs and he tasted warm and rich, he tasted like he'd missed her too, and she tangled her fingers in his hair and John laughed and said, "Fuck, man, she attacked you like that bug in *Alien*. Make she sure she doesn't implant something."

Without breaking her kiss, Sofia flashed John the OK sign behind Aish's neck. In the Monte, she'd explained to him—because it was only useful if he understood—that symbol meant asshole.

The other interns hooted and hollered as Aish kept kissing her—wholly and wetly, as if they were alone and he was inside her—while he walked them both toward the firelight. She gave a muffled yelp into his mouth when he grabbed her ass and swooped down to take a seat on a log.

She stayed straddling him, nestled closer as his big hand stroked down her uncovered thigh. She'd worn her ripped-up jean shorts and a tank top. She'd never felt more confident in her body than when he was touching her.

"*Mi fuego*," she breathed against his lips.

She opened her eyes to find his sparkling into hers. "*Mi estrella. Estrellita.*"

She'd been trying to explain to him that he couldn't make every word diminutive but he did make her feel small. His demanding hands, his long body, his thick penis, he made her feel tiny and necessary, like a far-off, life-giving sun.

She put her hands on his face, on those glass-cutting cheekbones, and pushed back his hair. "Where were you? You took forever." She pulled on his hair as punishment.

His eyes fell lazy with heat as he smiled. "With John. We finished our rounds then he wanted to hang out. He's the reason—" He shivered as Sofia stroked his plush bottom lip and she grinned. "He asked my uncle to put us on the same crew today." Sofia stopped stroking. "He missed me. When we were done working, we played for a little bit. He feels better. And he won't do that again."

Sofia looked up and saw John, a few feet away and in a circle of conversation, watching her. *Sorry*, he mouthed, then made a forlorn grimace with his big blue eyes. Sofia gave a nod. Apology accepted.

She knew when she returned her gaze to Aish that John would still be watching.

"Are you going to play?" she asked Aish, wanting to change the subject, wanting to shake off the weird certainty that, yes, John *was* going to do something like this again.

He nodded. "For a little bit. Not too long." The look he gave her made her toes curl in her boots. "I promise." They still had a few hours before they all were to report to their trucks at 3 a.m., to start driving out to the vineyards and picking up the grape bins that the vineyard workers filled.

They still had a few hours to find someplace dark.

With a soft nuzzle of his lips, she slipped off his lap and settled on the ground near him. She leaned back on her palms and stretched her legs out. His eyes took a long, slow, meandering crawl up her body.

"I'm going to play for a very little bit," he muttered. Sofia grinned.

When he pulled the pick from the neck of his guitar and started to strum, John stepped over the log to sit next to him, set the video camera on a tripod in the dirt and pressed record. The other workers moved closer.

Aish settled into a melody and John tapped out a rhythm against his thighs. Aish started to sing. The song was an easy and bright one Sofia hadn't heard before. She watched John as he joined in with Aish for a nice harmony at the chorus, his eyes closed, their voices blending smoothly because of the similarity of their registers.

The other girls thought John was hot. Sofia imagined he was, in a blond and square-jawed kind of way. But next to Aish, with Aish's one-of-a-kind beauty— black hair and lightning-struck eyes, long nose and a dimple—it was like comparing American vanilla cake to her village's *torrijas*, bread soaked in milk or sweet red wine, fried and then covered in honey.

John's voice compared the same way. Talking, he sounded a lot like Aish, a symptom of growing up in each other's pockets. Sometimes when she heard them out of her sight, she didn't know whose low voice was whose. But when they were singing, she could differentiate them in a second. While John had a perfectly fine singing voice, he didn't have Aish's range or depth. Or emotion, if Sofia was going to be bluntly honest.

Whatever drove John weren't the same things driving Aish.

When the song ended, one of the multiyear workers called out for a song that Sofia hadn't heard before.

"How about this one instead?" Aish said and began strumming.

But John smirked and said, "We don't play that one anymore."

"Why?" the woman asked.

John looked straight at Sofia. "'Cause."

His message was clear. It had been a song about another girl.

Sofia pulled her long braid over her shoulder, aware of everyone looking at her, and smiled. "I don't care."

"See, I told you she wouldn't care," John said, motioning at her. "We can't get rid of half our playlist every time you get a new girl."

Aish had called her his muse. His North Star. Of course he'd written songs about other women. And when this summer was over, he would shelve her songs for new ones.

Sofia believed that for about three seconds before Aish thumped the side of his guitar and turned to glare at John. "Fuck, man. I told you. The fact that I'm in love with Sofia has nothing to do with dropping that song. It's just a shitty song." He glanced at the person who'd requested it. "No offense, Lan."

Lan shrugged, enjoying the drama with the rest of the group. "I'm good."

Sofia could feel her heart expanding in her chest. It was going to burst if she didn't...touch him, talk to him. Kiss the shape of those words on his lips. After a lifetime of having her private pain displayed for the world, she refused to share this happiest moment with anyone else.

She stood up and caught Aish's attention when she took the pick from him, slid it in her pocket, then wrapped her hand around the neck of his guitar. She handed it to John without looking away from Aish's fire-lit eyes. She tugged him to his feet and pulled him away.

Aish walked docilely behind her through the moonlit grass as they headed toward the bunkhouse. "Sofia?" he said.

"Not yet."

Once they'd turned the corner, once they were out of sight of the goggling workers, she shoved him against the side of the barn.

"*Otra vez*, señor," she said, holding him against the wood by his shoulders.

His warm hands slid down her forearms, over her tattoo, making goose bumps break out in the warm night. "Sofia, what is it?"

"Say it again," she demanded.

"Yeah, I'm sorry about John. I know I said he wouldn't pull this shit again. I don't know what's gotten into…"

"No, not about him." He was driving her crazy; she wanted to tear open his shirt and listen to his heart pound out the words. "I don't care about that. Say what you said."

"What?"

The crinkle of his black eyebrows, the confusion on his gorgeous face, would have been adorable if Sofia wasn't suddenly horrified. What if she'd heard wrong? What if she'd had a ministroke? What if—*Dios mio*—what if she wanted him to say it so bad that she'd hallucinated it? What if…

Stop.

She might be young. She might be inexperienced in matters of the heart. But she'd been lied to her entire life, so in this—sensing what was real and what was pretend—she was a divining rod. Aish loved her and needed her and she could point the way for him.

She stared up at him and dug her fingers into his shoulders. "I love you, Aish. *Te amo.*"

Those shoulders slumped. "Shit," he said, and he looked so disappointed. "I know you do, baby. I love you too."

Sofia blinked. Breathed. And relaxed her grip on his shoulders. She straightened and dropped her hands to her sides.

"Sofia?"

She leaned back on one heel. "You love me?"

"Yeah. I do," he said with a sad half smile and a shrug.

She took a step back away from him. "Is this an illness you catch with every girl you're with?"

"No," he said, shaking his head and reaching for her as she took another step back. "No, I just—"

Sofia gave a resigned laugh. "Or the illness every girl catches when she's with you?" She was such an idiot. "They touch you and then they give you some cute nickname and then they fall in love with you…" She thought that she was special. "And then they become too needy because—"

"No, Sofia, that's not—"

"I mean, who wouldn't need all that, look at you, and then you have to break up with them because—"

Her back was against the wood so quickly that her head spun.

"No," Aish said, fierce above her, dark hair framing his eyes. "Don't do that. I've *never* said it to a girl before. Because I've never felt it. Ever. I've never felt anything like this. And I just wanted to... I wanted to make saying it special. John said I should wait and do something special."

Staring up at him, head still spinning, Sofia realized she might not be the idiot here.

She put her hands on his hard chest. "Why would you wait?" she asked.

"John said I shouldn't just blurt it out. John said you probably have guys telling you they love you all the time. So I asked my uncle for next weekend off and John and I had figured out..."

As he described an overcomplicated plan involving parasailing and a lighthouse, Sofia thought of the large pool hidden in the tunnels of her kingdom. One lounging night, she'd told Aish and John about the tunnels, about the pool, about the belief that the body of water was the principal gathering point of mountain runoff and the initial source of the Río Christo, the river that sustained her valley. Legend had it, she'd told them, that something dropped into the pool was a sacrifice to the river, would not touch air again until it bobbed up kilometers away.

Right now, she could imagine dropping John into that deep, dark pool.

Aish cupped her face in one big hand, squeezed her waist with the other. "I loved you the moment I saw you." His eyes were bright in the shadow of his hair, in the little cave for them he created with his height and width and dizzying warm scent against the barn wall. "I've needed you since the first second you opened your arms to me."

His hand slipped under her shirt, and its rub and grip against her body felt like ownership.

Sofia slipped her hands into his hair and anchored his eyes on her. "Don't wait to tell me words like that. I…" She closed her mouth, then opened it again. He was being honest with her. She had to be honest with him. "I need them, Aish. I don't hear them very often."

His heavy brow furrowed. "Fuck. I'm sorry, baby. I didn't think. With my parents… I hear them all the time."

And Sofia knew that, had heard "Love you, too" at the end of every phone call.

He pulled her up on tiptoe, against him. "I love you, Sofia." He cradled her face. "I love you, I love you, I love you, I love you, I—"

She stole his final *love you* when she invaded his gorgeous mouth. But she gave it back to him, covered his body in cooed *I love yous* when she fell to her knees and pulled down his jeans, gave him love in a way that had him crying out the words against the barn wall. She had him moaning *I love you* after he grabbed a sleeping bag and rushed her into the small woods on the edge of the property, riding him with *te amo, te quiero, mi amor, mi gigante*, making him writhe beneath her. He fingered the *I love yous* on her lips when he covered her mouth to restrain her screams, when he got comfortable between her thighs and showed her that her body could do that magical thing more than once a night.

He swore, "I love you," into her ear as she cried against him, as she felt—for the first time in her life—the impact of being deeply valued by someone she loved. He held her against him and continued to say it, in front of everyone, in front of John, with his arm slung over his best friend's shoulders as they walked to the waiting trucks in the deep of the night.

September 15

Aish followed Sofia's brother down the low-lit hallway to her suite, the ex-army ranger moving in that quiet but resolute way that made him look like he could bust cleanly through a wall. Aish imagined Roman Sheppard would bust through him if he tried to follow this path again. He was surprised he hadn't been blindfolded.

But the fact that Devonte emailed and Namrita approved and Roman led him to this midnight meeting meant that everyone was in agreement. It was time for Sofia and Aish to clear the air.

"Haven't felt your glares for a while," Aish murmured. He needed banter, anything to distract him from the teeter-totter of anger, guilt, and aching erection he felt for the woman he was about to talk to for the first time in four days.

"Been busy" was all Roman gave.

Yeah, Aish imagined he was. Bad news kept streaming out of the Monte. The blow by blow of their fight appeared in the press, the *public* blow by blow, and recent stories positioned the queen and the *Consejo* as the kingdom's saviors. Some tabloids had started a countdown clock to the end of #Aishia.

But fake countdown clocks were the least of Roman's worries. Someone had shifted from pain-in-the-ass words to pain-in-the-ass actions.

Random acts of vandalism had started in the village, with taverns reporting break-ins and shattered bottles, restaurants dealing with spoiled food from fridges left open overnight, and inns managing middle-of-the-night fire alarms. They were stupid kid moves and no one had been hurt, but they'd happened enough over the last few days that tourists and press were grumbling. Devonte told him that Sofia had been refilling fridges and paying people's hotel bills as fast as she could write the checks. But the business owners had started wondering if an expanded tourism industry was worth it. Right now, travel bloggers were calling them incompetent and unprepared.

A heart-eyed #Aishia would be a great distraction for everyone right now. But Sofia and Aish had stopped talking.

"So you're gonna catch the motherfuckers?"

Roman shot him a sniper's grin over his shoulder. "Never doubt it." The guy was good looking with his dark hair cut short and bottle-green eyes. And scary. He was missing half of his right ring finger and his left hand was scarred with burn. Aish's calluses from guitar playing couldn't compare to what this soldier-prince's hands had gone through.

He thought of another burly security type who'd been absent recently. "Henry's been busy with you guys too?" he asked, going for casual. He hoped the bodyguard who protected Roxanne Medina and her family had been, maybe, patrolling the mountains. Or even looking for bad guys in other countries. Anything was better than the thought of him holing up in Sofia's room. Especially after he and Sofia had…

"Yep," Roman said.

"Good guy?"

Grunt.

"He seeing anybody?"

Roman glanced at Aish. "Why? You wanna date him?"

Fuck it. "Is he with your sister?"

That stopped Roman's ground-eating walk. He turned slowly on Aish and stared at him. Then he made a circle in the air with his finger. "What do you think's gonna happen here?"

"Fuck if I know," Aish said. "I'm pissed at her and I want her like my next breath. It's exhausting."

Roman looked at him incredulously. "You just gave me more reason to keep an eye on you."

"I know," Aish said. "But I'm done pushing her." It was a declaration he'd already made to himself after that debacle in the cellar. "And I won't hurt her. I just to want to help."

He'd said it since he first arrived, "I just want to help," but now he wasn't sure how much he'd meant it. The first couple of weeks in the Monte, half of the time he had with her, he'd been certain that it was Sofia who had to change. And what had that given them? Two weeks of bad press and angry emotion. The only good news story had been the one Sofia orchestrated.

She'd told him repeatedly what she'd needed—space, calm, and respect of her wishes—and maybe if he'd given it to her instead of pushing for what he wanted, things wouldn't be such a mess now.

Maybe if he'd actually listened to her, instead of insisting that he was helping, he wouldn't have been hate-fucked in the dark by the woman of his dreams.

Roman gave him an x-raying once-over. Then he

turned and kept walking. "I'm waiting out here to kick your ass if she tells me to," he murmured as they neared a door at the end of the hall.

"I won't—"

Roman knuckle-knocked the door and then stepped to the side of it. "There's nothing going on with Henry."

Aish glanced at the steely eyed soldier before he heard the click of the door. Then he turned and forgot him entirely as Sofia filled the doorway with her glow: just showered, her hair swept back and still damp, her eyes huge, her cheeks steam flushed, braless and barefoot in baggy pants and an oversized sweater.

Neck-deep in resentment, he still wanted her. Wholeheartedly.

She nodded at her brother. "Gracias, *hermano*. Come in, Aish."

She held the door open for him and she smelled intoxicatingly good as he walked past her. She closed it and asked, "Can I get you a water?" looking at the minifridge instead of at him.

Feeling like he was trying to surf choppy waves, Aish shook his head.

Her suite was like his, a mix of rustic with its thick stone walls, cool terra-cotta floors, and heavy carved furniture blending with the luxury of white linens, silk embroidered pillows, and supple black leather. Her bedroom door was closed and Aish was glad; he didn't need the distraction.

He took a seat on one end of the buttery leather sofa without being invited and she sat on the arm on the opposite side, putting her feet up on the seat. With his elbows on his knees and fingers clasped, he noticed the tip of an inked wave peeking out at his wrist. He adjusted his long-sleeve cuff to cover it.

She'd done him a favor by insisting he cover his tattoos. He'd never imagined that she wasn't listening to the songs, hadn't seen his tattoos, hadn't known what they meant. He realized, only in the last few days, that part of his drive to become more famous than famous was so she would hear him, see him. So she would know.

Playing shirtless during the Super Bowl halftime had been easier than just picking up the damn phone.

Now he needed to keep his tattoos under wraps until... Well, until.

She broke up the silence with a sigh. "I've been searching for the words to tell you how sorry I am but I'm angry, too, so I go round and round and none of the words are right." Her lightly accented voice was soft in the lamp-lit suite. "But I'm ashamed. I'm horrified with myself. I'm sorry I did that to you."

Aish watched her with equal parts surprise and relief. She'd hunched over, crossed her forearms on her thighs, and she was looking down at her unpainted toes.

He wanted to cover them with his hand. "I think you just found the words," he said.

"Just like that?" Her head came up, eyes meeting his. "I haven't even said what I'm apologizing for."

"For using me as your giant dildo," he said and watched that divot appear between her brows, the skin so fine and soft there. "That was really fucking lousy, Sofia."

He didn't like to think about the time he'd spent in her cellar after she'd left, the lights on but all the warmth and air sucked out of the damning space. When his legs could carry him, he'd dragged himself to his room and argued with his hands and his cock, which

wanted to keep the scent and tacky feel of her. Ultimately, he'd showered under blistering hot water and
then called his mom. She'd filled the dead air once she
realized that's what he needed and didn't offer to pass
the phone to his dad.

Not like this, he wished he'd been strong enough to say
to Sofia. *Don't take what we had and make it into this.*

Her silence and distance after had been some kind of
relief. She'd sent no scripts, dropped no new punishments,
and had totally ignored him at workshops and meals.
Devonte and Namrita had worried how the interns would
perceive it—the international press was dancing with I-
told-you-sos—but the interns seemed to think she was
giving him an appropriate cold shoulder after a blowup
fight. The group of adults seemed to be evenly split between "He was only trying to help," and, as Amelia put it,
"You're getting what you deserve because she can speak
for her damn self." The interns believed #Aishia was
moving along like any blooming relationship.

While Aish had also stayed silent, struggling with
his own feelings of guilt, shame, and righteous pissed-
offedness, her speeches hadn't gotten less academic. But
she did seem more present, more real. Which shone a
big fucking spotlight on the fact that he needed to listen to her more.

"I've got to take some of the blame, too," he told her.
They were both hunched over, looking at each other.
"That wouldn't have happened if I hadn't chased you
down there."

"I…" She cocked her head at him like she was trying to figure him out. "Thank you," she said finally.

Her eyelashes were so pretty and long as she watched

him. Her mouth curved down. "What I said, though, about you…about John…"

Aish clenched his fingers together.

"That was unnecessarily cruel. I didn't mean it. I shouldn't have said it."

I wish you were the one who'd died.

She might not have meant it, but he had. He'd considered it a couple of times during the worst days, an option that was good enough for John. And he'd veered away from it, instantly, when he remembered that he had unfinished business with her.

"It's okay, Sofia," he said. Both of their voices had gotten quieter. "I'm sorry for pushing you. You've got enough going on. I'm not gonna push anymore."

Her lips fell open—surprise?—and, God, her mouth was soft and pink.

"This…this is going much differently than I imagined," she said. "I thought I was going to have to grovel. I was angry at you for it and you weren't even here."

He huffed a light sound of amusement, not wanting to jar this space between them where their words floated like clouds.

As miserable as their fuck had been, part of his shame was that he wasn't entirely sorry that it happened. There'd been something honest in the way their bodies had punished each other, working out a senseless decade of frustration. There was equal honesty in the gentleness of their apologies now.

They were separated by two leather cushions and ten years of getting it wrong.

"There's other stuff I need to apologize for—"

She straightened like he'd slapped her.

"More recent stuff," he fumbled quickly, sitting straight. "Non...breakup stuff."

She looked a second from yelling for her brother.

"The song. 'In You.' That was a private song and I shouldn't have let the label release it."

She crossed her arms over her chest. But she didn't kick him out.

Ten years ago, she'd walked into a bar to find a girl on Aish's lap with his tongue down her throat. And instead of apologizing, he'd told Sofia that maybe a breakup was for the best. He'd told her—after he'd promised that he needed her and that she could trust him—that he needed to focus on his music before he settled down.

Every time he'd tried to apologize for that now, it ended in disaster.

If he was really going to stop pushing her, he had to stop trying to force forgiveness out of her when she wasn't ready to give it.

He couldn't tell her, for example, that he'd written 'In You' during the rush of preparing for their first tour, a surprise invite that instigated the breakup. He couldn't tell her that he wrote it already suspecting he'd made the worst mistake of his life.

> *Moonlit as I slide inside you*
> *Back in the earth, you glow like a star*
> *You call me your fuego, I call you my baby*
> *Take me so deep, girl, I'll never go far*

"Why did you release it then?" she asked.

He ran his hands through his hair. "When we turned in our first album, they said we didn't have a hit. 'In You' was on my laptop. It...was discovered. By the time I showed up for the meeting the next morning, they were already freaking out about how great the song was and adding to our tour dates and John was so fucking happy…"

He grabbed his nape and squeezed. "Regardless, I should have pulled it. I should have said no."

She looked at him closely. He stayed still and let her look, let her take him apart with her serious scientist eyes. As a kid, he'd never hid from her, but he'd never believed he had anything to hide. Now, he just wanted her to believe him. Being under the intensity of her gaze again also made him want to lower her to the Turkish rug and show her what fucking after ten years was supposed to look like.

"Yes. You should have pulled it," she said simply. "Did John have anything to do with its discovery?"

The needle skipped on his dirty thoughts.

John had panicked and gone through Aish's laptop to find a song to give to the label. Aish had planned on looking himself, or even recording overnight, but had been felled by a bout of food poisoning. When he'd walked into the label offices the next morning, still nauseous but prepared to beg for another day, he hadn't known the laptop was out of his apartment.

He shrugged off her question now. "That doesn't really—"

"John didn't like me very much."

"What?"

"I didn't like him very much either."

Equal and opposite emotions spiked in Aish: the fierce desire to defend his now-dead friend and the equally fierce desire to hang on to this moment with Sofia.

"What happened to him was a tragedy," she said softly, as if she knew the words would hurt. "But I never trusted him. Maybe he wasn't as good of a friend as you think. Are you sure he did nothing to bring about the plagiarism claims against you?"

Heart hammering, Aish stood. "He's dead, Sofia." He was not discussing this with her.

She kept her relentless eyes on him. "Yes. And people have accused you of pushing him toward it. You might be a lying, cheating, self-serving fame whore, but you were loyal to John. You would have never hurt him."

Aish looked at her for a long moment and then gave a huff of a laugh. What the fuck else was he supposed to do? He slid his hands into his jeans pockets and walked toward her balcony doors, stood at the glass and stared out into the dark night.

The rumor had begun as seeds on Reddit boards and fan pages and the comment section of articles—easy-to-dismiss whispers that Aish had maligned, bullied, and shoved John into killing himself. They'd had no impact in the first sad months after John's death. But when two bands announced that they had irrefutable proof that Young Son had stolen songs, the seeds took root. The thinking was that Aish had harassed his best friend into taking the fall for the plagiarism. People posted daily, expecting an announcement from Aish placing the blame at John's feet.

While he would never do such a thing, hiding for a year had allowed the rumors to fester and grow.

It was up to Aish to make sure John Hamilton didn't go down in history as a song-stealing, suicidal victim of his best friend's jealousy.

And Sofia was wrong. He *had* hurt his best friend.

He wondered what proof she had against them. "All this shit we've been doing to each other, Sofia. Do we have to keep it up?" His words rang hollowly against the glass.

He could see her in the reflection. She studied his back, dipped briefly down to his ass before she looked away.

"No." Her brow furrowed as if she was surprised by her response. "As long as you stick to your promise not to push me."

He turned, hands still in his pockets, and leaned back against the glass. "I'm done with that," he said. "But we've got to start working together. We've both got a lot of baggage that we need #Aishia to distract people from."

She was quiet. Then she gave one decisive nod, her hair, now dry and showing all of its splendor of browns and golds, falling into her face.

What he wouldn't give to push it back for her.

"*Pero*...pretend only," she clarified, tucking her hair behind her ear. "What happened in the cellar isn't going to happen again."

"You really think I want that to happen again?"

He felt guilty when her eyes flickered with shame. She'd sincerely apologized. And he'd sincerely accepted it.

He pulled his hands out of his jeans and spread his arms. "Let's hug on it."

He'd gladly play the fool for her to watch her spine straighten, to watch her chin go up in that royal way that always flicked his Bic.

"Get out, Aish."

He left her room with the first smile—small, be-grudging, but real—that she'd given him in ten years.

September 16

Early the next morning, Sofia and Carmen Louisa
sweated at Sofia's desk while they studied the leaf water
potential readings taken the previous night from the Bodega Sofia irrigated vineyards. Several vineyards were
dry farmed; they relied entirely on rainwater. But those
with irrigation had turned on the misting systems, hoping a light amount of water would keep the not-quite-
ripe grapes from dehydrating or raisining. Too much
water, and the grapes could bloat. The readings, which
measured the water content in the vines' leaves, told
them they were getting close to the point when even ir-
rigating would no longer be an option.

As Sofia wiped the sweat from her forehead in her
winery—her supposedly temperature-controlled winery—she feared this heat wave would last beyond that
point.

"And the temperature never went below twenty-four
degrees last night," Carmen Louisa said, crushing her
wavy hair at her neck. "If we don't get a break from the
heat soon…" She flopped both hands down in her lap.

Sofia had never seen her so hopeless.

Years ago, when her brother was all but hiding in
the United States, Carmen Louisa had been the prin-

cipal grower who'd helped Sofia keep up the people's flagging faith that he would one day return. Carmen Louisa had led the charge to pull out underperforming Tempranillo vines for Mateo's new and improved breed, the Tempranillo Vino Real.

Sofia wondered if the faith the grower had always maintained for her prince was flagging for her princess.

"Weather reports predict cooling temperatures in two or three days…" Sofia said lamely.

Carmen Louisa didn't say anything. She didn't need to. Two or three days might be more time than they had. If the grape vines were stressed beyond a certain point, they would abort the fruit just to stay alive.

Sofia had drawn the eyes of the world to the Monte during a potentially disastrous growing season.

"Excellent!" Both Sofia and Carmen Louisa startled as a voice boomed in her office. "You both are here."

Juan Carlos strolled into Sofia's glassed-in office, a white hat set jauntily on his silver hair, a pale pink shirt unbuttoned dangerously low. His fingers and wrists were heavy with gold.

The black iron gate bearing her name might as well be invisible for how well it kept him out.

Juan Carlos saw the water readings on her desk. "Worried, señoritas?"

Pijo. Sofia gathered up the notes and tapped them into a neat pile as she held his eyes. "What do you want?"

"To free you from worry." He flared his bejeweled fingers. "The Consejo will buy your growers' fruit."

Sofia stared stonily. "Our fruit isn't for sale."

Juan Carlos offered a price per kilo as if Sofia hadn't spoken. The amount was twice what her winery would purchase the grapes for, which was discounted because the growers would receive a share of the winery's profits, and significantly more than what any other buyer would pay.

The price was Juan Carlos's bribe to lure her growers to finally abandon Sofia.

"That offer is only good until the sun goes down." He looked straight at Carmen Louisa. "Wait much longer and you will have no fruit to sell."

"My fruit isn't even ripe." Carmen Louisa scowled.

Juan Carlos shrugged. "You mix the raisined fruit with the under-ripe fruit, add in a little bit of this and that... My growers have already picked. We'll send our workers to you."

Since the first whispers of her winery, Juan Carlos and the Consejo had thrown every difficulty in her path to make her adhere to their winemaking rules that resulted in mediocre wine. And yet, he had the gall to stand in front of her and talk about adding this and that. He would follow the rules—aging in French oak and bottling for the prerequisite years before release. And while the wine aged, he would throw in powdered tannin to add texture and beet sugar to help it ferment and Mega Purple to deepen the color, all artificial enhancements that the Tempranillo of the Monte del Vino Real didn't need.

It was as much a crime to the integrity of wine as stealing notes and words were a crime to the integrity of music.

"I'm fortunate that none of my growers installed new vines," he said, shaking his head. "Tragic what's happening."

Sofia commanded him to shut his mouth as she stood. "*¡Cállate!*"

They'd only begun installing the Tempranillo Vino Real a few years ago, so many growers had tender one-to three-year-old vines that were suffering in the heat. Crop insurance that covered devastating losses wasn't available until vines were five years old. Her brother was getting as little sleep as she was, trying to come up with a solution.

He liked the old ways? Well she was princess and he was her subject. "Don't mock our people because this heat wave fits your agenda."

"My agenda?" Juan Carlos sneered. "We're in this situation because of the crazy ideas of you and your brother. You strive to disrupt what has worked for six hundred years and our people suffer for it. I offer your growers a way out and you spit in my face. Maybe *you* shouldn't be the one answering? Carmen Louisa, why don't you share what I've said with your compadres. Let them decide who truly has their best interests at heart—the delusional princess who will let their fruit burn to feed her fantasy or the Consejo that has been caring for them for centuries."

Sofia glared at him as she waited for Carmen Louisa's response. And waited.

She swiveled her head to look at her friend. "Carmen Louisa?"

Finally, the grower said, "My answer will not change. The other growers will come to you themselves if their answers are different."

Sofia didn't have to look up to see the satisfaction coming off Juan Carlos. "Perfect. Remind them not to dawdle; they only have until sundown."

As he left her office, her longtime friend and mentor met her eyes. "I can't make this decision for them." Carmen Louisa never shied away from what was hard. "I can ride out a couple of bad years. Not everyone can."

Sofia would willingly cover the losses of her growers. But these were proud people who cared for their vines like parents. They would rather see a year's labor go into something—even if it was Familia Pascual's jugs—then shrivel away to nothing. And maybe, with the continued negative press about the winery and Sofia's inability to fake #Aishia and the devastating effect of the heat wave, that's what Carmen Louisa believed Sofia offered them.

Nothing.

"You still believe we can do this, don't you?" Sofia whispered the words.

Carmen Louisa looked at her with troubled eyes.

Sofia's office door opened again.

"I think I have an idea."

At the sound of Aish's voice, the habits of two weeks and the emotions stoked for ten years crowded in Sofia's throat. But she gulped them down as he strode toward her in crisp black jeans, high-top Converse, and a black canvas work shirt.

"I think I've got something that can help," he said, steepling his long fingers on her desk.

Contrary to her wishes and wants, he stole her breath when he was this close, looking at her in that eager, lightning-flash way.

"Help with what, Aish?" Speaking to him normally felt like learning a new language.

"With the heat wave. My uncle used something at Laguna Ridge."

As Aish began to explain, it sounded impossible. Then unlikely. Then she thought that she needed Aish to talk to Mateo. And they'd need Roxanne's plane.

For all the ways she'd publicly scorned him and privately abused him, Aish was still here. She'd taken her pound of flesh and he'd still shown up, every day, on time, and seemed to find as much relief in giving her space as she'd found in getting it. His own apologies—taking part of the blame for what happened in her cellar, showing real regret for exposing her in a song—had been a shock. The Aish she'd known had never taken responsibility for anything.

The hushed conversation in her suite had gone a long way to heal the wound of what she'd done to him, a fresh wound she doubted they could playact around.

"What I did to you was the worst mistake of my life."

That wound still stung, despite the years of scar tissue, and they couldn't go anywhere near it if they were going to successfully get through this month. That he finally seemed to get that wove a strand of gratefulness into her dark, complicated emotions for Aish Salinger.

They might actually survive this month and come out ahead. As long as they could save the crop.

When she looked at Carmen Louisa, she was watching him with amusement as he paced. It was the first time she'd seen that gentle, laughing-at-the-world smile on her friend's face in days. Unaware, Aish continued to talk and strategize with flashing eyes and flying hands. He was equally mesmerizing in front of two as he was in front of two hundred thousand.

"Vale, chico." Sofia stopped him short, putting her hands up. "It's better than what we've got. *Venga.* Let's go talk to my brother."

Later, in the dying twilight of the still-hot day, Sofia
swiped her sweaty forehead with a red bandanna as she
stood on an open truck bed. Bodega Sofia workers, superstar interns, and—most importantly—growers stood
in the dusty road that ran between vineyards and looked
expectantly up at her. Her fifteen growers were gathered in a clutch, Carmen Louisa standing with them.
As the sun's last rays disappeared behind the Pico Viajadora, Sofia knew Carmen Louisa's decision. She'd
worked as hard as Sofia today making Aish's outland-
ish idea possible. But it was time for the other fourteen
growers to choose: secure a huge payout and a future
for this year's fruit by selling to the Consejo or spend
a sleepless night implementing an untested last-ditch
effort with no guarantee of success.

Namrita stood to the side of the road with a small
clutch of reporters and cameras. The growers' decisions
would decide Sofia's fate, and no amount of prettying it
up in the morning would change that. They'd decided
to allow the world to watch her fate unfold.

With one last wipe of her sweaty palms, Sofia stuck
the bandanna in her back pocket and said the first thing
that came to mind. "This is a crazy idea," she said, loud
in English.

There were a couple of awkward chuckles, as if people were as uncomfortable at her attempting a motiva-
tional speech as she was at giving it. Sofia didn't do
this. She didn't give inspiring eleventh-hour speeches;
she left those to her brother.

But facts and figures weren't going to raise spirits,
energize already exhausted people, and convince her
growers to follow the rebel queen instead of the selfish
but consistent rulers they'd relied on for years.

"Today, in my own office, I was accused of having lots of crazy ideas. And maybe I do. I don't know." She could hear the murmured translation for the few workers who didn't speak English, causing Juan Carlos's words to bounce back at her. She wanted to bat at them. "*¿Sabes que?* No. There's nothing crazy in helping the Monte del Vino Real adapt and thrive rather than allowing it to slip away until it's another lost village in the mountains."

She shook her hands at the daunting peaks around her and looked out at the crowd. People watched her hesitatingly. She probably looked like the *abuela* who had boisterous chats in the pews of the village chapel with people who were not there.

Aish's dark gaze felt like a touch.

"But what we're about to attempt, it's probably crazy." She motioned her thumb in his direction and addressed head-on one of the concerns of the growers. "Yes, it came from the mind of a rock star." Sofia pointed at herself. "It was approved by your party-girl princess. The idea was validated by the prince, who's responsible for some of you having young, vulnerable vines, and we used a billionaire's plane to fly to Bordeaux to get the materials we needed." She heard how damning the summary sounded from her own mouth and said her inner thought out loud. "It sounds more like we're putting on the world's best rave rather than trying to save this year's grapes."

To her surprise, there was true laughter from the crowd. It sounded like relief. It sounded like room to breathe. She pushed onward.

"I'm willing to try crazy if it will save us." She angled and focused all her attention on the group of growers. That's truly who this speech was for. "What I'm hoping and praying is that you are willing, too. We have the materials, we have the manpower, we have the equipment." She motioned to the spotlights stationed at the end of vineyard rows. They would allow everyone to work through the night to save the grapes. "But if you don't believe in me or this plan, I need to know now so that I can reassign workers. With the help of our interns—" She nodded at them. "We'll have enough hands, but we're stretched thin. If you decide to sell to the Consejo, they will supply you with their crews."

Her hopes began to falter as she saw the growers murmur among themselves. What had she expected, blind obedience? The pride of tradition was the mother's milk they'd been raised on; of course, they were going to question this untested plan.

A low voice hissed at her. She saw Aish standing at the edge of the truck, his fingers hooked around the bed.

"Tell them why," he whispered urgently.

"What?"

"Tell them why they should believe in you and this plan." He was dusty and disheveled from carrying the bolts of fabric off the plane and on to the trucks. The tip of a blue ocean wave could be seen on his wrist.

"He called me a delusional princess," she called out in Spanish as she straightened and turned back to them. "All of you, you know me, the real me and not the *princesa* they talk about on the internet, for two weeks if not for my whole life." Carmen Louisa moved closer to the intern group and began to translate for those who didn't understand. Aish and Devonte moved closer to the group as well, and Aish tilted his head without taking his eyes off Sofia.

For the first time, she drew strength from all the eyes on her.

"As we harvested together in the fields or argued over blueprints for the winery or you listened to me 'drone on' about winemaking—" She gave a nod to Aish, which surprised a few laughs out of the group. "Have I ever seemed delusional to you?"

She'd spent the last two weeks terrified of the needs driving her decisions. But she didn't have the luxury to doubt herself anymore. It wasn't the amorphous pressures of public skepticism or her kingdom's wariness bearing down on her, it was the sun, certain to circle around in about twelve hours and scorch everything in its path. Aish had given her a sure way to fight it, and she had to draw on her training, experience, intelligence, and royal destiny to make sure her people fought with her. For the first time, she was utterly confident that *this* was the right path.

"I created a multimillion-dollar product used by almost every winery in the world. Before I began building their competition, top wineries begged me to consult with them. I could get into this truck, drive out of the Monte, and never look back; my prospects would improve and my bank account would do better."

The attention on her was absolute. "I lay these facts out for you to make one thing clear—I don't ask you to do this for me. I love you, I love every hectare of this kingdom, but I am a wealthy, talented, and smart princess. I don't need you to secure my future.

"I ask you to choose this for the future of the Monte del Vino Real."

At that moment, headlights from a truck behind the crowd came on, lighting her up. Then headlights from another. Sofia realized then that only a slip of the day's light was still available. It was now or never.

She pointed at the bolt of fabric behind her in the truck bed. "*This* is the only way forward. Yes, it will provide either sure success or epic failure, and we won't know of either until the sun comes out tomorrow. But the old way, the Consejo way, leads to the end of the Monte. A few families will stay rich while the rest decline, our children will move away, and our way of life will be over. You must decide now. The possibility of a quick death or the certainty of a long, slow one. Aish?"

As everyone processed her words and Carmen Louisa caught up with the translation, Aish blinked like he was coming out of a daze. "Um…me?"

She smiled as he came closer into the light. "Yes, you. Could you organize our crew?"

"Me?" he asked again. He walked until the lowered tailgate stopped him; she moved forward until it supported her weight. He looked up at her as she looked down at him.

"Yes. You." She grinned. "This was your idea and you have experience with the shade fabric. You should lead our crew."

He looked up at her like she'd hit him with a mallet. His black hair was soft and mussed; there were fabric threads in it. She wanted to brush them out with her fingers. His eyes were deep and warm. He licked his plush bottom lip, and his Adam's apple bobbed in his strong, tanned throat.

She'd seen this look on him before. It was dazzled. It was dangerous.

She stepped back and looked away, around, heart racing, and noticed Carmen Louisa rushing toward

September 16
Part Two

Aish flipped on the generator and squinted away from the eye-searing spotlight as workers, interns, and growers gathered around him. Devonte, in jeans and the most casual business shirt he owned, picked up the corner of the long length of white cloth and handed it to him.

"So when you're cutting the cloth, cut it two feet longer than your rows so you can cover fruit at both ends," Aish told the group, holding up the open-weave cloth. He hooked a hole at the top of the cloth on to the trellis stake, just under the thick leaf canopy and just above the top of the grape clusters. Then he pulled the cloth to the next trellis stake and connected it.

He tugged on the fabric. "The goal here is to get a nice horizontal line that will keep out the sun without smashing the fruit."

He looked up and caught Sofia watching him, an intent expression on her face. He'd done this tutorial earlier for her and her brother Mateo—who was already hard at work with his crews putting shade cloth up in most vulnerable vineyards—but he never expected he entrusted to show her people. This wasn't rocket her. In that ten-second interaction, she'd forgotten that her kingdom's future was being decided as the world watched.

She jumped off the truck bed and took a steadying breath as Carmen Louisa reached her.

"*Vale.* They'll do it," the grower said in a rush.

"How many?" Sofia held her breath. Half of the growers would be good; they could still pull a vintage from half the expected fruit. Getting eleven of these growers to reject Juan Carlos's big payout would be a miracle.

"All of them," Carmen Louisa announced with her eyebrows raised.

"All of them?"

Carmen Louisa's smile told her she was shocked too.

But Sofia could waste time on shock later. They didn't have a moment to spare.

She jumped back on the truck bed.

"Okay, *vale*, excellent…" But then she had to stop. Because she had to wipe her eyes. She pinched her quivering lips together and raised one finger.

She just needed a second.

"*Vale*," she said again, clearing her throat. She saw others in the crowd wiping their eyes. "*Bien. Mil gracias,*" she said with a hand over her heart as she looked at her growers. But then she clapped her hands together.

"Now we get to work."

science; anyone could figure out how this shade cloth worked. But Aish was knocked out honored to be asked. She'd trusted his recommendation for this vineyard innovation that was still in the trial phase. She'd had him explain it to her brother. She'd sent him on the billionaire's plane to Bordeaux to make sure they were picking up what her phone call had purchased. She'd put him in this position of responsibility, training everyone, directing her crew.

It felt like being in a band again.

"My uncle liked crews of three. One person cuts the cloth and lays it out in the row, another person hooks it at the top, and then your third person hooks it at the bottom." Devonte, who'd also been part of the earlier demonstration, crouched down and belled the fabric under the fruit to attach it to the trellis stake. He stood, moved to the next stake, and crouched to attach it. Both knees cracked.

Aish said, "And make sure to switch off before the guy bending over wants to kill you."

Everyone laughed.

Aish's expertise with the shade cloth was pure luck. The cloth's French manufacturer had contacted his uncle during the growing season before John's death. They claimed their revolutionary fabric blocked out 50 percent of the sun's rays while still letting the grapes fully ripen, and they wanted Justin Masamune—who could have had Non-Traditionalist tattooed on his forehead—to test it out in his vineyards. The Russian River Valley was dealing with the same warming temperatures as other wine regions, and the fabric had worked to preserve the grapes in his sunniest vineyards. Thank Christ, Aish had been there to help roll it out.

The only problem, he'd told Sofia in her office, was that the white, treated, mesh cloth was still in the developmental phase because it was prohibitively expensive. That's probably why Sofia and Mateo hadn't heard of it.

Once she'd had her brother's buy-in—a buy-in that had come intimidatingly fast as Aish had tried to sound knowledgeable and confident standing in the man's fucking *castle*—she hadn't hesitated to buy all the material the thrilled manufacturer could provide at a moment's notice. The euro amount when Aish had signed the invoice as they'd loaded the bolts into the plane had made his eyes pop. He knew she was rich. *He* was rich. But he wasn't *that* rich.

And she'd dropped that fortune based on his word.

Fuck, he hoped this worked.

Sofia stepped into the spotlight. "So you know your crew assignments and where you're going. I've made recommendations on your sheets for rows or locations that are the most vulnerable. But growers, you know your vineyards best."

The spotlight outlined her body in a white shirt and dirty canvas overalls. She'd tied back her hair with a bandanna and the brown-caramel-blond stood up in tufts and curls. Her pointed chin was high; her neck was long and sleek and perfect.

His fingertips tingled as he listened to her command her army.

"I wish we could protect every grape in the Monte, but we can't. So please be mindful; this shade cloth is finite. *Buena suerte* and let's hope tomorrow's sunrise is kind."

The manufacturer only had so much shade cloth to sell. So Sofia and Mateo had to prioritize which vineyards and rows would be getting it: young Tempranillo Vino Real vines first, then vineyards on the Monte's eastern ridge getting the intense western sun, and finally, dry-farmed vineyards that couldn't be irrigated.

Aish shook Devonte's hand before the manager headed to the trucks with the growers, workers, and superstar interns who never thought they'd be participating in a life-and-death struggle for the survival of the Monte. Namrita had sent the press away after Sofia's speech.

He and Sofia were left in the roaring spotlights with their crew of nine. They broke into three groups to cover this quadrant of young Tempranillo Vino Real vines, and neither Aish nor Sofia fought the assumption that they would be in the same group. As the vineyard worker in their group went to cut lengths of fabric, Aish held up the loose cloth in the example row. "Who wants to go down on their knees first?" he asked.

Sometimes, being an ass was the only way he could get through the enormity of his feelings for this woman.

"Definitely you," she said, rolling her eyes with a smirk.

He could almost imagine they weren't at each other's throats a week ago.

She took the cloth from his hand and attached it, tight but not too tight, to the next trellis stake. She moved further down and Aish bent to attach it under the grapes. He could smell her, spicy and sweet, mixed up in the scents of green growth and ripe fruit.

"I should be annoyed that a rock star knows something about the wine industry that Mateo and I don't," she said.

He duck-walked to her in the dirt; the yoga he'd reintroduced into his morning routine made it easier. "I thought I noticed a tic in your brother's jaw."

"You saw that?" She grinned down at him. But then, as if realizing, her smile fell away and she turned her face back toward the canopy. One good day wasn't going to erase ten years of hurt.

"Everything I know is because of Justin," he said.

"You hadn't planned on staying involved with the winery," she said into the leaves, like maybe he wouldn't hear.

"That was before I met you."

They attached the cloth for a few yards in silence.

"What do I have to do with it?" she finally asked.

"You made the work interesting. Romantic." He sped up talking to cover up that word. "You were the first person to point out how much he wanted my involvement and how lucky I was to have someone need me that way."

He would call his uncle when he got back to his room and tell him he'd helped save a kingdom's harvest. Hopefully. "He's a successful Japanese-American winemaker whose mother was born in an internment camp. I don't want that legacy lost, or worse, sold off to a conglomerate when he's gone."

He glanced at the fruit before he hooked the cloth underneath it; there were a couple of tired-looking grapes on the cluster, but not the intense shrivel he'd expected. "And when you take care of something like this, watch it grow, year after year, you feel essential. Like being a parent. You know what that feels like."

Sofia had circled around the end of the row and Aish stood, flexed his legs, before moving around to join her.

She was staring stock-still into the canopy.

"Sofia?" he asked, concerned by the paleness of her profile in the spotlight.

She turned her face away and snagged the cloth on the pole. "Actually, I don't know what that feels like."

"Wha—"

"Bodega Sofia is important." She was moving down the row away from him, and Aish crouched and hurried to catch up. "But if it doesn't work out, no one will miss me if I'm gone."

He plopped to his knees then reached over to snag her by her overalls pocket before she could move further away. This far into the row, her face was in shadow, with only touches of light coming through the canopy hinting at what was going on in her eyes, on her mouth.

"What are you talking about?" he asked.

He saw the slightest raise of her small, world-holding shoulders. "They'll 'miss' me," she said, putting the word in quotes. "But I'm not essential."

He wasn't letting go of her pocket and she wasn't pulling away. "I was here when Mateo wasn't," she said in her academic away, diagramming it for him. "The villagers turned to me because they couldn't turn to my parents."

No wonder she hadn't heard his music. While Aish was singing her songs and tattooing his body, Sofia was trying to keep a kingdom together.

"You would have been so young," he said.

"When Mateo returned," she continued as if he hadn't spoken. "The villagers didn't come to me anymore."

Oh. Baby girl. First rejected by her mom. Then Aish. Then her people.

He could imagine her reaction if he offered pity, empathy, or to let her take him down to the cellar with a bullwhip. So he said, with a light tug on her pocket that he wished would topple her into his arms, "Well, you're essential now." He turned back to the leaves and hid the lump in his throat. "You're essential—" *To me* "—to the growers whose fruit you're saving."

They started working their way down the row again. "And you're essential to the relationship I have with my uncle," he said as he sought the little claw on the next trellis stake. "When everyone else thought I was perfect, you were the one person who expected more out of me."

He grunted, leaning into the greenery. Dammit, he couldn't find—there it was. He hooked the cloth. He shuffled a couple of feet to the next stake.

"This shade cloth was a good idea," she said quietly. "It was our only good idea."

He paused and looked up. Her voice sounded daunting.

She was very deliberate as she attached the next section. "But I don't want to discuss the past. That part of our rules still holds true."

The fucking ground rules. Her mentioning them was like the twang of a broken guitar string. But, for once, he swallowed his frustration.

"Anything else?" he said tightly.

She dropped her hands against her pants and looked up into the dark sky. "I'm not...threatening you. I won't do that anymore. #Aishia is the only thing we've still got working for us."

Her dark eyes were troubled when she looked down at him. "*Pero...seguiremos fingiendo*, Aish." She stroked the leaves like they comforted her. "It's all pretend. Regardless of what we... I did to you in the cellar...the only way this can work is if we both agree it's pretend."

But it isn't pretend, he wanted to demand. He needed her and, at the very least, she desired him. He wasn't blind to the way she'd looked at him that evening.

But he'd already made her miserable this month with his impatience.

"Of course," he said, his voice steady. "It's pretend. We won't talk about the past."

They worked the rest of their way down the row in silence. He promised he would listen to her, he promised he would trust her wishes. He promised himself he would take responsibility for some of the fuckups that had happened here.

That didn't make the work-warmed smell of her, the steadiness of her breath, the weight of her imprint in the soil any easier to bear. When they reached the end of the row, he marveled at how much temptation could be packed into a hundred feet. They had many more rows to cover before dawn.

Unfortunately, the night lasted longer than the cloth did. They were still a couple hours from sunrise as Aish sat on the open tailgate of a Bodega Sofia truck, trying not to look as mentally and physically exhausted as he felt as Sofia paced in front of him, on her cell phone to discover who needed help and if anyone had extra cloth. She'd already sent one crew to another vineyard, let the other crew go home, and now, he and Sofia were alone. They'd turned the spotlights off halfway through the night and Aish's headlamp next to him in the truck bed created a dim glow in the deep darkness of the night. The stars were gorgeous, a million pinpricks in the sky high above him. But here, on the ground, he could barely see his hand in front of his face.

Sofia slid her phone into her overalls pocket, crossed her arms around herself, and rubbed her fingers across the line between her brows. It was the first time all day she'd shrunk to her normal size.

"Any luck?" he asked.

She stood near his knee, but the glow of the lamp barely touched her. She shook her head without looking up. "Everyone is running out of cloth and heading home."

He wasn't going to ask the questions racing through his mind. How much of her crop got covered? What was the weather report for the morning? There was no point. They'd made their one play; only time would tell if that play worked.

But he wasn't going to just sit there as this tired and worried princess rubbed her forehead. "This is going to work, Sofia," Aish said, voice strong with conviction he didn't feel. She liked going after him for his sunny American outlook, his baseless positive assertions. He'd give her a target.

But instead of smirking at him like he'd gotten used to, she kept rubbing. "Is it?" she asked. And it was the first time he heard this giant of a woman sound afraid. "I hope so." Her breath shuddered and it fucking killed him. "I don't know what we'll do if it—"

No contract was going to keep him from touching her now. He grabbed her by her hand and pulled her to him.

"Hey, you've been going hard all day, and now that you can take a breath, you're starting to spiral." He settled her between his knees and briskly rubbed her arms, from shoulder to elbows. He could feel her warmth and tensile strength and trembling exhaustion. She didn't look at him. "You're tired, Sofia. Let's get you home. Don't make yourself miserable; you've worked too hard to let doubts kick your ass now."

He'd watched her all day make huge snap decisions,

drop buckets of money in a flash, direct and strategize and inspire a group of people who felt the universe was working against them. She'd been mammoth.
Right now, she was fragile under his hands, between
his knees. Right now, with the nostalgic scent of soil
in his nose and the rustle of the breeze in his ears, she
was the girl he'd fallen in love with and the woman, his
instincts yelled, who needed him.

She listed forward, like a vine bending to the wind,
and pressed her forehead against his chest. The heat,
the pressure, felt a million times better than her desperate basement blow job. He put his hands on her narrow back, slowly, like touching a skittish animal, and
began to rub her, comfort her by kneading with his
palms when she didn't shy away.

"Hey, hey," he said. He had strong hands. He was
good at this. He could give her this. "It's gonna be okay.
Tell me what you need."

She gave a tight, hysterical laugh that made her more
naked than he'd seen her in a decade.

"Sofia, tell me—"

She put her hands on his thighs and squeezed. "*Por
favor*, stop saying that."

He couldn't say anything. Hot, hot hands on him
made him lose the power of speech.

When she raised her head and looked at him, beautiful and steady and serious and regretful looking right
into him, his whole body flushed hot. The feeling was
rare. And remembered. This was exactly how he'd felt
when he'd stuck his head into a wine tank and seen
a half-naked girl cleaning it, her tiny body stretched
out on her toes and her long multicolored hair beating
against the back of her thighs.

"This is all pretend, *verdad*?" she asked, her voice so treasured and ephemeral he could have been dreaming it.

He gave a quick nod.

"It's not fair of me to ask it of you. I shouldn't—"

"Sofia," he said, digging her name out of his chest, but it tried to stick low and gravelly in his throat as he fit his hands to her waist. His hands were a belt, a corset, the structure that would keep her upright if she wanted it. In the open sides of her overalls, only a thin cotton shirt separated her skin from his.

Her mouth trembled in reaction. She sank her white teeth into her bottom lip to hide it. He wanted to command her to stop it and claim her lip as his own.

"I don't want to think, Aish," she said, her strong fingers digging into his thighs. "That's what I need."

He promised he would listen to her. He promised he would trust her wishes.

This was all pretend.

"Yeah," Aish said, low. "I get that." He'd spent a year in his house; he knew all about not wanting to think. What if she'd been locked away with him? What happy, wild creatures they would have become.

He didn't even realize he was pulling her toward him until she twisted her chin away.

"Don't… I'm sorry but I can't…don't kiss me on the lips," she gasped.

Her words punched him in the gut. He glared at her fine jawline as she denied him that wide, wet, pleasure-giving mouth. And he felt, couldn't help but feel, her fingers make swirling, random, soft patterns on his thighs. She didn't want to want him. But she did.

He leaned forward and bit her jaw. Nipped her to let her know he was irritated. Then he licked her earlobe and sucked it into his mouth, fondled it in that way that used to send her into full-body shivers.

It still did.

"More rules, Sofia?" Aish said into her ear. God, he loved her haircut. It made her ears, her neck, her pulse, all those places that made her boneless, so fucking accessible.

Then he lifted her chin with his thumb and made her look into his eyes. "I got a rule, too, Sofia." Slow and deliberately, making her watch him do it, he unclasped one side of her overalls. "I'm not going to fuck you until we agree this is more than a one-time thing."

She gave a tremor, just like she used to, at *fuck* falling out of his mouth.

He slipped his hand under her shirt, stroked up sleek skin, and groaned at what he found: soft, warm, naked roundness. Her breast was bare under her shirt. Her nipple, that sweet eager bit of her that he'd missed so much, was diamond hard.

"But don't worry, pretty girl," he said, stroking her nipple, watching that mouth fall open and those eyes go half-mast as he did it. "I remember all the ways to make you come." He said *come* through gritted teeth and it made her gasp, made her roll her hips between his knees.

He scooted forward on the tailgate to press against her.

Years of fantasies and one-days and memories that at times haunted him so cruelly that he just wanted to forget them, and now she was here, against his body and under his hands, smelling like she'd been fashioned from the soil specifically to please him. This was nowhere close to paradise. But her nipple was hard between his fingers and her neck had goose bumps when he rubbed his nose against it, and she molded her hands—those delicate and mighty hands—against the muscles of his thighs. She had her rules but she needed him and she was giving herself to him and he would take her. Any way he could get her.

She didn't want to think? He'd tease and touch and taste her until he'd cleared her mind of anything but him.

He lifted one side of her shirt so he could expose her breast to the warm air and his eager mouth. He had to see her again.

But he only caught a glimpse—caramelly skin, that sweet boob with its dark nipple, the bright lines of a tattoo at her hip—when Sofia gasped, "Light. No light," and leaned over to fumble at the headlamp. The light clicked off, and the darkness surrounded them.

It didn't stop Aish from getting his mouth on her. He hunched over and sucked her into him, wringing a moan out of her.

"Fuck, your taste…" he said against her softness, his nose pressing against all that warmed-up Sofia smell. He remembered what his girl liked and he did it, wet tonguing to her nipple, soft sucks to the flesh around it mixed with bites. The teeth and the hair tugging—neither of them minded a little pain with their pleasure. "Remember when you'd lean over my face, tease me with these tits then slink down until just breathing on me would make me blow?"

He hadn't known fucking could be an art form until Sofia showed him. She whimpered and dug her hand into his hair, shoved him against her body.

It helped to cool the possessive punch he'd felt when he'd seen the edge of that tattoo. It was new. At least, new to him. And she didn't want him to see it.

He had to keep his head in the game. He flicked at

her nipple like he used to play with her clit while he ran his palm down her, into her overalls, then swept his finger over her warm, wet slit through her panties.

Sofia sighed "Yes," then staggered to give him room.

"Yeah," he said, feeling like a king and conqueror and peasant at her feet as he rubbed his middle finger over this secret adored place, this place that had represented more than a good—great—lay for him. "Spread your legs for me, Sofia."

She did, good girl, then twisted her hand in his hair until it stung.

"Don't tease me," she moaned above him as he found her clit through her panties, tight and eager, and circled it. "*No me provoques. Por favor.* Aish, *por favor.*"

And, fuck, he had to shake off her hand and let go of her tit because—fuck. Fuck her and her fucking mouth.

Her silence when they'd fucked in the cellar, when she'd poured hot, wet retribution over his cock, had been a blessing in disguise. They'd been chatty little Cathys in bed when they were young, so that silence had been one more thing that separated that fucked-up act from the true lovemaking they'd done as kids. Right now, her breathy words, her demanding desperation while she trusted him with the reins, felt like warm rain washing away that chilling reunion.

Still, this was so much less than he wanted. He wanted her to turn to him for more than a moment of forgetfulness.

He pushed into her panties, and for just a moment, held her. Held her crinkly hair and soft puffy lips and wet, warm cunt, protected this heart of her with his hand.

And then he stroked his middle finger.

She pressed her forehead to his neck and wrapped

her arms around his shoulders. She held him—Sofia was holding him—and she kissed his neck. "*Asi, asi, Aish*. Like that, so good. *Más, por favor.*"

He had to stop again, tug his head away from her again.

"No…talking," he growled. He'd weaned himself from coming too soon with her when he was twenty-one, and he didn't need to start that shit again now.

He began to thrum at her, all his guitar-strumming skills focused on her eager little clit. "No kissing, no fucking, no light, and no talking." He bit her neck for punctuation. "You wanted rules, Sofia. You got 'em."

And he needed to lay down some speed bumps. He had to be more than a warm body she pretended with.

But he fondled her neck and loved on her pussy, let her dig her fingers into his shoulders as she panted into the air. "Do you still like it when…yeah," he murmured into her skin. She still liked it when he played with her little hood, nudged and nudged it. "Your clit's so happy to see me, just right there, out on my finger, I can't wait to say hello with my mouth, I'm gonna taste her until she's trembling against my tongue and—"

"You—" Her voice was high and tight and that was fucking magnificent. "You said no talking."

"No talking for you," he growled, then pushed into his girl.

In the fragile darkness before dawn, Aish squeezed her in his arms and stroked her breasts and kissed her neck and took his time pleasuring this woman he feared he'd never touch again into an agonized, bliss-filled orgasm that rang off her mountains.

September 18

Two evenings later, Sofia stood on the *hospedería* pool deck with her sister-in-law and Henry and tried to be surreptitious as she watched Aish laugh with his manager and the interns. He held a club soda and lime now. But earlier when she'd led the toast, she noticed that he clinked with a glass of her Tempranillo rosado that she'd poured to celebrate the success of their "crazy idea."

The shade cloth worked. The Monte would lose about ten percent of that year's harvest, but the cloth had protected the majority of the vulnerable fruit during the next day's harsh sun. Without it, the losses would have been catastrophic.

Last night, the winds from the Bay of Biscay—tucked between Spain and France and just north of the Monte's mountains—had finally found their way through the Picos de Europa to sweep away the heat wave. Temperatures had settled back to their September norms.

Harvest would start within the week.

This party thrown together quickly, with a village band playing in the corner and a spread of *pinchos* and *paella* on the other side of the pool, was as much a sigh of relief before the madness of harvest as a thank-you to the interns. Without them, Sofia had told them during her toast, they couldn't have covered the numbers of vines they did during the critical short window.

The video of Sofia talking to her growers as well as the success of the shade cloth was the cleansing her image needed. In forty-eight hours, she'd gone from "Princess Prick Tease" in the international media to "a shining light for the beleaguered Monte del Vino Real."

In a surreal turn of events, she had her dark-haired ex to thank for it.

He looked like a bad boy tamed for the occasion in white denim pants and a cream summer sweater that showed off the width of his shoulders. When he threw back his head and laughed, his throat was tan and strong, so different from that strung-out rock star who'd shown up at her winery launch. The sunset cast a rosy gold glow and sparks of it caught in his hair.

"...so then I saw this dragon flying over and I thought, whoops, someone's gettin' canned, 'cause you know about dragons and fire," Henry said and Sofia blinked and looked up at him.

"Sure, sure," Roxanne murmured on Sofia's opposite side. "But dragons usually hoard gold so if they're in the vicinity, you've got to balance win-losses."

Sofia swiveled to look at her. "What are you two talking about?"

"There she is!" Henry boomed, drawing a few looks with his Texas-size voice.

"We were talking about how devastated we were to be ignored while you were eye-fondling the rock star," Roxanne said, grinning evilly.

Sofia scowled and lowered her voice, hoping the two would do the same. "I wasn't—"

"Were," Henry said.

"And don't worry," Roxanne said, tilting toward her. In an off-the-shoulder red peasant dress that highlighted how kickboxing was a good antidote to childbearing weight, Roxanne looked like a swimsuit model and not a mogul and mother of two. "He's been sneaking glances, too. He looks at you like I looked at my first million."

"Except when I do shit like this…" Henry said as he slipped his arm around Sofia's waist and pulled her against his thick, muscle-y side, covered in a black polo shirt and jeans. She leaned against him, because it was easy and comfortable, because their friendship had always been tactile after an attempted kiss in the first few months let them know they'd never feel lust. "When I hug you, that little guy thinks he can take me."

Henry was twice the width of Aish and Aish had never been jealous of anyone because men who perceive themselves as golden idols don't envy ants and both of her pseudo siblings were acting like annoying teens so Sofia had no idea why the defense "He's not little," popped out of her mouth.

She was as shocked as they were thrilled.

Maybe turning to the boy she once loved for a distraction orgasm hadn't been the best idea. But that's all it was. Aish Salinger, more beautiful with hours of hard work on his long frame, had been a handy alternative to falling apart in the middle of a vineyard. An orgasm was an orgasm, and although this was the boy who showed her that she could have them, there was no reason it should outweigh other stress-relief orgasms she'd had in her life.

"I got a rule, too, Sofia. I'm not going to fuck you until we agree this is more than a one-time thing."

It wasn't going to be more than a one-time thing. She smoothed her hand down the hip of her white linen sheath dress as a reminder.

"It's all pretend," she'd told Aish, and she couldn't allow their pretend flirtation to turn into real…itch scratching. Filling the 24-7 news cycle along with Sofia's video was a photograph of Aish and Sofia. It showed him looking up at her on the truck bed while she'd looked down at him.

It was a photo Sofia didn't want to see more than once.

But social media was raving about the warming temps between the princess and the rock star. Bodega Sofia *finally* had some good press, and Aish was too important to that continued momentum to allow their arrangement to get complicated.

As if he was the voice of *el diablo* on her shoulder, Henry drawled, a touch quieter, "You know, it's okay if you want to try to get to know him again. When the cameras aren't around."

Sofia straightened and pushed herself out of his hold as she raised the wineglass to her lips, calmed and centered herself with the taste of the savory rosé she'd made from her brother's grapes. For a second—unintended and unwanted—she wondered what Aish had thought of it. He'd said nothing about the half glasses he'd sampled.

"Why would I do that?" she said quietly.

She could feel the telegraphing messages being sent between Henry and Roxanne over her head.

"Well, I know we don't talk boys or curl each other's hair," Henry said, and was that a dig for her not sharing with him what had happened with Aish all those years ago? "But I've never seen you look at a guy the way you look at him."

"He hurt you," Roxanne said. *A lo hecho, pecho*, what was done was done and her sister-in-law never hid from it. "Maybe spending some time with him would help you let go of some of that hurt."

It wasn't their fault. They didn't know how cruel they were being. But if Sofia told her and Henry what had really happened, how he had left her alone and terrified in a hospital in a foreign country, neither of them would be talking about reacquainting herself with Aish Salinger. They'd be dragging him up into the mountains and throwing him from the highest peak.

If they knew what Sofia had begged of him—in the vineyard, in her cellar—despite what he'd done to her, they might throw her off right behind him.

Sofia had to be better than a lost cause.

It was of course now, when she was submerged in dark emotions, that Henry tapped her hip and she saw Aish and his manager making their way across the pool deck toward them. Aish looked flinty-eyed at Henry.

Sofia focused on Devonte so she wouldn't get caught up in the ludicrous idea that Aish was jealous.

"Princess, I'll be taking off in the morning. Just wanted a chance to say goodbye," the manager said.

Surprised, she let Roxanne and Henry murmur their thanks and move away to join the party before she took Devonte's huge hand between both of hers. "*¿Te vas?* I can't believe you're leaving just when we're starting to have fun. You'll miss harvest."

"Duty calls," he said. He really had a charming smile for such a bulwark of a man. "And this one—" he nodded at Aish "—claims he doesn't need his 'lap dog' anymore."

Sofia refused to cringe at what she'd called the manager during that confrontation in her office. Her assessment hadn't been wrong. What was striking now was how it had evolved. Aish had christened the vines and winery with a decent amount of his sweat, and Devonte had taken off his suit jacket, rolled up his sleeves, and sweated right alongside him.

"You've been a tremendous help when you could have just been a tremendous *dolor en mi culo*." Devonte chuckled. *Pain in the ass* was understandable in all languages. She went up on tiptoes to kiss his cheek. "You're the only friend of Aish's I'd let in the kingdom."

Devonte stepped back and eyed her. It was a long pause for such a flippant remark.

Sofia glanced at Aish. He shrugged.

Finally, Devonte said, "You weren't a big fan of John's, either?"

"What?" Aish scowled. "What are you doing?"

The majority of partygoers were on the other side of the pool deck around the food table, leaving Sofia, Aish and Devonte alone by the second-story railing. Twilight was settling in around the foothills and lights strung around the deck sparkled on.

"Getting another perspective," Devonte said, his jaw set. "I can't be the only one who never trusted John."

Aish's head snapped back. "What the fuck are you talking about?"

Devonte rubbed his hand over his jawline as he reached for words. Whatever was happening here, Sofia didn't want to be involved.

She raised her empty wineglass. "I'll just…"

"Sorry, Princesa, but I gotta know." Devonte looked resigned to the course he'd set. "Why didn't you like John?"

She glanced at Aish's hurt expression. "I don't really think it's my place to—"

"Don't be shy," Aish said, and now there was anger building behind his words. He glared at Devonte. "We've had nothing but one-on-one time for an entire fucking year but at a party when he's about to leave is when he decides to drop a bomb. Go with it. Tell Devonte what you told me."

In her room that night, when she'd apologized for using him, was the only time she'd revealed her true feelings about Aish's best friend since diapers.

"John didn't like my connection with Aish," she said, dropping her eyes to her empty glass. Acknowledging their past in this intimate way felt treacherous. "I think he actively worked to break us up."

"No way," Aish interjected immediately. "No fucking—"

"It wasn't overt," she said, looking directly at Devonte. He *was* a better friend to Aish than John. If he needed something from her, she would give it to him. "It was *cuchicheos*. Whispers. He wasn't a good person."

"Sofia, how can you—"

"He made me pay off a family once." Devonte's cold words shut Aish down. "A single mom making threats and her sixteen-year-old daughter. I had to bring an envelope to this apartment outside St. Louis that was just…" He shook his head. "The girl had gotten backstage, wanted to show him some lyrics she'd written. He let her show him the lyrics…then he showed her a few things."

"What are you saying?" Shock and betrayal ravaged Aish's whisper. Sofia nudged their little group until Aish's back was to the party. He didn't deserve on-lookers to this.

Devonte made a disgusted *snick* with his tongue. "The girl tried to rip the check out of her mom's hand and give it back, told me she loved him. But she was *six-*teen. An *obvious* sixteen. Two weeks later, he's show-ing you those lyrics in the studio and telling you they're his. I realized then I wasn't paying for statutory rape. I was paying for those goddamn words."

Sofia's shock was a cement block in her chest, sus-pended as she watched this terrible truth play out be-tween Aish and his trusted manager. She wanted to leave; she wanted to believe she didn't belong here. In-stead, horribly, she knew she had to stay.

"Why is this the first time I'm hearing about it?" Aish asked, leading with anger and defensiveness, the animal snapping his teeth from the corner. "Why didn't you tell me then? Why did you agree to deliver the money?"

Devonte slid those bone-crushing hands into his ex-pensive suit and looked Aish straight in the eye. "I have a juvie record. I was told to hurt a couple of guys…and I did." Finally, like that was all he could risk, his dark eyes dropped to the tile. "My record was expunged but somehow John found out. If I didn't keep his secrets, he threatened to tell everyone. Tell you."

And that was the worst threat, wasn't it? That Aish, with his perfect upbringing and gleaming American ideals, wouldn't understand a life of hard choices. That he would take himself away.

"There were more secrets?" Aish asked, his voice

cracking. Even when she'd glimpsed him in that video, even when he'd emerged from his town car in her court-yard—pale and worn—Sofia had never seen him look this devastated.

"That was the worst one," Devonte said.

"Why are you telling me now?"

Instead of looking at Aish, Devonte looked at Sofia. "Because she knows what I know about John. He wasn't good enough for you. He didn't deserve all the devotion you gave him." He took two steps and propped his arms on the railing, looked out over the darkening foothills and the still-white peaks of the mountains.

She leaned on the rail next to him, felt the railing shimmer as Aish fell back against it on Devonte's op-posite side.

"You buried yourself in your house and worshipped at the shrine of John for the last year, and I had to nurse you through it knowing he was a piece of shit," Devonte said quietly. "Committing suicide and somehow mak-ing you feel responsible for it was his last 'fuck you.' And I couldn't tell you because, if you kicked me out, you'd be all alone. I wasn't going to leave you all alone in that house."

Sofia pressed her lips together to hide their trem-bling.

"Now you're finally getting better and I've got to go so you can stand on your own two feet. But you need to know the truth so you can heal the rest of the way, even if it means you're gonna fire me. I'm telling you in front of her so, if you do fire me, she understands what you're going through. I'm leaving you in her hands."

She refused to look at Aish, but felt Devonte squeeze

her shoulder. "I'm sorry, Princesa, but I'm asking you to keep an eye on him. Just…call me if you need me."

He let her go and thunked Aish's chest. "Sorry, man," Devonte murmured. And then he left, leaving a Devonte-wide space separating the two of them.

A breeze pushed the scent of the ocean past her, and Sofia knew that wasn't coming from the Bay of Biscay. She couldn't look at the torn-apart man standing two feet from her.

"I can't—" he started then stopped.

Sofia was squeezing her glass so hard she was afraid it might shatter.

"I gotta go."

The smell of salt and sand dissipated as she listened to the slap of his shoes against the tile. Sofia wrapped a hand around the railing.

She couldn't follow him. She couldn't help him. She had duties and responsibilities here. She knelt to put down her glass then gripped the railing with both hands.

Aish now had to face what Sofia had proof of all along: that John stole songs. After Aish had broken up with her, she'd been a mess, weeping as she'd grabbed her things from the piles between his and John's beds and thrown them into her footlocker. Only later had she realized she'd grabbed a flash drive that belonged to one of them. She'd been falling apart in a high-end San Francisco hotel when, wanting any connection to Aish, she'd opened it to discover audio and video recordings of other people playing songs she knew John had passed off as his own. The recordings even captured John hitting on girls or ordering a beer as the street musician or open-mike band played. She hadn't cared about the thievery; she'd kept it and—shamefully—put it in her treasure box because it also had recordings of Young Son performing. Of Aish.

Now Aish had to face that song stealing wasn't John's only crime. He'd blackmailed Devonte, slept with an underage girl. What else had the friend he'd built a life around, the partner in his life's passion, been hiding? Sofia hadn't had proof of John's manipulations, but she'd sensed them. Why hadn't Aish?

Feeling the cold iron dig into her palms, Sofia convinced herself that she would deny Devonte's request and let Aish be. She would leave him alone with his shock and sorrow. In a hotel. In a strange land. While his family was a world away and his friend was headed to the airport.

It was a cool, calm, deliberate decision.

Sofia was across the pool deck and pushing open the door into the *hospedería* before she'd fully settled on the cool, calm, and deliberate decision that—regardless how much she'd hated him over the last decade—she wouldn't leave him alone now.

September 18
Part Two

The third time Sofia knocked on Aish's suite door, she quietly called his name.

With the party in full swing, there was no reason any of the interns should be in their rooms. Still, it was best if no one caught her pawing at the rock star's door.

When he still didn't answer, she pulled out her master key card.

And saw him across the room in the lamplight, angry amazement overtaking the haggard look on his face as she pushed the door open.

"What the fuck, Sofia," he said, glowering at her.

She stepped in and shut the door behind her.

"I knocked."

"I know." He turned his back on her and continued to pace. His stride was too long, too fast, for his hotel room, causing him to double back too quickly in front of his balcony door. The stone walls caged frenetic energy that needed to get out.

"Aish, what John did to you, the way he misled you was—"

"I don't want to talk about it," he growled without

stopping. The thick swoop of his black hair bounced on his forehead.

"But it's not your fault that John—"

"I don't want to talk about that, Sofia."

She crossed her arms over her linen shift to staunch her frustration, while he continued to march a trench into her *hospedería* floor. He was a gathering storm in his summer cream sweater and white pants. She couldn't just leave him alone.

"*Vale*," she said, dropping her arms helplessly to her side. "What do you want to talk about then?"

When he swung on her with his sparkling, black-eyed glare, it caught her off guard. "Let's talk about Henry," he said, aiming that too-long, too-fast stride at her. "Let's talk about why he keeps putting his hands all over you when you're begging orgasms from me."

He was coming at her. Her heart was pounding. "Jealous?" she asked, raising her chin.

"Fuck yes," he said, and then his big, hot hands gripped her shoulders. "It kills me to watch him touch you with the freedom I want." His gaze scorched her lips, her cheeks, her eyes. "I want to wrap my arms around you. I want to stroke you and feel you lean against me."

His words were like a sip of the richest wine. "You've been paying close attention," she said, and felt his re-action—a fight of his impulses—in the squeeze of his fingers, the subtle dominating shift of his shoulders.

"Don't, Sofia," he warned, deep and growly. "Are you in love with him?"

Her body throbbed in anticipation. He'd never been jealous over her before. He'd never had reason to be; her devotion had been absolute and slavish. She wouldn't have known what to do with him like this as a girl, with him angry and holding back a desire to assert himself. But now she was a woman and having his big body wanting to master hers—within the boundaries of their rules—suited her just fine.

She smiled at his ludicrous question. "Would you have denied me orgasms if I did love him?"

He wrenched her hard against him. "No and you know it." And maybe he was going to break her rules and maybe he was going to taste her lips and maybe he would fuck her through the floor and maybe she would face the consequences later. In the morning.

His bite on her lower lip was sharp. She gasped, eyes and mouth flying open, pain and want getting all mixed up, and the look in his eyes got darker and more determined, his hold on her tighter, as he tilted his head to kiss her jaw. The bite there was kinder, slower, and toe curling. She felt the delineation of his strong, white teeth.

Looming over her and warming her like a furnace, he held her against him and began to make out with her ear, her neck, the skin between her clavicles—wet, soft flicks and nips and hot, nerve-scoring lip drags—mocking her mouth for all the kissing, sucking, and biting it was missing out on.

"Your beautiful fucking neck," he murmured, thumbs holding back her chin, tilting her head back for his exploration. "Your neck makes me crazy…the only skin you'll let me see… I fuck my fist thinking about your neck… I come fantasizing about kissing it."

Why did his filth make her so hot? When he began pulling up the calf-long hem of her dress, she felt molten.

A final, desperate flail from her dying self-preservation reminded her what Aish would see on her hip.

"Apaga las luces," she gasped, not wanting to think, not wanting to stop. "Turn off the lights, Aish."

Like a cord had been snipped, he sagged against her, making Sofia stagger then straighten to take his weight. She grabbed his hip, grasped the back of his neck when he buried his head against her shoulder.

She'd gone from bending beneath him to being the only thing keeping him up.

"I've been in the dark for so long," he said, tight and low into her skin. His hands came around her and clung to her back. "I can't go back there tonight."

As a boy, he'd caused her so much pain. The worst misery in a life that had a fair share of it. She hadn't wished him evil in return; instead, she'd tried to erase him from her mind entirely. Seeing him crumbling now, she should be dancing on his ashes.

She slid her hand to his chest and pushed him upright. He gritted his teeth, thinking it was a rejection. But she swept his hair out of his eyes then tugged his head back with a soft grip so he was looking at her.

She let him go and walked backwards to a silvery grey chaise, took a seat on the edge of it, and pointed the toe of her basket-weave wedge sandal. "Would you help me with my shoe?"

She wouldn't leave him alone in the dark. Neither did she want to be touched by his light.

He approached her cautiously, unsure, but when he slid that long body down onto his knees, it started a low flame in her belly. When he dipped his hands under the hem of her dress and traced slowly up the criss-crossed satin ribbons to the bow at the top of her calf, that flame grew.

When he untied the bow, Sofia murmured, "Could you tear off one of the ribbons?"

He did, effortlessly, the veins in his guitar-playing hands bunching as he ripped the wide ribbon loose, then handed it to her. When she held it up to him, pulled taut between both hands, understanding knocked the dreamy expression off his face. The white satin ribbon was as wide as her palm.

Hunger filled his eyes as he lifted his chin and leaned his face toward her.

She settled the ribbon over his eyes before he could see the jolt of excitement, of power, his acquiescence gave her and tied it at the back of his head. "*¿Estás bien?*" she murmured, running her fingers over the slick fabric, already warm from her body and now from his, making sure it covered his eyes and was secure but not too tight.

It was a creamy, glistening white barrier against his tanned skin and black hair, banning her from his lightning-storm eyes and making his leonine nose, the slash of his cheekbones, and those plunderable lips even more erotically upsetting.

He tilted his head toward her ear. "I'm good," he said, a purring rumble from his chest. "And no more talking, Sofia."

A thrill shook her as he regained his bravado. He moved closer and slid his fingers up the back of her calves, untied her other shoe and tossed it away. He spread her knees and made room for himself between them.

"I can't see you, just a glow," he murmured as he feathered his fingers against the sensitive skin behind her knees. It was overwhelming to see him, watch those lips move, study him this close and vulnerable without the threat of him looking back. "I promise. I swear. Can I get you naked? Let me touch you naked."

And she wanted it, the pressure and pleasure of his hands on her body without seeing the weight of what it meant in his eyes. It was every fantasy she'd swear she never had.

She wiggled the dress up her thighs, over her body and tossed it away. It made a soft thump against his rug and his hands painfully squeezed her kneecaps.

"Lay down," he murmured, and he moved and pressed her knees together, swung them up on the chaise as Sofia leaned back, her head flat against the chaise's long seat. The material was cool and velvety against her skin.

As a fully clothed Aish Salinger leaned over her nearly naked body, the ribbon of his blindfold dripping down to tickle her shoulder, his broad shoulders highlighted in gorgeous cashmere that slipped aside to reveal the edge of a tattoo—the gridlines of a map?— Sofia had to press her lips together to hold back hysteria. She had to press her hands against her thighs to keep herself from lifting them, from spreading them and begging.

"Shake your head yes or no, Sofia," he said, voice low but commanding as he skimmed one hot, callused finger over her shoulder, across her jaw, and then over her lips. She opened her mouth for him as his teasing stroke made her lips tingle. "Did you ever do this with him?"

"With who?" she sighed.

The slow birth of Aish's feral smile made her remember. Henry. He was asking about Henry. While he was blowing her mind. *Cabrón. Gillipollas.* She jerked her lips away from his touch and he let her, instead stroking his thumb against her chin and the long line of her neck.

"No talking," he said, and his blind grin hovered over her like the X-rated version of the Cheshire cat. "Do you want to do this with him?"

Sofia hesitated. But then shook her head no, made sure his thumb could feel it. It was a fair question; this was only a game, and he should know that no one would get hurt by their play.

"Do you want to do this with me?"

That's when she realized that while she lay all-but-naked for him—she still wore her nude-colored panties—he'd only touched her shoulder, her face, her neck. In the time that he'd been in her kingdom, Aish had unrelentingly pressed her for more, pushed her for reaction and answers and emotional intimacy she'd been unwilling to give him.

Except in this. In this, in desire, he'd never pushed. *Come on, baby* had been omnipresent with men. But not with Aish. Never with Aish.

"Do you want to do this with me?" He'd made himself vulnerable when she would have let him take.

"Yes," she groaned, the restraint in her fraying and snapping, arching up her back. "Yes, please, *por favor*, Aish. I need you to touch me, *por favor, tócame, tócame ahora.*"

One hand covered her mouth, rough skin muffling her pleas, while the other hand skimmed down her body to find her breast. His mouth bent to her nipple, licked, bit then pulled as her back arched sharply and she gave a cry against his palm.

"No talking," he commanded again, sucking against her skin, savoring, and she pried her eyes open to watch it, watch him blindfolded and bent over as his whisker-shadowed cheek hollowed to pleasure her. He opened his mouth wide, like he would swallow her whole, and his mouth and tongue were wet and voluptuous over her breast.

"You taste so good…like, fucking…you taste like cinnamon candy, Sofia." His tongue slid down her sternum. "You've always been my favorite flavor."

When he rubbed his lips against the fine hairs along her abdomen, Sofia couldn't help but spread her thighs. Her hips began to move helplessly as she knocked his relaxed hand from her mouth. "Keep going, Aish, please, *te necesito,* lower, lower, Aish, I need you, it's been so long…"

"Keep talking and I'm stopping," he said cruelly. "You follow my rule if you want my tongue in your pussy. Is that still your favorite, baby?"

He teased into her belly button like he would lick at her clit, and Sofia had to jam the back of her hand against his mouth as her hips begged *porfavorporfavorporfavorporfavor.*

"Remember the taste of your cunt," he cooed as his nose skimmed over her quivering stomach, rubbed into the hair above her panties. "Remember wanting to eat you for days."

She pressed her lips against her teeth as he bit her hipbone; if he saw what she'd tattooed there, the reminder that should have kept her from this, he'd realize she remembered something about him, too.

His kiss, between her legs, was soft through her panties; it jolted her like an electric shock. To watch his handsome face, once so beloved, against this essential part of herself—terror twined with pleasure when he licked hard, in this upside-down way, almost sitting next to her on the chaise, and Sofia's hands needed him, dipped under his sweater and began tracing up his gorgeous, wide, rippling back... She caught the sight of ink—he was tattooed here, too—before he pulled away from her and moved to the end of the chaise.

Aish Salinger, blindfolded and more magnificent than she could have dreamed he'd become, kneeled between her legs, gripped the wisp of fabric at her hips, and slowly pulled her panties down and off.

She didn't know whether the tremors as he smoothed his hands up the insides of her thighs came from her or him.

He separated her pussy lips gently and traced her like he was looking with his fingers. And then he was leaning over and the long ends of the satin were trailing over her skin and his hard shoulders were muscling between her legs and his harsh breath was warming her most intimate place.

Things fell apart in her as she stared at him, blindfolded and vulnerable and masterful between her thighs.

"I missed you," he said before his mouth tasted her.

Kisses. Wet, soft, licking, sucking kisses. All the kisses she denied her mouth he gave to her pussy. With his fingers holding her open, he kissed and kissed her, turning his head, stroking and touching, humming against her, until he pushed her thighs up and spread her. Kissed her harder and deeper. All with a wet, searching tongue.

She knew then that the eager, hungry boy wasn't just a figment of her hated fever dreams. His tongue flicked at her clit like her pleasure kept him alive. His fingers turned and slid inside, finding her bumpy G-spot then come-hithering it.

That was a new trick. It made Sofia want to scream.

"Good, baby?" he groaned into her skin. "Like that? Push my hand away if it's too much. Tell me…yeah, oh God, yeah." Sofia felt it, too, the flood of moisture that celebrated what he was doing. "Fuck. Soak my hand, pretty girl. Gorgeous…" His tongue joined his fingers at her entrance. "Why do you have to taste so good? Why do you have to feel so fucking good?"

Sofia couldn't stand it, had to bury a hand in his hair while she buried her teeth into the thin skin of the back of her other hand.

Why do you have to be so good at that? she wanted to scream at him. *Why do you have to be so beautiful? Why*—she wanted to praise him, flay him, worship him, and kick him in the face—*do you have to be the one that tempts me most?*

His fingers began to move faster as he sucked on her clitoris and it wasn't Sofia's fault that out of her mouth poured, "*Eso, así, así, más, me gusta, te necesito, adalante, adalante, mi fuego.*"

He reared up, grabbed her by her biceps, pulled her up against him.

"What did you call me?" he demanded, and she could see his eyes moving behind the blindfold, feel the desperation in his hold.

Her body trembled on the edge of an explosion. She knew instantly when she'd said it mindlessly. *Mi fuego.* My fire. Her fire, the loved word she'd named him, the one he'd abused in his song.

He'd have to beat her to hear it again.

His breath chugged in his chest like he was working to get ahold of it. After several moments, his hold on her gentled.

He tilted his head.

"You're not very good at following rules," he said. His black hair flopped over his white blindfold and he gave her his lopsided grin. It was strained. His lips gleamed with her.

She was literally vibrating in his hands. "I'm as good as you are," she said through clenched teeth. She was on the verge of humping him.

"How about this?" he asked, and he wiped his thumb across the gleam of his lips. And then that motherfucking *cabrón* licked his thumb into his mouth, sucked it clean with a *pop*. "You give up one of your rules and I'll give up one of mine. Let me kiss you. Then I'll let you talk."

She'd tried to hobble him by hiding his eyes. Instead, she'd only left herself defenseless, focused all her attention on his beautiful mouth, that thin but sensitive upper lip, his plump lower lip she'd once liked to tease plumper with nips and sucks.

She wanted his mouth. She wanted to babble. To help him forget.

It was just this one last time.

"Yes, Aish," she said because she could now, pulling him to her. "Kiss me. *Bésame*."

She was prepared for their kiss to be hard. Hot. Explosive. What she wasn't prepared for was for Aish to feather his fingers across her mouth like he was saying hello to it. For him to trace her lips slow and sweet. When he finally leaned in, only his breath touched her lips. He inhaled her. And then he gave her the barest, silkiest brush of his warm lips, one finger still fondling the crease like he was checking for confirmation.

Every nerve ended at Sofia's mouth.

His tongue touched her bottom lip, next to his finger, before it retreated, like the taste was too much. Too good. She could hear him swallow. His pink tongue returned, to stroke again, to flick inside, and she touched her tongue to his. Licked his finger to let him know yes, she wanted this. Yes, this was real.

He touched her jaw then cradled it like she was glass then he kissed her, at last, pressing that unforgettable mouth against hers, giving her warmth and breath and endless sunny sea. She sobbed helplessly into his mouth and he soothed her with his tongue, pressed inside and pleasured what had been empty.

He gathered her naked body up in his arms and kissed her for the first time in ten years, plunged his tongue inside and gave and tasted and took. The nineteen-year-old girl with her oath flailed inside her, just for a second, before pure pleasure burned her up. Tomorrow. She would think about it tomorrow.

Tonight, Aish Salinger was kissing her.

Pleasure quickly emolliated his restraint as he gripped her ass and stood, still kissing her, and then sat with her straddling him. She pressed naked to his hard, cashmere-covered torso. He sucked on her tongue before he commanded, "Get my cock out," against her lips, and she responded as eagerly as if she'd demanded it, eyes closed now and as blind as him as she undid his button and zipper and got him out—long, hard, hot cock she stroked up against his sweater—and she pressed up against him.

He grabbed her by the bend of her knees and moved

his hips until the length of his cock nestled between her juicy pussy lips. Even though he wouldn't go inside, there was relief in the heat he pressed against her.

She began to roll her hips, grinding her clit up and down all those thick, hard inches.

"Yeah," Aish moaned, between kisses and bites. "Yeah, slick me up with your pretty pussy, baby. Sofia. Fuck...*fuck*." He cursed and she felt him shudder. "So soft and good. So warm. Ride it, baby. So good at stroking that shaft."

And Sofia was moaning right back. "There, *allá, allá,* Aish, just like that, *no te detengas,* don't stop." And groaning. "*¿Por qué,* Aish? *¿Por qué?* Why is it so good? So...perfect."

She'd grabbed his hair to lock together their mouths and he'd grabbed her back to lock together their bodies, and when he began to groan against her lips—"Fuck fuck, I'm going to..."—she held on tight and rolled her hips faster and he chanted his orgasm into her mouth. "Fuck...ahhh... Sofia... Sofia... Sofia—" as his come splashed over her belly.

The feel of him, desperate and wet and filthy and so familiar, flung her over the edge as well, made her jolt and spasm and cry out as she got him wet, too.

When he fell back against the chaise, she let him take her with him. When he reached for the blindfold, she stopped his hand. But she got up on quivering legs, turned off the lamps, and then climbed back on top of him.

With her head against his soft sweater and hard chest and his flaccid penis tucked between her thighs, she tugged off the sweat-soaked ribbon and threw it to the floor.

She'd leave. As soon as her legs stopped shaking.

But she fell asleep and so did he and when her ringing phone woke her up in the middle of the night, she was confused about the warm body beneath hers. Then horrified. She stumbled off, away, snatched on her dress, then answered the call.

The only reason she answered it was because the caller was Mateo.

When she hung up, she could see Aish staring at her, still and wary, in the dim light of her phone. He was probably as shocked by her grin as she was.

"It's time, Aish," she said. And knew, gratefully, they'd soon be too busy to fixate on dead friends and stolen songs and not-quite sex that shouldn't, couldn't, wouldn't happen again.

Relieved, she grinned wider. "Harvest has begun."

September 22

Sleep was disregarded and laughed at during the next several days in the Monte del Vino Real. Those whose lives centered on the fields and fruit—the growers, vineyard workers, and winemakers—were joined by friends and family who made their living other ways. The former mandate from dictatorial Monte rulers that every man, woman, and child work in the fields one day per harvest had softened to a tradition; during the height of harvest, every villager chipped in, even if it was only to deliver cold water bottles and hot coffee to the tireless workers. Curious tourists learned quickly not to stop and gawk unless they wanted to spend the morning carrying grape bins.

Those few souls who tried to sleep found it almost impossible. Chatter and good-natured ribbing constantly floated in from the fields, trucks hauling fruit to the wineries rattled continuously by, and lights from the village square shone all night long as restaurant owners stayed open twenty-four hours to provide hearty, simple meals to anyone needing quick sustenance.

The superstar interns suddenly found that this lark they'd embarked on two weeks ago, an all-expense-paid trip to a pretty corner of Spain with front-row seats to a sordid celebrity romance, now mattered to them. The princess they'd doubted had gotten under their skin with her steadfast beliefs, grandiose ambitions, and refusal to play the game the way everyone thought she should play it. They'd abandoned all objectivity in their desire to help her. The training she'd given them made them feel fit to serve.

The twenty interns were split into two groups. Half were deployed to the fields in the middle of the night, when the flavor compounds of the grape were stable, to cut off grape bunches gently but quickly with razor-edged shears. Although they would never be as quick as the hyperexperienced vineyard workers, it still was a matter of pride how many bins they filled and how fast they raced them to the end of the rows to dump their bins into the truck that would deliver the grapes to Bodega Sofia.

The other half of the intern corps helped to weigh and process the grapes arriving on flatbed trucks at dawn. The cavernous processing side of the winery, so long dim and quiet, now roared with noise, its bay door letting in sunlight and eager bees as forklifts drove bins into the winery and carefully tipped the fruit into the sorter. Interns stood over the sorting table, their eyes growing dry and backs aching as they watched eagle-eyed for leaves, bunches that shattered, or grapes that had raisined in the heat wave. They removed this detritus before it could spoil the batch in the crusher-destemmer. This machine ejected the stems and lightly broke open the berries, releasing the juice so that it could start to mingle with the skin and seeds, giving the future wine color and tannins.

It was here, in the organized chaos of crush at her

winery, where Sofia reigned, relying on Carmen Lou-isa to oversee the picking and delivery of harvest. As she tasted samples of the grapes and lightly pressed juice, she made her first decisions about the wines that would define her legacy: Would she ferment the juice, skin, and seeds in steel, wood, or concrete tanks? Did she jumpstart fermentation in the tanks with cultured yeast or did she rely on naturally occurring yeast from the grape skins? After fermentation, the two to four-teen days when the sugars transformed into alcohol, how much time did she give the juice on the skins and seeds, which provided color and tannins?

She discussed these questions and decisions with her interns and staff, sought their input or made sure they understood her reasoning. Or sometimes, in dirty overalls and a kerchief tying back her hair, she'd stand with them in the bay doors as they waited for the next load of grapes and chat, joke, or dance along to what-ever music they were adding to the playlist that boomed through the winery. It was in the arms of a Chilean grower hopelessly trying to teach her the *bachata* that the woman told her they were listening to a Young Son song. Seconds later, Aish confirmed it when he came running from inside the winery, wide-eyed denial on his face. Sofia had smiled, nodded without saying any-thing, and let the song play on.

Now, the interns, those scamps, seemed to be play-ing Young Son every third or fourth song, caught up in the same #Aishia excitement as the rest of the world at the easing tensions between the couple.

The fates that had been lined up against her now seemed to be directing things her way. Her growers were storing the shade cloth for future years' use and praising her for its performance. A well-known documentary filmmaker wanted to produce a multipart series on the Monte del Vino Real. Reservations for Bodega Sofia's *hospedería* were sold out for six months following its grand opening in the spring.

And a vice president from the Mexican conglomerate Trujillo Industries had contacted Roman; they wanted to support Bodega Sofia, however needed. Roman had rescued the kidnapped daughter of tycoon Daniel Trujillo when he'd been a recently discharged army ranger establishing a security business. Later, he'd convinced the industrialist to invest in the Monte when the kingdom needed capital, and Mateo had paid off the bulk of that investment in the intervening five years.

Sofia didn't know why the billionaire who dominated Mexico's auto industry wanted to get involved with a concern as tiny as her winery, but it felt like another cog aligning in her kingdom's favor.

Juan Carlos and the Consejo were still agitating for her failure, with ever-shorter news stories appearing further and further away from the main page, but even he and his band of lazy winemakers were too busy with harvest to cast many stones. The vandal hadn't been caught, but neither had the vandalism continued, probably because of the Monte's current always-on status.

Behind the walls of the winery she'd built, creating wines she was proud of, surrounded by the kingdom she might actually save, Sofia could let Aish's songs play and listen or not listen as the moment allowed. When she did listen, when she did discover herself humming tunelessly along like she was now as she walked the fifteen-foot-high walkway checking the temperatures of the giant steel tanks, Sofia found control by behaving like one of his songs was like any other.

Usually, however, she couldn't feel the singer's hot gaze on her as she hummed.

She glanced up and found him, through the open door, watching her as he sprayed out just-emptied bins. He didn't drop his ardent stare as he let loose one of his slow, aching grins.

He grabbed the end of the spray nozzle, twisted it to lessen the pressure, and raised it to send water cascading down over his head.

Sofia let out a surprised huff, watched the water slick back his hair and melt his long-sleeve black T-shirt to his shoulders, then ducked her head to study the temperature readings she'd written on her clipboard. Or, at least, pretend to study them.

The buzz of her phone was a welcome distraction. She pulled it out of her pocket, read the text, then looked toward her office. She didn't look at him again as she made her way down the stairs.

Rushing into her office, she closed the door behind her, shutting out his music and the noise of the machinery. The only sound now was the delightful one of shrieks and giggles.

"Can't you think of a way to entertain them that doesn't involve tossing them around?" she asked Henry.

"What?" The man who should know better, their bodyguard, was standing and slowly spinning in the open space. "They like it."

Indeed, her three-year-old niece and nephew did like it as they hung from Henry's huge hands and he spun like a helicopter propeller. It was a testament to the strength of his shoulders and arms how high he could hold them, their chubby legs in shorts kicking in the air, their heads flung back as they laughed and screamed.

"*Tía Fía, Tía Fía, mira, mira*," they called. "Faster, *tío*."

Sofia raised her eyebrows. "If you go faster, Helen is going to know." She made the motion of spinning something over her head and launching it. He stopped on a dime.

Helen had been Roxanne's personal assistant and consigliere until the twins were born and she'd informed the billionaire that she'd be moving laterally to take charge as the kids' nanny. No one argued with the indomitable former army nurse.

Henry began using the next prince and princess of the Monte del Vino Real to perform bicep curls.

"What are they doing here?" she asked as they whooped.

"Favor for Helen. They've been buggin' her about coming to see the *cantador*." His accent was exaggerated as he said the singer.

"So I said I'd bring 'em."

A quick flare of anger burned away Sofia's smile. "That's not your decision to make."

Henry's dark blond brows rose up into his hairline. "O...kay." He gently set the twins down. "Sorry. Misread the room. I thought things were getting better between you two."

Sofia went to her knees to steady the twins as they wobbled, and Henry joined her on the floor. Liliana leaned one chubby arm on Sofia's shoulder and swiped back her tawny, sweaty hair from her flushed forehead. "That was tiring," she huffed in English for Henry's sake, the *r* in *tiring* transformed into a *w*.

Sofia wrapped her arm around her niece's waist and nodded seriously. "I could see you were working hard." It killed Sofia every time these little babies behaved like mature people. She tugged her niece against her and soaked up her smell of fresh-baked *pan*.

"Sorry," she said to Henry, muffled in Liliana's hair.

He settled back against the sofa, letting Gabriel climb up on the cushion and then onto his thick shoulders. Henry was Gabriel's favorite jungle gym. "Where'd I get it wrong?" he asked.

She didn't have much in common with Henry and they didn't go places together. Sofia didn't have friends like that. The big American was her best friend because he chose her. He wasn't family or a villager, people that had to withstand her presence in one way or another. He sought her out when his job was in the vicinity, lazed around, asked her opinions, and laughed at her jokes. He'd shown her, in a hundred ways over five years, that he wanted her company and needed its constancy.

She leaned back against the sofa next to him and pulled Liliana into her lap, gave her a *Wine Spectator*. Liliana Sofia Esperanza y Medina loved looking at the pictures.

"Things are better," she said tightly.

In the long nights and early mornings, between the shared lugging and sneaked staring, during the easy conversations and moments turned thick with memory because of a snippet of song, Aish Salinger's sweat and grit were washing away a decade of hate. But that didn't mean she wanted him to ingratiate himself into her life more than he already had. That didn't mean, when he was gone, she wanted him to haunt new nooks.

"I don't want him…too close. And I don't want

them—" she smoothed her hand through Liliana's curls "—to be disappointed when he's not around."

"You sure they're the ones gonna be disappointed?" She narrowed her eyes at him over Liliana's head.

He chuckled. "You can shoot me all the dirty-diaper glares you want. I've seen the way you look at him."

She'd seen the looks, too, in the daily media round-ups Namrita continued to send: her glance when he was working, her smile when he was entertaining the group with a story. They'd caught her staring at Aish in sil-houette with a broom in his hand, and she'd looked like a ballet aficionado watching Misty Copeland.

Her eyes were lingering too long on Aish Salinger.

"*Parra*," she said quietly, asking him to stop. "Why do you keep going on about this? It's an act. I'm sup-posed to…"

"Sweetie, you're not that good of an actress," he drawled over her words. "And I noticed the looks be-cause there was a time I was hoping to get 'em."

Shocked, Sofia met his blue-sky eyes. It was the first time she'd seen insecurity on this man built for big burly joy and bravado.

"I've been over it for a while, so don't worry. But when you said that kiss didn't work, it didn't work for *you*."

He *tsk'd* a laugh and then pushed his finger against her chin to snap her mouth closed.

"Henry, I'm sorry I…"

He chuckled and shook his head. "Don't do that. That'll just make it weird. I'm only telling you to get you to pay attention. I don't know what happened in the past, but in the present, he's stickin'. He's staying and fight-ing and that's the last thing I expected from him. And you're… I don't know…stronger and warmer when he's around. And that's the last thing I expected from you."

Sofia didn't want to think of the implications of her looks or Aish's fight or the awareness from someone she deeply admired that she was changed when her ex was around. Of course she was. That was why she'd obliterated the thought of him for a decade.

So she just wove her arm around Henry's massive bicep and leaned her head against it. With her eyes closed, as he squeezed her thigh, she tried to tell him without words how sorry she was she couldn't fall in love with her best friend. It wasn't personal. She wouldn't fall in love with anyone.

And it was—of course—at that moment that the office door opened.

"Sorry." She heard Aish's discomfort over the blast of music and equipment. "I…there's been a long lull. They asked me… I said I'd check to see when the next load is coming in."

Sofia opened her eyes and the kids began to yell and wiggle free and Henry pinched her thigh and she tried to untangle her arm as she watched Aish take in what looked like an intimately domestic scene on her office floor.

In his knee-high muck boots, grape-stained jeans, long-sleeve T-shirt that clung to his shoulders, and wet hair shoved haphazardly back, this hardworking laborer couldn't look any different than that heroin-chic rock 'n' roller who'd stepped onto her cobblestones three weeks ago.

She'd forgotten how starkly the hard planes of his face showed emotion.

"Sorry, I'll just…" He began to close the door but the

kids were running toward him, gleeful shouts of "Aish, Aish" coming from their baby mouths and he was startled as they grabbed his jeans and couldn't help it as he was pulled inside.

Sofia finally got up on her feet as Aish squatted down to take in the kids' babble.

"*Te hicimos una canción. Puedes ponerlo en tu album,*" Gabriel said, tugging on Aish's wet shirt.

"We wrote you a song," Liliana said, translating for her brother. Her hand was on Aish's shoulder and she was looking seriously into his eyes. "It's for you, for your next album."

As Sofia walked behind them to close the office door, she realized this was the first time Aish was getting to see Liliana and Gabriel without their caps and sunglasses. There, in that squat he'd kept up in the vineyard, he was looking into her niece's hazel green eyes, seeing her wavy hair the color of Sofia's. Gabriel, with his big brown curls, sometimes looked more like Roman than Mateo.

Many people didn't understand that you had to get down to a child's level to really enjoy them.

Aish glanced behind his shoulder toward Sofia, but she just took out her phone to text Carmen Louisa about the next truck of grapes.

Henry stood and went over to lean on Sofia's desk.

"Okay," Aish said hesitatingly. "Um…do you want to sing it for me?"

They both nodded excitedly. Too young with lives lived with too much love to know shyness, they began to sing. The song was in Spanish, a convoluted tale about the cocker spaniel they had to leave back in San Francisco where the family lived half of the year so

Roxanne could be close to her headquarters. The song also mentioned their devotion to *chocolate y churros*.

Their voices were high and warbly, Gabriel got a pouty lip when they disagreed on the words, and what Liliana lacked in tune she made up in volume.

But there was no artifice in Aish's room-filling shatter of applause when they were done. "So good," he praised, still clapping. "This is definitely going on the album."

Sofia walked around to stand in front of him, and pulled Gabriel against her legs. While Aish singing to them left her bereft but suspicious, his enthusiasm for their singing left her weak kneed.

"*Que bueno,*" she bent over to whisper into Gabriel's curls before she kissed them.

Liliana leaned her whole weight on Aish's side, so he had no choice but to put his arm around her.

"What's the name of your dog?" he asked her, her head close to his.

"Benito," she said.

"I'm sorry he pooped in your room."

"*¡Casi vomito!*" Gabriel exclaimed.

Aish grimaced theatrically. "Yeah, it's gross. I would have almost thrown up, too."

Henry called from the other side of the room, "How'd you know what they were singing about?"

Sofia was slower to put it together. But when she did, she looked down at Aish.

He looked up at her steadily. "*There never was a good time to mention that I'd learned the language,*" he said in flawless Spanish.

Sofia was bombarded by several emotions. Anger that he'd never told her. Panic over what she'd said in his presence when she thought he couldn't understand. Lust at those perfectly formed words coming out of his beautiful mouth.

And a full-body-warming surety that he'd learned those words for her.

The buzz of her phone surprised her. She looked down at it. "Carmen said there's no more grapes coming in today. Everyone can take off."

Henry came over to them. "I'll let 'em know. I got to get the kids back to Helen before she sends out the cavalry." He hunched down and picked up one bemoaning child at a time. He stood and looked at Sofia.

"You two, um…" Devilment glittered in his eyes. "Have fun."

Sofia stayed standing and Aish stayed squatting as the door closed.

She crossed her arms. "Did you enjoy listening at keyholes?" she asked.

"Enough of the interns and journalists speak Spanish that no one said anything revealing." He rested his elbows on his thighs, let his big hands dangle between them, like he was prepared to stay in that uncomfortable position at her feet all day. "Me knowing the language felt like the biggest reveal."

Neither broke their stare.

"*I want inside you so bad I'm dying,*" he said, softly in Spanish, conversationally, as if the children were still in the room.

Sofia gripped her elbows. "You said you wouldn't fuck me until it was more than a one-time thing."

"*I also said I wouldn't let you tempt me with your voice.*" He licked that delicious bottom lip. "*And you*

*said I couldn't kiss you. Our rules work best when
they're broken."*

Helpless to it, Sofia said, "This is a really bad idea."

When his mouth tilted up wickedly, she realized how
far her answer was from "no."

"Tell me you don't want to feel it again," he said, his
black eyes beckoning. *"Tell me you don't want to know
if it's as good as we remember."*

She scraped her teeth against her lip. "I'm afraid it's
going to be better."

And that was the thing, with an exhale of air, that
knocked him back on his ass. He fell back to the floor
and covered his eyes with one arm, covered his crotch
with the other.

He was so dramatic. And she in no way wanted to
rip open his jeans and palm his beautiful hard dick and
sink it inside her, ride him in the afternoon sunlight,
enjoy him and make him howl in full view of every intern and employee and reporter who cared to watch.

Harvest was winding down. Soon, all the grapes
would be in and she'd begin the measuring, blending, and aging to turn the alcoholic juice into world-
renowned wines that would reinvigorate her kingdom.
It was the task she was put on the planet to do.

But perhaps tonight would be best spent letting some
of the air out of her growing fascination with Aish Salinger.

"Tonight," she said. But then stopped. Breathed.
"Would you like to come to my room after dark?"

"Yeah," he muttered, his arm still over his eyes, his
voice gravel. "Okay." And his fist, dangling over his
crotch, was white knuckled before he unclenched it,

stretched for just a moment, and then white knuckled it even tighter.

She wanted to get each finger wet with her mouth and then insert them into her body.

She forced herself forward, stepped around him and headed to the door. "Tonight," she threw over her shoulder before she walked out of her office.

Sofia wanted to lay the ghosts of their painful past to rest. They could calm the allure of their current desires if they simply gave in to them, touched each other until their former touches no longer haunted, and then allowed themselves to fade into pleasant footnotes in each other's stories. Tonight, she would take him into her bed and body and make him like every other man she'd entertained there. They would throw out his last rule, and have at each other for the rest of the month, while maintaining hers. She would only have sex with him in the dark.

In a cool and methodical way, Sofia would strip Aish Salinger of his power to ever hurt her again.

September 22
Part Two

Aish had eaten, showered, slept—which was pretty shocking considering the vibrato of lust rattling him ever since Sofia had invited him to her room—put on good clothes and even styled his hair by the time he watched the last centimeter of sun slide behind the mountains from a hallway window.

He turned to tap on Sofia's door.

She opened it before he could, and they both startled.

"How long have you been here?" she asked. But then her eyes were moving over him and he leaned back on one shiny black loafer and let her look at his pompadoured hair and clean-shaven jaw, the crisp white shirt with collar unbuttoned just enough to tease at his tattoos, the perfectly tailored black tux, the silk pocket square as deep red as her flushed, pretty pussy.

"How long have you been by the door?" he countered, as pleasure—warm and excited and throbbing—filled him. She'd dressed for him, too.

He'd known it was possible that he come to her in his dressed-down tux and she'd be in overalls. But she wasn't in overalls. She was in roses. Her dress was an explosion of red roses against a black, wispy-looking fabric, roses exploding over her torso and around her cinched waist and down the skirt to mid calf. Her arms—her beautiful, golden-toned, muscular arms with her *The Queen is Dead* tattoo—were bared by cap sleeves. The dress's deep V showed off the sleek skin of her chest and soft sides of her breasts.

So much delicious skin.

Her tawny hair was softly swept back from her face and her wide mouth glistened with gloss and she'd put little shiny black stones in her ear and she'd done this for him and he just wanted to…just wanted to… He was seconds from falling to his knees.

Her voice, when she whispered in Spanish, sent shivers over his skin. "*Do you want to go at it right here in the hall or would you like to come in?*"

He kept his shit together. "*I think I'll come in. It's drafty out here.*"

He watched her pause, press her delicious lips together. Then she stepped back.

"Let's stick to English," he said, a touch of gruff in his voice, as he walked past her. She smelled so sugar sweet.

"Yes, let's."

He could glory later in what the tapes and tutors and true fascination with the language had earned him— her surprise, hopefully her admiration, and maybe her insight into how much she'd meant to him. Perhaps she even realized that he'd hoped—planned—to share his new linguistic skills with her one day. But right now he couldn't speak Spanish with her, not with the way it made her look at him. Right now, he couldn't give her the green light to speak it, not with the way her voice sparked over his body.

He was an amateur at this long game, so he needed to keep his act together before he began blubbering everything he needed and wanted into her rose-covered lap.

If through her body was the way back to her heart, then he had to be deliberate in his journey.

When he turned to look at her, her hand was already on the light switch.

"What are you doing?"

"Making it dark."

"Wait, wait, wait."

He walked quick steps back to her, pulled her hand from the wall and against his chest, tried to think fast when his brain felt stuck in a molasses of want and hope. The twilight glow coming through the sheers of her closed balcony doors gave him something. "It's not dark enough yet. And...um..." The palm pressed against his chest, the fingertips that had ended up just inside his collar and touching his skin, weren't helping him think.

Why wasn't he pushing her up against the wall and lifting that dress?

"And, yeah." He kept a hold on her wrist as he tugged her into the room. Away from the wall. "I had a rule and..."

The smile growing on her face, amused and sexy, stopped him short.

He cupped her hand and kissed her cinnamon-scented palm. "This is more than a one-time booty call, Sofia."

"*Vale*. Okay," she said, still sweet, still amused, before she slipped her hand from his hold and moved to a heavy black sideboard where decanters of wine and water and a tray of fruit, of crostini, queso and cured meats waited.

It settled him, centered him, that she'd anticipated at least a break in their lovemaking—a quiet moment to eat and drink—instead of expecting him to fuck her then get out.

When she pointed at the decanters with a questioning look, he asked, "Is the wine yours?"

She nodded.

"Then pour me a glass." She turned away from him quick enough, but he still saw the pleased quirk of her lips.

When she walked back carrying two glasses, he took in the soft *swish* of her dress and the smoky look in her eyes. She handed him a glass and then took a seat on a black-leather-topped wooden bench near the balcony doors. Here they could both watch the light. Sofia urging it to fade to black and Aish using every bright second.

He unbuttoned his jacket and sat next to her, swirled the wine in his glass and took a sniff before drinking. He felt her eyes on him as he did it.

He nodded down at her arm, inches from him. "Your tattoo hasn't faded." The neat script, the blood-red words *The Queen is Dead* on the inside of her forearm were as sharp as ever.

She ran a thumb over it. "I keep it vibrant with vitriol and malice."

Because he couldn't help himself, he ran two fingers over it, too. The skin was seductively silky. "Thank you for letting me see it again." She let him stroke her, feather back and forth over those angry words, and the comfort and ease of it was jarring. Mind-blowing.

She'd granted him this little bit of a second chance. He was so fucking lucky to be here.

She moved her arm away. "You'd never mentioned wanting your own tattoo," she said.

And he hadn't. At twenty-one, Aish could no more have imagined covering what he'd thought was a pretty ideal body with ink than wearing a blue wig over his hair. But after his first sex with someone other than Sofia, he'd staggered still stinking from the show into a tattoo parlor in Dallas and gotten a compass on his forearm in the same spot as Sofia's tattoo.

He'd been such an idiot to think it would lead him back to her.

But that story would have her shutting down and kicking him out. So instead, he just said, "I liked yours. I got one. Then I didn't stop."

Her *hmm* of a response had Aish wondering for the first time *why* she'd insisted he cover his tattoos. He'd assumed it was another degrading restriction in a list of them, the clear line to announce what she thought of him and how little she trusted him. But maybe she liked the idea of ink tracing over his body too much.

It wasn't time to heat up. He took a sip of wine to cool down and savored the taste.

"Do you like the wine?" she murmured.

"Yeah," he said. The sky outside had become plum. "What…um…what do you like about it?"

He turned to look at her. Then he stood up, straddled the bench in his tux pants, and sat down facing her.

"Sofia," he said, his grin growing. "Are you hunting for compliments about your wine?"

She wouldn't drop her chin or her gaze from the window. He should have been sitting this way the whole time. She looked so pretty and indomitable, sitting here with her stubborn chin and heavenly dress in the hotel she created.

He thought about the other thing he'd been craving since harvest began.

"I'll tell you what I think about your wine if you tell me what you think about my music."

It had been a lucky break when she hadn't blamed him for the Young Son songs pouring over the winery's sound system. He knew the acoustics in the large facility made it difficult to hear them. But he had noticed her, more than once, humming along in her tone-deaf way. Did she like the songs? Had she heard any of the lyrics?

He scooted gently closer, until his knees touched the softness of her skirt.

She dropped her eyes to her glass. "That's not a fair bargain, you know."

"Why?"

"I have told you what I think of your music."

Aish opened his mouth to object. But quickly closed it.

She'd spent hours and hours that long-ago fall listening to his music, playing him her favorite bands, critiquing a lyric or a hook, listening and loving every chord he strummed on the guitar, every note he sang. She'd believed entirely in him. Her faith in his destiny had been absolute.

He'd treated her praise like it was his due.

She didn't want the apologies he felt like he could scoop out of himself in buckets. So he picked up the pale red wine that he'd been savoring because he wouldn't pour himself another glass although its taste made him want to.

He sniffed it again, caught something sweet. Vanilla-ish. "It's spent some time in American oak," he said. She nodded.

He took a good drink.

I could drink a case of you, Joni Mitchell sang in his favorite song.

"My palate's gotten used to fruit bombs, those big chewable Napa Valley cabs and Sonoma County pinots," he said. She tucked her hair behind her ear; she was listening although she wasn't looking at him. "This is…restrained. Delicate. Unique. You've got a little tobacco, a little acid. They balance each other nicely."

He could see the pleasure on her cheek even if she didn't smile. Then she stood, slid her leg over the bench and faced him too, letting their knees touch as her skirts fluttered around her lap. She could have slapped him, her move provided that much power and surprise.

"I was impressed by the variety of instruments you've incorporated into your music," she said softly, eyeing him. "I always thought you planned on being more of a four-piece American rock band."

Because he couldn't not, he gently slipped his hand under her skirt to cover her knee. When she didn't pull back, he slid two fingers under the bend, feathered them across the thin, ticklish skin. "We *were* an American rock band. With, like, fifteen pieces."

She tilted her head to smile at him. "And a bagpipe."

He dug all of his fingers between her leg and the leather, loving the weight and warmth of her, being able to claim and hold her this way, and took another drink of wine. Her eyes, as still and watchful as a cat's, followed him.

He wanted to press her back and whisper love words about aroma and mouthfeel and finish against her skin.

He rolled the wine around in his mouth and swallowed. "You know what I really think, Sofia?" He gripped her knee and made his thumb memorize the bones. "I think your wines are fucking incredible. I think you already know that. And I don't think you need to hear it from me or anybody."

"No, I don't," she said imperiously, lifting her nose and exposing all that gorgeous skin—her neck, her chest, the sides of her sweet tits—to the lamplight. "But you owe me some fawning."

He finished his wine in two big gulps. Then he thunked the glass on the floor and, his hands now free, slid them over her thighs, over the delicious fabric and warmth and softness, to her hips. She was so small in his big hands. Her waist looked as delicate as the wineglass stem. He met her eyes.

Her smile, the challenge and excitement in it, reminded him how that little nineteen-year-old girl had mastered him entirely.

"You want some fawning," he said, lifting her and pulling her onto him, her thighs sliding over his, her weight in his lap. He gripped her thigh in one hand and her waist in the other as he looked up at her.

Slowly, lazily, she laid her arms around his shoulders. As if, of course, yes, like a thousand other men, she knew he adored her.

He smiled up at her with all the joy of being here. "You're an artist with the grapes. Tasting what you created makes me want to cry. Once people get their heads out of their asses, you're going to be queen of the wine world and I'm going to be some has-been in your liner notes."

She shifted, just a little, but enough to push her closer

to where he was hardening up for her. "You don't get to feel sorry for yourself, not with the music you're capable of." She leaned in and feathered a kiss at the top of his cheekbone, letting him get lost in the smell and tickle of her hair. "You have a talent and a skill that's a gift from God." She kissed his bridge, the tip of his nose, rubbed her lips over an eyebrow. "If you waste it, or let this scandal distract you from it—" her hands, those small world-dominating hands, tugged back his head so she could smooth her mouth along his jaw "— then yes, you're just a sad little man who buried that bold joyous boy."

She bit the vein of his neck and he let his hands meet over her skirt and under her tight little ass so he could push her tight against him.

"Is it dark enough now, Aish?" she purred in his ear.

Without even looking, since her room was the same layout as his, he reached over and slapped at the light switch by the balcony door, bathing the room in darkness that he didn't even care about as he wrapped his hands around her neck and took her mouth with his.

Her tongue welcomed his with a smooth lick as she gripped his wrists and rolled her hips, tasting him and letting him taste as her soft, flower-covered pussy got him ready.

She tugged her head back and smacked a hand against his chest when he tried to follow. "So are we going to do this, Aish?" she said, and he could feel her breath against his open, gasping mouth.

"Are we going to fuck in the dark until the month is over?" Her voice sprinkled over him like Spanish fly.

"Are we going to take each other until it's out of our systems?" He could feel the slightest silk of her lips, the barest tease of her tongue at his mouth. But she wouldn't give it to him. Not without an answer.

"Yeah, Sofia. Yeah." Then he pulled her in rough and hard and invaded her mouth, wholly and wetly, and trapped her with muscles he'd reformed for her, and kept his tongue busy so he couldn't say what was vibrating through him.

Never, Sofia. You'll never be out of my system.

He felt nimble fingers at his shirt buttons.

He let go of her mouth with a wet suck and then opened his eyes, looking up at her. But there was only the vaguest suggestion of her outline and the swing of her hair—right, the dark—so he couldn't see what was on her face. But, fuck, he could feel.

His girl was undressing him.

She tilted back a little to get to the last buttons then, when his shirt was all the way open, she tugged it wide. His stomach, his chest, the whole story he'd inked there, were exposed to the dark, the warmed air between them, the sacred atmosphere of her room. He was still in his tux coat.

When she put her hands on his stomach, his abs contracted under the touch.

"Are my hands cold?" she asked softly.

"Are you fucking kidding, Sofia?" he groaned, not soft at all, and she laughed and he wanted to die and she slowly, lingeringly stroked those much-loved hands over his stomach and ribs and pecs and sides and treasure trail and belly button and sternum and armpits and collarbone and shoulders and down his arms, tracing legends she couldn't see, pushing everything off until he had to lurch away from her hands and tug off his cuffs himself because he was about to come in his pants.

His cock did jump beneath her, did get wet at the tip, when he straightened again and heard her give a soft, involuntary coo of pleasure.

"You're so…" She sighed and *fuck*. It was too much, too good and too bad, that she liked what she saw when she could barely see him. He didn't want to be an anonymous good lay for her. He didn't want her to lose track of what this meant.

He wrapped his hand around the back of her neck and pulled her up against him. "Your beautiful fucking neck," he growled against it, licking up the long line of it, wanting her to hear his voice, wanting her shivers to belong to him. "I took for granted all the beautiful skin you used to show me. Now all I get is your beautiful fucking neck. I'm obsessed. It's my newest kink." He sucked it filthy where it met her shoulder, just to prove him true, and she quivered under his mouth. "I can't see your legs," he said, working his mouth slowly over the skin. "Or your tits…or your ass…or your pretty, pretty cunt. So I think dirty, dirty thoughts about this beautiful…" Biting it. "Gorgeous…" Sucking it. "Fucking…" Loving it. "Neck."

She was gasping, boneless, nerves trembling just under her skin against him. She mumbled something against his shoulder.

"What, Sofia?" he asked. He tilted up her chin. Now he had her attention, now he could be tender, sweet. He softly kissed her lips. "What, baby?"

"Take off your pants," she said.

Guh. This woman. He dipped his hands under her skirt. "You first," he said, hands stroking up her legs to reach for her panties. Stroking up taut thighs, round hips, and soft warm panty-free ass.

Fuuuuuuuck. This woman.

With a growl, he lifted her up against him as she gasped and laughed, squeezed her ass and gave it a slap, then took her mouth. She buried her hands in his hair and pulled it just like he liked.

"Get naked, Aish," she commanded against his mouth. "Get me naked."

And he did, pulled her free of all that gauzy dress, over her head and her shaking out her hair like a cloud. Smacked away her hands when she tried to help with his fly, lifting her high, naked, nipple in his mouth as he took care of it himself, stood and struggled out of pants and socks and shoes, never letting her go, then straddling the bench again, warm leather against his ass and thighs, hot Sofia straddling his lap and in his arms.

Her skin, God, her skin, the bright glow of it against him even if he couldn't see it in the dark. Overwhelmed, he pressed his forehead against her neck and mouthed at the smooth plane of her chest. She was silky smooth. She was so warm. She smelled like home.

"Aish," she murmured, into his hair, and she stroked her strong fingers down the muscles of his back. Dug into the muscles above his ass and tilted her hips against him.

The trim bush that stroked his cock was already wet.

"*Que bonito, que guapo,*" she murmured in the secret air between them. "The feel of you, Aish. So good, so long and hard and gorgeous."

She lifted up, brushing dampness up his contracting abs and the head of him jerking as it felt her, nothing but naked wet hot her and she wanted and she was asking and there was something, there was something he'd meant to…

Fuck. He wrapped his hands around her slim waist and held her suspended above him. "You asked me if I was safe, Sofia," he breathed in the dark. "Are you?"

After a lifetime of caution—he'd only skipped condoms with Sofia after they'd both been tested—he'd gone inside her in the cellar uncovered. Between the astonishment and horror, protection had never crossed his mind.

"Yes, Aish, yes," she said, desperate, her waist, her hips, weaving in his hands. "I've never gone bare with anyone but you."

His heart lurched. Neither had he, not in ten years, but he was obsessed with her. What was her fucking excuse?

The Aish of a week ago would have howled and pushed, would have jumped up and turned on the lights and gone down on his knees and demanded that she acknowledge it, explain it, admit that it had to mean something, right, beg that she put him out of his misery and give him some fucking hope that, just maybe, there was some infinitesimal chance that he had another shot with her.

The Aish of right now pulled his sweet-skinned girl against his naked body, held her head in his hands as he kissed her precious mouth, and gently and carefully tilted his cock so the love of his life could sink down onto it. The Aish of right now would focus on the miracle of this moment, even if it never happened again.

When she was all the way down, when he was all the way deep, she leaned back, just a little, and pressed her hand against her stomach.

Fuck. He'd forgotten how she used to do that. "Are you okay?" he whispered. He realized then how quiet they were both being. Her breath was coming in little gasps. His chest was moving too fast.

"*Sí,*" she whispered back. "You're so big."

And all of it hit him right then, her skin and her smell and her silky wet heat and he was inside her and she wanted him there, and he groaned, loud and naked, surrounded her in his arms and began to rock her, up and down on top of him, needing to fuck her and needing to get fucked, and he growled, "C'mon, Sofia," and she was riding him, oh fuck her perfect pussy, she was riding him so good and hard and crying out, "*Así, así,* like that, Aish, yes, yes…*gigante,* so deep," her hands grabbing him, needing him, and he crashed her back against the leather so he could give her what she needed. He spread her thighs so he could give it to her, getting in so good and as deep as she wanted, commanding her, "Tell me…like this…like this," using his fingers and cock and hips and balls and when she shrieked, when she showered him with her orgasm and her legs shook in his hands, he pulled out and flipped her over and slapped her ass and shoved in again because it wasn't time yet, wasn't time yet for him, and she called him names, filthy names, as she clawed at the leather and he grabbed the edge of the bench, and shoved in and in and in, calling her names, too.

"*Belleza,*" as he bit her neck. Beautiful.

"*Amada,*" licking at the sweat between her shoulder blades. Beloved.

"*Mi princesa, mi única estrella,*" as she locked up beneath him, shaking and sobbing and coming, and his own helpless orgasm shot down his spine.

My princess. My only star.

10 Years Earlier

Sofia was happy and a little buzzed on the wine they'd guzzled in the parking lot and the pot clouds floating around her as she sat on a blanket in Golden Gate Park, running her hand through Aish's sun-warmed hair as he rested his head in her lap and sang along to the band that was playing on the festival stage. The other student-workers who'd come with them were in the beer tent, which America's archaic liquor laws and the glaring black X on the back of her nineteen-year-old hand prevented Sofia from enjoying.

No matter. She'd worked hard all week funneling wine from the fermentation tanks to the barrels and shoveling out must. She'd even covered a couple of Aish's shifts when he'd been up late drinking and writing music with John. So she was going to savor today, with her man's head in her lap and his best friend at her side, who'd kept her laughing with a steady stream of stories about their childhood.

"…And he's so proud of himself because he's hit the ball and everyone's yelling, but they're yelling because he's running the *wrong way*. Right to third base. A week later, our moms take us out of baseball and put us in basketball…"

Aish's silky hair smoothed over her bare thighs as

he turned to look at John and say, "And you stopped dreaming about being the next A-Rod and started talking about being the next Kobe."

John grinned, and the sunlight glinted off the white teeth, blond hair and true-blue eyes he'd used to seduce so many. "Gotta dream big," he said.

Things had gotten better with John in the last month. She'd worked to be more accepting of his third wheel in their company, less possessive of Aish's time, and John had stopped flicking at their relationship. He'd even helped Sofia out a few times, covering Aish's shift when she couldn't, and sending a friend he knew in San Francisco to pick her up when she'd been stranded at Fisherman's Wharf, wandering around with a bouquet of balloons when Aish had forgotten their date to play a last-minute gig in Santa Cruz.

Aish being a musical genius, John had explained, meant that he could be a relationship idiot.

If he was an idiot, he was *her* idiot, and Sofia didn't love Aish any less for revealing that he was as fallible as any twenty-one-year-old boy. She trusted that he loved her, that he respected and needed her. She didn't know what was next for them and tried not to think about the fact that they only had a month left in the internship. Sofia would start at the University of Bordeaux in the spring thanks to his uncle's influence. His home was in LA, hers was in Europe. She...was grateful for the love he gave her now.

She refused to beg for more.

The worst thing a girl can do to herself, her mother had said, weeping as Sofia felt choked by the thick scent of perfume, *is fall in love.*

Sofia shook off the ugly memory and buried her hand in her love's hair.

John was frowning down at the festival program in his hand. "Moriah's Trick is playing," he said.

Aish jerked to look at John, making Sofia inadvertently yank. "Sorry," she said, untangling her fingers.

But Aish hadn't seemed to notice. "How the fuck did they get on the bill?" He propped his weight on his elbows, lifting off Sofia's lap to glower at John.

"They signed with Steadman," John said, still studying the program. "I've always said he'd be a great manager." He paused. "Should we go talk to them?"

"We should," Aish said. Then he shot Sofia a look. What was that expression?

He pushed up to sitting and swung his legs around to face her. "We know this band from LA," he said, entwining her fingers with his. "We're gonna talk to them for fifteen minutes and then we'll be right back."

Sofia smiled at him, confused. "I can't go?"

Aish gripped her fingers. "The lead singer…she's into me. Nothing's happened and nothing's *gonna* happen." The big hot hand he ran down her leg wasn't fair. "But I can't go back there with my gorgeous girlfriend and expect the singer to say nice things about me to her manager."

She could see his point. And appreciated his honesty.

And it was only fifteen minutes. She nodded her head. "*Vale*," she said, pulling her long hair over her shoulder and crossing her legs.

When Aish leaned forward to kiss her, deep and hard with a hand squeezing her shoulder, it settled the butterflies in her stomach. John stood and held out a hand to pull his friend to his feet.

"Don't worry," John said, patting Aish on his chest. "I'll make sure he gets back to you without letting her take too many bites."

And all the butterflies started fluttering again. But she didn't let Aish see them as she waved him off, leaned back on the blanket, and kept her eyes on him until his dark head was swallowed by the crowd.

Two hours later, sweaty, headache-y, and frantic, Sofia shoved through a drunken clump of twenty-somethings, the skunky smell of pot clinging to everything, to finally grab at the correct blond man's shoulder—she could smell John's heavy cologne meters away.

"John," she said, her fingers digging in so he couldn't get away. "Where have you been? Where's Aish? What happened?"

John's eyes went wide. "He's not with you?"

Sofia shook her head, feeling naked with desperation. She wanted to put her hands over her face and hide. John cursed and grabbed his phone out of his pocket.

"I've already tried that," she said.

When John got the same results as Sofia—straight to voicemail—he grabbed her arm and said, "C'mon. We'll find him."

John's urgency made her panic get worse.

"He said he was heading back to you, so I hung with some of the other bands," John said as they wove hurriedly through the crowd. "Wanted to give you some alone time."

"Did you talk to the lead singer?" she asked.

John was quiet a beat too long before he said, "Yes."

"*¿Y qué pasó?*"

"What?"

"What happened?" She didn't shriek. But she could have over the noise of the alien crowd, the roar of the unknown music, her own unfamiliar worry and lack of control.

"He…" This close to the stage, the crowd was denser, and John had to shove with his height and shoulders and tug her behind him. She felt like a thinly stuffed doll dragged behind an uncaring child.

Finally, they broke into a gap of space and air at the side of the stage.

John had to shout in her ear. "She introduced us to their manager, and we talked." His cologne added to Sofia's nausea. "Then Aish said he was going to say goodbye to her before he got back to you."

At the expression on her face, John urged, "Don't freak out." He turned and spoke to a beefy security guard standing near an entrance to the backstage.

Sofia's stomach dropped when he shook his head.

"He's wandering around somewhere," John promised. "We'll find him." She followed on his heels, skirting the edge of the crowd until they could breathe and hear again.

"You're special to Aish," John said, scanning the crowd as they walked. "He wouldn't do anything stupid."

Oh God. As fifteen minutes had ticked into thirty and then an hour and an hour and a half, Sofia had worried about him being safe. Her imagination had gone wild with thoughts about him being attacked by a drunk festivalgoer or overly officious backstage security. She believed only something catastrophic would make him abandon her, without a word, in the middle of a crowd of strangers. She hadn't considered…anything stupid. It'd seemed outside the scope of possibility. Until John implied it was the one thing she should be worrying about.

"Was the lead singer still into Aish?" she asked, making sure to look away, far, far away as if Aish could be found on the horizon.

John gave a begrudging laugh. "Every girl is into

Aish." Then he seemed to remember who he was talking to. "But it doesn't matter who is into Aish; he's into *you*. And as long as he doesn't drink too much, he's cool."

"Was he drinking backstage?" she asked before she could stop herself.

John gave her a side eye as they continued walking. Finally, he said, "Not that much."

It was one characteristic of Aish that she was not a fan of and that, fortunately, didn't happen very often. He could overindulge to the point of foolishness. It never happened when it was just the two of them. But being from a kingdom of wine, she had little patience for people who could not manage their alcohol.

How much had he had to drink backstage with a gorgeous lead singer who wanted him?

"Fuck…finally," John cursed, before he was charging toward the beer tent. Sofia was right behind him when she saw what he'd seen: Aish, sitting on a bench outside the large tent, looking sweaty and miserable as he swayed and gripped a half-empty bottle of water.

Sofia wanted to rush to him, wanted to throw her arms around him and pull his lolling head against her, wanted to start pouring gallons of cold water down his throat. But she didn't. She slowed as John moved to Aish's side.

"Fuck, dude, where've you been?" John cursed, punching his shoulder.

Aish winced as Sofia stood in front of him. "I couldn't find you guys," he groaned.

"You told Sofia you'd go back in fifteen minutes. You told me you were going back."

"I wanted to." Aish's forehead clenched in misery. "But I started feeling shitty and…"

"I told you not to do those shots," John said.

Aish squinted up at him. "We were doing shots?"

"You," John said, looming over his best friend. "You were doing shots. You're lucky she didn't roofie you."

Sofia watched these two indolent boys as the American sun beat down on her head and dehydration made her skin feel two times too small and endlessly old. And tired.

"Sofia?" Aish said, focusing on her.

She watched him and said nothing.

"Sofia," he repeated, more urgent. He lifted the bottle over his head, upended the rest of it, and she realized then that his hair wasn't sweat soaked. He'd been trying to sober up.

"I'm going to grab more water," John said quietly before walking away.

Aish gripped the bench to keep from swaying as he looked up at her. "I'm sorry," he croaked. "I fucked up."

She dug her fingers into her biceps, squeezed her arms against herself.

"Could you...could you sit down? If I keep looking up, I'm going to hurl."

She sat as close as she normally did, a stupid force of habit, and instantly smelled the strong scent of patchouli. It was coming off him. Aish—who never wore cologne, who smelled like salt and skin and sun, who had become her favorite scent—now smelled like another woman.

She quickly slid away from him and gripped her knees.

"Sofia..." It came out like a moan.

"What happened?"

"I...fuck... I don't know. We went backstage and talked to the manager and it went well and then she gave us beers and, I swear, I know I only had one but shit started to go wonky and then...goddammit, I don't remember doing shots…" There was real misery in his beloved voice. Sofia fought the horrifying inclination to soothe it. "The next thing I remember I was out here looking for you guys."

"So you don't know what happened with her?" She stared at the dirt between her sandals. Maybe she'd had too much to drink; she felt like hurling, too.

"Nothing happened with her."

"You smell like her."

"Fuck," he cursed again, sharp and bitter. Like someone else had done this. Like he wasn't responsible for this nightmarish moment. "She hugged me. She…kinda…was hanging on me when we talked to her manager."

Then he'd gone back to say goodbye, did shots with her, and "forgot" what he'd been doing for the last hour and a half.

Sofia shot to standing. And found herself just as quickly in Aish's lap.

"Don't, don't, don't, don't," he chanted low, pleading, against her neck, nosing under her hair and getting to skin, his long strong arms belting around her waist and holding her against him. "Please, please, don't, I swear to God, nothing happened, I know it didn't, my body knows it, it couldn't have, I love you, I love you too much."

He was heat and strength and safety plastered up against her, rocking and squeezing her, and she had to bite her lip to keep from sobbing.

"Please, please, I know I fucked up but please, let me fix it, we gotta fix it." His breath was hot and vibrant against her back, her shoulders. She clenched her eyes shut against the sensation. "Please, Sofia, *mi estrella, estrellita*, I need you, tell me, tell me what we can do to fix this."

Her traitorous body was melting into the urgent curve of his. He'd made love to her this way, forcing her to sit still with him deep inside her, his hands free to touch and pleasure her everywhere. She'd come explosively without one thrust, sucking on his fingers as he fondled her clit.

"Tell me," he'd purred into her ear. *"Tell me what you want."*

"I gave him everything," her mother had sobbed. *"And he treats me like trash."*

She tried to get up and he pulled her back.

"Oh god, don't, Sofia, please." His voice was broken. "Please, tell me…fuck…fuck, I know…" And he dumped her on the seat next to him, his big body wild as he reached for his back pocket and then came back empty handed to punch at his thigh. "Fuck, I don't know what happened to my phone."

Then he was on his knees in front of her, gripping her hands in his huge ones. People walking by snickered and hooted.

But he focused on her like she was the only person in Golden Gate Park. "I've been looking for apartments for us in LA." He looked manic, pale and wide eyed.

"What?"

"Yeah, I bookmarked them and I can show you… come live in LA with me. Then when you go to Bordeaux, I'll live with you." His black eyes crackled. "I mean, if you want. I'll have to fly home a lot…"

"Dude!" John had come back with more water bottles. He glared furiously at Aish. "You told her about the apartment? The manager *just* said having a girlfriend is a bad idea when you're starting out."

"That guy doesn't know what he's talking about," Aish said, swiping a bottle from him. His eyes were focused and ardent on Sofia. "We can make this work. I know we can. I love you. We can make this work."

"I…" She was stunned. Shocked. Whiplashed. Everything she ever wanted was being laid out for her on a platter. All she had to do was reach for it.

He squeezed her hands like he could get their bones to meld. "I fucked up, Sofia, and I'm so, so sorry. I'm such a fucking idiot for letting her put a chink in your trust." He reared up and pulled her forward, nestled as close as he could get to her without being inside her, cradled her face in his hands and trapped her eyes. The catcalling was a distant, uninteresting buzz.

"Nothing like that'll ever happen again. You can trust me, Sofia, you know you can. I'll never let down my *estrella*. I need your light. Say you'll come to LA with me. Be with me. Stay with me. I need you."

"Why doesn't he love me?" her mother had cried.

Aish loved her, proved it by defying his best friend and this manager, and Sofia could put aside the idea that her mother's tragic story was a blueprint for her own. He was going to fuck up. So was she.

But that didn't mean she had to reject the dream he was offering her.

Trembling, speechless, she nodded and placed her hands on his glass-cutting cheekbones, pressed her lips to his, and accepted Aish Salinger and the promise of his constant love.

September 26

Sofia was surprised and impressed by the amount of
sex they were able to squeeze in amid the million and
one tasks of crush. When she'd spent half the day side-
eyeing Aish as he performed punch-down, his muscles
flexing as he used the metal, flat-headed tool to break
up the cap of skins and seeds that formed at the top of
fermenting juice, she'd eventually had to grab him and
shove him behind a tank, strip off just enough grape-
streaked clothes to access the needy parts, and plant
hands over his eyes and mouth as she rode him hard.
When they'd been hauling barrels out of the cooper-
age, she'd suddenly found herself in a dark corner, one
small window letting a thin beam of light into the stone-
walled room, bent over a barrel as Aish tasted then took
her from behind. She'd felt pummeled by the scent of
toasted wood and ocean-soaked man.

And at night, whenever nights happened for them,
sometimes at 2 a.m. and sometimes just before dawn
and sometimes seconds after the sun slipped away,
they'd be in her bed, the countdown clock to the end of
the month their excuse for attacking each other again
and again, even when it wasn't attack, even when being
with Aish was slow and delicate and enormous. She

traced him like she was blind, smoothing over the planes and outline of him to record in her mind's eye something more perfect than what he could ever be in the light.

Something more permanent.

He murmured and kissed and held and gripped her and tried so, so hard to stay in her bed until the bright light of morning. Even if she fell asleep against him—sweaty, euphoric, once just passing out on top of him while he was still inside her—some preservative sense always had her waking up and kicking him out before morning fully arrived. His gorgeous body was a ghost of sleek muscles and indecipherable tattoo ink as he grumbled and gathered his clothes.

Her decision to allow them to have at each other was paying off in more than mind-blowing orgasms. #Aishia was a sensation. Happy, flirty pictures of the two of them painted every available corner of the Internet. The servers of a popular fanfiction site had crashed after they'd received a torrent of stories focused on Aish and Sofia happily-ever-afters. An American cable network had announced an unauthorized biopic about their long road to love.

More importantly, Bodega Sofia's *hospedería* was now booked for a year after their spring launch.

In a matter of a few days, days when Sofia's morality or talents or goals hadn't changed, fickle world opinion aligned on her side and dragged the wine world along with it. Namrita was busy organizing late fall private tours, *hospedería* stays, and Sofia interviews for some of the world's top wine writers and producers. A Burgundian winemaker Sofia had known for years, who'd been too busy to take her call a couple of months ago, told *Wine Spectator* that Bodega Sofia was a textbook example of how to lead with innovation while honoring tradition. Letting bygones be bygones, Sofia had sent him a quick email promising him a case of their first official vintage.

All this because she'd decided to let Aish bone her whenever their little rabbit hearts desired.

She'd muttered that once, her forehead resting on the sleek skin of his pelvis, the epic blow job she'd been giving interrupted by the urgent and repeated ring of her phone and the five-minute conversation she had to have with a *New York Times* reporter before they went to press. Aish collapsed laughing to the seat of the Bodega Sofia truck, parked in the large, dark garage where they'd hid, and Sofia found him so irresistible that she blew him until he begged.

He never once brought up the fact that he'd been right about the potential of #Aishia if they worked together. She never once mentioned how intolerable the thought of #Aishia had been.

People didn't "know" they were fucking. Namrita had coached during the worst of times to stay coyly mum about the specifics of their relationship, and she doubled down on that advice now. But they weren't doing much to hide their fascination with each other. Why should they? They were two consenting adults. Even now, as Sofia stood in the ancient courtyard of El Castillo, their family's six-hundred-year-old castle designed by Moorish architects as a gift from Queen Isabella, Sofia knew their behavior was drawing the curious eyes and teasing grins of everyone attending the annual end-of-harvest party.

"Hate your dress," Aish murmured as he handed her a glass of wine. Globe lanterns and up-lighting transformed the already magical courtyard of tinkling fountains, intricately patterned tiles, and lemon trees into something fairylike. Aish looked like a rock god Dionysus in the middle of it, devilish and tempting with his dark scruff, perfectly coiffed hair, no tie, and one-button grey suit that sleeked over his long body.

His smile was so banal he could have been talking about the weather. "Your dress makes me wanna rip it off, sink my teeth in to hold you still, and fuck you in front of all these people."

Sofia smiled calmly to hide her shiver. "I'm not stopping you," she murmured. "There's a reason I'm naked beneath it."

She watched his tongue tap at his thin upper lip. Met his dark eyes to see how close to the edge she'd pushed him. Then he moved in a whisper of languid body and fitted suit and sun and salt smell to stand by her side.

"Just came," he said, low and dusky as he took her arm and wound it through his. "Feeling better."

Sofia tucked her laugh into her wineglass.

He said he liked her neck, so Sofia gave him her neck in a shoulderless silk dress that matched the summer tan of her skin. It covered her torso and arms sleekly, banded at her waist, and fell to the ground. But it left her shoulders, chest, collarbones and neck bare. She'd emphasized her nakedness by loosely pinning back her hair at her nape, leaving off necklace or earrings. She'd put on a light touch of bath oil to make her skin gleam.

She'd dressed up for her people, the tireless villagers and growers and employees and interns celebrating the success of what could have been a tragic season. But she'd selected this dress for him.

She raised her glass to Manon, the French hotel executive who was watching the two of them, and gave a sympathetic grimace. Manon was stuck in a conversation with Juan Carlos Pascual and the queen.

Manon winked back.

"What's he doing here?" Aish asked, openly glowering at Juan Carlos.

Sofia couldn't help the cheap thrill it gave her. "He has every right to be here," she said. "Whatever our differences, Consejo board members are still my people."

"That asshole doesn't know how good he has it," he grumbled. "He doesn't deserve your devotion."

The declaration warmed her through.

The Consejo had been surprisingly subdued in recent days, either bowing to the direction of the wind or simply too consumed with their own duties to harass Sofia. While most of the Monte's residents could relax until the next growing season began with pruning in late winter, winemakers and their employees would be busy the next few weeks with fermenting the must, pressing to separate the wine from the skin and seeds, transferring the wine into barrels for aging, racking the wine to clarify it, blending when warranted, and, ultimately, bottling for longer aging.

The extra hands of the superstar interns would be sorely missed at Bodega Sofia when they left in four days.

Sofia had four days with Aish standing tall and solid and supportive by her side.

When she realized the queen was closely mimicking their stance, her naked bronzed arm wound through Juan Carlos's, Sofia tried to withdraw her own. But Aish caught her hand and gently held it against his bicep as he looked down at her.

"She should be so proud of you," he said quietly.

"Not…" He nodded at the spectacle of Queen Valentina in a teal gown cuddled up to a man who'd said horrible things about her daughter. The king and queen had separated to opposite ends of the party the instant they'd arrived in a blast of fanfare trumpets blown by men in livery. Her parents had clung to those red-and-gold flouncy uniforms like misers when her brother tried to eliminate them.

She couldn't track when she'd given up on having a relationship with her father. Maybe she'd never entertained the notion. But her emotions for her mother were complicated. Sofia cursed herself for still needing affection…admiration…something from her after so much proof that she was never, ever, ever going to get it.

"You've got to be one of the more accomplished princesses in the long line of them," Aish said.

Sofia tried to shrug off the intensity of his gaze. "Don't be so sure. Princesa Margarita founded a leper colony and washed the children herself. And it is said Princesa Fabiana invented the radio five years before the Americans. Princesa Martina de Rosa conquered more women than Casanova."

Aish huffed. "Okay. Other than Martina de Rosa, you're more accomplished. Why does your mom have to be such a bitch?"

Sofia lowered her eyes to her wineglass. "I know her secret."

"What's that?"

He was too close and his gaze was too direct and his hand was too comforting. She met his eyes again. "Why would I tell you?"

To his credit, he didn't flinch. But his hold on her hand became less possessive and he straightened.

"I was getting pushy again," he said, and Sofia could just hear his low voice through the merriment of the party. "Sorry."

She would not let his respectful retreat make her feel guilty.

Yes, he would be leaving in four days. And Sofia would wave him goodbye, following the exit strategy Namrita had planned in the initial #Aishia negotiations. They would allow distance, careers, and banal press releases about "still friends" and "hopes for the best" do the work of their "breakup."

Because regardless of the amount of sex they'd been having and the perfection of the orgasms they shared and the fact that Aish had truly committed to the work here, she still hadn't forgotten what he'd done to her. She would never forget, and if all of these laughing, smiling, winking, nudging people knew what he'd done, what he'd said to her as she lay terrified in an American hospital, they wouldn't have thought of this as some fairy-tale reunion either.

They would see it for what it was: a cold business arrangement with a positive outcome, her winery and his reputation pulled out of the mire and given a sparkly glow. She tapped her wineglass against her hip as a reminder. He had no right to ask questions about her feelings, her challenges, the obstacles in her life.

For the next four days, she and Aish could have closeness. Physicality. But they would never again have real intimacy. She would never again reach toward the fire for warmth and only get pain and a palmful of ashes.

Her grey thoughts were interrupted by Roman, Namrita, and Carmen Louisa coming toward them, their gorgeous party outfits disrupted by the worried expressions on their faces.

Aish saw them, too. "Should I…?" He began to motion with his thumb out of the area, but then stopped.

Sofia realized she was squeezing his bicep harder. She let go but said, "No. Stay."

He'd been helpful before. Whatever this was, he could be helpful again.

Roman, Carmen Louisa, and Namrita surrounded them.

"One of the workers was attacked at the winery," Roman said, low. "He's going to be fine, just a mild concussion and a few bruises. But I'm taking my team over now. Castle security alone will have to manage the coverage here."

"What happened?" Sofia asked, her wineglass cool against her racing heart.

"He said he was doing some last-minute checks before he came to the party, thought the winery was empty, then was surprised by some guy trying to mess with one of the tanks. The guy roughed him up and then ran."

Carmen Louisa asked, "Did he recognize him?"

Roman shook his head. "Said he wasn't local. Brown hair, early thirties. He didn't speak so we don't know what language."

"How did he get in?" Aish asked.

That was a good question. Her walls were actually pretty good at keeping out pests. Except Juan Carlos.

Juan Carlos. She leaned back from the group to shoot a glance at him now. The winemaker looked relaxed in his circle of sycophants. Would he really be so afraid of Sofia's success that he ramped up his intimidation tactics to include breaking and entering, sabotage, and violence on her workers?

"Not sure," Roman said, drawing her attention back. "Since everyone's taking a day off tomorrow, we'll have downtime to review security and fill the holes."

He licked his full lips and slid a hand into his slim-fitting suit pants. Her soldier brother had become a bit of a *fashionista* in the time she'd known him, and she appreciated the dichotomy of it, enjoyed seeing him in something other than his bodyguard black. Right now, she hated the guilt on his face.

"We never did catch that fucking vandal," he said, his green eyes troubled. "I'm real sorry about this, Sofia."

Her half brother was adept at bearing the weight of the world. He was a war veteran who'd saved his platoon, an entrepreneur whose company protected movie stars and human rights advocates, and a retrieval specialist who'd entered the international spotlight when he'd rescued a Mexican teen heiress after others had abandoned the mission. The only thing he'd been unwilling to take on was his role as a member of the royal family.

Although his relationship with Mexican tycoon Daniel Trujillo, the heiress's father, had provided loans to get the Monte through the worst economic times, Roman still acted like a guest whenever he was in the kingdom.

"*Basta, hermano,*" Sofia said, patting "enough" on her brother's chest. "You've done so much for us. You're a huge part of the winery's success. In fact, this is probably just a byproduct of the success, an overeager tourist who snuck in then panicked. I have every faith you'll figure out what happened. The only thing I feel bad about is that you can't stay for the party. This is your celebration, too."

As always, her brother gave her his steady nod. But both she and Mateo still had a lot of work to do to get him to embrace that he was an essential member of their family.

As he turned to go, Sofia pulled Namrita and Carmen Louisa close. "*Beberse todo, mujeres,*" she said, grabbing wineglasses from a passing waiter and handing them to them. "Drink, laugh, dance. You've worked so hard." She kissed them both on their cheeks. "Roman will find the attacker and shore up our security. I want to see you smile."

Both women looked surprised by Sofia's enthusiasm.

She would visit the worker tomorrow, make sure he was comfortable and well compensated, and invite him to the castillo's dungeon with her once Roman found whoever dared to hurt one of her people. She liked to keep the manacles oiled down there specifically for such a purpose.

But Sofia wanted to stay riding high on the wave instead of drowning under its weight. All their hard work had paid off. The world's excitement about Bodega Sofia would translate into a brighter future for her kingdom. For once, her need to be needed was a benefit to the people she cared about, and not a burden.

With the guitar strum of her homeland's music drifting over the crowd and glasses of her wine in the hands of laughing and chatting interns, an unfamiliar bubble of hope filled Sofia's chest. When she looked at Aish, he looked back like he'd never taken his eyes off her.

He tilted his head and gave her the gentlest of kisses. But beyond him, just before she closed her eyes, she saw Juan Carlos watching.

Two hours later, with the party in the courtyard roaring along as the wine flowed and the band played, Sofia tried to look regal as she held up the edge of her long skirt and fast-walked along the ancient terra-cotta tiles that lined the hallways of her childhood home. Just like when her brother used to sleigh her along these slick floors on a blanket, she hoped she didn't get caught by any El Castillo staff. They were loyal, hardworking, and willing to adapt to Mateo's budgetary restraints and an overall minimizing of pomp and circumstance.

Seeing the *princesa* they adored tipsy and horny and rushing through the halls to screw a rock star in her canopy bed might put them over the edge.

She'd given Aish a head start. She hoped he could read the directions she'd scrawled on the cocktail napkin.

He'd stuck to water as they laughed and danced and mingled, and that discipline in a man whose drunken slurring had landed him in her kingdom, in a boy who encouraged her to run naked into rainstorms, had proven irresistibly provocative. She didn't want to wait to get back to the *hospederia*.

As she kicked off her Pradas, hid them behind a suit of armor, picked up her skirts, and ran through this endlessly long wing of the castle, she realized that sometimes discipline could be overrated.

Finally, she reached the hallway leading to her bedroom. At the end, her door was closed. Hopefully, Aish was behind it.

Her eagerness to find out meant that she didn't notice the open door of a never-used sitting room. But she did hear the regal command that issued from it as she passed.

"Sofia. *Ven.*"

Joder. She turned to see her mother sitting in a tall,

carved-wood chair, the slipcover thrown to the floor beside her. When was the last time her mother had been in this portion of the castle? Titi had soothed their childhood fears and nightmares since the king and queen had installed their suites in a separate wing. It was the one thing Mateo hadn't changed with his cost-cutting measures.

Sofia glanced at her closed door before she sighed and, head held high, walked into the sitting room steeped in the mustiness of stale air and ancient furniture. She knew from vast experience that it was easier and faster to let the queen have her say. And don mental armor as the queen said it.

Her mother tapped rhinestone-studded nails against the chair arm's carvings. "What do you think you're doing?" she asked in Spanish.

"Sneaking away from a party to fuck my lover," Sofia replied. "You know all about that, Mother."

The queen stiffened in her teal silk as Sofia eyed her. She was wearing an Elie Saab gown, not new but well taken care of. Sofia was almost impressed how straight and silky her mother's platinum sheet of hair looked. She was naturally a wavy-haired brunette, and she no longer could employ a team of stylists.

Rather than the responsive rage and slaps Sofia had come to depend on, her mother stayed seated. "Lover. Interesting word. Do you love him?"

Sofia frowned. "What?"

Her mother smiled the smile that Sofia recognized in the mirror, the smile she'd practiced to obscure everything she didn't want anyone to know. That smile was her most effective mask. She'd erred in forgetting it now and, instead, giving her mother an opening with her surprise.

"You obviously loved him once," her mother said. "Do you love him again?"

The question, out of her mother's lips, was strange and jarring. Not once in her entire life had the queen asked about her emotional state.

"Mother, having spent your child-rearing years striving to be as far from me as a private jet would allow, you have no gauge on what is obvious about me."

"That's still not an answer."

Sofia rolled her eyes. She was a millionaire and had dual degrees in enology and wine chemistry. But conversations with her mother could still drag her back to her thirteen-year-old self.

"No… I…not that it matters to you, but no, I don't love him." She hated that she'd stuttered. She settled herself into her more dependable emotion of disdain. "I learned the tragedy of that mistake from you."

Again, her mother surprised her.

"Did you?" the queen asked calmly. "I don't think so." She tilted her head, sending that sheaf of hair over her bare, bony, shoulder. And despite it all, the dye job and the tan and the plastic surgery and the self-hating artifice, Sofia still found her so pretty.

"Do you know why our relationship has been difficult?" the queen asked.

"You mean, why you hate me?"

The queen nodded. "Perhaps."

Now. They were doing this now, while a gorgeous man who would be gone in four days was waiting, hopefully naked, down the hall.

Sofia squared her shoulders. "Because I know what

you don't want anyone to know. I know that you love your cheating, humiliating dog of a husband."

That night in deep winter, that time of the season when the Picos de Europa declared their dominance over the sun and forced residents to remember they were tiny mortals living among forbidding mountains, Sofia had been so young, only seven or so. She'd still believed she could find a magic combination of words, deeds, and princess prettiness to draw her mother's attention away from the trips and soirees and boy toys and drooling dukes. Discovering from staff that her mother was in residence, she'd crept into her suite—she wasn't supposed to be in there—to recite the French she'd learned. Her mother liked non-Spanish things and her tutor told her she looked adorable when she spoke it.

Sofia had heard her mother before she'd found her, in a robe on her dressing room floor, sobbing in a pile of gauzy clothes she'd ripped off the hangers. An empty crystal decanter and broken shards of a perfume bottle glittered near her. The heavy ambergris scent of the perfume was choking in the small space. Her mother had been bleeding and Sofia rushed in to grab a towel and press it to her. The queen started slurring between moans and tears, telling her about how she'd been the timid teenager of a wealthy grocery store chain owner, how she'd felt so blessed to be selected for a young king when all she could offer him was a share of her family's fortune. The king had made her weep in both good and bad ways on her virginal marriage bed, and then left that bed to have sex with her cousin, who he'd stowed away on their honeymoon yacht. After that initial humiliation, he heaped them upon her by never trying to hide his affairs. She discovered she was only a con-

duit for heirs and money, and, horrifyingly, she loved
him anyway. The king was a compulsion she couldn't
shake. So she'd turned herself into what the king admired: a perfectly carved woman who used herself as
a tool to garner men, money, and influence. She made
herself into him.

And he still didn't love her, she'd wept before she'd
passed out among the silk and chiffon, her cuts no longer bleeding.

"You're perceptive as always, Sofia," her mother said
now. Plastic surgery had removed the faint scarring
along her forearm. "It's one reason I find your presence unpleasant."

Sofia had stopped flinching years ago.

"But there's another reason," her mother continued
airily. "I hate that you never need anything. You are
smart, beautiful, composed, kind, accomplished...all
on your own." Only her mother could make the compliments drip with insult. "You certainly don't need
me. As you grew, in that first flush of womanhood
when the average girl is consumed with crushes, you
made it clear you didn't need a man. And I hate you for
that." As she spoke, her words became sharper. "How
dare you have more than me when you come from me?
How dare you position yourself as better than me when
I have worked so hard and sacrificed everything to be
the woman I am?"

The queen's fingernails were clenched into the wood.

Then, like a sieve, the queen let her fury fall away.
She relaxed, leaned back in the chair, and raked her
nails down her long, shining hair. "But now, I see you
with this American rock star and maybe I've been
wrong all along. Maybe you do need. Maybe you will

prove to be as weak and stupid as I am. I wouldn't wish it on my worst enemy, but, Sofia, I might enjoy watching it happen to you. You're falling in love with a man who's going to destroy you."

Sofia felt the punch of her words like a witch's curse. There was martyr's blood and pagan rituals mixed into the stones of this castle and those who respected that did not make predictions lightly.

Her mother meant every word.

Only three decades of training allowed Sofia to pull off the world's best performance now. "Will that be all, Mother?"

But the pleased smile on her mother's face showed that she wasn't fooled. "For now, *hija*."

Sofia turned on her heel and focused on taking measured steps out of the room. Back in the hall, away from her mother's gaze, she faced again her childhood bedroom door, all of her enthusiasm for entering it drained away.

Her mother had ruined it for her.

Just as her mother had ruined perfumes and pretty, girly dresses for her. Because later, years later, Sofia finally paired her childhood memories with adolescent understanding to realize that those cuts on the inside of her mother's forearm and at her hip, where she said she had a birthmark that the king used to kiss, had not been an accident. Sofia probably had that empty decanter to thank for the cuts not being deeper.

Her mother had loved her useless husband so much that she'd been willing to take herself away from a little girl who had actually desperately needed her.

September 26
Part Two

Aish fingered the fluttery silk that fell from the gilded wood top of the canopy bed, thinking how much this pink princess bedroom must have chapped young Sofia's hide. She was nowhere to be seen among the claw-foot Louis XV furniture, pink silk, and crystal chandeliers. A beady-eyed ballerina doll stared back at him from a mound of pillows on the bed when he knew for a fact that Sofia preferred chemistry sets and was only a so-so dancer.

The only thing in the room that even hinted at her was the wooden box on the floor near her dresser, the size of a couple of shoeboxes, carved and inlaid with ivory. It was a haphazard spot for something that looked old and precious.

He'd believed he'd made her omnipresent in Young Son's first album, with his guitar tuned to the microtones she'd introduced him to, with lyrics full of stars and cinnamon and tempting skin. He'd sung about the rub of soil against her body and the green of the vines she'd been surrounded by.

But as he sat on the edge of her bed and surveyed this

silk and lace room, as he thought about the woman he'd
gotten to work alongside and laugh with and make love
to and admire over the last several days, he realized for
the first time that those songs no better reflected her
than this room did. His songs were what *he* wanted her
to be; just like this room was what the queen wanted
her to be. And he'd shown up in her kingdom still wanting that girl he'd set in the amber of his lyrics: smart,
hardworking, pushing him to do better, yes. But also
unquestioningly adoring. And loving. She'd loved him
without reserve because he told her she could, that she
could trust him.

And then, when push came to shove, when the manager said they could have the tour spot but only on the
condition that Aish broke up with his girlfriend because "leashed dicks don't fill seats," when Aish had
to choose between Sofia and all the things he wanted
for himself, he'd chosen himself. Yeah, John had harassed and hounded him, had shoved the girl into his
lap when Sofia had come into the bar, because Aish had
already waited a week and the manager was threatening to walk. But it was Aish, stone-cold sober, who'd
broken up with her.

He'd never worked as hard at anything as getting
famous. Never had to. Surfing, the state-tournament-
winning three-point shot, sex, it all came easy. But each
song, each performance, each multiplatinum-earning
album, had to be fucking perfect. Because he'd given
her up for them. He needed to be more famous than famous because of what he'd sacrificed to have it.

When he'd stood at the edge of the stage, battered
by the screams of thousands, arm around John, he believed he'd earned it. When he'd fired the manager the

instant he had some leverage and hired Devonte instead, he thought he'd been making amends.

When he sang into the camera for every video and showed off his tattoos during every televised performance, while never once trying to contact her, he assured himself that he was doing everything he could to win her back.

And then he'd stepped into her kingdom thinking *she* was the one who needed to change.

He knuckled the pang growing painful in the middle of his chest.

He needed her here with him, right now. He needed to lock the door and keep her away from him.

He would tell her that he was writing again. He'd already scheduled studio time for when he got back. He would tell her that he had her to thank for the newly flowing lyrics and melodies.

He would tell her that he'd been wrong.

Fuck.

After a lifetime of believing he'd been pretty near perfect, he was wrong, and he'd tell her. He was actually the selfish, self-involved man-child she'd accused him of being. He was wrong for showing up here with his preconceived notions of her and he was wrong—and, let's face it, a coward—to go ten years without telling her he thought of her daily.

He was wrong to have believed that anything—his music, his career, John—was more important than her.

He startled to standing when the bedroom door opened and although all the things he had to tell her were on the tip of his cowardly tongue, he stopped short. Saw the look on her face—anger, distress, even a little fear—as she aimed herself at him in a rustle of silk then pressed her face against his crisp, white shirt. Her arms burrowed under his suit jacket and clung to him like he was a tree keeping her grounded during a storm.

Stunned, he slid his hands over her silk-covered back and embraced her, gathered her tight against him. "Sofia?"

She raised her lips to him. "Kiss me," she demanded, that little line of stubbornness between her brows. He didn't know who she was defying. But it wasn't him.

"Of course," he said, rubbing his big hands over the delicate muscles of her, over her back, shoulders, arms that carried so much. He would reassure her. He would keep her safe. "As many kisses as you want."

If anything, that made the line dig in deeper and, fuck, he didn't want to be the reason for her distress, so he gathered her face in his hands and kissed her with all of the devotion he had.

He wanted it sweet. He wanted to soothe her. But his kiss caused a wounded sound in her throat, and that, that had to end right fucking now so he pushed his tongue into her mouth, strived to heal whatever was hurting with slow, wet plunges.

His hand slid over the glistening, creamy-tan silk, silk turned erotically warm with her heat, and over one pebbled nipple. That's right, she was naked under this silk. Restraint was already slipping when she pulled back with a wet suck and looked into his eyes. Hers were as sultry as just-turned earth after a summer rain.

"I want to make love with the lights on," she said, and holy fuck, if that didn't almost send him to his knees. "Get out your cock so I can see it."

And...*unh*...down to his knees he went.

She huffed in surprise and excitement, and Aish nuzzled through the silk into the apex of her. "You first, Sofia," he murmured, cupping her small, firm ass to hold her, to allow him to breathe and nose and kiss at the heart of her where she'd sworn she was naked for him. "I'm dying to see this pretty pussy. Please, *princesa, por favor*, let me see your gorgeous cunt. I need it."

And her hands clenching into his hair, the sugar-salt bloom of the smell of her beneath her skirt, told him she was as desperate as he was.

But when she stepped back from him, she was the *princesa* he'd just called her, regal and restrained, with all the control she'd learned from being a representative for her people when her parents were dicks, from being dismissed as a party girl when she was actually a self-made millionaire, from having to deal with a media circus when she was just trying to create a better future for her kingdom.

Princesa Sofia Maria Isabel de Esperanza y Santos began to raise her skirt. He loved naked bodies, loved each stripper and groupie and socialite and movie star who'd slowly taken off their clothes to show him theirs. But not one of those experiences had him like this, down on his knees and panting as his princess raised her gilded skirt to show him delicate bare feet, a part of her that highlighted how small she was, even though she always seemed gigantic. She showed him the fine bones of her ankles and the glistening line of her shin. When she revealed her knees, he tried to duck down and kiss them, but she nudged him back, *tsk-tsked* him for being so impatient and Jesus fucking Christ he really needed to find out if she liked roleplay. These were the first knees he'd ever found irresistible. Then her thighs— smooth, tanned thighs—which meant she'd been hanging out poolside at some point and fuck every minute someone else got to look at those thighs. He wanted to snatch up those minutes like they were Matchbox cars he was too selfish to share.

When he realized he'd been staring at the gentle slopes of her inner thighs with his fingers clawing into his pants, when he realized she'd paused pulling up her skirt, he looked up at her. She was staring down, down at his crotch, where his cock was being obscene between his white-knuckled hands.

"Eso parece que duele," she said and he felt a spurt because, yes, fuck, it did hurt, especially when she spoke Spanish to him in that satin-wrapped voice. "Maybe you should take it out."

"I will," he said, pressing the heel of his hand to it. "I will, Sofia, but *fuck*, c'mon, don't tease me, c'mon, Sofia, I need…" He was officially begging.

With a regal nod that had his cock thumping against his hand, Sofia backed away slowly, not lowering her skirt but not raising it any higher either, and sat on the edge of her pink frilly bed. Without taking her eyes off Aish, the silk still held by one hand, she tossed the ballerina doll to the floor.

Aish was glad to hear the crack of its lifeless porcelain face against the tile.

Pushing herself up the bed until she was ensconced among all the satin-and-lace pillows, she tapped a spot at the foot of the mattress with her toes.

"Siéntate, guapo," she commanded, and Aish was standing, toeing off his shoes, and kneeing up onto the bed between her feet like the most obedient of palace guards.

He leaned back on his heels. He let her admire him with those dark, liquid eyes as he worshipped her.

Her legs, those gorgeous, hardworking, miles-of-skin legs, were bared to him from her unpainted toenails to the creamy silk dipping between her thighs. He put his hands around the delicate bones of her ankle in fascination, amazed to see this again, to be allowed to touch her this way again.

He raised his eyes and saw her, his sun-stroked princess, so smart and filthy and serious and proud, sprawled for him because she wished it, sleeping with him because she chose it, listening to him because she allowed it. He was wrong in assuming she'd been the one who'd needed to change when he came here, but he would make amends now by changing for her. If she needed to move mountains, he'd help her push. If she needed quiet to let that big brain work, he'd shoot singing birds out of the sky. Her wants were beneficial and generous in a way Aish's had never been. She deserved her wants, and he would help her achieve them.

He would tell her. He only had four days left.

"Take it out, *guapo*," Sofia purred, shifting the skirt over her thighs so that it made a hissing sound. Or maybe that was Aish. "I haven't gotten a good look at that big, beautiful dick in a decade. Let me see it, *amor*."

His toes curled at that word—*amor*—and he put his hands on his zipper. "You too, Sofia. C'mon, raise that fucking skirt for me, baby. I need it. I need to see your pussy so bad."

Her bare toes tickled at his hips like she was restless and needy, both crazy with all the fucking teasing, but she started to shift her skirt incrementally higher as Aish carefully slid down the zipper. The sound of the clothes—silk over skin, the buzz of the zipper—was the hottest soundtrack he'd ever heard.

With his zipper down and the bulge of his hard-on pushing his grey boxer briefs through the opening, he got a glimpse of light brown curls before she put a hand over herself.

"Sofia," he groaned.

She kept the skirt trapped at her hip with her other hand. "*Pull it out, Aish,*" she said, and her voice was like magic. "*Pull it out and I'll spread my legs and you can see how wet I am, so wet, and I'll use my fingers so you can see it and hear it, but you have to pull it out, pull it out, please, please, and touch it for me, fist that perfect hot cock, my handsome love…*"

And every humming, spell-casting word as she spoke and he watched her face and her lips and her fingers, fluttering over where they hid her, was in Spanish. And he was ashamed and embarrassed and vibrating like a kid on the verge of coming because he knew, he knew as he gingerly pulled his cock through the opening in his briefs and she slowly slid her hand up to her stomach, showing him light brown curls, trimmed now in a way she wasn't a decade ago, that for all of his noble pretension, *this* was why he'd learned her language.

He'd hoped and prayed and wished for this chance, a chance to touch her again and understand her lust-soaked words in her native tongue.

She made a delicious sound, like she was licking flan away from the spoon, as he fisted once down his cock and held it at his base. Held it up for her.

"Spread your fucking legs, Sofia," he growled, because he was done, fucking done, she'd promised and he needed it, needed the wet and heat and pink and softness of his memories and current reality, needed to finally marry the two, and she did, almost like she wasn't paying attention, her teeth digging into that lush bottom lip and her earthy eyes hungry on his cock, but his were just as hungry as those kissable knees widened and those sleek thighs spread and then, lovely curls parted to let him see her. Smell her.

She moaned, hurt, when a bead of clear precome came from his tip and ran down his shaft, dribbled over the back of his hand.

Fuck.

Yeah, she was beautiful, rosy and puffy lipped and peacocking her arousal for him in the mellow light of the overhead chandelier. Yeah, she was gloriously shiny. And yeah, she smelled good, she looked good, she looked like forever.

But he didn't give a fuck about the look of her pussy. What he cared about was that she was showing him. In the light. In her castle. In her kingdom. Breaking every rule that had ever kept them apart. She was spread out and vulnerable and giving it up for him. To him.

With a restraint he'd never had, Aish carefully let go of his cock to crawl over her, watching her heavy-eyed approval as his shadow fell over her glowing body, and put his hands over her dress on her hip, helping her hold the material against the tattoo that she still didn't want him to see, that he pretended he didn't know was there.

He'd never, ever, ever again ever insist anything from her that she didn't choose to give.

She was already nodding when he pressed her into pillows and said, "I need to be inside you," and he was kissing her luscious lips as he was searching for her, his free hand holding him up, and he was stroking over silk skirt and soft hair and velvety moisture and then his hot, iron-hard cock sank into the hot plush hug of her body and her thighs were coming up to grip his hips, still in his suit pants, and he was in heaven, pushing deeper into the soft, wet give of her, in her pillow-thick princess bed as those capable chemist's hands tilted up his chin and she stared into his eyes.

Staring into him, her eyes held a million stars. She tilted her hips and then slowly, with absolute power and control, she gripped him inside her. He gritted his teeth to keep them from chattering; the intimacy, the pleasure, was agonizing.

"Sofia…baby…love." He couldn't stop panting. "You blind me. You're star bright."

He began to move, he had to show her, he had to prove to her, he could give her what she needed. He needed her. He only had four days.

The slide of his cock—he was thick and long and could move his hips and it was all for her, all his practice to please this princess who'd earned it—got him a reward: she tasted the inside of his mouth, bit his chin before she pulled back, still holding his jaw. "*It's you. What it feels like…with you.*" She poured every hot word in Spanish over him as he pulsed and thrust into her, pushing her deeper into the pillows, deeper into the center of her where she lit him up. "*What it always felt like with you. Say it again, Aish.*"

And he knew what she was asking for as he collapsed against her, dug his arms under her to hold her close, wrapped her tight while he rode her hard because she could take it, it's how she wanted it, drowning in her eyes. "*Estrella,*" he said clearly. "My star. Always. Drawing me and guiding me. *Estrella.* So strong and bright and making me…fuck…" He pushed deep and made her still against him, losing it in the amazement of all of this. He held her precious body and made sure she saw every naked hope in his eyes. "Sofia, my shining star… I need you. Always have. Always will."

And for the first time ever, it was his words, his English, that made her come.

"*Mi fuego*," she cried out, and she was light-filled pleasure in front of his eyes and gut-shuddering pleasure down his cock, and beautiful, beloved woman falling apart in his arms while he watched his favorite words pour out of her mouth: "Aish" and "*mi fuego*" and "*amor*" and "*amor*" and "*amor.*"

After, she kicked him out of her room.

It wasn't a surprise; Aish didn't fight leaving.

He was feeling pretty fucking overwhelmed, too. He skirted the party and found their driver. On the silent drive back to the *hospedería*, his hands were trembling. Something mattered, really fucking mattered, and for the first time in his life, he might not get it.

What was a surprise was the early dawn phone call from Devonte, after he'd just drifted off.

"Tell me you didn't do this," his manager demanded.

Just six words and an hour of sleep and Aish was wide awake. He'd never heard him more disgusted.

"Do what?" Aish asked, already panicking.

"Don't fuck with me, motherfucker."

And Aish wanted to die.

"I trusted you. She trusted you. Tell me you didn't set all this up just to destroy her and help you."

Aish shoved out of his bed and strode across his room naked, grabbed for the first jeans he saw. "Dude,

I don't know what you're talking about. Please, man," he begged into the phone cradled against his neck, already looking for a shirt, shoes.

Devonte was silent for too long. Finally, he said, "I'm heading to the airport now. I'm on the next plane out and you're gonna have to lie to my face.

"But there's proof. There's a flash drive proving John stole songs. They're saying Sofia released it to get back at you. That you had a blowup fight after you two left the party, and she was always jealous of John and the band... With all the pictures of you two googly eyed and how hard you were working at the winery, they're making *her* out to be the traitor. Vindictive, small minded, the woman scorned...man, the bullshit they're slinging about her."

Devonte's sigh was full of remorse. "If you made me part of a plan to destroy a good woman who didn't want anything to do with you..."

"I didn't," Aish insisted, his heart tommy-gunning in his chest. His eyes shot around the room, looking for his key, his phone. Yeah, fuck, he was using his phone. "I didn't, I swear to God, but man, I gotta go."

Go, go, go. Oh Jesus fuck, he needed to go.

"Man, I gotta go find her."

But when he threw his door open, he realized he wasn't going anywhere. Because already keeping watch in the hall was his old guard dog, Roman Sheppard, looking every bit the soldier, with his shoulders thrown back, his fists clenched, and murder in his eyes.

September 27

Sofia rested her fists on the glass wall of her office and looked out over the afternoon dimness of her wine production facility. The lights were off and the winery was still. The day after the end-of-harvest party was always a day of rest in the Monte. Tomorrow, the facility would be bustling again as employees and interns took measurements, racked wine, and hauled barrels down to the cellar for long-term storage in the wine caves.

She'd planned to go to every single intern this morning, apologize for wasting their time, and offer to change their plane tickets to allow them to leave early. But before she'd had the chance, working her way down Namrita's methodical list of to-dos to plug a leak in a crumbling dam, Amelia Hill found her. Acting as emissary for the group, she'd told her that not one of the nineteen interns believed that Sofia had handed over the flash drive. They would stay until the internship was over. They would support her once they were home.

Sofia had replied that the interns should support the winery and the Monte. Supporting her was a lost cause. The IT techs had called to report a dangerous surge in server activity as people canceled their *hospedería* reservations. A major American wine distributor, who'd been willing to work around the Consejo to get the wine out of Spain, had emailed to say he was no longer interested. And Mateo had begrudgingly revealed, after Sofia had harangued him that she needed to know the full impact, that two new fruit buyers had pulled their contracts.

Was there any use in finishing the wine that right now sat in the steel and oak vats on the quiet processing floor if no one was going to drink it? The quiet that had settled over the Monte didn't feel like rest, Sofia thought as she settled her forehead against the cool of the glass.

It felt like mourning.

Mourning the fact that their princess's desperate bid for attention was every bit as destructive as their queen's. She'd tried to make herself necessary and valuable and, as a result, damaged her kingdom. The queen's blowups and affairs had never netted a result this disastrous.

"They're bringing him over now," Namrita said from behind her, her voice strained. Acting as the kingdom's mouthpiece, trying to set the story straight, had worn it out. It had been a useless effort. The international media had the story they liked. Sofia was a betraying bitch who—in the midst of a royal temper tantrum—tried to ruin the legacy of one man who'd sacrificed himself to the Mississippi River and the career of another man who'd been working hard to save hers. She'd poured gasoline on the world's favorite love story and lit the match.

It was funny; Sofia had invited the world press to her home because she thought she could manipulate it. She couldn't cry over shattered grapes when Aish proved to be the better manipulator.

They'd packed up his room—apparently the prima
donna had refused to help—and kept him away from
his electronics all day. Roman's security team was es-
corting him here and then straight to the airport. Namrita felt they should try to discover what he was going
to say to the media, what he planned next.

He had no reason to lie to them now; he'd accomplished what he'd come here to do.

She'd been dumbfounded by the information Namrita gave her this morning while she'd stood in a
T-shirt in her childhood bedroom doorway, her dress in
the closet and her face washed clean but her hands still
tingling from Aish's scruff, from the way she'd cradled
his face as she let him see every irretrievable emotion in
her eyes. She'd been so intent on defying her mother's
curse that she'd actually allowed herself to ignore her
vow and believe that maybe…for a second….

She'd sent him home before that second could stretch
any further.

Or at least, she'd thought she'd sent him home. Instead, it looked like he'd escaped. Let himself free so he
could unleash this story that Namrita relayed, dark eyes
full of sorrow, just after dawn: the contents of the flash
drive leaked, blame heaped on Sofia for the reveal, Aish
and John somehow left blameless for the theft. Sofia had
actually been shaking her head in the doorway, no, he
couldn't have…there's no way he would have…when
she'd first seen the box, made in the fifteenth century
and purloined from another part of the house by a little
girl who hated her pink room, sitting on the floor out
of its hiding place in the dresser.

He'd had so much time in her room before she'd
shown up. She wondered how many of her private

spaces he had searched—her office, her suite—before finding the box.

She'd trusted him in all of them. Her craving for him once again had made her peel off restraint and skepticism so she could warm herself with his fire. The shock that she'd done this to herself—again—left her dispassionately cool as she sat in the ashes.

She felt nothing as she heard a winery door open, turned to watch Aish take huge strides toward her office, her brother and two of his men hustling to keep up. Carmen Louisa, Namrita, and Henry had been keeping silent vigil by her desk. Henry moved to stand in front of her. She could just see Aish over his shoulder.

He looks terrible, she thought before she put her hand back against the glass and soaked in the cold.

He was in old jeans, a dirty long-sleeve shirt, and flip-flops. His black hair was standing on end. He appeared to be going for the insanity defense; she felt sorry for whoever had to sit next to him on the plane.

He jerked her door open and got out, "Sofia, I didn't do this—" before her brother and another guard caught him by the biceps.

"Not a fucking word," Roman growled. She turned around and watched them walk him into the room, shove him down on the couch.

Aish's eyes, black and sparkling, never left her over Henry's big shoulder.

Namrita and Carmen Louisa looked equal parts furious and ill at ease. But her PR representative walked until she was standing directly in front of Aish. "Mr. Salinger, what do you intend to do once you leave the Monte?"

"Leave?" he shot back. "Fuck you, I'm not leaving.

You can drag my ass out and I'll be on the next fucking plane back because *I did not do this!*" His shout was equal parts madman and beast and Sofia watched Carmen Louisa wrap her arms protectively around her waist.

He needed to play out his little melodrama; the least Sofia could do was limit his audience.

"If everyone could give us five minutes," she said evenly.

Four people turned in shock and started arguing with her as Aish dropped his face into his hands and started muttering, "Fuck, thank God, yeah, just five minutes, thank you, just give me…"

Sofia put up a hand. "Now," she commanded, and the room went quiet.

Standing behind the couch, Roman put a hand on Aish's shoulder and said, "You keep your ass on this couch. If I see you going for her, I will kill you."

Namrita shivered. Not one person in the room thought he was talking in hyperbole. But Aish stayed focused on Sofia. "I won't, man, I promise," he said fervently. "I don't want anything from her she doesn't want to give."

Sofia felt the frown on her face, the line he used to try to soothe, before she cleared it away and raised her chin. The people who loved and protected her, the people she'd let down, left her office. They closed the door behind them but hovered, talking quietly in a clutch, just outside the glass.

The reality that everything turned out just as bad as she knew it would by letting him back in her life felt like a calming straitjacket as she looked at him. What had she ever been afraid of, in looking directly at him?

His ardent stare and jumping jaw and white-knuckle grip on his forearm were the histrionics of a rock star used to making enough drama to satisfy millions of screaming fans.

"I shouldn't be surprised," Sofia said, standing away from the glass wall and sliding her hands into the pockets of her oversized pants. "You came here to manage the rumors and save your career. And…that's right… 'soak in that Spanish air.' Bravo. You got everything out of this month you wanted."

"Sofia!" he spat, like the shock of it could drown out her words. "That's not true. I don't know where that motherfucking flash drive came from!"

She smiled, exhausted, and ran one hand through her hair. It probably looked as crazy as his. "You don't know that it came from my room, where you had plenty of time to look for it. You don't know that it came out of a box that you clumsily left out of its hiding place. You had no idea what was hidden on it although you left me quickly enough so you could review it and then send it on."

"Left you?" he squawked. Sofia pinched her leg inside her pants pocket; why had she said it like that? "Sofia, I didn't want to leave you. You asked me to leave! I wanted to stay wrapped in you all night. If it was up to me, we'd still be tearing up that stupid princess bedroom."

She ignored the crackling in his eyes, the ugly anguish on his face, the way he gripped the edges of the couch so he could keep his promise to her brother. "Where'd the fuck you get that drive? Why did you keep it?"

Sofia noiselessly breathed through the hot jolt of emotion that question caused.

When she'd discovered the secret inside her, she'd listened to Aish's performances over and over again in her San Francisco hotel. The addict going back for her fix.

She'd kept it in her treasure box like the addict who believed she'd recovered, who believed she was strong enough to keep something on hand. Just in case she needed a hit.

How Aish must have laughed when he'd sifted through the other items in that box—the torn condom wrapper, a corner of a pizza box, the pick he'd been using the night he declared he loved her. Or, more likely, he hadn't recognized those items at all.

She needed to wrap the cold around herself tighter to stop the slide back to that stupid, stupid girl who assumed he had any emotion for her.

She gave him a bland smile. "Since you're not going to fess up and I'm not going to answer your questions, I don't see any reason for us to…"

"Sofia, 'cause, fuck, look, if the reason you took that drive was because you wanted songs, I have a million songs for you." His fervent eyes, his big body, was straining toward her as he kept himself on the couch. "'In You' wasn't my big secret; all the songs were. Every song I've ever written is about you. Or, at least, I thought they were. I've been figuring out since I've been here that I was writing them for me and what I wanted you to be. I came here wanting you to be that girl from ten years ago. But you're too brave and smart and strong for the mold I was trying to fit you into. Sofia, I was wrong."

Aish gripped his knees like he wanted to get down on

them and beg. "I was wrong for believing I had to trade you in to have a music career. I was wrong for never contacting you to tell you that. I was wrong for thinking a bunch of songs could do the hard work I needed to do. *I* was wrong, Sofia," he said, banging his chest. "Nobody else. Just me."

There was a crumbling wall in the village plaza, the last remaining limestone rocks of a medieval barrier that once protected the young hamlet of the Monte del Vino Real. Sofia called upon those ancient rocks now to leave her impenetrable against the arrows Aish was shooting.

What he saw on her face made Aish grip both big hands in his black hair.

"Why would I write all those songs if I was just planning to fuck you over?" He huffed a breath like he was running. "There are a lot of ways to screw you that don't include being haunted by you every time I pick up a guitar. Ten years, Sofia, and every single, lazy song was the hope that you'd give me a second chance."

Elbow deep in the work of her winery, Sofia had finally allowed herself to enjoy what she hadn't heard in ten years: his deep, melodious voice, his smart and lusty turn of phrase, the American pop and soul rhythms now imbued with the global chords she'd introduced him to. She'd given herself sips of his talent while she was surrounded by walls her ancestors built and she'd fortified.

But she'd dismissed the lyrics like echoes, unwilling to reflect on what the recognizable words and phrases of their love affair meant in his songs. Verses might have nudged their way in, and she might have hummed them in the repetition of winery work.

She'd shaken them off every time.

It was time to shake him off now.

She took two steps back and rapped her knuckles against the glass.

Aish jerked like she'd shot him as her brother instantly turned and put his hand on the door handle.

"Fuck, oh fuck, no, Sofia, c'mon, c'mon okay...," and he was wrenching at the snaps of his dirty shirt as her brother opened the door and Aish was wrestling out the fabric and tearing it off his arms, and then getting up to his knees on the couch, still on the couch, stretching out his arms and saying, "Look, Sofia, please, please look, you don't have to love me, but please look, know I wouldn't do this to you, please..." and Sofia put her hand up to stop her brother in the doorway.

Aish was shirtless in front of her and what she'd denied herself in the dark—in trying to ignore his existence and then insisting he cover up—was right out in the open. He was low-slung pants and endlessly long, muscular torso and veiny, work-hardened arms and frantic energy, circling awkwardly on the couch so she could see the entire story of his full torso tattoo, covering him from wrists to collarbones to hip cuts and across his incredible back.

As he babbled, "...don't owe me anything, I know, just please, know, why would I do all this if I wanted to hurt you, just please, believe that I only came here to help..." she saw a thin, forlorn skeleton, wreathed in a single flame, up the left side of his back, reaching across a nautical map, across tormented waves and broken guitars and an empty pizza box to a vineyard paradise on Aish's front, fruitful and fertile in black ink, surrounding the constellation over his left breast, the constellation of la Osa Menor, the Little Dipper. The grid of nautical map and ocean covered his arms, along with a multitude of compasses whose arrows all pointed North. But the compasses were all turned so that North was directed right towards his heart.

Over his heart, at the tip of the constellation, was a brilliant, bursting North Star. It was a flame of a million colors, the only color in all the black ink of his body.

His body told the tale of a lonely burning man reaching across the ocean and sky for his *estrella*.

Forever. This would have taken forever. Years, a thousand hours in a chair, and a million hours of after-care. When she'd staggered away from his body a decade ago, he hadn't had a drop of ink on it.

"All this time, you think you're not essential, Sofia? Look at me, look around you, look what you've done for your people. Even the queen, she doesn't ignore you. She torments you for your attention. They all need you, but they can go fuck themselves because I need you more." His mouth twisted into a grimace of desperation. "You're essential to me, Sofia, and you have been every hour of every day since I left you.

"I never forgot, Sofia." Still on his knees, Aish was her supplicant. "I never gave up hoping." He turned his wrists up to her, looked willing to bleed. "You're my first love. You're my last love."

His eyes were black sparkling pools. "You're the only woman I'll ever love."

Sofia covered her mouth with a hand, her other arm wrapped over her stomach.

She began to laugh.

The door opened. She saw that her friends were coming up behind her wide-eyed brother.

"Get...out," she choked out between laughter that was getting worse.

"Sofia—" Roman began.

"Get out," she said again, and maybe she screamed it. Who could tell between all the laughing? But they were giving each other alarmed looks and Sofia continued laughing, waving them away. "Come back...come back in a few minutes...just get out...get out."

And they did because...because she was a grown woman who'd fucked up and she didn't need any help getting it wrong and when they left her, she was still laughing and she could turn her eyes back to Aish and he looked green, like he looked during one of his infamous, stumbling drunks and that look, that memory of how she'd believed he hadn't fucked around with that lead singer, set her off again, leaning back against the glass and laughing as all of her emotions broke their bonds and came roaring out—anger and despair and heartbreak and, most of all, the great irony that he believed they were a story to be written in the stars, regardless of how much he'd hurt her, when he was the worst mistake of her life.

"Never," she gasped. Stopped. Sucked in her breath while she grinned. "I would *never* fall in love with you again." It was like sucking down the finest vintage, the raw anguish on his face as she smiled into it. "I never forgot, either, Aish. I never forgot how you broke up with me in a crowded bar. I never forgot how you threw me away. And I never forgot how you left me alone in that hospital bed. I will never, ever, ever forgive you."

The anguish fell off his face. "Hospital bed?" he said.

Him echoing it back shoved her from hysteria to pure fury. "I was nineteen years old," she roared. "And you left me alone in a foreign country. With no one. I was terrified. I was in so much pain. They told me I might die. And you told me to handle it. You told me you had a tour schedule to keep."

The blood was draining from his face as he shook his head and slumped back on the couch. "Sofia, I don't…"

And, oh God, maybe he didn't know. Too high. Too drunk. Too preoccupied. Or maybe just too much of not giving a fuck about one burdensome girl.

Astonishment blazed through her as she, too, shook her head. "You remember getting caught making out with that girl, right? Breaking up with me after you'd asked me to move in with you?" Because she remembered it in cinematic brilliance: walking in on a cloud, crashing into the darkest pit when she saw his arms around a girl, his tongue deep in her mouth. He seemed drunk, yes, but not sloppy. He'd said he was sorry, but as he looked away from her shocked tears, suggested that maybe it was for the best. Mumbled halfheartedly about John, about what he owed him, about the manager's insistence that girlfriends made for bad rock business, that he needed to give his all to the music before he settled down.

She'd no more expected him to give up his music and its demands than she was going to give up her University of Bordeaux education. They'd figure it out. And she'd never thought him being with her was settling.

"That was the biggest mistake of my life," he said, fervently. "I never should have—"

She steamrolled over him because she was so tired of his excuses. "*Vale*, stick with me, *guapo*. Do you remember the call, oh say, three weeks later? When I told you I'd miscarried?"

He looked at her like she'd stabbed him. "You were pregnant?"

With three words, he flattened her. She had no more righteous fury or cold reasoning, she had nothing left. He scooped her out and left her empty. Exhausted. Without even a glimmer of hope. *This* was the one who'd ruined her for love? What a sad, pathetic creature she was.

She'd become exactly what she despised.

She closed her eyes and lowered her head, slumped back on the glass.

"Yes, I was pregnant, and I'd planned to get an abortion," she murmured. "I told you that on the phone. But I started miscarrying before I could, and then I went into septic shock."

She'd been bleeding and shaking and quivering with fever when the ambulance technicians had pulled her gurney through the fancy chrome and glass lobby of the hotel while businessmen gawked, and the noise and pain and fear had blurred for hours until the nurse in the ICU asked if there was anyone Sofia could call. It had been a blinding moment of clarity. There was no other person she needed, no other person she wanted by her side.

She'd had no doubt he would come.

"You told me it was my problem. You told me to handle it. You told me you had a tour schedule to keep." He was making a sound, some kind of sounds on the couch. She didn't care. "The contractions and the back pain and the fever, it all hurt so much. They said I was there for ten days; I don't remember much until the last two. That's when they told me that the infection had damaged my uterus to the point that I can't have children." He made another sound. "You told me to handle it and

I did, that whole experience, all by myself. I still am handling it; you're the only person I've told this much to and I imagine you'll forget about it when you go back to your rock star life."

He was muffled now. She looked up and saw that he'd buried his face in his hands. His muscles were shaking. She didn't care.

"You know what, you can stay until the internship is over. I don't care if you leave. I don't care if you stay."

Staring at him, half naked and ink covered and crying on her office couch was like looking at a bug on a vineyard leaf.

"You're my first love, too, Aish," she said, pushing herself off the glass and walking to her office door. "You're also my last love." She opened the glass and tossed her last statement over her shoulder. He probably wasn't paying attention anyway.

"Because you're the reason I'm never going to love again."

September 28

Devonte had told Aish that he was going to have to lie
to his face. But Aish hadn't had to utter a word when
his manager pounded his heavy fist against his suite
door later that night. Instead, when Aish staggered to
his door and threw it open, eager for whatever firing
squad was behind it, Devonte took one look at him,
cursed, and then strode into the room and threw his
overnight bag into a corner.

"Talk to me," he'd commanded. "Tomorrow, we'll
fix it."

Early the next morning, Devonte was still passed out
on the couch that looked comically tiny beneath him as
Aish stood at his balcony doors, showered and drinking coffee he hoped the staff hadn't poisoned, watching
the sun peek over the top of Sofia's mountain for what
might be the last time.

Even if he could fix this for Sofia—no, he *was* going
to fix this—even *when* he fixed this for Sofia, he knew
she would never want to see him again. He would never
be invited back to this kingdom that he'd begun to think
of as a second home. He would never be embraced again
by this community of people who showed him the value
of honoring something bigger than personal ambition.

He would never explore her mountains, hand in hand with her, finally getting to discuss the future and not the decade that had passed.

"Why won't you let me apologize? Why won't you let me try to make this better?" he'd asked her. Now he knew. There was no making this better. Now he understood the hell he'd put her through by coming here, by breaking her ground rules and insisting on intimacy, by forcing her to look at him, talk to him, touch him. Now he understood how truly brave she was, how much she was willing to endure for the sake of her kingdom.

"You told me it was my problem," she'd said. *"You told me to handle it."*

He put his hand against the glass to steady himself as nausea churned through him, but then quickly took his hand away from the warmth. He stepped just out of the rays of her rising sun; he didn't deserve to feel anything but cold and empty.

"What time is it?" Devonte croaked from the couch.

Aish shrugged and then nodded at the steaming cup of coffee he'd already placed near him. They had work to do.

He continued drinking his coffee, let his manager spend a few minutes mainlining his, as he watched sunlight grow across vineyards he would never get to see ripen again. Then he sat in a chair across from Devonte, who was hunched over his cup in an undershirt and jeans.

"So how do we make me the bad guy of this story instead of Sofia?"

Devonte huffed humorlessly into his cup. "After all the motherfucking time we spent trying to make you look like a knight in shining armor," he said, mournfully shaking his head.

Aish grabbed the nearby coffee pot to refill Devonte's cup. "I looked like the douche in shining armor. Remember that metallic vest your stylist tried to put me in?"

Their chuckles had no laughter in them. Last night, he'd shared everything Sofia had revealed: the pregnancy, the miscarriage, her alone and bleeding in an American hospital believing Aish had turned his back on her. Devonte had needed a breather on the balcony after. Now, both of them understood how revolting their rock star display was when Aish first showed up in the Monte.

"You deserve your knocks but you know who the bad guy should be?" Devonte said. "John. He's the one who stole the fucking songs."

"I know," Aish said, slumping back in his chair. "But I can't get her off the hook by blaming a dead guy."

Devonte looked at him funny.

"What?" Aish asked.

Devonte's dark eyes narrowed. "When I said that John was the bad guy, you just said 'I know.' Like you just didn't throw away the last year of your life and almost torpedo your career defending and mourning him." Anger and a bit of hurt started to build up in Devonte's broad forehead. "I told you about John making me pay off that family and you let me leave here without knowing if I had a job the next day, much less my friend."

Aish shoved off the urge to blame shock or surprise. "I'm sorry," he said. "You were never going to lose your job or your friend. And I'm sorry I didn't tell you what I've known for a while. John was a piece of shit."

Devonte opened his mouth but no sound came out. Aish realized his leg was jumping up and down like crazy. He stood, circled behind the chair for a little room to walk. He had to be moving to tell the rest of this story.

"You know all those rumors, that I was involved in John's death, that I somehow got him to kill himself." He turned back to Devonte, put his hands on the back of the chair, and forced himself to face him. "They're true."

He had to press on, get it all out now, and finally deal with what he'd been pushing away for a year.

"I found out John had stolen songs. I confronted him about it in Memphis, told him I was going to tell you and the label. I knew the label would get squirrely, maybe even try to pay off the bands and suppress the info. But you…you would keep us on the straight and narrow."

Devonte scoffed, and Aish knew it was self-mocking. Devonte had already known about the plagiarism, had already been manipulated by John to do something that went against his nature. And that was John's gift wasn't it? Using people's weaknesses against them. Aish's greatest weakness was his arrogance, the belief that he was perfect and would always remain so. It had made it so easy for John to do whatever he wanted in the gutters while Aish kept his head up in the clouds.

When he discovered the plagiarism—when he'd walked into that bar in Santa Rosa, near his uncle's winery, and faced the lead singer who jumped off the stage snarling at him about how he'd stolen their song, when the singer played him an early recording and talked him

through how they'd developed the song and showed him
the cease and desist letters from Young Son's attorney,
an attorney Aish had never heard of—he waited a month
to confront John. He didn't want it to be true. Because,
if it was true, then John had tarnished the fame Aish
had traded in the love of his life for. Aish didn't want
to believe he had this darkness woven into a glow that
he needed to be pristine.

Ultimately, though, it had been thoughts of Sofia
that had forced him to confront John. She'd always demanded the best out of him; no way he'd ever get her
back if he let this slide.

So, in Memphis, he told John that he knew and that
he still loved him and that he understood the pressures
of creating a hit and that he would stand by his friend.
But they had to make this right.

"It was the first time I ever saw John cry," Aish said.
"He begged me to wait a week. Let him get his finances
in order, tell his parents. The morning his week was up,
you came pounding on my door."

John's body was never recovered from the Mississippi River. But a witness came forward to confirm
she'd seen John jumping in. She'd been in too much
shock to stop at the time, she'd said, too guilt-ridden
later to come forward immediately.

The coroner's pronouncement of death *in absentia*
six months later—due to the suicide note, the clothes
left on the bank of the river, and the witness—killed
any hope that Aish had that he could make amends.

"So they're not wrong," Aish said, staring at the
veins Sofia liked to caress on the back of his hands,
thinking about the blood pumping through them. "My
hands are all over John's back. That's the guilt I've been

trying to hide from. That's my fucking legacy: lead singer pushes best friend to commit suicide.

"I'd sit in my basement studio and think about that, think about how I owed him a whole life, and I tried to squeeze that debt onto a fourth album." He huffed a humorless laugh. "No wonder I was a little blocked, right?

"And the funny thing is, now that I know what he did to Sofia, he wouldn't have had to jump into that river." He squeezed his hands into bloodless fists. "I'd have thrown him in myself."

"Wait…what? What did he do to Sofia?"

Aish swung his head up, let Devonte see how far the last year and yesterday's revelations and his own self-disgust had pushed him from that golden California rocker everyone loved. "Haven't you figured it out, yet, man? That phone call Sofia said she made from the hospital? The guy she said she spoke to? That wasn't me. I might be a fuckup in all ways, but I *loved* her. I never stopped loving her. That first year of Young Son's debut, right on the heels of our breakup, when 'In You' was this phenomenon and we went from playing bars to stadiums in six months and I should have been on top of the world, I was *fucking* miserable. If I'd known she needed me, if I'd gotten a chance to hear her voice again, I would have tossed everything away. John, the band, the songs, the tour…everything.

"John knew that. I thought he was taking care of me, the way he pushed girls and guys and booze and drugs on me to fix it."

"And you two sounded so much alike." Devonte looked at Aish, thunderstruck. "She was talking to John."

Hearing Devonte give voice to the realization that

Aish had woken up gasping to made his heart pound and his stomach roil, made fury build in his head and disgust burn in his soul. He'd been so willfully stupid for so fucking long.

"John would fuck with my phone. Steal it. Forward my number to his. He'd say he did it so I could concentrate on the music. Let me handle the creative side while he handled everything else. I let myself believe him. I let myself be grateful. And he told Sofia to handle the fact that she might die, all alone."

"Holy fuck," Devonte breathed.

She'd almost slipped away from him. She would have been alone and scared and so young and so undeserving of Aish's actions and inactions.

Suddenly, his friend had a hold of his biceps. "You've got to tell her," Devonte said, only the chair keeping his manager out of his face. "You've got to tell her, everyone knew you sounded alike when you were talking, you've got to explain to her—"

"No," Aish said, shrugging out of Devonte's hold and stepping back from the chair. "No, I'm not going to tell her. And you aren't either."

Devonte's powerful arms fell to his side. "What the fuck?"

Aish stared at his friend's bewilderment and had to shake his head. People had been giving him a pass for so long.

"I'm a thirty-one-year-old man who's just come to the realization that I let my best friend manipulate me for the better part of my life. I allowed him to manipulate me and use the glow he got off me to hurt other people. My rich, good looking, and popular were his tools. Do you think he got to do that because I was too

stupid to know better? You think he took advantage of
me? 'Cause that's a story we could go with and maybe
I could keep making music. But it won't get me back
Sofia. She knows better. She's been calling me on it
since the second I showed up here. Called me a man-
child who blames everything on others, and she's right.
John manipulated me because I let him. I can be pretty
fucking wily when I want to be—ask Sofia—but it was
a fuck-ton easier to let him push me where he wanted
me to go than to plant my feet in the sand and take control of my own fucking life."

Maybe he was shouting a bit, but it wasn't at Devonte.

"Yeah, John pushed, fuck knows he pushed, but I
chose to dive in. I *chose* to pick the music over Sofia
and not do the work to have both. I *chose* to put 'In You'
on the album and I *chose* to ignore the rumors about
stolen songs and I *chose* to reveal Sofia on that video
and I *chose* to come here even though she made it clear
she didn't want me."

His words were heaving out.

"I've made choices and the worst one was to keep
my head in the clouds. People got hurt because I'm a
passive, childish, entitled, lazy asshole. I'm the worst
thing that ever happened to Sofia. The only way I can
make this right is by giving away the best things that
ever happened to me."

Devonte had sat back down on the couch during
Aish's diatribe. He stared at him now.

"You've changed this month, man," he said.

Drained, Aish huffed. "Yeah? Losing your career
and your one true love can do that to a guy."

"I like you better now."

Aish rolled his eyes. "That's good. Since I'm probably not going to be able to pay you for much longer."

Devonte shrugged those massive shoulders. "All I've got on my resume is representing a band that stole songs for a decade. Finding a new job'll be easy."

Christ. When Aish fucked up, he did it spectacularly.

But Devonte kept that wide and bright smile. "Okay, man, how are we going to fix this for her?"

By that evening, Aish's suite looked—and smelled—like a dorm room, with plates and cups and bottles stacked on any available surface, notes spread over tabletops, and both laptops practically smoking from overuse. Room service begrudgingly brought drinks and *albóndingas*, little spicy meatballs, but no one had been back to clean anything up.

Aish knocked over a stray glass when he pressed send with a flourish.

"Got another one!" he announced, thrilled to have connected with one more media outlet who would be present tomorrow afternoon when Aish torpedoed his music career.

But Devonte hung up his phone with a frustrated grunt. "Goddammit," he said, throwing his phone on the sofa and striding over to his bag in the corner. He started to pull clothes out of it. "She's still not answering. I'm going to have to go track her down."

Ready or not, Namrita and Sofia were going to have to deal with the press descending tomorrow for Aish's press conference. Devonte had been trying to get through to the PR rep all day to let her know their plan, but she was ignoring him.

"You keep going through that list," Devonte said

as he began unbuttoning his shirt. He was apparently going to strip down right in front of Aish. That was no problem; Devonte had seen him just about as naked as he could be. "Get ahold of as many people as you can. Make sure they know hauling their asses to the Monte one more time is going to be worth their while."

And it was.

For the first time in his life, Aish was going to stand alone in front of the media. He was going to open his mouth and lie his ass off. He was going to tell them that he'd known about the song thefts all along (which he didn't) and that he was equally as culpable as John (which he wasn't) and that they would relinquish all claims on current and future earnings of Young Son's royalties to pay settlements to all the victimized bands. That last part was true. He was also going to claim responsibility for releasing the evidence on the flash drive, claim it was a ploy to lay the blame at his deceased bandmate's feet that had misfired.

Sofia, he would tell the world, was the only one creating something real and authentic.

Manon had stopped by his room to see if there was anything he'd needed, and he'd told her a stripped-down version of his plan and asked her to share it privately with the interns, in case any in the group were holding Sofia at fault. She'd assured him that Sofia had all of their support.

Every song he'd written, every song he'd not yet gotten to, cried out at the thought of how he was about to aim a depth charge at his career. Writing, playing, and singing were the only things he knew how to do, the only things he wanted to do besides loving Sofia, and his life was going to stretch out long and lonely without either music or Sofia to occupy it.

Then he thought about how she'd held her niece and nephew and knew that this was a sacrifice he owed her.

"… But the thing I can't figure out is who *did* share that flash drive?" Devonte's monologue interrupted Aish's thoughts as the man pulled clean pants over his stellar ass.

Aish shrugged. The focus on *who* had done the deed had gotten lost in the damage the deed had wreaked. "She said it'd been in a box. I think I saw the box, it was in her room, but I didn't see anyone else as I was sneaking there to…"

Aish cut himself off as heat rose on his skin.

"Fuck?" Devonte finished for him. "Declare your endless love?"

Aish looked back down to his media list while Devonte put on his shoes.

"You're letting her go too easily," Devonte said.

Aish raised his head to glare at him. "I'm trying to do the first unselfish thing in my entire fucking life. Don't ride me on this."

Thankfully, Devonte nodded. It had been a long, hard day, and tomorrow was going to be longer and harder. Aish didn't need Devonte reminding him of all he was going to lose when he gave Sofia her winery back.

Devonte slipped on a blazer, grabbed his phone. "Don't wait up. You need your beauty rest if you're going to be in front of a bunch of cameras tomorrow. Namrita is going to listen to me even if I have to shout through her suite door."

Aish smirked at him. "How do you know where her suite is?"

Devonte *snick'd* back. "Businesspeople have business meetings. Get your head out of the gutter."

As the door closed behind Devonte, Aish's smile faded away. He desperately wanted to follow his friend. He desperately wanted to run through the halls and pound on his love's door and beg, fucking beg, to get another chance.

He gripped his fist on the desk like it could tether him there. There was a very real chance that he would never see his love's face again.

A knock sounded at the door.

"Did you forget your key?" he called, pityingly grateful for the distraction as he approached the door and opened it. But it wasn't Devonte, as he'd expected.

It was Manon again. The French hotel executive now looked frazzled and anxious, not anything like the elegant and carefully coiffed executive he was used to seeing. She was standing next to a man wearing the Bodega Sofia uniform, a maroon polo and khakis. Brown hair, blue eyes, he smiled benignly at Aish. Behind him was a large laundry cart with a few linens.

"Aish, I just wanted to say how sorry I am about everything that's happened," she said, surprising him by moving into his doorway and putting her arms around him, pulling him into a hug. He stared at the hotel worker in confusion as he awkwardly bent down to return her hug.

"Uh…it's okay, Manon…we're figuring it out."

He startled when he felt her lips brush against his ear. "I'm so sorry," she whispered.

He'd barely felt the needle slide into his side when he started suffering from the effects.

He slumped in Manon's arms.

"Whoa, I got you, buddy," said the hotel worker, grabbing on to Aish, hauling him toward him. "I've always got you, man."

That voice. Aish knew that voice.

It sounded like his own.

Aish mumbled against his shoulder, trying to call out, his limbs useless.

"Shh, shhh, don't worry, I'm going to take care of everything," the hotel worker said as he picked Aish up. Aish felt like a bag of bones as he was flung into the laundry cart. "You know I never let you get in your own way."

Then the man, that unknown face with that lifelong familiar voice, hovered over him as everything else started to go dim.

"Or let you get in mine."

September 28
Part Two

Crunched up into the corner of Roman's couch, Sofia punched Decline on her mother's incoming call for the second time in ten minutes. Whatever harassing, cruel, mocking thing the queen wanted to say could wait until Sofia returned to the Monte.

With her one-way flight out already chartered for the next morning, she planned on that being months, maybe years, away.

Carmen Louisa pulled the phone and empty wineglass from Sofia's hands and then tucked the blanket tighter around her as if strangling her would keep her in the kingdom. She refilled Sofia's glass and then downed half of it herself. Sofia held her hand out, but Carmen Louisa stood in her white button-up shirt and figure-flattering jeans and stared down at her.

"Just stay until the press conference," she said, the strain of the last few days showing around her pretty hazel eyes. "See how people react."

Sofia retracted her hand and pulled the blanket back around her shoulders. "If it goes well, then Bodega de la Gente will benefit." That's what she told the growers they should rename Bodega Sofia. She was already calling it that—winery of the people—in her head. "If it doesn't go well, I won't be here to make it worse."

The grower couldn't get it into her head that Sofia was leaving to save her.

To save all of them.

Carmen Louisa had shown up an hour ago at Roman's mountainside home with Namrita and Devonte so they could tell her that Aish was going to throw himself on the pyre. He was going to take full responsibility for the plagiarism and the release of the flash drive. He was going to swear that Sofia had nothing to do with it, that she'd been an unwitting victim of his dastardly plan.

They had threatened to call Mateo when they heard Sofia's response. She wasn't going to change the press release scheduled to go out the next morning that relinquished all her rights to and involvement with the newly christened Bodega de la Gente. She wasn't going to cancel her departure.

And, she'd told them, if they tried to sic Mateo on her, she'd just leave early. She didn't want the Monte's future king—the kingdom's only hope—anywhere near her.

She'd made herself numb to the dejection on Namrita's face when the woman left—she'd worked so hard to save the unsalvageable—but Carmen Louisa had stayed.

Sofia rested her temple on her knees and blocked her friend out. Carmen Louisa paced away with a frustrated sigh.

She could let Aish take the fall for the debacle that her winery launch had become. But now she understood how temporary a solution that would be. Aish wasn't the illness. Sofia was, Sofia and her vast unquenchable need to be needed. She'd tried to satiate it with her mother's attention, Aish's affection, and her people's devotion. Each attempt had been slapped away, making her more and more desperate. What had it led to this time? Positioning herself as the savior of her people and insisting everyone bow to her ideas. And when no one was convinced, she sank her kingdom into this ludicrous, devastating scheme. What crazy thing would she do next to prove she was essential?

She would take her desperation away so that it could no longer hurt the people she loved.

Sofia jerked as the blanket was shoved down, her hand pulled out, and her wineglass slapped into it. The violence of the movement sloshed the contents of the nearly full glass on her shirt.

"*¡Joder!*" She looked up at Carmen Louisa looming over her, fiery-eyed. "*¿Qué pasa?*"

"What?" her friend shot back. "You don't want to do anything but sit and drink. So there. Sit. Drink. Get on a plane tomorrow. Abandon us again."

"Abandon you?" They'd all been walking on tiptoes around her. Carmen Louisa's anger was shocking. "That's not what I'm—"

"No? You're fleeing the kingdom. Again. What would you call it?"

Again. She snapped down her glass, kicked out of the blankets, and stood. "I'd call it killing the bacteria before it can spread." What did she want from her? "I'm trying to help you."

"How?" Carmen Louisa had never accepted a no in her entire stubborn life. "By taking away the best winemaker the Monte has? By removing our *princesa*'s warmth and encouragement and making us stumble around in the dark?"

She felt herself twitch at the description of herself. "That's not what I'm…"

"All this time, you think you're not essential, Sofia?" Aish's words flickered punishingly. *"Look at me, look around you, look what you've done for your people."*

"You're this kingdom's life force," Carmen Louisa said. "You make us strive to be more than a sleepy village in the mountains. You make us thrive. And everyone can see that but you."

Sofia bit down hard on her lip. How dare she? How dare she sketch out everything Sofia had ever wanted. But her outrage evaporated when she saw Carmen Louisa angrily swipe at her eyes.

She never wanted to make her cry.

She reached for her. She took her hand.

"When I left…before…" Sofia was whispering. She didn't know why. Roman was in the next room, but she didn't fear him. "You had Mateo back. You had Roxanne." It was a wonder she could hear her at all. "You didn't need me anymore."

When Sofia had taken Carmen Louisa's hand, she thought she was doing it as her *princesa*. But when Carmen Louisa gripped it back, she knew she needed the sure handhold of the best mother she ever had.

"We weren't going to continue tormenting our young *princesa*, with her own hopes and aspirations, with our problems. But while your brother has planted the seeds, you're the light that helps us grow."

"Mi estrella," Aish had groaned in the lamplight against her skin, almost fully clothed yet indescribably naked for her. *"So strong and bright…"*

No. No. No, regardless of the career he said he would sacrifice.

"But…" She flapped her hand at the village lights seen through Roman's living room window. "This mess. It's all my fault."

"And would you have said success was all your doing?"

"Of course not," she said instantly.

"Then how can one be true and not the other?"

Carmen Louisa was better than any soul alive at leaving her without a response. The grower stared with soft, hopeful eyes. "Stay, *princesa*," she said. "Fight."

"He's staying and fighting and that's the last thing I expected from him," Henry had said about Aish. *"And you're stronger and warmer when he's around. That's the last thing I expected from you."*

Both women jumped when a heavy hand pounded at the door. Roman poked his head out of the kitchen doorway—looking for the all clear from them—before striding across the living room.

"*¿Qué pasa?*" Carmen Louisa asked in wonder as the fist continued to pound.

What now?

Roman opened the door and Henry pushed past him, leading a pale-faced Queen Valentina into the room.

Her mother wasn't wearing makeup. Her mother always wore makeup. It startled Sofia enough that she said, "*Reina*," urgently, stopping her mother short. She never called her queen.

They stood and stared at each other. "What's happened?" Sofia finally asked.

The queen put her hand over her heart—she was out of the castle in her exercise clothes, a tank top and yoga pants, her platinum hair in a haphazard ponytail—and although she opened her mouth, nothing came out. Her dishevelment, the fear in her eyes, her inability to say one cutting word, had Sofia gripping her hands into fists. "What's happened?" she demanded again.

"*Mi hija*," the queen finally choked out in Spanish. "He's taken Aish."

Sofia understood the words individually. Together, they made no sense. "What?"

"He… John. John is alive. He's kidnapped Aish. I don't know where he's taken him."

Sofia suddenly found herself sitting back down on the couch. She saw Henry and Carmen Louisa rushing toward her. But her mother got to her first.

Her mother was down on a knee in front of her, a steadying hand on her arm, another on her leg. "*Mi hija*, I'm so sorry. I had no idea he would go this far."

Sofia stared into her mother's face as Carmen Louisa translated for Roman and Henry everything her mother just said. An unplugged part of herself noted that she'd never had her mother's undivided attention this way before.

"When?" Roman barked.

"She thinks in the last couple of hours," Henry said, all trace of her good-times-and-brewskis friend gone as he relayed the details, as daunting as Roman at his most soldierly. "The family is at the castle; they're on lockdown. God only knows what else this asshole is gonna pull. Security has already started searching the *hospedería*. Manon snatched a rental car and left an hour ago."

"Manon?" Carmen Louisa gasped.

Sofia turned chilling eyes back on her mother. "What did you do?" she asked.

Sofia suddenly realized that everything she'd lost in the last twenty-four hours might only be a drop of what she could potentially lose.

Her mother's eyes were naked wounds on her face. But she lifted her chin and took her hands off Sofia. She folded them in front of her like she didn't have the right to touch her daughter. "I didn't instigate it. Juan Carlos came to me. He wanted to stop you. He said it was for the good of the Monte. I wanted to stop you because… because you are everything I can never be." Sofia was stunned to watch her mother struggle to swallow her tears. Tears were usually her best weapon. "Juan Carlos didn't recognize John when he approached him. He's had—" she waved her hand in front of her face "—work. But he said he would help us if we gave him information, access. He had one of your interns under his thumb before she arrived."

"Manon broke into your room the night of the party and stole the drive," Henry said. Then he shook his head, his bone-crushing hands on his hips. "That whole fucking break-in at the winery was just a diversion. They wanted to minimize the security at the castle so she could sneak through without gettin' caught."

"*Dios mío*," Carmen Louisa said, her eyes stricken. "I'd taken her on a tour of the castle earlier in the week."

"You didn't know," Sofia replied commandingly as she looked at them both. She refused to have one more person feel guilty in all of this. "How could any of us have known?"

Manon. Manon had been working with John, sharing detailed information of the internship with the press, using her media experience and contacts to spin everything and make it reflect negatively on them.

"How did they know about the drive?" Sofia asked her mother.

The queen settled back on her heels, crossed her arms over herself as she looked away. "I like spending time in your room. I like to imagine brushing your hair as you tell me about your day. Sometimes I pretend I'm Roxanne or her—" she sniffed at Carmen Louisa "—when the idea that my own daughter would talk to me seems too farfetched for imagination." She shrugged and dropped her gaze to the wood floor that had to be uncomfortable on her knees. "I found the box. I'd go through it and make up stories you would tell me about the things in it, if I'd been different. If I'd treated you differently."

Sofia was astonished to discover that her mother, too, wished things had been different between them.

"I never knew the significance of the flash drive until John asked about some proof he'd heard you mention while you were in the cellar with Aish."

In the cellar. With Aish. The only time she'd been in the cellar with him was when she'd fucked him. Her skin crawled at the idea that John had been there, in the dark, listening. Listening to her assault his "best friend."

"Juan Carlos called me this evening, frantic, with a wild story." Her mother ran a trembling hand down her ponytail and Sofia distantly recognized it as a move she'd once used to comfort herself. "He said that the man we'd been working with was Aish's dead bandmate, that the man had lost his mind, that he was going to make it so Aish would never be seen again. Juan Carlos said we had to get our story straight so we couldn't be held responsible."

Sofia suddenly had trouble catching her breath. Something was filling her chest, pressing against her lungs, clogging her throat. She put her hand against her heart. She looked up, confused, at Carmen Louisa, at her brother and Henry. She opened her mouth, but could get no air in or out.

Oh God. Aish was lost in her kingdom with a psychopath.

Henry's blue eyes went wide before he was charging toward her and shoving her forward, forcing her head between her knees. "Breathe, girl," he barked. "You're having a panic attack."

She felt other hands on her back, rubbing up and down. "*Respira, mi hija. Cálmate, mi amor.*"

Instant tears popped into her eyes. She let her head hang and let her mother rub her back and tried not to think about never seeing or touching or kissing Aish again.

On her first full inhale she said, "We've got to... we've got to go save him," she finally gasped out, head still between her knees.

"You're not going anywhere," Roman said. "I'll find him."

She had no breath, or time, or need to argue with him.

"If you knew...the Monte like I do...you would have caught him already." Because who else could the vandal and the person who'd assaulted her worker be but John?

It was a low blow but *never* was *wah wahing* in Sofia's ear. Never seeing or touching or kissing Aish ever again. She'd said *never* over and over again during the last decade, stroked her hip again and again as she repeated it like an incantation, an incantation that had apparently worked because it had kept her shielded from Aish's world-dominating fame. *"I will never fall in love with you again. I will never, ever, ever forgive you."* But, for all of her denial of his existence, her *never* still involved Aish existing, out in the world somewhere, playing his music, living his life, filling someone else's days with his love and spirit and warmth.

Only now, she discovered, that within her *never*, she'd always hidden the possibility of *maybe*.

This *never* was Aish gone. His fire extinguished. The space his big spirit took up in the world icy cold.

He'd broken her a decade ago. Then he spent the next ten years writing her songs and learning her language and inking odes into his body. Was that simply the response of a guilty conscious? Or something more? What would he have said if she'd allowed him to complete the apologies he'd attempted so many times? Could she forgive him?

He'd planned on sacrificing his career for her this afternoon. *"You're my first love. You're my last love. You're the only woman I'll ever love."*

They'd dived effortlessly into loving each other as children. Maybe they needed a chance to see if they could do the hard, mountain-climbing work of loving each other as adults.

Her breath was coming easier now. She straightened and closed her eyes, gripped her hip, fortified herself with big inhales of air, taking in the leather-and-gun-oil smell of Roman's home, the aroma of her wine, the soft scent of her mother because for once she wasn't drenched in—

Sofia's eyes snapped open. Cologne. That rank whiff of it when she'd been in the cellar with Aish. She'd smelled it earlier, too. When? In the basement of the bar when they almost kissed. When someone took the photo.

She asked Carmen Louisa to find the picture from the news story. Then she pointed at Roman. "*Dime otra vez*, what businesses had the vandalism?"

They both looked at her like she was losing her mind. "*Rapidamente*," she urged.

As Roman rattled off the businesses, Sofia tracked their location in her mind. *Joder.* Of course. She couldn't believe she hadn't put it together before.

When Carmen Louisa handed her the phone, it was the verification Sofia needed.

"I know where he has Aish," she said, flipping the screen around. She pointed at the photo. "We thought one of the interns took this picture. But the angle is wrong; this was taken from the back of the room. Where there is a gate that leads into the tunnel. The tunnels connect all of the vandalized businesses and the winery; *that's* how John has been getting around and how he snuck into Bodega Sofia. That's where they've gone now."

Carmen Louisa nodded eagerly. "Yes, yes, Manon was asking about the tunnels."

A cold certainty dropped into Sofia's stomach. "And if John wanted to get rid of Aish so we could never find him, I know exactly where he'd take him." Those careless stories she'd shared about the tunnels so long ago. She swallowed her fear as she looked at her brother. "We need to go right now."

With one nod, Roman pulled his phone out and began contacting his team.

She bit back a laugh of hysteria. After all her bemoaning and complaining, her self-pity and sadness, Aish certainly needed her now. She was the only one who could save him. But she wouldn't have known he needed rescuing if not for the woman kneeling in front of her.

"You could have kept quiet," Sofia murmured to her mother as Roman and Henry rallied the troops over their phones. "You could have let him die and kept your involvement secret."

The queen, always such a dominating presence, appeared small and uncertain. Still, a lifetime of being rejected by her made the next words almost impossible to get out. "You don't have to talk to an empty bedroom."

Her mother looked at her with the tiniest quiver of hope. "Can I be forgiven for my mistakes?"

Sofia had every right to disdain and condemn. It's what the queen had given her her entire life. It's what the queen received her whole life from the man she loved.

"If you can forgive me for mine," Sofia said as she gripped her mother's hands and helped her stand with her. "When I have him back, we will talk."

With a tremulous yet tender smile, her mother nodded.

When she said the next words to her mother, they sang inside her with hope. "We still have time to be different."

September 28
Part Three

The gun prodded Aish in his kidney again, just above where his hands were bound behind his back, and he groaned around the cloth shoved into his mouth and secured with duct tape. He didn't know how John had gotten him down into the tunnel system that ran below the Monte, but he felt like John had dragged him over every stair and stone and stalagmite before he'd slapped him awake. They'd left behind the cut-stone archways, endless rows of dusty wine bottles, and ancient iron gates signaling some hope of civilization, and not even the jab of that fucking gun could keep Aish moving forward into what looked like an endless black hole.

They were beneath acres of sunlit vineyard rows Aish had gotten to know intimately over the last month. But down here, the Monte was hostile, hard and careless stone. The black was immense. The headlamp John wore cut through the darkness about as effectively as a butter knife through concrete. Aish was a kid who'd grown up in the sun, so it made sense how uncomfortable he was in this dark underground tunnel. He held on to "uncomfortable" because it was better than the utter fucking panic he was fighting off with every step into this cold and alien world, with his cold and alien best friend poking a gun into his back.

John jabbed again, but this time with a chuckle. "I've been shoving you where I want you to go your entire life. You think now, when I'm holding a gun, you're going to stop following my orders?" It was the first thing he'd said to him beyond grunted single words; they were deep enough in the earth that John wasn't worried about their voices seeping up through some-one's basement. "Don't make me use it. I'll just shoot off whatever gets you walking again."

That voice as familiar as his own saying surreal things in this dead place—Aish swung around to see him, to make what was happening real.

He was instantly blinded. John chuckled again.

"Still can't believe it, right, buddy? What a fuck-ing idiot you were? Get a good look." Keeping the gun aimed on Aish, John slipped the headlamp off his head and pointed it at his face.

Aish blinked to clear the spots from his eyes and then focused on the altered face of a person he'd trusted like a brother.

John had never had a problem getting laid with his classic square jaw, straight nose, thick blond hair, and bright blue eyes. The plastic surgeon had made him a regular face in the crowd, made his nose broader and built bulk around his cheekbones. The shorn-close brown hair hid John's thick waves. John had gone from an All-American prepster to a Jersey dockworker.

Those rich blue eyes, though, those eyes looking back at Aish with so much smug satisfaction, they were the same.

"He did good, right?" John said, grinning. The surgeon had even put a chip in his gleaming smile. "Found him through a sob story from one of the girls waiting for you backstage—she told me about his oopsies with underage patients. Got him to do the work for free and burn my records."

John put the headlamp back on but tilted it up so it cast a residual light on their faces and then motioned with the gun. "Go."

Aish grunted, gave an emphatic jut with his jaw.

John smiled again. "Got something you want to say? Cool, cool. No one can hear you."

He ripped the duct tape off along with a decent amount of hair. Aish shoved out the disgusting rag and then bent over, gagged, spit on the ground.

"You've been roofie-ing me since we were kids," he croaked, not a question as he focused on not puking. His body ached, his head pounded. During the walk, he'd been trying not to throw up and choke himself. Aish recognized this particular hangover. When he'd get embarrassingly drunk on just a couple of drinks, or get a bout of food poisoning or stomach flu when everyone else was fine, he thought it was the dues he paid for his rock 'n' roll lifestyle.

He'd felt this way twice since John "died." Once at the festival with the gin maker and the hidden camera. Once when he'd hoped to calm his nerves with a drive through the Spanish mountains.

He'd been such a fucking idiot.

"Why?" Aish demanded as he straightened, taking big breaths through his mouth, his bent back shoulders screaming.

John smiled like a papa proud of Aish for figuring

it out. "It was my favorite way to put you on ice. Aish Salinger, the guy everyone loved, slurring and puking like an asshole. Manon's going to tell everyone she saw you drunk, crying, stumbling down to the cellar." John was so fucking happy. "I asked you to do one thing. I set it all up for you.

"All you had to do was tell everyone that I stole those songs."

Aish looked at him sharply. In the text John had sent him that horrible morning, the text Aish had found after Devonte pounded on his door, he'd asked Aish to tell the world. Begged to let him correct his mistake and take the blame away from Aish. Steamrolled with guilt, Aish had kept the message for a month, then deleted it.

He'd been the asshole trying to preserve his best friend's legacy.

"And you, you stupid fuck, you couldn't even get that right." John shook his head then motioned with his gun.

Aish lifted his chin.

John smiled wider. "Turn around. Keep walking. You stop again and I'm shooting off pieces. I'll start with those famous, guitar-strumming fingers."

Aish grimaced, but turned, walked. Even with his back to a gun, it was easier than facing John's smug smile and his effortless words of violence.

John straightened his headlamp and cast it into the impenetrable blackness in front of Aish.

He'd go slow. He'd buy time. Someone had to notice he was missing by now. Someone had to be looking for him. Sofia knew these tunnels.

Would she care to look?

"If you'd done the only thing I'd asked you to do, we wouldn't be here." John's voice bounced around him.

"You tell everyone that I did the stealing, that I felt so guilty I killed myself...how many bands are going to sue us when we've got a sob story like that? The public feels sorry for us, the label pays a couple of little settlements, and our slate is wiped clean.

"But you had to be a pussy. You wouldn't spill it when I started the rumor that you were involved with my death, you didn't tell that guy at the festival. That's what I paid for him to get on tape." John's audible frustration had Aish hyperaware of the gun. "If I couldn't get you to open your mouth, we were going to get big-time sued, or worse, the label was gonna drop us, and then what? I can't have the John Hamilton estate coffers getting lean."

Aish moved to spin around, but he was sore, drugged, lumbering and John punched him, hard and sharp, in the kidney.

"Fuck!" Aish shouted, almost going to his knees, before stabilizing himself. Body vibrating with pain, he groaned, "That's what this is about?"

John's parents, a COO for a small LA company and a middle school teacher, had been surprised when they were told his fortune would go into an estate that would benefit a variety of charities. Grief-stricken and financially comfortable, they hadn't fought it or sought more information. Aish, too, hadn't thought about where the royalties from their songs—all credited to Hamilton/Salinger and split fifty-fifty—would go. No one had followed up to investigate who the executor was. Or whether any of those charities had seen a dime.

"This whole fucking thing is about *money*," Aish spat.

John grabbed him by his hair and breathed stale breath against his face.

"You're such a spoiled little shit," John said, shaking him, and the pull on his hair had tears coming to Aish's eyes. "It's not about *money*. It's about millions. It's about keeping my investment in the glorious Aish Salinger. I've enjoyed the ride on your coattails and you're not going to take that from me just because I stole a couple of songs."

The whole simple, senseless explanation echoed off the kingdom's primordial stone.

He shoved Aish forward.

Aish couldn't run, couldn't fight back. All he could do was keep him talking.

Slow him down. Someone will come. Sofia will come. If he died down here, the chance to make things right for Sofia died, too. Her reputation, her winery, and her efforts to save her kingdom would wither right along with his corpse.

He worked hard to calm his breathing. "So…you fake a suicide, keep me making music, and live off the royalties on the beach in Cabo?"

John huffed. "Something like that."

"How long have you hated me, John?"

That got a pleased chuckle out of him.

"For a real long time, Aish. A real long time."

Aish thought of the girls who asked John to vouch for them and the smaller trophies John would put next to Aish's big ones and the backup vocals and the bass playing.

And then he thought of Sofia and any guilt evaporated.

"What are you doing here?"

Their words had taken on a hollow quality, losing their echo, and Aish saw, ahead of them, the tunnel widening.

"I needed to keep an eye on my boy, didn't I?" John answered. "Make sure you didn't fuck it all up and turn the public against us? I told those old guys I could help them out. But then I hear you and Sofia in the cellar, the fighting, the fucking, I forgot how hot it was listening to you two, and she mentions the evidence she had. Finally, after she almost ruined us, that royal bitch was going to be the answer to my prayers."

Pure, throbbing rage blocked out the ache in his shoulders, sent feeling back into his bound hands. But he couldn't fight, and he couldn't run, so all he could do was verify one last awful truth.

"She almost died from her miscarriage," he said through his clenched jaw.

"Huh," John said. "She didn't tell me she was dying." Not even an attempt to deny it. "Wouldn't have made any difference. The road was calling, man."

The tunnel opened up and they were walking into a massive cavern. It would have been magnificent, something to behold, if John's headlamp wasn't focused on the huge pond in the middle of it. He nudged Aish forward with a hard jab of the gun when Aish hesitated, finally understanding. Their footsteps struck hollowly against the stone, like the black pool sucked up all the sound and light and life that came near it.

When they were at its edge, John came up beside him, the headlamp tilted up from his face and the gun pointed at Aish's side.

"Remember when Sofia told us about this?" he said, looking into the pool. "The source of the river. You wanted to see her kingdom so bad. Now you're going to be, like, fertilizing it."

John looked at him, now a stranger inside and out.

"I never wanted it to end this way," John murmured, motioning Aish toward the pool with the gun. "But you can't give away our money."

Aish had to stall. He needed to buy more time. And he was getting really fucking annoyed at the lazy way John was trying to kill him.

"What, you think I'm just going to get in?"

John rolled his eyes and smiled. "Yeah."

Because wasn't that what Aish had done his whole life? How many hallways and pathways and stadium tunnels had he followed John down, letting his "friend" hold doors for him and walking through, so assured of his own perfection and graced life that he never stopped to look where he was going? Of course John thought he could lead Aish to his death.

Of course he thought he could force Aish to abandon Sofia once again.

Like he'd summoned her with his desire to finally put his foot down, he heard the most glorious and terrifying yell in the world behind him: "Aish, no!"

"*No*," he groaned back because, fuck, he never thought it would actually be her saving him, her literal vulnerable self, and Jesus Christ he hoped her brother and that behemoth were with her because all he could do as John started to whirl around was slam his shoulders into the smaller man.

"You pathetic fuck," he got out, rearing back to slam into him again, hoping to make him drop the gun, hoping to send him into the pond, hoping to make him shoot a hole a foot wide into Aish, anything other than letting John hurt his girl.

John's look of shock and his shaky hold on the gun gave Aish a second of triumph.

Just one second.

John steadied himself and the end of the gun barrel suddenly looked wider and blacker than the pool.

Thank God Aish could swim like a fish.

He turned and dove into the water.

A bullet winged near him, almost meaningless against the arctic cold and ancient dark that swallowed him, an electrocution of pain to his aching body. He kicked hard with his hands behind his back, trying to stay near the surface, trying to keep John's gun aimed on him and away from Sofia. But he could feel the pull, the whirlpool trying to sacrifice him to the river. With his hands tied, his battered body was not cooperating in the freezing water.

And soon, too soon, he had to breathe.

He tried to mermaid up to grab a sip of air. But he couldn't get his head back above the surface.

He could see lights bouncing above him as an invisible force tried to drag him down.

Maybe those ghosts Sofia talked about were real.

Maybe he'd join them and one day get to tell her that he was sorry. That he loved her. That, in a happy and blessed life he hadn't earned or deserved, she was the happiest and most blessed thing that had happened to him.

That he'd never felt more worthy than when he was striving to be perfect for her.

Feeling the last of his breath burn up in his body, Aish closed his eyes and began to sink.

The water moved beside him and slim arms surrounded him. Those hermetic monks were welcoming him to their ranks.

But instead of going down, Aish felt his body being

lifted up. His head broke the surface and then he was given a slap to the back of his head.

"*Respira, idiota*," said the most lovely voice he'd ever heard. "Keep…treading."

Aish was never going to be manipulated again. He was going to stand on his own two feet and bear the weight of his own decisions. But in this, for this woman who showed him how to carry a kingdom on her shoulders, he would do what she said.

He opened his mouth and breathed deep, moved his legs to help her fight the whirlpool's claim on them.

His coughing spasms made him slip through her hold before she clenched him again.

"*Román*," he heard her call, saying her brother's name in the Spanish way, and although he felt like he was kicking through quicksand, he kicked harder to soothe the panic in her voice. They were fine, he wanted to tell her. They were together.

Everything was going to be fine.

Seconds or minutes later, a bright light shone in his face as hands hooked under his armpits. "I got him," Sofia's brother grunted, and Aish sucked in with pain as he was dragged over the sharp rim of the pool and every muscle in his body howled. That didn't stop him from struggling to rise once solid stone was beneath him. "Get her out, gotta get her out, gotta…"

Before he could even struggle to sitting, a dripping Sofia was kneeling next to him on the stone. "Roll over," she said, her teeth chattering. "I'll free your hands."

When he rolled over, he realized why he could see her dripping and chattering and wide-eyed beautiful. Glow sticks had been snapped and scattered around them. John was on his stomach, knocked out, his hands bound behind him. Roman was kneeling and rooting through a backpack.

Aish felt the bind give behind him. His shoulder screamed as he rolled to his back, brought his arms forward, grabbed Sofia's face in his big hands.

"I'm sorry. I love you. I need you. Nothing's brighter than you." He was shaking so hard he was afraid she couldn't understand him.

But her wide, liquid eyes, her trembling smile as she hovered over him, told him that she did. She grabbed his wrists as she tried to control her own shaking.

Roman dropped a Mylar emergency blanket over her shoulders. "Okay, lovebirds, let's get you two warmed up."

Aish wanted to fight her brother when he pulled Sofia's hands down and swaddled her in the blanket. But he couldn't get the words out, and then Roman was pushing Aish up to sitting, wrapping him in his own blanket, rubbing his chest and back through the sleek material, and Aish thought how nice it was to have a big brother. He rested his head on Roman's shoulder. He loved the Esperanza family.

He heard a sweet sound, opened his eyes, saw Sofia's tooth-bitten grin. He realized he might have said that out loud.

Her brother grumped but patted his head. "We love you, too. I think." Roman raised a walkie-talkie to his mouth. "Now let's get outta here."

I think. Aish kept his eyes on Sofia as exhaustion weighed his lids. He wasn't going to be disappointed that Sofia hadn't said it back. She didn't have to love him. She didn't owe him anything. Just as soon as he took a little nap, he'd make sure she knew that.

Even if she didn't return his love, she would always be the best thing that ever happened to him.

September 30

Two days later, the last day of September, the last day of Bodega Sofia's superstar internship program, the Monte del Vino Real was in an uproar. No villager was home. Instead they were filling the *tabernas* and partying in the town plaza with the tourists and reporters that mobbed the small kingdom, reveling in the wild story and sharing new tidbits. John Hamilton was alive! He'd kidnapped and tried to kill Aish Salinger! Princesa Sofia and her bodyguard of a brother had saved the day! The media—who'd been curious about Roman Sheppard, the reluctant half prince who'd famously rescued an heiress years ago—were now mad to interview the ex-army ranger. Any reservations the people of the Monte had had about the quiet and stalwart American were now gone. Roman Sheppard would be in their nightly prayers for helping their *princesa*.

Not that their *princesa* needed help, they bragged to reporters. Their *princesa peleadora* had saved the harvest season, had reinvented the Monte winemaking industry when all odds were against her, and now had rescued a rock star. They were proud to have a brave and bold princess who never went down without a fight.

The liberal toasting in the streets to their warrior

princess—a nickname quickly overtaking party-girl princess—meant that rumors were flying wildly, although none could compete with the spare bits of truth shared in two press releases, released jointly by the rock star's manager and the princess's PR rep. John Hamilton was in custody for kidnapping and attempted murder. Juan Carlos Pascual and two additional members of the Consejo Regulador del Monte also were in custody for aiding and abetting, and authorities were seeking hotel executive Manon Boucher for questioning. Both Princesa Sofia and Young Son's Aish Salinger were in good health and would give complete accounts of what happened to them at an afternoon press conference.

The world waited with bated breath for this 4 p.m. press conference, having spent thirty days watching the courtship of #Aishia stutter then fester then bloom then teeter precariously. After the drama of the last month, not even the most hardened cynic believed the relationship was faked. Would the warrior princess and the devoted rock star finally get their happily ever after? Would Aish go down on one knee? Would Sofia? Or, now that the internship was over, would they shake hands and go their separate ways, leaving the world heartbroken and howling?

As viewers at home bit their nails and watched their clocks, wine flowed throughout the Monte, locals cheered with tourists, and reporters anxiously prepped themselves for the story of their lives.

In the cellar of Bodega Sofia, however, everything was calm and quiet. Quiet, except for the clang of Aish's boots against the metal steps as he reached the bottom of the stairs. Calm, except for the nerves obvious in his handsome face as he rounded the steps and made eye contact with Sofia, who was sitting behind a white marble bar in the middle of the majestically lit cathedral space.

"Sofia?" he asked, staying near the stairs.

She hated the deep purple bruise high up on his sharp cheekbone, hated the way he held his normally languid body stiff with his aches and bruises. She wished she'd been able to get to John before she'd had to jump into the pool to save Aish from drowning, gotten in a couple of kicks before Roman's security team had dragged him away.

But she loved the way Aish stood there on her black marble floor under glowing lights, tall and breathing and here and alive, in his long-sleeve black button-up shirt, his black rock star jeans and boots, his blue-black hair pompadoured and perfect. What a glory it was to stare at a beautiful man.

"Come here, Aish," she called, motioning to the two filled glasses and the bottle of wine she'd set on the bar. Her wine. One of her best.

He stayed where he was. "Shouldn't we get ready for the press conference?"

She sank her teeth into her bottom lip to hold back her smile. This was a boy who'd asked if he could make her wet within minutes of meeting her, who'd barraged her with questions and touches when she'd seethed at his presence, who'd been ready in an instant to throw away his career to save her dreams. She'd never seen him wary, never witnessed him hesitate.

He truly didn't know how today was going to turn out.

"We're doing the press conference here," she said, picking up her wine. Aish wasn't the only one with a few nerves. "The cellar is the heart of Bodega Sofia, but you've only had bad experiences here. I wanted to show it to you in a better light."

Aish reached up to wrap his long hand around a metal stair rung. "Okay."

Helpless, she let her smile loose. He was so gorgeous, so vibrant and male. She wanted to warm herself at the flame of him. He was so far away. "Aren't you going to come here, Aish?"

His hand clenched the rung. "I don't want to demand anything you're not willing to give. And if I'm close to you..." He dropped his head, sent that thick pomp of hair tumbling against his forehead.

There'd been no time for just the two of them since they'd been helped out of the tunnel by Roman's team. They were rushed off to separate hospital rooms for treatment, interviewed by the *guardia civil*, then petted, praised and scolded by Mateo, Roxanne, Henry, Devonte, Namrita, and Carmen Louisa. There'd been no time for Sofia to tell him what she'd realized. What she wanted.

Now, she could see the muscles jumping in his sleek jaw as her own body quivered at the temptation of him, the unbelievable reality that she'd gotten to him in time. He steeled himself and looked back up, caught her in his sparkling black gaze. "If I'm in touching distance right now, Sofia... I'm gonna touch." She felt his eyes stroke over her. Felt the same disbelief that they'd made it to the other side. "And I don't know if that's something you want. I don't know if that's something I've earned."

Sofia ran her hands up through her hair—she'd left it loose and soft—and pushed off the bar stool to stand. She walked to the end of the bar, trailing her fingers

over the marble, and then stood to the side of it, letting
Aish see her from head to toe. Let him see the black
baby doll dress, embroidered with bright flowers, that
covered her arms and the tattoo she was thinking about
removing, but left her long legs bare from the top of her
Doc Martens to upper thigh. Let Aish see all the skin
he talked about coveting.

"I know it was John I spoke to that day in the hospital," she called across the cellar space. "I heard him
say it in the tunnel."

Aish stared at her. His eyes moved over her like he
was seeing a mirage. And then, careless if the fantasy
was real, he was coming at her, a big man on long legs,
barreling toward her and crashing into her, tunneling
his fingers into her hair, bending her back over the bar,
sleeking a hot hand up her thigh as he took her mouth
in a life-confirming kiss. A kiss giving her his heat and
breath and pulse.

"Holy fuck, Sofia," he gasped into her mouth as he
pulled back to stare in wonder at her. "Holy fuck, you
saved me. How did you fucking find me?"

Her hands moved over him, greedy for the feel of
him in her arms again. "It was John. He's so stupidly
arrogant, he went to the trouble of changing his face but
not that horrible cologne he always wore." She buried
her nose in Aish's neck and inhaled the cleansing scent
of him. "I realized I'd smelled him, down here and when
we were at the bar." She squeezed his biceps, hot and
full of tensile strength, in her fury. "Roman's security
team was coming up the main route but I know a short-
cut. *Gracias a Dios*, you got him talking, I could keep
track of you as we were getting close. When I heard
him tell you to get in the pool…"

She pulled her head back until she could look into his eyes, take in that spark that she'd been terrified she'd never see again. When she'd watched him dive in and heard the gunshot, she'd felt the nightmarish despair of true *never*, total and endless. This wasn't a cold she'd wrapped herself in; this was a dark emptiness that would go on forever.

Driven by "He needs me!", she'd sprinted out of the mouth of the tunnel with Roman on her heels and dove into the freezing water. She'd found Aish's waving black hair and closed eyes in her headlamp. She thanked the hours of squatting to pick grapes for her ability to swim them to the surface and resist the whirlpool's tug.

It had been anger, not despair, that had her smacking him upside the head. *¡Absolutamente no!* Not after everything. He wasn't allowed to leave her now.

Now, she pulled him down to kiss her again, to cover herself in his warmth.

His hungry kiss ended too soon, though, when he picked her up and sat her on the bar top. His hands gripped the marble near her hips and he stared grimly into her eyes.

"My apologies thirty days ago would have been for the wrong reasons, apologizing for the wrong things. Can I try to tell you I'm sorry the right way now?"

She nodded solemnly.

Aish took a steadying breath. "John's not to blame for what happened to us. I made the decision to break your heart after I told you to trust me, and I put you in the position to believe him when he answered my phone. If I hadn't hurt you so bad, you would've known it wasn't me. Then you wouldn't have been…" Aish stopped, shook his head, and pressed his face into the bend of her neck.

"I'm so sorry," he whispered into her skin, and Sofia rubbed her cheek against his hair.

She let his words soothe the wound.

"I'm so sorry you were alone. I wish I'd been there." He nuzzled his face in, but then sniffed and straightened. He cleared his throat then looked her in the eyes again, ready to take a bullet. "I let you go," he said. "I didn't fight for us. I used you in my songs, but I didn't contact you. John didn't do that; I did that."

"Why didn't you ever reach out?"

"I was afraid," he said immediately. "I'd convinced myself I *was* reaching out, with the songs and the tats, that I'd done the work and the ball was in your court. But really…" He shook his head. "I was just chicken-shit. If I never tried, then I could live in hope of one day. But if I tried and failed, it—" He stopped, and his gaze ran over her face like he was afraid it was one of the last times he'd have the privilege.

He took his hands off the bar and stood straight, so tall and fierce for a languid boy. "When I say what I'm about to say, I don't expect anything in return. Know that. I don't think you owe me because of what happened ten years ago or what's happened this month or because you're glad I'm alive. I'm not going to demand anything from you."

He swallowed and clenched his fists. It made her flutter, silly, like a girl, that golden-boy-rock-star Aish Salinger was nervous over her.

"I love you, Sofia. I've always loved you. I'll always love you. There is nothing I need more than you, no song or friend or tour, and if…if it's too far gone and

I've hurt you too much and waited too long for you to love me back then I'll accept whatever you're willing to give me, even if it's just…friends or, coming back here to help with harvest or…"

She reached for his clenched fist and gently pulled it into her lap. "Won't your uncle miss you at harvest?"

He moved closer, a flash of hope on his face. "He'll understand," he said. "He was tired of me raving about how brave and brilliant you are when I was being such a coward."

That made her lower her head, stare at his hand. "Brave and brilliant?"

He tucked her hair behind her ear so he could see her face. "The bravest. The most brilliant."

She turned his hand over and unsnapped his cuff. "I would have said needy and desperate. I thought I was weak." She folded up his cuff, ran her thumb over the thick blue veins of his wrist. "I thought my desire to be… How did you put it? Essential? I thought my need to be essential led me to make bad decisions." She began rolling up his sleeve. "But I tried 284 chemical compositions to eliminate cork taint until I found the right one. I built a winery and enacted a wild and successful plan to save my kingdom."

With his sleeve folded up to his elbow, she turned his forearm back over and slowly traced the compass there, the needle pointing to his heart. "And I found you. You were a needle in a haystack and I found you."

His free hand was tender as it stroked over her jaw. It was gentle, undemanding, as it tilted up her chin.

"My need makes me brave," she said as she looked into his sparkling eyes. "It makes me attempt the impossible."

"Like loving me again?" he asked. "*¿Es eso lo imposible?*"

Is that the impossible?

This man, this gorgeous man with a Midas touch, looked like he would give her whatever she wanted. But he had to know the truth before he made any promises.

"I can't have children, Aish," she said, looking into his eyes for the impact. "I can't have your children."

His eyes went wide like she'd slapped him, and both hands came up to surround her face. "Jesus fuck, I was just hoping you'd let me sleep at the end of your bed. I wasn't even praying for…family. Fuck, Sofia." He gripped her hair. "Family. We can be the favorite aunt and uncle or we can adopt but…family, Sofia. I just want you to be my family."

She put her hand on his chest, over his heart, over the star that flamed there. "If I hadn't miscarried, if we had stayed together, I still would have gotten an abortion."

He nodded. "Yeah, and I would have driven you to the clinic and taken care of you afterwards. Sweetheart, I'm not going to romanticize what could have been."

She smiled. He got her. He saw her. "Okay," she said. "I just don't want it to be confusing when not being able to have children aches sometimes."

"Let me share it with you, baby," he said. "All this success and happiness in my life, it's not meant shit without you to share it with. Let me share your sadness, too. I love you."

As the cellar door above them opened and feet rang on the stairs, as she quickly kissed Aish but pulled away from his hold and jumped off the bar, she didn't miss the disappointment on his face that she didn't say it back. She shook out her dress and casually mentioned that he should roll up his other sleeve, let his tattoos shine, as Namrita, wine blogger Amelia Hill, and a crew of camera, lighting, and sound technicians came down the stairs.

"Sofia?" Amelia asked in wonder as Sofia walked toward her, kissed her on the cheeks. Namrita directed the camera and sound people to set up at the bar with the barrels aging Bodega Sofia wines as backdrop.

Sofia led the woman toward Aish. "You had every right to be skeptical when you arrived here, Amelia, and you pushed me to do better." When they met Aish by the bar, he too looked at her with curiosity. "We're all a little tired of the spectacle of #Aishia. You're the best person to tell the real story of Sofia and Aish."

"This is the press conference?" Aish asked.

Sofia smiled. "If Amelia doesn't mind…"

The wine blogger had to shake her head to free herself from shock. "I…you want to hand me the story of the year? No, no, I don't mind at all."

Ten minutes later, the lights were set up, Aish and Sofia were seated together on matching bar stools while Amelia faced them, and a technician was counting down with her fingers *three…two…one…*

Amelia spoke into the camera, introducing herself, the name of her popular wine blog that was about to go very viral, and then introduced Sofia and Aish. The feed, whose web address had been announced five minutes earlier, was going live worldwide.

Amelia's first questions were about the kidnapping, and Aish and Sofia spoke candidly about what had happened, about the interference of John and the Consejo in the winery launch, and about what charges had already been brought against the responsible parties.

"I understand the Consejo has decided to dismiss the current board and elect new members. They've requested you lead it?" Amelia asked.

Sofia nodded, her hands crossed over the bare thighs her dress showed off. It had been a while since she'd dressed this way; after the press conference, she'd probably reserve it for more intimate moments with Aish. She liked her winemaker garb.

"The Consejo has asked, but I have declined, for now. I suddenly have an overbooked *hospedería* and wine member list with a two-year wait to get on it. Instead, I've asked my mother, Queen Valentina, to serve on the board and represent the interests of Bodega Sofia."

Aish looked at her sharply. There was still so much she needed to share with him. Like the morning tour of the winery she'd given her mother, and the awkward but sincere conversation that their future could be different than their past.

"There's a tremendous demand for Monte del Vino wines internationally. Will Bodega Sofia be able to satisfy it?"

Sofia grinned. "We won't have to. Thanks to our new partnership with Mexico's Trujillo Industries, the kingdom will be able to offer low-interest loans to anyone in the Monte interested in starting a new winery or modernizing older ones." That's the favor Sofia had called in, and the vice president of the company had answered with a yes in less than half a day.

Once again, Roman's connection to industrialist Daniel Trujillo benefited a tiny kingdom a half a world away from Mexico. And yet, no one in the Monte had ever met the man.

Amelia turned her attention to Aish. Sofia looked

at him, at the ocean waves and compasses that licked down his forearms, and marveled that he was there.

"Aish, you'd had a press conference planned when you were kidnapped. What did you want to say?"

"Mostly, I wanted to get the heat off Sofia. She didn't do anything wrong. She has more integrity and bravery in her little finger than I have in my whole body."

Sofia slipped her hand into Aish's—because how could she not—then saw how the sound person wiped his eye, how the camera operator put a hand over her heart.

Aish continued, "I'd known since right before John died—I mean, when I thought he'd died—that he'd stolen songs. I didn't *know* before then, but I also wasn't following up on all the rumors. And I've got to take responsibility for that. So, I'm sorry to every hardworking musician who heard me sing a lyric or play a melody that you wrote. I'm relinquishing all royalties to Young Son's songs; we're gonna use it to pay those bands we stole from. And I'm…breaking up the band. Young Son is over."

The squeeze on her fingers let Sofia know how hard this was for him. She squeezed right back. She'd be here for him.

"Will you continue to make music?" Amelia asked.

"Definitely," Aish said immediately. "I can't not. It's going to be up to you guys to decide if you want to listen to it."

Sofia squeezed his hand again, this time in excitement. Aish, on his own, out of the shadow of John and with no directives other than that of his fiery, artistic heart. She couldn't wait to hear every song inside of him.

Amelia smiled, looked at them both through her big glasses. "So now, the question that everyone's been waiting for…" She put up her hands. "What's going to happen to #Aishia?"

Aish looked over at her.

"I don't want to demand anything you're not willing to give."

Sofia took her hand from his and clasped both of hers in her lap. She could see the worry on Amelia's face, saw the wide eyes of the camera person. She took a deep breath. She was about to declare to the whole world, adamantly and definitively, what she needed.

"From the beginning, Aish has literally worn his emotions on his sleeve," she said. "I'm the one people are unsure about. I'd like to clear up any doubt about my feelings now."

She pushed off the bar stool and stood. "I fell in love with Aish Salinger when I was nineteen years old. He broke my heart, and I swore to myself that I would never fall in love again."

She began to lift the hem of her short dress. "I swore it as I walked into the tattoo shop in Madrid, six months after we'd parted." She leaned on the wobbly legs of her wild child as she began to reveal her upper thigh. "I swore it as I showed the artist what I'd drawn, what I wanted her to ink on me." She'd worn black, high-cut briefs, no more revealing than a swimsuit, but high enough to show what was on her hip. A hip she was showing to the world now, holding the skirt up on one side.

A hip she was showing to Aish.

"For those of you who don't know," she said, "*Aish* means fire. It means passion and inspiration."

She looked down at it, at this constant reminder she'd inked on herself, thinking it meant one thing when it actually meant something else, this tattoo on the same spot where her mother had tried to cut away her ability to love. It was a flame two hands' width long, at the bend of her thigh and up her waist, a gorgeous flame of yellow and oranges and blue black that reminded her of Aish's hair. Of the star he'd inked into his chest.

Just beneath the flame, in simple black ink, was one word: *Siempre*.

Always.

She thought she wanted a reminder, forever, for always, that Aish's love had burned and scarred. But the understanding that Aish hadn't turned his back on her when she needed him, the belief that he would have been at her side in an instant, and the knowledge that he'd mourned her absence every day for the last ten years—just as she'd mourned his—helped her realize what her heart had been hiding.

She would never hide her brave, brilliant, loving heart again.

Keeping her skirt high, she turned her head and looked directly into Aish's eyes. "I swore to myself I'd never fall in love again. It was an easy promise to keep. I couldn't fall in love again because I'd never fallen out of love with you."

Then she turned her back on the camera. She turned her back on the crew and the lights and the world and focused on the only thing that mattered: his stunned, open, glorious gaze as she surrounded him in her arms.

"Me too, Aish," she murmured against his mouth.

"I've always loved you. I'll always love you. Let's make the impossible come true."

Then in the heart of her castle, in the heart of her kingdom, Princesa Sofia kissed the man who would always be her always.

* * * * *

Reviews are an invaluable tool when it comes to spreading the word about great reads. Please consider leaving an honest review for this or any of Carina Press's other titles that you've read on your favorite retailer or review site.

To purchase and read more books by Angelina M. Lopez, please visit her website at www.angelinamlopez.com/books

Acknowledgments

Hoo boy, thank you Kerri Buckley for being honest about what this "first book written under contract" needed for improvement, and for believing that this debut author could pull it off.

Paloma Beneito Arias, I met you at a party and you don't even read romance. And still, you went over the Spanish culture and language in this book with a fine-toothed comb. Thank you for your enthusiastic assistance, your diligence, your thoroughness, and your overall joy in a novel that still needed A LOT of work when you saw it!

And thank you to Peter, Gabriel and Simon, who've been so supportive on this journey, even though having a writer-on-deadline in the house has certainly changed our lives. You listen, you support, you cheerlead—it's what everyone deserves but certainly not what everyone gets. I'm so appreciative I get it from you!

About the Author

Angelina M. Lopez wrote "arthur" when her kindergarten teacher asked her what she wanted to be when she grew up. In the years since she learned to spell the word correctly, she's been a journalist for an acclaimed city newspaper, a freelance magazine writer, and a content marketer for small businesses. At long last, she found her way back to "author."

Angelina writes sexy, contemporary stories about strong women and the confident men lucky enough to fall in love with them. The fact that her parents own a vineyard in California's Russian River Valley might imply a certain hedonism about her; it's not true. She's a wife and a mom who lives in the suburbs of Washington, DC. She makes to-do lists with perfectly drawn check boxes. She checks them with glee.

You can find more about her at her website, www. AngelinaMLopez.com, and at @AngelinaMLo on Instagram and Twitter.

**And available now from Carina Press and
Angelina M. Lopez**

A marriage of convenience and three nights a month.

That's all the sultry, self-made billionaire wants from
the impoverished prince.

And at the end of the year, she'll grant him his divorce…with a settlement large enough to save his beloved kingdom.

Read on to be swept away by Lush Money, *the first
book in Angelina M. Lopez's Filthy Rich series and
the story that started it all…*

January: Night One

Mateo Ferdinand Juan Carlos de Esperanza y Santos—
the "Golden Prince," the only son of King Felipe, and
heir to the tiny principality of Monte del Vino Real in
northwestern Spain—had dirt under his fingernails, a
twig of *Tempranillo FOS 02* in his back pocket, and a
burning desire to wipe the mud of his muck boots on
the white carpet where he waited. But he didn't. Under
the watchful gaze of the executive assistant, who stared
with disapproving eyes from his standing desk, Mateo
kept his boots tipped back on the well-worn heels and
his white-knuckled fists jammed into the pits of his UC
Davis t-shirt. Staying completely still and deep breathing while he sat on the white couch was the only way
he kept himself from storming away from this lunacy.

What the fuck had his father gotten him into?

A breathy *ding* sighed from the assistant's laptop.
He granted Mateo the tiniest of smiles. "You may go in
now," he said, hustling to the chrome-and-glass doors
and pulling one open with a flourish. The assistant
didn't seem to mind the dirt so much now as his eyes
traveled—lingeringly—over Mateo's dusty jeans and
t-shirt.

Mateo felt his *niñera* give him a mental smack upside the head when he kept his baseball cap on as he entered the office. But he was no more willing to take his cap off now than he'd been willing to change his clothes when the town car showed up at his lab, his ears ringing with his father's screams about why Mateo couldn't refuse.

The frosted-glass door closed behind him, enclosing him in a sky-high corner office as regal as any throne room. The floor-to-ceiling windows showed off Coit Tower to the west, the Bay Bridge to the east, and the darkening hills of San Francisco in between. The twinkling lights of the city flicked on like discovered jewels in the gathering night, adornment for this white office with its pale woods, faux fur pillows, and acrylic side tables. This office at the top of the fifty-five-floor Medina Building was opulent, self-assured. Feminine.

And empty.

He'd walked in the Rose Garden with the U.S. President, shaken the hand of Britain's queen, and kneeled in the dirt with the finest winemakers in Burgundy, but he stood in the middle of this empty palatial office like a jackass, not knowing where to sit or how to stand or who to yell at to make this *situación idiota* go away.

A door hidden in the pale wood wall opened. A woman walked out, drying her hands.

Dear God, no.

She nodded at him, her jowls wriggling as she tossed her paper towel back into the bathroom. "Take a seat, *Príncipe* Mateo. I'll prepare Roxanne to speak with you."

Of course. Of course Roxanne Medina, founder and CEO of Medina Now Enterprises, wasn't a sixty-year-old woman with a thick waist in medical scrubs. But "prepare" Roxanne to…

Ah.

The nurse leaned across the delicate, Japanese-style desk and opened a laptop perched on the edge. She pushed a button and a woman came into view on the screen. Or at least, the top of a woman's head came into view. The woman was staring down through black-framed glasses, writing something on a pad of paper. A sunny, tropical day loomed outside the balcony door behind her.

Inwardly laughing at the farce of this situation, Mateo took a seat in a leather chair facing the screen. Apparently, Roxanne Medina couldn't be bothered to meet the man she wanted to marry in person.

Two minutes later, he was no longer laughing. She hadn't looked at him. She just kept scribbling, giving him nothing to look at but the palm tree swaying behind her and the part in her dark, shiny hair.

He glanced at the nurse. She stared back, blank-eyed. He'd already cleared his throat twice.

Fuck this. "Excuse me," he began.

"Helen, it sounds like the prince may have a bit of a dry throat." Roxanne Medina spoke, finally, without raising her eyes from her document. "Could you get him a glass of water?"

"Of course, ma'am."

As the nurse headed to a decanter, Mateo said, "I don't need water. I'm trying to find out…"

Roxanne Medina raised one delicate finger to the screen. Without looking up. Continuing to write. Without a word or a sound, Roxanne Medina shushed him, and Mateo—top of his field, head of his lab, a goddamned *príncipe*—he let her, out of shock and awe that another human being would treat him this way.

He *never* treated people this way.

He moved to stand, to storm out, when a water glass appeared in front of his face and a hair was tugged from his head.

"Ow!" he yelled as he turned to glare at the granite-faced nurse holding a strand of his light brown hair.

"Fantastic, I see the tests have begun."

Mateo turned back to the screen and pushed the water glass out of his way so he could see the woman who finally deigned to speak to him.

"Tests?"

She was beautiful. Of course she was beautiful. When you have billions of dollars at your disposal, you can look any way you want. Roxanne Medina was sky-blue eyed, high-breasted and lush-lipped, with long and lustrous black hair. On the pixelated screen, he couldn't tell how much of her was real or fake. He doubted even her stylist could remember what was Botoxed, extended, and implanted.

Still, she was striking. Mateo closed his mouth with a snap.

Her slow, sensual smile let him know she'd seen him do it.

Mateo glowered as Roxanne Medina slipped her delicate black reading glasses up on her head and aimed those searing blue eyes at him. "These tests are just a formality. We've tested your father and sister and there were no genetic surprises."

"Great," he deadpanned. "Why are you testing me?"

Her sleek eyebrows quirked. "Didn't your father explain this already?" A tiny gold cross hung in the V of her ivory silk top. "We're testing for anything that might make the Golden Prince a less-than-ideal specimen to impregnate me."

Madre de Dios. His father hadn't been delusional. This woman really wanted to buy herself a prince and a royal baby. The king had introduced him to some morally deficient people in his life, but this woman... His shock was punctuated by a needle sliding into his bicep.

"*¡Joder!*" Mateo yelled, turning to see a needle sticking out of him, just under his t-shirt sleeve. "Stop doing that!"

"Hold still," the devil's handmaiden said emotionlessly, as if stealing someone's blood for unwanted tests was an everyday task for her.

Rather than risk a needle breaking off in his arm, he did stay still. But he glared at the screen. "I haven't agreed to any of this. The only reason I'm here is to tell you 'no.'"

"The king promised..."

"My father makes a lot of promises. Only one of us is fool enough to believe them."

She took the glasses off entirely, sending that hair swirling around her neck, and slowly settled back into her chair. The gold cross hid once again between blouse and pale skin. She stared at him the way he stared at the underside of grape leaves to determine their needs.

Finally, she said, "Forgive me. We've started on different pages. I thought you were on board." Her voice, Mateo noticed, was throaty with a touch of scratch to it. He wondered if that was jet lag from her tropical location. Or did she sound like that all the time? "I run a multinational corporation; sometimes I rush to the

finish line and forget my 'pleases' and 'thank yous.'
Helen, say you're sorry."

"I'm sorry," Helen said immediately. As she pulled
the plunger and dragged Mateo's blood into the vial.

Gritting his teeth, he glared at the screen. "What
self-respecting person would have a kid with a stranger
for money?"

"A practical one with a kingdom on the line," Roxanne Medina said methodically. "My money can buy
you time. That's what you need to right your sinking
ship, correct? You need more time to develop the *Tempranillo Vino Real*?"

Mateo's blood turned cold; he wondered if Nurse
Ratched could see it freezing as she pulled it out of him.
He stayed quiet and raised his chin as the nurse put a
Band-Aid on his arm.

"This deal can give you the time you need," the billionaire said, her voice beckoning. "My money can keep
your people solvent until you get those vines planted."

She sat there, a stranger in a tropical villa, declaring herself the savior of the kingdom it was Mateo's
responsibility to save.

For centuries, the people of Monte del Vino Real, a
plateau hidden among the Picos de Europa in northern-
most Spain, made their fortunes from the lush wines
produced from their cool-climate Tempranillo vines.
But in recent years, mismanagement, climate change,
the world's focus on French and California wines, and
his parents' devotion to their royal lifestyle instead of
ruling had devalued their grapes. The world thought the
Monte was "sleepy." What they didn't know was that
his kingdom was nearly destitute.

Mateo was growing a new variety of Tempranillo

vine in his UC Davis greenhouse lab whose hardiness and impeccable flavor of the grapes it produced would save the fortunes of the Monte del Vino Real. His new-and-improved vine or "clone"—he'd called it the *Tempranillo Vino Real* for his people—just needed a couple more years of development. To buy that time, he'd cobbled together enough loans to keep credit flowing to his growers and business owners and his community teetering on the edge of financial ruin instead of free-falling over. He'd also instituted security measures in his lab so that the vine wouldn't be stolen by competitors.

But Roxanne Medina was telling him that all of his efforts—the favors he'd called in to keep the Monte's poverty a secret, the expensive security cameras, the pat downs of grad students he knew and trusted—were useless. This woman he'd never met had sniffed out his secrets and staked a claim.

"What does or doesn't happen to my kingdom has nothing to do with you," he said, angry at a computer screen.

She put down her glasses and clasped slender, delicate hands in front of her. "This doesn't have to be difficult," she insisted. "All I want is three nights a month from you."

He scoffed. "And my hand in marriage."

"Yes," she agreed. "The king has produced more than enough royal bastards for the Monte, don't you think?"

The king. His father. The man whose limitless desire to be seen as a wealthy international playboy emptied the kingdom's coffers. The ruler who weekly dreamt up get-rich-quick schemes that—without Mateo's constant monitoring and intervention—would have sacrificed the Monte's land, people, and thousand-year legacy to his greed.

It was Mateo's fault for being surprised that his father would sell his son and grandchild to the highest bidder.

"I'm just asking for three nights a month for a year," Roxanne Medina continued. "At the end of that year, I'll 'divorce' you——" her air quotes cast in stark relief what a mockery this "marriage" would be "—and provide you with the settlement I outlined with your father. Regardless of the success of your vine, your people will be taken care of and you will never have to consider turning your kingdom into an American amusement park."

That was another highly secretive deal that Roxanne Medina wasn't supposed to know about: An American resort company wanted to purchase half the Monte and develop it as a playland for rich Americans to live out their royal fantasies. But her source for that info was easy; his father daily threatened repercussions if Mateo didn't sign the papers for the deal.

In the three months since Mateo had stormed out of that meeting, leaving his father and the American resort group furious, his IT guy had noticed a sharp rise in hacking attempts against his lab's computers. And there'd been two attempted break-ins on his apartment, according to his security company.

Billionaire Roxanne Medina might be the preferable devil. At least she was upfront about her snooping and spying.

But have a kid with her? His heir? A child that, until an hour ago, had only been a distant, flat someday, like marriage and death? "So I'm supposed to make a kid with you and then—what—just hand him over?"

"Didn't the king tell you…? Of course, you'll get to

see her. A child needs two parents." The adamancy of her raspy voice had Mateo focusing on the screen. The billionaire clutched her fingers in front of the laptop, her blue eyes focused on him. "We'll have joint custody. We won't need to see each other again, but your daughter, you can have as much or as little access to her as you'd like."

She pushed her long black hair behind her shoulders as she leaned closer to the screen, and Mateo once again saw that tiny, gold cross against her skin.

"Your IQ is 152, mine is 138, and neither of us have chronic illnesses in our families. We can create an exceptional child and give her safety, security, and a fairy-tale life free of hardship. I wouldn't share this responsibility with just anyone; I've done my homework on you. I know you'll make a good father."

Mateo had been trained in manipulation his whole life. His mother cried and raged, and then hugged and petted him. His father bought him a Labrador puppy and then forced Mateo to lie about the man's whereabouts for a weekend. Looking a person in the eye and speaking a compliment from the heart were simple tricks in a master manipulator's bag.

And yet, there was something that beckoned about the child she described. He'd always wanted to be a better everything than his own father.

The nurse sat a contract and pen in front of Mateo. He stared at the rose gold Mont Blanc.

"I know this is unorthodox," she continued. "But it benefits us both. You get breathing room for your work and financial security for your people. I get a legitimate child who knows her father without...well, without the hassles of everything else." She paused. "You understand the emotional toll of an unhappy marriage better than most."

Mateo wanted to bristle but he simply didn't have the energy. His parents' affairs and blowups had been filling the pages of the tabloids since before he was born. The billionaire hadn't needed to use her elite gang of spies to gather that intel. But she did remind him of his own few-and-far-between thoughts on matrimony. Namely, that it was a state he didn't want to enter.

If he never married, then when would he have an heir?

Mateo pulled back from his navel gazing to focus on her. She was watching him. Mateo saw her eyes travel slowly over the screen, taking him in, and he felt like a voyeur and exhibitionist at the same time.

She bit her full bottom lip and then gave him a smile of promise. "To put it frankly, *Príncipe*, your position and poverty aren't the only reasons I selected you. You're…a fascinating man. And we're both busy, dedicated to our work, and not getting as much sex as we'd like. I'm looking forward to those three nights a month."

"Sex" coming out of her lush mouth in that velvety voice had Mateo's libido sitting up and taking notice. That's right. He'd be having sex with this tempting creature on the screen.

She tilted her head, sending all that thick black hair to one side and exposing her pale neck. "I've had some thoughts about those nights in bed."

The instant, searing image of her arched neck while he buried his hand in her hair had Mateo tearing his eyes away. He looked out on the city. *Jesus*. She was right, it had been too long. And he didn't need his little brain casting a vote right now.

She made it sound so simple.

Her money gave him more than the three years of financial ledge-clinging that he'd scraped together on his own, a timeline that had already caused sleepless nights. The only way Mateo could have the *Tempranillo Vino Real* planted and profitable in three years is if everything went perfectly—no problems with development, no bad growing seasons. Mother Nature could not give him that guarantee. Her deal also prevented his father from taking more drastic measures. The chance for a quiet phone and an inbox free of plans like the one to capture the Monte's principal irrigation source and bottle it into "Royal Water" with the king's face on the label was almost reason enough to sign the contract.

Mateo refused to list "regular sex with a gorgeous woman who looked at him like a lollipop" in the plus column. He wasn't led around by his cock like his father.

And that child; his far-off, mythical heir? The *príncipes y princesas* of the Monte del Vino Real had been marrying for profit long before Roxanne Medina invented it. He didn't know what kind of mother she would be, but he would learn in the course of the year together. And if they discovered in that year they weren't compatible…surely she would cancel the arrangement. After the initial shock, she'd seemed reasonable.

Gripping on to his higher ideals and shaky rationalizations, he picked up the pen and signed.

The nurse plunked an empty plastic cup with a lid down on the desk.

"What the…?" Mateo said with horror.

"Just the final test," Roxanne Medina said cheerily from the screen. "Don't worry. Helen left a couple of magazines in the bathroom. Just leave the cup in there when you're finished and she'll retrieve it."

Any hopes for a reasonable future swirled down the drain. Roxanne Medina expected him to get himself off in a cup while this gargoyle of a woman waited outside the door.

He stood and white-knuckled the cup, turned away from the desk. Fuck it. At least his people were safe. An hour earlier, his hands in the dirt, he'd thought he could save his kingdom with hard work and noble intentions. But he'd fall on his sword for them if he had to.

Or stroke it.

He had one last question for the woman who held his life in her slim-fingered hand. "Why?" he asked, his back to the screen, the question coming from the depths of his chest. "Really, why?"

"Why what?"

"Why me."

"Because you're perfect." He could hear the glee in her rich voice. "And I always demand perfection."

Don't miss Lush Money *by Angelina M. Lopez Available now wherever Carina Press ebooks are sold.*

www.CarinaPress.com